LEAN

David Walker has had a remarkable career. A country boyhood in Scotland led to Sandhurst, carefree Army service with The Black Watch in India, aide-de-camp to the Governor-General of Canada in the last year before the Second World War, when he married Willa Magee of Montreal. He was taken prisoner with the Highland Division in 1940, escaped three times from German PoW camps, and was eventually committed to Colditz Castle in 1943 for the remainder of the war. Afterwards he returned to India as Comptroller for the Viceroy, Field Marshal Lord Wavell, whose close friend he became. In 1948 he emigrated to Canada, where he and his wife rebuilt an old farmhouse, to be called Strathcroix, and where their four sons grew up beside the great tides of the Bay of Fundy.

David Walker began writing when he was thirty-six. Since then he has written nineteen diverse works of fiction, and now his memoirs. His work reflects the saying of the chief character, Simon Skafe, in *Where the High Winds Blow*, his novel of the Canadian Arctic: 'Life is an adventure, or it is nothing.'

*By the same author*

POT OF GOLD
ASH
BLACK DOUGAL
THE LORD'S PINK OCEAN
DEVIL'S PLUNGE (*in USA* CAB-INTERSEC)
COME BACK GEORDIE
MALLABEC
WINTER OF MADNESS
STORMS OF OUR JOURNEY (*short stories*)
WHERE THE HIGH WINDS BLOW
HARRY BLACK
DIGBY
THE PILLAR
GEORDIE
THE STORM AND THE SILENCE

*For young people*

SANDY WAS A SOLDIER'S BOY
DRAGON HILL
PIRATE ROCK
BIG BEN

# LEAN, WIND, LEAN

## *A few times remembered*

DAVID WALKER

COLLINS
8 Grafton Street, London W1
1985

William Collins Sons and Co. Ltd
London · Glasgow · Sydney · Auckland
Toronto · Johannesburg

BRITISH LIBRARY CATALOGUING IN PUBLICATION DATA

Walker, David, *1911–*
Lean, wind, lean.
1. Walker, David, 1911 – Biography
2. Novelists, Canadian – 20th century – Biography
I. Title
813′.54 PR9199.3.W33Z

First published 1984
This trade paperback edition 1985


ISBN 0 00 217588 6
Photoset in Linotron Ehrhardt by
Rowland Phototypesetting Ltd, Bury St Edmunds, Suffolk
Made and printed in Great Britain by
William Collins Sons & Co. Ltd, Glasgow

To
Martin Gilliat

# CONTENTS

BOOK TWO:
*The Leaf on the Birch*

# LIST OF ILLUSTRATIONS

# PREAMBLE

Introductions are usually to be skipped, at least by me. But there are a few things that I must say about these eclectic memoirs, which took a year in the writing and a few more months for delays and revision.

They are slivers of memory, no more than that; and I have divided them into two parts. Book One begins in a German prison camp, goes back to my childhood, and climbs on by home, youth, Sandhurst, India, Canada, and into war, all that interwoven with, and subordinate to the kernel, which is Germany from 1940 to 1945.

I could have written chronologically from a first recollection at the age of three but that would have aspired or presumed to autobiography, which was far from my intent. So I wrote stealthily with many switches back and forth in time and place. That this will be interruptive to the reader I am aware, and do not apologize for it. But I have tried to help by putting the relevant year or years at chapter headings.

It is necessary to mention, too, that they are written from the viewpoint of an immediate present, much as diaries are written. Thus, Douglas Bader, a friend since prison days, was still much alive when I mentioned him early in the book, to die later on.

Next, as is obvious, the conversation is all invented. One needs talk to bring the thing to life. For much the same reason I have embellished minor incident here and there.

But in all essentials, both parts are as true to my faulted recollection as I could make them. Memory is odd. The humdrum can be a total blank or a kaleidoscopic haze; but some things remain astonishingly vivid: for instance, a few days and a few nights at large and after recapture in Bavaria in 1943. My escaping partner, Patrick Campbell-Preston, godfather to our first son Patrick, who died in infancy, and again to our fourth son David, cannot correct me. Word of Pat's death came to us as we sat above the snow in the warm spring sun on the terrace at Strathcroix.

The sharpest memory of all was the epic escape of the Second World War – or perhaps of any war – over the wire at Warburg in August 1942. It was, and would remain, the superlative venture for all of us in our lives.

As to sources and some detail, I am much indebted to a book called *Detour*, compiled with perfervid zeal and dispatch after the war by an admirable Canadian, the late Jerry Wood.

I am grateful to my Colditz messmate, Philip Pardoe, for letting me read that part of his prison diary which concerned the Warburg wire escape. I asked that favour because I needed a check upon my own recollections. But although mine is much more detailed and explicit (no wartime security reasons to inhibit me), the two accounts are virtually identical.

Book One ends with the miracle of freedom.

Book Two is different. It begins with farewell to Field Marshal Wavell, the man who was to become a central figure in it, goes back to golden moments of reunion, and thereafter moves on more or less chronologically to a hard Arctic journey in 1956.

There were other things, many journeys before and later, and many good people, not mentioned here, who helped me on my way. I would like to thank them.

So this book ends almost thirty years ago. Last evening, until boredom took over from bafflement, I watched a television programme about the fifth generation of computers, soon to come and do our original thinking for us. That means, if I have the general idea right, that the fifth generation will programme us rather than the other way round.

I must be one of the few remaining imperfectly literate human beings who have never encountered Generations One to Four. If the car or the television set has such little beasts built in, they were never programmed by me, thank God.

But who knows, there might yet be a strong idea for a novel in me before Generation Five arrives to do a better job of it.

Strathcroix, St Andrews
*April 1984*

# BOOK ONE

## *Let us fly together*

# ONE

# 1982 and 1942

From my workroom, I look through the window above ground or human level at *Amelanchier Canadensis*, our first and most beautiful blossom, which lines the edge of every field and every open woodland ride. For these few days the *Amelanchier* may be better here than anywhere on earth, or that is my conceit. It has many names, locally the wild or robin pear (it is not a pear) and it is called the shadbush, saskatoon, or service tree. But the names do not matter. What matters are the pure white blossoms and the ruddy leaves on many modest trees. What matters most is that when high summer comes the sweet red berries will be a feast for every fruit-loving bird.

Down beyond the wild pear and our untidy forest is the estuary of the St Croix river. The crossing arms of water, or the suggestion of a cross which caused men to give it that name, are a few miles upstream of here. We pronounce the river St Croy, as in boy, just as the name of our house is rather less of an etymological bastard than it might seem, Strathcroix called Strathcroy, a strath being a wide Scottish river valley, or its bottom lands. Still, as the one who dubbed it, I occasionally feel at odds with our Scottish-anglicized-French name.

Across the river, about two miles from my armchair, is the notable state of Maine.

That is the here and now. We have a journey in mind to make, not first to a beginning, but to a place and time which quite arbitrarily suggested themselves, and to a particular memory. Again by chance, it is a memory of this month of May forty years ago, at a prison camp at the edge of the north German plain. It was a large camp, about a mile in circumference within the wire, and it held some thousands of British prisoners in wooden huts scattered all about the sordid place. The communal latrines were pits in the ground, the stench abhorrent, the white creepy-crawlies that waddled from them in warm weather of indescribable loathsomeness.

But all was not loathsome. Someone had brought a blanket, and the four of us lolled on it in quite a pleasant grassy place away from the huts. We were Tom Stallard, Patrick Campbell-Preston, Martin Gilliat and myself.

We talked idly to pass the time until darkness fell. We were idle in speech but not in thought. All the camp electricity – the hut lights, the lights along the wire, the searchlights in the raised sentry boxes – were controlled from a fusebox in the guardhouse at the bottom or north-east end of the camp. So, presumably, the Germans thought. But two captive electrical wizards thought otherwise. We were waiting to find out whether they were right. Now dusk had gathered, now it was surely time; and the lights came on.

The electricians allowed a minute or two, then they put their conductor across bared leads in the camp barber's shop and every electric light in and around Oflag VI B went out.

'So it works,' Tom said. He was to be our leader, a brilliant, selfless, diffident man, a leader whose word no one ever questioned, in fact a leader.

The barbed wire that held us in was not a single high fence but two fences about seven or eight feet apart, between them dense coils of the thicker barbed wire called dannert. It looked impenetrable but one or two intrepid people had cut their way through. Our idea was a different one – to blitz our way over.

By that early summer of 1942, air raid warnings were frequent. The sirens would ululate and the whole camp, inside and out, would be in darkness. But for an escape such as the one we began to plan, air raids were unpredictable acts of God and of no use for our purpose. We could not have ladders and bridges erected in advance, or teams of people dressed for escape with loaded packs, or diversions ready for action, or highly elaborate stooge systems to give warning of German activities in the camp, which activity instantly increased when the sirens sounded and the lights went out. A stooge in prison was not a foil but a sentinel of prime importance.

In a few minutes that evening the camp lights came on again. There had been no alarm, no Teutonic screams. The master fuse in the village of Dössel a mile or two away had been re-set and all was normal, and we were soon screamed at to get into our benighted huts.

Now, it happened that the barber's shop stood apart from the other huts and power poles, and it happened that the nearest source of supply for it was the main cable outside the camp fence. So the Germans, not wisely, had tapped into that main cable before it reached the camp fusebox.

It was a foolish lapse. It was a fluke. It was our key to darkness. Months of planning and training were before us, but we had our key to darkness.

## TWO

# 1914 to 1927

My first memory is of a jolly surgeon, Mr Greig, who operated on the tubercular glands in my neck when I was three. My second memory is of the same year, 1914, when my young brother was born. I think I remember our cousin Harry leaving for war that August, soon to be killed commanding a Black Watch battalion.

The first-recorded Walkers of our family were portioners or small farmers at Pitlair in the kingdom of Fife at the beginning of the seventeenth century. But in about 1800 they became jute-spinners, first at Cupar, Fife, and later across the river Tay in Dundee. Jute is a coarse fibre, largely grown in what is now Bangladesh, and used for making sacks, the backing of linoleum, and other things. In the United States it is more commonly called burlap.

Our family prospered during the nineteenth century, no doubt at the expense of their employees. When I was a boy, the poverty among the mill-people of Dundee was terrible. The barefooted urchins in their only playground, the dirty street, were called 'keelies', a term of contempt. Looking back now, I feel shame at the way the likes of us must have exploited them. But to my parents' generation, the other half (a massive half) were not quite the same kind of human beings as ourselves. Even my sensitive liberal-minded mother, who never harmed anyone and spent her life doing kindness, would speak of 'those people'. They were the lesser orders who, if a generous employer installed a bath for them, would be sure to use it as a coal bin.

My grandfather built Pitlair soon after 1900 on the same land that we once had farmed, near the farmsteading itself, agreeably named Daft Mill. Grandfather Walker was an unusual man, a semi-invalid most of his life, and chess champion of Scotland. One of the less usual things about him was that he owned two country houses, eighteen miles apart as the crow would fly, one in Fife and one across the estuary of the river Tay in Angus. There is nothing out of the ordinary among those who have prospered in having two houses – usually one in lowland country, the other a shooting lodge in the Highlands. But Pitlair and Balgersho were in almost identical flat agricultural land and he divided his year between them. I have never understood it, and never did ask why.

I remember little of Grandfather, with his aquiline flare-nostrilled face and burgeoning moustaches, a kindly impersonal man, I would say. He had an unforgettable parlour trick, which was to spin his napkin ring on edge down one side of the dining room table, round the centrepiece and back like a boomerang to his hand. I have another mental picture of him, sitting outside the library window at Pitlair, muffled in rugs, feeding his pet robins and titmice. He loved animals, even to the extent of keeping delicious morsels on his own plate, and holding that down to the dog. I have been devoted to some dogs but do rather draw the line at sharing plates.

Until I was twelve, we lived on the outskirts of Dundee, in what one might call suburban countryside, with an acre or two of garden and field. Our gardener was named Mackenzie, a short square man of distinction, as square as my Irish grandfather was rotund. Mackenzie was a lovely man.

In a young people's book called *Sandy was a Soldier's Boy* (not one which as a whole rests well with me), I wrote:

> . . . There was a building too, a greenhouse sheltered from the north and open to the sunny south, but no sun this murky afternoon. On the top near corner of the roof a grey squirrel sat as cheeky as you please. It was not nice like the red squirrel with the cocked-up tail. It was bigger, and it had a ratty toothy face, killing red squirrels, eating robins' eggs, killing baby blackbirds, a Foreigner. It did not see Sandy, silent stalker in the bushes.
>
> I'll teach you! Sandy thought. Dash blank something murderer. He knew some good bad words. He put his left hand into his sporran pocket and took out the catapult. Then he put his right hand into his sporran pocket and felt for a round pebble . . .

> Third time lucky, he thought, and his bullet went fast as the wind this third time. So did the wicked squirrel. So did father blackbird with his orange bill, and brown mother blackbird and the smaller birds. Nobody left here but Sandy McBain, listening to the clatter and the tinkle and the crash.
>
> Where the top centre pane of glass had been, there was nothing now, not even spiky bits of glass. Sandy gave one grunt. Then he started shooting the end out of that greenhouse. At first he listened to the bad grand music of the glass each time. But he got quicker and quicker, a shooting machine with silent gun, one still falling as the next one went, a red glow on the greenhouse on and on and nothing could stop it, like Highland Laddie; and then it stopped, as even Highland Laddie stops.
>
> The wooden frames were there – twenty-seven, he counted them; sad corner-slivers of glass were there; Sandy McBain was here among the rhododendrons, back here from wherever it was that he had been. He did not know where it was that he had been . . .

There may or may not have been an extenuating circumstance in my case. It was certainly not a grey squirrel because they did not then exist with us. Or if it began unintentionally, I was probably firing my catapult at some innocent bird, frightful killer that I was. I went back to school, and was not accused of the crime, but when I came home next weekend I encountered Mackenzie in the garden. 'Davie,' he said, 'yon greenhouse – would it not be avoiding worse trouble if you just owned up?'

So I did, and received mild punishment for my act of vandalism across our neighbour's wall. Father should have beaten my backside on numerous occasions but the most severe castigation he could bring himself to inflict were a couple of token slaps on the hand with a Sam Browne belt that he wore in the Volunteers, with the time-honoured comment that it hurt him more than it hurt me, certainly true.

So far in this dander through early days, I have made myself out (apart from murderous propensities with catapults) to be a nice mischievous little chap. At my best, I suppose I was that, and quick-witted, which amused older people. But all was not sunny. There were the dim times which have always burdened me, a sort of *Weltschmerz* that only action seems to rout. I also had a hellish temper. The worst tantrum occurred at a wayside station named Achnasheen on our way back from fishing at Loch Maree where, aged eight, I had caught a two-pound trout and should have been in a sunny frame of mind. I have no idea what caused that exhibition, but Achnasheen was never forgotten in the family. David Harry are my names, and when those rages occurred my redoubtable Aunt Isabel (Father's unmarried sister) called me *David Heinrich*, *Da-veed* in the German way, not a popular language at that time.

Then, in 1923, we moved out and up in the world. Father bought a house in Fife with eight hundred acres, only two miles from Pitlair. There were two Rankeillours, Over Rankeillour and Nether Rankeillour, ours was Over. It had originally been called Rankeillour Hope, having been owned by a branch of that distinguished family.

It was (and is, although we long since lost it) a rectangular Adam house, facing south to open parkland. Behind were woods, a mixture of conifers and hardwoods, and shrubberies in which to lurk. The noblest of the trees were beeches, two hundred and fifty or more years old, some with trunks as thick as the spread of a man's arms. Of all the places that I have known, Rankeillour had the most pleasant seat.

A book of mine, *Black Dougal*, was about an indigent Scottish landowner faced with the inevitability of selling out. In fact, Dougal saved the situation by somewhat unconventional means. But at the beginning he thought: 'My trouble was that I loved the place. Perhaps few human beings are any longer blessed and burdened with one particular place to love from early childhood, and through youth, and to come back to. You can call that sentimental, and it is. Nostalgia must be sentimental.'

In my case it was not early childhood. I was a boy of twelve, but there was an added blessing, my young brother. His names were Barclay Clibborn, after two lots of Irish relations.

Soon I was sent to school in England, at Shrewsbury, but in the holidays Barkie and I were hardly ever separated. We dug up juicy wasp maggots for bait and got stung together (so many painful early encounters may account for my present allergy to stings). We fished together with timeless patience and negligible success in the lethargic Rankeillour burn and a few meandering miles downstream where it was the Pitlair burn. We shot together. We made most satisfying explosions with black powder together. We made hides in the marvellous secret woods together. We played golf together on the lopsided Cupar course. We laid tacks together across the main road to puncture passing cars (never successful, I think). But blow-outs or burst tyres were common in those days and we had one quite successful gambit – we hid behind the roadside wall, and whenever a car came past we fired our loud cap pistol. Quite often the driver stopped and got out, to find that it was a false alarm. But so many false alarms on the same stretch of road led to suspicion and an irate farmer to pursuit, and we had to give that up.

We went about our fishing and shooting occasions at home on foot. Almost everything else we did by bicycle – three miles to Cupar for library books, and sometimes much further afield than that. But most of our cycling was done on the many mossy paths in the woods near the house. We raced up them, down them, round them for tireless hours, skidding the corners with rare skill. It was perfectly pointless and quite dangerous, and the greatest fun. By the time Barkie was thirteen, he played games and did all physical things better than I did, and so it remained for the rest of his life.

I suppose that it is common enough for a pair of brothers, entirely different in temperament, to click, to hit it off so completely as we did. The credit lay with him; he had a most complaisant nature, which I certainly did not. I do not remember any disagreement, any ill-feeling ever between us. We were as close as a pair of collie dogs, linked invisibly to the shepherd's heel but minus the shepherd.

Our parents were somewhat remote from us. Our elder brother, Willie, and our sister, Huldah, were almost grown-up by the time we went to Rankeillour, and so Barkie and I became a self-sufficient unit. Our closest companion and friend was John Keiller, the gamekeeper, who always came shooting with us except on our evening expeditions to stalk rabbits with a BSA air rifle, and later a .22. Barkie became such a crack shot with it that he could shoot a running rabbit cleanly through the head. So much killing, but that is what we did.

The people who worked at Rankeillour and their families – the keeper, the gardeners, the forester, the chauffeur, the maids in the house – were unfailingly kind to us, and sheltered us from parental displeasure when necessary. It would be untrue to say that they treated us as they would treat their own children. The difference (I mean of indulgence, never subservience) did always lurk but we lived in comradeship with them, and as neutrals in a small rural world of faction. Some families got on with one another; some did not speak; some were at daggers drawn.

An idyllic boyhood, I am saying, and so it was. Barks and I were a proper pair of spivs, never being called upon to do any labour of any kind. When our own sons were that age or younger, I used to make them help me clear our tangled woods, which they did willingly enough, and they all learned to be good workers. But this is Canada, where every tree beyond the garden is seeded by the Lord; and that was Scotland, where almost every tree had been planted by man. Nevertheless, we might have been set to thinning plantations or the like, to making some contribution to the affairs of paradise.

Four months of each year in Eden, eight months at school. I cannot say that I look back on my five years at Shrewsbury with any pleasure in myself, or with much pleasure about the place. We learned, I suppose, to some extent to play the game, which meant the team game. We learned about a stiff upper-lip, no bad thing. There were a few thoroughly civilized schoolmasters, and some boring pedagogues.

In my day, the boys were fed by individual houses and the fare provided depended upon the circumstances and inclination of the housemaster. Mine was a worthy man and a gifted organist. He was also a poor man with seven children and our food was appalling.

It was not until much later that I learned about hunger, a good test of which, for those of European eating habits, is whether you have all the bread you want. To digress for another moment, when I came back from prison in Germany at the end of the war, I went for a walk and on the village street I saw a large wire trash basket full of discarded loaves. That told me all I needed to know about the hungry British.

The majority of Shrewsbury boys came from moderately well-off families in the English Midlands. None of my school friends – I had few, in fact – were country people, and if they came to stay at Rankeillour were not at home in our rustic life. One even mistook a wood pigeon for a duck, to us an unbelievable gaffe. Another difficulty was that the broad Fife dialect was a foreign language to them, as broad Yorkshire would have been to me. So those visits were not much of a success, and when we left school our ways parted.

# THREE

# 1925 to 1929

Romance was fairly rife at Shrewsbury. Big boys fell for appealing small boys, and the other way round. But in so crowded and regimented a society there was not much opportunity for assignation. Almost none of it was true homosexuality. We were simply deprived at an age when maidens were to dream about. Things were not much better at home because likely girls were scattered thin in Fife, and I was so acutely shy that I dreaded the parties at which we met them.

But at Rankeillour that problem did not occur. Either we were blowing off steam with physical exertion, or I was lost in a book. I think that I began on John Buchan when I was eight, and read insatiably thereafter.

My taste in novels is a bit better now, in fact choosy, even as to thrillers, but then I read anything and everything, good or bad – Walter Scott, Jack London, Percy F. Westerman, Sapper, Ballantyne, *Some Experiences of an Irish RM*, Balzac and the *Decameron*, RLS, Kipling galore, Mason, Ian Hay, Galsworthy, Dornford Yates, even my sister Huldah's schoolgirl stories by Angela Brazil. You more or less name it, I drank it in. Shakespeare was an exception at that time. He was two hundred melancholy lines of *Hamlet* to be digested for tomorrow's English Literature in the Modern Fifth. But later when I went to India and began to have a feeling for poetry and language, I read much of Shakespeare.

The food at Rankeillour was beyond compare – an inaccurate statement, because I expect it was comparably good in thousands of other British homes. I can better say that it was plain and perfect, from the farm cream so thick that it would hardly pour on to the salted porridge – sugar on porridge was a barbarous English habit and a loathsome taste – to the tender beef, the game, the vegetables and fruit from the walled garden a quarter of a mile away. It was perfection, and perhaps the most perfect of that perfection – after tactfully asking Mackenzie's permission (he had come from Dundee with us) – was to pick and eat a downy delicious peach from the south-facing wall.

The size of the garden was four acres, given over in only an ancillary sense to the growing of fruit and vegetables. My mother was a gifted and artistic gardener. When one went through the door in that high sandstone wall, her herbaceous borders astride the grass walk stretched away in harmony of scent and shape and colour to an infinity of meeting at the other end.

She would have liked (and so would I, although boys pay but intermittent heed to natural beauty) to have her flower garden round about the house. But such was not the Scottish custom, in part because of rabbit-proofing, in part because in a fickle northern climate a walled garden stores the sun's good heat and tempers wind. She did have two low rectangular enclaves on either side of the grass tennis court in front of the house. She called them the Forts and grew gentians and favourite rock plants there.

While I am remembering the holidays, I may as well explain how my hero, *Geordie*, came to win the shot-putting at the Olympic Games. Like Geordie, I was small for my age and longed to be big. Unlike Geordie, my efforts were not to be rewarded.

But despite short stature I was well enough muscled and assiduously practised putting the shot for bigger and better development. I particularly enjoyed putting it against our local minister when he passed our way on the bicycle-round of his flock. He was a large man of about six foot three, not well muscled, or not well coordinated might be the better term, and I used to beat him easily.

When Geordie had already achieved vast dimensions, Henry Samson (The World's Strongest Man), his mentor, wrote to advise him to take up shot-putting. Not having a sixteen-pound metal ball, Geordie found a suitable boulder and started practising. This is what ensued:

> . . . 'Hallo, Geordie,' said a familiar high-pitched voice.
>
> Geordie turned round. It was Reverend MacNab, the minis-

ter, sitting on his bike on the road with the toes of his boots touching the ground. He had on his black suit and his black hat and the usual cheery grin on his red face.

'Hallo, Minister,' said Geordie, a bit sheepish at being caught playing with stones, and him grown up.

Mr MacNab got off his bike and came over. He was quite a pal of Geordie's in a way, not that you could be real pally with a chap who had to swear off sin. But certainly the holiness didn't hang heavy on the minister. He could have a hearty laugh for all his arsey-tarsey collar.

'So you've got on to putting the weight, Geordie,' he said. 'I'll watch you.'

Geordie cursed inside. He didn't want to go making an exhibition of himself at something he hadn't learned the way of. But he marked the starting line again, which was getting smudged, and took a few more putts.

'Here, Geordie,' said the minister. 'Hold it like this, close into your shoulder, wrist straight, so it goes with the force of your body.'

Geordie did what he said, but not very willingly. What would a minister know about shot-putting, and him just a wee bit of a chap beside Geordie? But it did seem to go better with the stone held close.

'Hold it in your fingers,' said MacNab; and that didn't do any harm either.

'Too low, Geordie. Throw higher. You know, I believe you'd make a shot-putter if you learned how to do it.'

'That's what I'm to do,' said Geordie. He dropped the stone with a thud on the grass. He was a bit fed-up.

'I'll have a competition with you,' said MacNab. He took off his jacket and waistcoat. He had on a pair of bright blue braces which didn't seem right somehow. The minister was a whole head below Geordie, not more than five foot eight perhaps, but broad; you could see he had strong wee arms on him when he rolled up his sleeves.

'You go first, Geordie,' he said.

Geordie did a good one, the best yet. They marked the spot with a stick.

Then it was Reverend MacNab's turn. He nestled the big stone in his shoulder, and swung his left leg back and foward getting balance. Then he launched himself at the line and the whole of his body spun in a half turn and the stone flew up and away and over and down a good six foot beyond Geordie's.

That was one of the biggest surprises of Geordie's life.

The minister had been smiling all the time before, but now he bubbled over with delight. He laughed with a high cackle, and bent over in his mirth and gasped for breath. He was just about busting he was so pleased with himself. And Geordie began to laugh too. He couldn't help it, with the wee fella' giving him such a beating.

I knew a man like that minister once but never anyone like Geordie. He simply came to life for me, as large as life to me. But this may show how a fictional idea can stem from the reverse of fact.

Then the long day's journey by train from Perth, change at dismal Crewe, and on to school for another term. Looking back upon what I have written, I see that I have not done justice to Shrewsbury which, except in the vital matter of food, was a good school of that era, and I daresay that I enjoyed much of my time there.

But some things do not rest well in far retrospect. For instance, house monitors were allowed to inflict corporal punishment and some of them beat small boys for the most trifling offences, in fact for pleasure. They were no light beatings either, administered with a cane at full strength on the bottom. I myself was once beaten by the same monitor four nights in succession for next to nothing. And I myself once beat a boy I disliked on a trumped-up charge. There was a lot of minor sadism and the idea of protest, or of complaint to the housemaster, was unthinkable.

For a second instance, we were bound in dress and deportment by an absurd intricacy of unwritten rules. Junior boys had to have all their jacket buttons done up. If they wanted to put their hands in their trouser pockets, the flaps of their jackets must be forward. Incidentally, boys, large or small, were never referred to by one another as boys, but as men. I forget at what stage of eminence these rules were progressively relaxed. But if anyone transgressed them, and hardly anyone ever did, swift retribution was meted out upon his backside. The ultimate Olympian might be seen, jacket undone, flaps back, hands in pockets, velvet First Eleven cap on the back of his head, strolling across a school lawn (also forbidden to the common herd).

These rules – and there were many more – were harmless enough, if ridiculous, but were linked to a fetish of athletic prowess. If a man among the men was a brilliant scholar and did not excel at any sport, he was written off as a 'sap', so much for him. Although Shrewsbury had an excellent scholastic record, this games worship was extraordinarily pervasive and compelling. It was not until I had left school that I came to realize that being able to hit a ball or to kick a ball did not a human being make.

When I was sixteen I had a bright idea for getting a week away, so I went to Jesus College, Cambridge (where my elder brother had been and my younger brother would later go) and passed the Littlego exam for entrance. But soon after that an extraordinary thing happened. Ambition seized me and headed me on quite a different course. Until then I had swanned through school, doing just well enough to pass. Now suddenly there was the Navy, and now suddenly I began to work. Most people went in much younger via Dartmouth but there was a small Special Entry at school-leaving age, about eighteen, in my year limited to ten vacancies.

The Royal Navy, my golden purpose, my golden dream – for the first time in my life I drove myself. There were difficulties, the worst being mathematics, at which I was hopeless. Elementary physics, not so bad; French all right; English much better.

After more than a year of it, a slave at school, being crammed in the holidays, I went in the summer of 1929 to London to take the Navy exam which, except in compulsory subjects, was the same examination as for the Army. My father and mother came down from Scotland to ensure fair play in the wicked city and we stayed at the Langham hotel in Portland Place.

When the papers were all over and I knew that I had done quite well – exams were never a bother to me – and I knew that the parents had gone to bed, I stole downstairs and out to the night to meet a fellow examinee from Shrewsbury and to pick up a pair of tarts. She was an amiable whore but it was no sublime initiation; let us leave it at that and sneak back to the Langham, undetected.

Next day to school, soon to say goodbye to school. At the last evening chapel of the summer term, some clerical master would address us with noble sentiment about the world at our parting feet, that world from which we would look back to Shrewsbury, our beloved guide throughout these happy formative years. Sometimes it had been Cyril Alington, once our headmaster who had gone on to Eton. He was a strikingly handsome and theatrical figure, rightly noted for his fables at Sunday evening chapel. Or it was our incumbent headmaster, Canon Sawyer, a formidable tubby man who beat me once, six strokes punctuated by six deep grunts. He was good at it. Canon Sawyer had no choice but the cane because I had been sent up to him for cheating.

*Cabbing*, we called it, slightly wrong but venial, like exceeding the speed limit or outwitting the Customs. The master was a decent fellow, a man we liked, and also admired for a most important reason – he was a brilliant soccer player. But he played a damned dirty trick on me.

'Walker,' he said. 'Did I see you cheating in that exam a week ago, looking at Smith's answers?'

Perhaps he expected me to deny it. But cabbing was one thing, lying another. 'Yessir,' I said, honourable cheater and bloody fool. *That isn't fair*, a boy's ultimate plaint. But six on the backside from the grunting Canon did work and I never cheated again. Pay heed, enlightened educators.

But we were saying goodbye to school. The inspiring address was over, the closing hymn had been sung, *Abide with me, fast falls the eventide*, and beautifully sung. The singing at Shrewsbury was wonderful, thunderous in hymns like *Hills of the North, rejoice*, exquisitely muted as it died away to *O Lord, abide with me*. The blessing had been given. The choir and clergymen had walked down the aisle.

And now the school filed out, starting from the first pews, starting with the exalted men, praepostors and school monitors, the Upper Sixth Forms, the Lower Sixth Forms, and so on.

Most of the first men would be leaving and it was not difficult to tell which men would be Old Salopians tomorrow. A manly tear, if not *de rigueur*, was quite the thing. Mysterious people, the tight-lipped British.

# FOUR

# 1929 to 1931

The ten vacancies for the Navy were one too few. I came in eleventh, forty-eight marks behind the next man. The irony was that in the Officers' Training Corps at school I had failed to pass Certificate A, a rudimentary test which gave a bonus of fifty marks in the Service exams. So that boring bad joke, the Corps, cost me my Special Entry. My own stupidity cost me it.

The thought of the Navy was heaven. The thought of the Army was hell. I had never longed for success before and now first time off I was a failure. To make matters worse, while being a naval also-ran I had been quite an army winner, passing high into Sandhurst, the Royal Military College at Camberley. I had qualified for Cambridge two years before, so there was that way of escape. But my parents put on the pressure for Sandhurst, and I cried once, I remember. I cried one late time in the billiard room at Rankeillour – not the slop tears of farewell to beloved Alma Mater but the genuine strangulated article, aged eighteen – and I yielded.

Father and Mother were a shrewd couple in their reticent different ways, and perhaps they realized that the wayward one would never settle to making jute. The wayward one realized that too, so the magical bridge and quarter-deck fell astern and the bloody barrack square loomed ahead.

The first two months of a Gentleman Cadet's life at Sandhurst were far more regimented than life at school had been. They were a nightmare of drill, first in plain clothes, then canvas, *Wot a bleedin' orful clumsy lot you are, Gennelmen, a cart-'orse would turn over in 'is grive*, of march to have uniforms fitted, march back, counter march, double march, go-crazy march. But we did not go crazy. We endured the process of being smartened up.

The smarteners up were mostly Guardsmen, unbelievably

smart themselves. CSM Robinson was ours. *Staff*, we called him to his face. *Yes, Staff. Right, Staff. Sorry, Staff*, standing strictly at attention. *Robbo*, we called him behind his back. *Lite one more time, Mr Walker, Sir, I'll tike your nime*, he called us. One could not imagine Robbo ever making a mistake in drill, or ever transgressing his iron code in anything. He was perfection, and a very decent human chap. Our riding instructors were human too in their raffish lordly cavalry way. Only the physical training instructors were somewhat less than human, muscled sub-men of the body beautiful.

One came quickly to a condition of dream-like automaton swoon, being harried (and yet not bullied) from dawn to dusk. Whether it did us overall good, I would not know. In terms of alertness and precision, certainly yes. In terms of thinking about the inequities of life, certainly not. While our contemporaries at Oxford or Cambridge were questioning and rebelling (some of them), we were doing and obeying, a square lot on the square, that soulless expanse of pebbled tar macadam on which we had to show competence before being allowed beyond the college gates. Another prerequisite for freedom was learning to polish leather. It was no mean skill. One began with a heavy hand and too much polish, the result a cloudy mess. But with the lightest touch of Kiwi, a dab of methylated spirit, water, silk handkerchief for polishing cloth, one gradually learned to woo a bootcap or a belt to mirror brilliance. I still feel self-satisfaction, even aesthetic pleasure, in being able to clean shoes better than most people.

We were never free of that square for the whole of the eighteen months but the worst of it was over and we now drilled extremely well. A few people were physically incapable of matching opposite arms and legs, or of marching in step, and when this became apparent to the kindly Robbo he hid them as inconspicuously as possible within the ranks.

Still, the prison of the square was over, and we were GCs on the local loose, riding our bikes wherever we wanted out of working hours. Passes were also available to make pilgrimage to Mecca, that being London, thirty miles away. The thing was to have a high old time and sober up enough in the bus coming back to be able to sign in before the officer on duty that evening. Most of them were indulgent about it, and provided one did not weave too evidently and could scrawl a signature with owlish solemnity, all was well.

I think that the best things and the worst things for me at Sandhurst were horses. The worst horses were those of the inanimate variety in the gym, padded, neckless monsters over which one had to project oneself, an eager-beaver PT instructor standing guard to prevent broken bones. The best horses were equine, most of them plugs, old stagers who had taught thousands of cadets to jump with crossed stirrups and stay in the plate.

Riding was new to me and I loved it. We had several equitation periods a week, sometimes in a closed manège or riding school, sometimes on the large area of blasted heath called Barossa. There were also local livery stables where one could hire horses for hunting with the Garth or other packs of hounds. I fell off many times (and was fallen with) as I learned to ride at Sandhurst and became no more than an apprentice horseman. Later, in India, I improved.

The spirited horses, the difficult rides, were given to the real performers, contenders for the Saddle which was awarded to the best horseman of each term. So the easy horses were given to the likes of me. But they were not all plugs. Sometimes I was allowed to ride a chestnut named Limerick. Light in the mouth, gentle-mannered, fast, an effortless jumper – to be taught by Limerick was pure bliss.

Unlike a man whom I shall soon mention briefly, I was late in getting started with the women, with the nice girls, I mean. London had plenty of bad girls for occasional relief. But I knew hardly anyone in the south of England, and was still much too shy to pursue the belles of Surrey or to make the acquaintance of nice girls at the Camberley Golf Club, where Patrick Campbell-Preston and I played wildly and ripened an acquaintance with whisky and soda.

But I met one attractive in-between girl and took her to a cinema in Reading. We made a good beginning during the film and were progressing nicely in the local train coming back. There was no corridor and we had a third class compartment to ourselves, the train trundling along at modest speed, when of a sudden there were urgent hammerings and a face at the window. The door opened and in tottered a Gentleman Cadet known slightly to me. 'Saw you get on,' he said, totally pie-eyed. 'Thought I'd join you.'

To push the bugger back out where he came from would have been murder, if under dire provocation. So he fell asleep while she and I cooled off in opposite corners. The next time I asked her out, she was sorry. It might have been that she did not fancy the company I kept. Much more likely, she had found something better.

Life at Sandhurst (or at the RMC, as we called it) has been vividly and amusingly described by David Niven in his *Moon-Balloon* reminiscences. He was a year ahead of me, a senior in my junior term, an Under Officer to boot, and I saw him in his eminence from afar. But Niven was the wag of the place. While we sat in the Camberley cinema waiting for the show to begin, he, near the front middle with a buddy on either side, would entertain us. I cannot remember anything he said but he was funny, madly funny.

Twenty-five years later, when I had written a few novels, a letter arrived out of the blue from David Niven, saying that he had enjoyed one of them, *Digby* (the film rights of which had been bought by MGM for Spencer Tracy. Tracy eventually lost interest and the film was not made). Niven hoped that someday I might write a story and a character which he could play. That also never did come about.

*Geordie* was a fable of love and truth, of that kindly Scotland which is a dream of Scotsmen. But *Digby* poked a bit of fun at the people of the sacred land. It was an unpopular shock, not at all what had been expected of me. After it had been published, we were staying with the Campbell-Prestons in Argyll and I went along with Pat to Oban and into the bank where he introduced me to the manager, adding: 'He wrote *Geordie*, and we all loved it. He wrote *Digby* too, and we know what we think of *that* one, don't we?' This from an ancient friend to a perfect stranger. One growls and bears it.

In my last term at Sandhurst, the autumn of 1930, I was a Junior Under Officer, a help toward being accepted for a regiment. One of our company instructors was W. S. P. Alexander (a brother of the Field Marshal) who had taught me the long jump, at which I was a fair performer for my size. Alex arranged for me to be offered a commission in his regiment, the Irish Guards. Although I was half Irish, and therefore had some connection, it was a most unmilitary one because my mother's immediate relatives were Quakers from Dublin and Cork. Both her brothers drove ambulances in France in the First World War but they could not be soldiers. The Irish Guards was a splendid regiment, in which I would have been an interloper; and London life, still more spit and polish – neither would have suited me. So when, late in the proceedings, a firm vacancy was offered me in my home regiment, The Black Watch, I jumped at it. If one must be a soldier, that was the kind of soldier for me.

My final marks at Sandhurst were bad, a far drop down the list from the beginning. Once again I had been at my old trick of swanning along just well enough to pass. Sandhurst was a good fair boring place. It served its limited purpose of machining us into young officers. The best thing may have been that, while humbling us from being conceited senior schoolboys, it never failed to respect us as men.

Early the next spring Donald Nicol (who had been Senior Under Officer of our company) and I joined the Second Battalion at Colchester.

In January, before the Sandhurst results and postings had come out, I went skiing with first cousins, the Charlie Walkers, at Saanenmöser in Switzerland. There I began to make up for lost time, having two romances in a fortnight. The first charming girl left and the second charming girl arrived. With her came trouble. She was a member of the British ski team, a brilliant performer, which was the trouble.

If you have never skied before and have not even taken lessons (they were not then much in vogue), the lady champion is a hazardous target. All a chap can do is his very best, and I did mine. She floated away, she simply floated, doing those graceful new-fangled Christiana turns, and in deep snow those elegant old-fashioned Telemarks; she floated downhill and out of sight, heading for the foot of the cog railway to take the next train up.

My object was to get there in time to share a seat for the climb, and perhaps prevail upon her to spare a few minutes from racing practice while I encouraged myself with a glass of Glühwein. I knew no turns, not even a stem. There was but one thing to do – point the boards down, feet wide apart, a duck-like stance, and go for it. In the course of that week I wrapped myself round trees, dug holes in the piste, screamed 'Track!' to the terror and fury of people in my path, broke two pairs of skis, and survived unscathed. It was as good a madness as I can remember. One amiable old chap at the hotel (he was probably about thirty-five) said: 'You're the sort of bloody fool who gets the VC.'

I was to learn later, and to my shame, that I was anything but the sort of bloody fool who gets the VC. But keep trying is the thing, and so I did, and always have. Jeannette was her name, and dancing in the evenings Jeannette and I met on more equal terms.

I saw her only once again. It was that next summer at a ball, at Hurlingham or Roehampton. I took a girl, with whom I was by then infatuated. It was on a lawn in the evening light and I came face to face with Jeannette, the beautiful dark champion girl. I stared at her and she stared at me. If I had smiled at her she would have smiled at me and we would have spoken. But I did not smile at her, what a miserable poleaxed creature, I turned away to join the new one. I have been looking through that window, seeing it so clearly, as if at this moment now just past, not forty-nine years ago.

But home again, and the results came out. The regimental tailors, William Anderson and Son, always Wullie Anderson to us, were in Edinburgh across from Fife, and one took the train by the great Forth bridge, or one took the car-ferry just below it. There were many uniforms – mess kits, khaki, blue patrol, two kilts, two sporrans, tartan trews and tartan breeches, white spats, diced hose, and so on and on. It cost Father a pretty packet, something like two hundred and fifty pounds. That so much money should be squandered on one fledgling officer's gilded uniforms at a time of depression and mass unemployment was fairly disgraceful, come to think of it. But the fledgling officer certainly never came to think of it. In fact, trying on his scarlet mess jacket, starched shirt, mess kilt, gold-tasselled sporran, diced hose, skean d'hu and gold-buckled shoes, he could hardly help fancying himself a bit, right handsome in the looking glass.

It occurs to me that it is quite a long time since I last admired my mirror-image.

## FIVE

# 1942

At Warburg in 1942, we had discovered that, so long as certain wiring remained unchanged, we were, in the negative sense, masters of electricity inside and out at Oflag VI B. It was a discovery of enormous importance, or it could be that for an escaping scheme well-planned and practised.

First, the planning: was it to be a small affair, one ladder, one bridge, one team of, say, ten? Would it be a mass escape? But that would be uncontrollable. Or a larger escape over several ladders, say, four teams of ten? We moved to favour that. And we moved to favour one launching place. That was the only way to monitor the foot sentries patrolling their beats – sometimes quite widely apart, an open chance to seize. And we decided that the best place to do it was at the northern side, between two huts that were long-end-on at right angles to the wire.

People who were never involved in escape attempts from established prison camps tend to think of them as slapdash affairs of derring-do. But, apart from very rare opportunities to be spontaneously seized upon, they were far from that. The successful escapes were meticulously planned and planned and planned, with no thought of glamour. Many unsuccessful attempts were planned just as well and failed.

The risks were imponderable, however soundly you prepared. Would he use his machine gun from the box? Or would he be deterred by the risk of shooting his own men? It was a gamble, to be cold-bloodedly assessed. That we were fanatics, with but one purpose from wake to sleep, is true, and sensible people who heard rumours of some such wire-storming venture said that it was suicidal madness. But through a maze of imponderables and with our one closely-guarded secret, we thought it risky, certainly not madness.

We walked and talked day-in day-out anti-clockwise round the wire. The few eccentrics who made a clockwise circuit were a nuisance because one had to pause while passing, pause from the invariable topic.

Planning was one thing. Practice was another, no less important. In this camp of several thousand people there was a small hut that served in the capital cause of Culture or *Kultur* as music room. In it were an old piano and sheets, largely of classical music, spread carefully on two shelves. In the hut there even appeared one day two stout wires about seven or eight feet above the floor and a like distance apart, from which hung more sheets of music by their spines.

The music room was beside the main Lagerstrasse, winding gradually down from the *Kommandantur* gate at the west end to the guardhouse gate at the north-east corner. The stooging system was in operation. This was an easy watch in broad daylight. Later, much later, in darkness before action, the stooging system would be of extreme complexity. Now it was simple enough.

'Shall we begin?' Tom Stallard said, one of his orders, not one of his questions.

The music sheets were whipped off long shelves, loose extra slats removed, the ladder placed up against one wire, the bridge laid from it to the other wire, the team of ten lined up. Thumping his loudest, the pianist could not drown the twanging rattle of our passage, which was tremendous at close quarters. First man up the ladder, on to the bridge, number two holding the near end of the bridge while number one went through the dropping space at the further end, and so on.

'Forty-five seconds. Not bad, but you must crowd one another still more. Never fail to hold the bridge for him, but never get on until he's off. Let's go again.'

Sooner or later would come the 'Goons-up' signal, and if the storming of our imitation wire fence became increasingly fast, the restoration of the music room to its soberly cultural self became increasingly magical.

'Goon up!' The pianist played on, stopping reluctantly after the German officer had come in. The rapt audience straggled to its feet with typical reluctance, but it stood.

*Bitte*, said the security officer, a casual salute, an indulgent wave of hand to indicate: 'Play on.' It was almost all German music, ultimate *Kultur*; but his eyes wandered round the music room, the people in it. He was on the job. If he had been more intuitive he would have read those faces.

'They say that the Seventh is the apotheosis of the dance. I say the last movement is the apotheosis of conquest. Give us the run of it on the piano.'

The pianist was very good, so good that his music transcended our escape in escape to victory.

One of the Germans said one time or other: *Warum kämpfen wir nicht . . .* ? 'Why are we not fighting shoulder to shoulder against the sub-men?' It was an old Teutonic cry, and the thought lay deep in all their minds.

It could usually be elicited in the cause of deception, as it was now, and it could be put in its place by those boneheads, good men and true, who could not tolerate playing up the enemy. 'That's your problem, isn't it?' said someone short and sharp, and the atmosphere stiffened dangerously.

'Why not play us that lullaby, Schubert, isn't it? *Schlafe, mein Prinzchen*.'

He played and sang it, so beautiful, so peaceful. *Ach, du lieber Gott*! The German went away and soon we had the 'Camp Clear' signal.

All that summer we practised, four teams of ten, one from each battalion. First we practised unimpeded by homemade packs – we stitched those from canvas or clothing or whatever stout cloth could be stolen. Then we practised with packs on, each loaded with bricks, fifty pounds or so. Then we practised laden with our eyes shut. By the end, ten blind burdened men flowed over the practice run in less than forty seconds. We went about it cheerfully but totally disciplined in earnest. Only the RAF team, with a smattering of glamour boys, thought it was a piece of cake, that the earth-bound soldiery took practice and themselves too seriously.

It was at Warburg that I came to know Douglas Bader. I liked him from the start, a flamboyant 'Give-em-a-squirt, boys' type, a bloody nuisance to the Germans and sometimes to us. How could a man with two aluminium legs (or one and a half, to be accurate) possibly take part in an express-train climbing venture? He could not and so we vetoed him. Douglas was the apotheosis of the fighter-boy, and still is to this day. Try being driven by him at night through the West End of London as I was lately and you will see what I mean.

Now, in long retrospect, I think that we may have been wrong to bar him. With his determination, his strength, his extraordinary balance, he might not only have been able to keep up but might have put a compelling spur to the slap-happy Royal Air Force.

While we practised blitzing over, many people were burrowing under. Some of us had started a commodious well-revetted tunnel in the winter but it was in unstable sandy soil and a rainstorm put an end to that. Frank Weldon and Hamilton-Baillie got out just before it collapsed. They were not on the wire scheme. We shall meet Frank and H-B later in another camp.

Solid clay was difficult and slow to dig but it was safe. The next tunnel I entered was during that summer, the brainchild of an Australian mining engineer, who went deep, found clay, and used no revetting. If you bisect a hen's egg, the wider half of the shell will more or less represent the shape of that tunnel, the floor flat, the roof an arch. It was safe from fall-ins, the spectre of which lay in the mind of every tunneller except perhaps there in that disagreeably cramped small groove, already over two hundred feet long when I was asked to go into the thing. There was an occasional turning place, otherwise it was a belly crawl, the air growing worse along the way until a fat-lamp would not burn and one lay at a turning place coughing desperately for oxygen. Claustrophobia never bothered me until that time (or after) but I tried to think of other things and collected myself and pushed on.

In all those tunnels, except the very short ones, ventilation was provided by a fan, usually constructed from the works of a portable gramophone, the handle wound continuously, the air pushed through a pipe made of powdered-milk tins. Up to a point, or for some distance, it worked well. The air grew still worse until suddenly it became much better. The Australian engineer had bored a discreet hole upwards into the middle of the camp fence. Now the tunnel rose to the face not far ahead.

As I have said, I had had no part in that tunnel and was not invited to escape from it. I was invited to be the letter-out, that is, the man whose unenviable job it was to watch and wait and give the shoulder-tap to the next man to go.

I went back and out and looked at it from above ground. The tunnel ended only a few feet beyond the wire, a dangerously short distance from the German in the corner sentry box. I did not see how from his raised vantage point he could fail to detect movement at such close quarters and I said so, and I was right. If they would go fifty feet further into the still-green and growing crop of grain, I would do it, otherwise not. They yielded, as anyone with any sense would yield, and dug further and the Germans soon found the tunnel.

It was bad that a splendid venture ended in failure but I do not remember ever questioning my own decision. I must have been fairly sure of myself in those days.

During the waiting months that summer another drama happened to me, quite by chance. A tractor came in daily, hauling a trailer of cookhouse coal which it left in the middle of the camp. There was a space, probably a spare-wheel compartment between the back wheels, into which a man could squeeze. One did in the afternoon, expecting the tractor to return for its appendage, by then unloaded. But the tractor did not come and overnight the unfortunate occupant became cramped beyond endurance, beyond his physical ability to move at all. He had to be extracted. But the coal cart remained there, empty and inviting.

The word shot round the camp: was anyone ready to escape? It happened that I was – pack, food, copied maps, and so on. At about midday, when people like tractor drivers would be having lunch, I was bundled in.

Being small, I fitted with a pinch, tightly enough to know what the many hours must have been like for my predecessor. But very soon the tractor arrived, hitched up, and we were off, through the west or *Kommandantur* gate unsearched, and on a bit, and we stopped.

I heard him unhook and go away. For a first time in the two years I was on my own outside a German prison camp, funny good feeling, if increasingly uncomfortable. I could see nothing except a few feet of road ahead below me.

The tractor came back, linked itself again, and we were off, really off this time. I knew the road to the village of Dössel because we had slouched along it on our way to Oflag VI B. It ran straight for a distance, then took quite an abrupt turn to the right between trees.

The place to get out was obvious, if now invisible to me. The driver was sure to be looking ahead as he approached the turn. I gauged it right, pushed out my pack, stretched for a handy bar or plank, a difficult move to ease myself forward and get my legs and body out. The wheels passed safely on either side and I rolled into the ditch, a copy book impromptu job.

But there was an astonished voice, not a Germanic scream, not even a shout. Between me and the tractor was another trailer containing a work party of skeleton Russians from their small starvation camp nearby, and containing a German guard whose muzzle wavered about me as I stood up and raised my hands. Another surrender from the surrendered, there was nothing else to do.

The guard may have been too surprised to shoot me, just as I may have been too surprised to feel much afraid, although I shudder now at the recollection. With very few exceptions, our own guards would not have fired in such a circumstance but the brutish custodians of the Russians were another matter. They had to be brutish to endure the horrors that they inflicted. I was lucky. It must have been the nearest I came to being shot in four years and ten months of captivity.

He was a solid sort of oaf, saying nothing, removing his right hand from the rifle and beckoning me and pack aboard, God bless him. Instead of turning right for Dössel, we turned left for the guardhouse. En route, I got rid of map and German money as best I could behind my back; a waste of effort, they would be picked up later while I waited for interrogation. Now I rode in sort of solitary state at the tail end of the procession like a ridiculous sort of royalty. It was not unfunny.

'How did you obtain this money?' asked the *Hauptmann* in English.

'It is my duty to give my name and number, Herr Hauptmann, and it is my duty to escape, and it is my duty not to answer that question,' I replied pompously and properly in German, fair German by that time, and disconcerted him.

He asked about the map in English and I gave the same answer, abbreviated, in German.

'Your name is David,' he said. 'It is a Jewish name.'

'Yes,' I said in English, and he soon gave up. The interrogation was a formality required of him. A fat square German guard escorted me with screams past the cooler (where I would soon do my ten days) and to the guardroom gate, back into the camp. He was a perfectly loathsome little beast, appropriately named Viereck, square man, as broad as he was long, and he hated us. He was dangerous too, at least once taking a pot shot from the sentry box at someone who pointed out his harmless intention and popped over the trip wire (a few feet back from the camp fence proper) to fetch a strayed football. He hated me and I hated him. I disliked a good many Germans but I do not remember ever hating one except that small monster Viereck. Others who survive will remember him and wish him long in Hell.

Meanwhile we practised on at the music hut, and meanwhile the Germans found tunnel after tunnel all over the camp. Our plan was to wait until late summer when there would be full darkness to protect us on our way, and a nearly full waning moon rising soon to guide us on our way.

But there were new difficulties to add to all the others. First, we learned from tame Germans, suitably bribed with cigarettes, that sentries had been posted at night out of sight and well beyond the confines of the camp. That involved extra details and extra work for the guard company and therefore was unpopular with them. The rumours became persistent until we were sure that the Deep Field, as we always called it, did indeed exist. 'Deep Field' is a cricketing term meaning a fielder who is posted far out yonder against a bashing batsman. A man at the 'Warning track' might be the equivalent term and position in baseball.

The Deep Field was a risk that had to be taken. Much more alarming were increasingly persistent rumours that the camp was to be moved. We were fully trained but had only the prototype ladder and bridge. Furthermore, in the chaos of a suddenly ordered move the elaborate and essential stooging system could not possibly work.

The odds had changed to be a good deal longer against. Tom Stallard called a meeting and spoke of what we already knew; about the Deep Field, about the lack of complete darkness in August. Some top-rate people assessed the risks and opted out. They were among the best men on the scheme and I honour their decision, a harder one to make than ours to go on with it.

We still had forty trained men, one prototype ladder and bridge, yet one more negative risk to be taken. We constructed the remaining three scaling ladders and hid them inadequately above a hut ceiling. I remember, the day that was being done, a decent chap, I knew him well, coming up to me with the old Cassandra song: 'It's suicidal,' he said. 'But the best of luck.' Who on the Warburg wire scheme was not told that? Or perhaps no one ventured to say it to Tom Stallard, that godlike man.

SIX

# 1931 to 1932

Meeanee Barracks in Colchester were old and grey and dismal. But the people who accepted Donald Nicol and me into their company were anything but that; a more entertaining, competent lot of young men could not be found. Our seniors, although they drank much more habitually and behaved much less wildly, were not very different. On parade was on parade. Off parade everyone except the Colonel was, with reservations, equal. I believe that in some regiments newly-joined subalterns were treated with disdain for the good of their stripling souls but in The Black Watch it was blessedly otherwise.

We were mad about two things, or two objects, I am not sure in which order of priority. One was cars. They ranged from Keith Dick-Cunyngham's black blaring Bentley down to a tired jalopy that someone bought for seven pounds. Most of them were touring cars, as open machines were then called. Mine was a Wolseley Hornet, a semi-sporting two-plus seater for which Father, generous as ever, paid up with a grumble. My spendthrift ways were a worry to him. The Hornet would do about sixty-five, near which speed the needle hovered, to London and back, to Scotland and back, a reliable small car until I had a high-compression head fitted to increase performance. Thereafter it blew gaskets every hundred miles. The most seductive and productive vehicle may have been Donald Nicol's coupé SS Swallow – a precursor of the Jaguar – in which the other things or object of our madness could recline with pleasure. The girls round Colchester were a lively lot.

Rankeillour was not a social place. My parents hardly ever went out for meals, and dinner parties at home were an extreme rarity. But there was a brief change in 1931 when we had a house party for the Perth Hunt Balls. We motored up from the south, with or without the young ladies of the moment. Among the unattached was Thomas Rennie, our adjutant, at thirty-two a good deal older than the rest of us.

He was a big dark-headed craggy individual, what we call a Black Scotsman. On the military job one had to watch one's step with him. Out of working hours he was great carefree value.

After the ball Thomas went on north, leaving behind him by chance or convenience a pair of the white kid gloves that we wore on dress occasions. Passing again, he had to pick them up, which helped about picking up my sister Huldah. I think that there was no hesitation in either of them from first meeting: and so much truth to come of it. I am pleased to admit that the notion had occurred, my sole venture as a matrimonial agent.

But after nine lively months at home, I was posted to the First Battalion in India. All the other partings had been for brief periods. This one was different, a long journey to a mystery land six thousand miles away. It seemed, and was, a long long step from Rankeillour in midwinter, from people who had been the anchors of my life thus far. And yet the place and the people were to remain my anchors quite far into the unknown future, until Father's death in 1951.

But this was the beginning of January 1932, and we sailed in a troopship, the *Nevasa*. I had longed desperately to be a sailor. By the time we were in the middle of the Bay of Biscay, I longed somewhat less. It was my first ocean voyage and we ran into the worst storm I ever encountered in many times at sea. It was my fate, on the first night of it, to be the duty officer, who had to go round the troop decks once an hour to make sure that all was well. The poor soldiers were abominably crowded in their hammocks and every man was sick. The groans, the retching, the stench, the slime underfoot, the threat from overhead, were appalling. I suppose that may have been my first meeting with the horror that life can be. Having a job to do, albeit a hideous job, probably helped and I did just survive without being seasick. After each tour I lay down on a deckchair, wedged in a corner of the heaving deck, and closed my eyes and felt a little better.

But the next day, trying to sleep it off in our four-man cabin, pitching, rolling, corkscrewing, and that frightening race of the propellor out of water, I succumbed. Only one of us was not sick, and he laughed when the failed sailor said, 'I wish the bloody thing would sink.'

We came through that storm and turned into the Mediterranean which was in its bluest, most tranquil mood. The only diversions for us young chaps were drink and gambling and playing deck games. The ancients, people like captains and majors of forty-five and their weatherbeaten wives, had a row of cabins on an upper deck, and as we steamed into warmer climes so did their behaviour warm. They swopped infidelities or slap-and-tickle with a coy gusto that we found distasteful, incongruous, inexplicable in dotage. I have noticed that even the modern young (whose Pill-smoothed ways can hardly be called monastic) take a dim view of licentious behaviour among their elders. We are all prudes, looking up and down.

*India, so marvellous, so maddening.* I wrote that much later, but it would describe my thoughts about the country from those first days on. They were, and would remain, an outsider's thoughts.

The officers of the Indian Army, the Indian Civil Service, and so on, served India while ruling it, and on the whole they served and ruled it very well, with dedication, with an integrity that might not be matched anywhere in the world today. They were a part of India and many of them came to know the languages, the customs, the history better than Indians themselves.

But we in the British Army were apart, a potential riot squad against internal trouble and external threat. I say *potential* because in my five years there before the war we were never called out to aid the civil power.

We had our Indian servants, and Indians worked for us in numerous ways. We did not work for them at all. But let a fictional Indian say it for me in a novel, *Harry Black.* This is Rabat Singh who has been serving an attachment to Harry Black's battalion. They have just finished an excellent dinner at Firpo's in Calcutta and are driving to the elephant lines:

> They paid and went downstairs and on to Chowringhee to the car. The beggars came. Rabat routed them with harshness. He was Indian in that. He was an Indian, after all. Some of the

Indians attached to British regiments were complete flops. Rabat, during his year, had become a sort of regimental pet. Mr Rabbit, the troops called him with affection, and would follow him.

Harry sang *Night and Day* for the benefit of Calcutta, for the benefit of late babus who looked with hostility at him and Rabat in the open car . . .

'Will you miss your India?' Rabat said the 'your' with a hint of a Hindu little edge now suddenly for the first time.

'Polo, shooting, Mr Rabbit, this and that and so on. Yes, of course.' But Harry did not think he would miss India very much. There were new things, places, people to enjoy, with the Regiment as family and home wherever it might be . . .

'I tell you one thing, Harry,' Rabat said. 'This year with the Battalion has been strange for me. Into Saturday Club and Bengal Club I am not allowed, but with you people I have been a very special Wog belonging to the family.'

'Woggy, wog,' he said. 'Come off it, Rabat. You've had too much champagne.'

'Enough,' said Rabat. 'Not too much. No, Harry, it is just that you have all been good to me, and I am Woggy-wog, a human being, not a Wog, and I have seen the English as Indians do not see them, and now I am rather English too, so now what am I?'

'I don't quite understand.' He did, in fact.

'You are very intelligent, and you hardly ever think. Why not? Because you are young, of course, but mostly because you are a pukka British Sahib and sure of yourself and protected by the Regiment, and you do not have to think. I am intelligent and almost sure of myself with you people as a semi-English Mr Rabbit, but I am not sure of myself really as Indian at heart, and so I must be thinking all the time beneath, not belonging to anybody quite, and not agreeing with my emancipated sister who hates all English guts.'

'Does she? Why? Are we so awful?'

Rabat rolled about the seat with laughter. 'Awfully wonderful! Particularly British Army people of crack regiments. India is what you call your oyster for fun and games, and you don't pretend like Indian Army and ICS that you want us to be Indianized or have self-rule. You simply are not interested. It is of not the least importance. I like that very much.'

> 'But surely they want you to have self-rule – eventually, I mean.'
>
> 'That we do not believe. Now you are thinking: *What a bore old Rabat is.* Well, I am boring this once to you and not again because you are the one who took me under wing from the first day, and this year has been the best time of my life for which I am truly grateful, and I thank you sadly for awful fate of almost understanding British point of view.' Rabat laughed again. He laughed in hilarious waves, which was one of the numerous endearing things about him . . .

That fictional evening ended with an elephant ride down The Lane, as Kreyer Road was called, the shady lane, and to Number One-Three-Eight, a fashionable house, of which Cora was entrepreneuse and head prefect.

But Rabat Singh's comments about the British Army were fair enough. We worked hard when we worked, which was not very much, and India was our playground. We met few Indians in a social way, and the ones we did know were usually well-anglicized members of the Army or the ICS. Most of us learned only enough Urdu or Hindustani for our practical needs, ordering: *jeldi jao* (go quickly); *idhar ao* (come here), a peremptory smattering. And we had our Muslim bearers to come to the rescue when vocabulary ran out.

But if we knew little of the diverse people of that diverse land, we came to know the land itself much better. In the cold weather we shot duck and snipe, which migrated in enormous numbers across the plains, or went after blackbuck, or sought big game in the jungles to the north.

And we had polo to learn, golf of a sort to play, squash, occasional tennis, soccer with the Jocks. It was almost totally a physical life.

We were stationed at Meerut, not far from Delhi, the hub of things. The winter climate there, from December to late February, was wonderful; warm days, crisp nights – wonderful for us, less wonderful for the Indian peasant with his cotton blanket. The girls were out from England then, so our social life was brisk. They were called, rather unfairly, the fishing fleet. But it is true that most of them were in their early-middle twenties, husband high. Anyway, they were great fun before the long womanless void of a bachelor hot-weather.

I soon caught dysentery, only of the bacillary variety but an unpleasant ailment; and that was cured in hospital as March went by, the nights still cool, the days stoking up. The hot-weather was coming, and with it came the birds of heat – the coppersmith tonking all day, a pleasant monotony, a wearying monotony; the brain-fever bird by night: *brain fever*, quietly, wheezingly. *Brain fever*, louder and higher. *Brain fever*, querulous and mounting. *Brain fever*, up up up, insistent to its broken peak of desperation, to other muted starts interminably. *You're going to die* were other old words for that feverish call.

We had a hill detachment to which the fortunate were sent. And a good many of our elders went home on six months' leave. Among the few left to hold the hot-weather baby were Neil Blair and myself. We were so few that for a time Second Lieutenant Walker was commanding two rifle companies. In fact, the company sergeant majors corrected me with tact and did the real commanding but it was responsibility at the age of just twenty-one.

A hundred degrees, a hundred and five when you felt the burn of heat on your lips, a hundred and ten, and still it grew. The nights were not much better and could be worse. I slept in the parched bungalow garden, an electric fan at the foot of the charpoy, a towel across my middle section. In late May, as the monsoon dawdled up through India but was still south of us, violent dust storms would arrive in the middle of the night to blast us into the sealed airless house, and up at five-thirty before dawn to a mere hint of freshness, to another furnace day.

It was a drastic change from the benevolent climate that we knew and we were homesick and grumbled a good deal to one another. But we had one long weekend of relief.

Neil's father had been killed in Russia after the First World War and his mother had married again. Brigadier Ling was at Army Headquarters which moved to the hills in the hot-weather, as did the whole central government of India. We took the night train to Ambala, and to Kalka, where the mountain railway started its leisurely climb to Simla, seventy miles away and seven thousand feet up. I have lived in hot climates often since then and have not minded them, we seem to be compatible, but I have never forgotten the bliss of that first gradual escape to coolness.

The Lings were a delightful couple and Neil's comfortable kindly Mum had a soft spot for me. It was good with them there, and again in Delhi in the winter. My memories of Simla are a jumble of that time, and of other times after the war. I suppose that it remained essentially the same place as Kipling's Simla, the trim bungalows, and the tumbledown hovels perched precariously on hillsides, the panting emaciated rickshaw coolies, the massively hungered and minutely privileged hotch-potch that was India.

We went walking; we went to a race meeting; we went drinking; we went to a garden party at Viceregal Lodge, and there I saw someone who was seen by the poet, Gerald Poynder, in a novel I wrote called *Mallabec.*

> . . . 'The Indian girl, did you ever know her?'
>
> 'No,' he said. 'I did once see a girl. It was in the hills at Simla at a garden party. My first year in India, and the plains were hideously hot just before the monsoon broke, and I had four cool days leave. Talk about bliss. I was wandering about at this viceregal shindig, not knowing a soul, and there was a long table with a white cloth on it, outside a marquee, *shamiana*, they call it. And there alone was a Hindu girl in a green sari edged with gold, real gold, I suppose, she had that look. She was as pale as you, except her eyes, and she was eating a small pink cake with coconut icing. I can't endure the stuff, but I went and took one too, very sweet it was. And I looked at her, and she looked at me, eating our coconut cakes, and she licked the thumb and first finger of her right hand, and so did I, and then she smiled and she said: *I must say good-bye*, and went into the shamiana. That was all.'
>
> 'She gave you your poem?'
>
> 'The germ of it,' he said.
>
> 'So simple,' she said. 'So exquisite, the English boy and the Indian girl, rain for the meeting, rain for the loving, rain for the parting, rain tomorrow, rain thundering on the roof, a doom of rain until the hillside broke.'

'I saw that happen at Darjeeling. Forty inches in three days, and then a landslide.'

'The girl – was she so beautiful?'

'Yes,' he said . . .

My girl never spoke to me but otherwise it happened, that moment come and gone, not gone.

It was hotter than ever back in Meerut. There had been brief small rains, the *chota barsat*, but the monsoon stayed away. Black clouds gathered in the south and vanished, and it did not come – a hundred and eighteen degrees on the verandah in the afternoon, a hundred and two at midnight, and still it did not come. And then at last on the eighth of June it came. My memory may be wrong, but I think that was the day at Meerut in the year 1932.

I stood naked in the rain, in the cool miracle of rain, in gouts and plouts of rain. And overnight, brown India was turning green.

Although damp heat suited me better than dry, monsoon weather was also burdensome. The incessant sweating brought on prickly heat, a maddeningly itchy rash. A myriad bugs swarmed at every lamp and mosquitoes whined, lusting to get through the net. Snakes were flooded out of their holes, so one had to light one's way by night. Everything mildewed and cigarettes became unsmokable.

These were minor banes amid the magical rebirth of the land. It was about then that I bought an ancient army-surplus T-Model Ford, with an open truck or lorry body. I christened it Arabella, and became most attached to her. With a couple of basket chairs in the back, Arabella chugged us in grand style to play golf or polo, or simply chugged us for an evening ride. Push down for low, let up for high, push another pedal for reverse, the parking brake half on for neutral – Arabella's gears were odd. She was no speedster but a trusty steed with impeccable manners except in one respect: there was no starter, so one had to crank, wary of a broken wrist from vicious backfires.

That September I drove north on leave, by Roorkee and through the Siwalick foothills to Dehra Dun, which lies in a plain immediately below the beginnings of the Himalaya. My intention was to leave Arabella at Mussoorie, the hill station close above

Dehra, and from there go on foot into the Indian state of Tehri-Garhwal.

Unfortunately, and typically, I had omitted to check the oil and she seized up solid at Dehra Dun. That may have been just as well because a T-Model was better suited to flat country than to mountain roads. So I left her to be repaired and climbed by other means.

That was a first long shooting trip, alone with my bearer, a patriarchal rogue named Adil Hussain, and with a shikari from Garhwal. My licence allowed me to shoot black bear and ghooral, a species of mountain goat.

The bear proved elusive, but after weeks of negotiating cliff and steep jungle the shikari came on fresh tracks, which we followed all morning on a narrow path. My borrowed rifle was a double-barrelled .470, a monster and heavy. The tracks petered out; we had lost the bear; so I handed the rifle to him and led the way to swing back for home.

That was another one of my mistakes. I rounded a corner of rocks to be met by a roar and, face to face, a great six-foot bear on its hind legs. It did not attack but made itself into a black cannon ball, rolling over and over down the hill, as is the way of bears, out of sight.

The rifle was back in my hands but the bear had gone. Not so. It came back uphill in a businesslike fashion, just as fast as it had rolled down. I shot the bear. One close shave and one lesson learned. One will not reach the end of the lessons until one is no more.

The second close shave was not my fault. We were moving along the side of a steep valley. They were all steep, in fact, and in those days I was not too bad a mountain goat, careless of heights that would paralyse me now. I was ahead, carrying the blunderbuss, when I saw something at eye level to my left. At the same moment the shikari punched me in the back.

I recovered and turned to the big brown and green snake, coiled, its head raised to strike. *Bahut karab wallah*, 'very bad one', from him. I shot it with the right barrel and reloaded instantly and instinctively, as soldiers do. But there was a mate, not coiled to strike, coming for me. I blew the head off it too, and I blew myself back down the hill. That rifle had a nasty trick. If you fired one barrel the other often fired itself out of sympathy, and the two barrels of a .470 approximate the kick of one Clydesdale horse.

The shikari was quite shaken, so I suppose that the snakes were bad ones. They were not cobras, which I had met already.

The only Europeans I saw were four lady missionaries who spent a night at a *dak* bungalow nearby and asked me to dinner. Four lady missionaries – rather earnest ones at that – seemed a bit much to me, but I went and made stilted conversation.

Leave was nearly up, the monsoon nearly over, and I headed back. Birds did not much interest me then, but no one could fail to notice the party of scarlet minivets, the males bright red, the females yellow, vivid small creatures darting from one patch of forest to another.

I had been alone but not lonely, driving my body hard, revelling in the mountain coolness, strong again after a first hot homesick summer. I ran and walked along green hills loud with water, and came one evening to the bright lights of Mussoorie.

They were not neon-bright but they would do. In the cabaret at the hotel there was a gentle Anglo-Indian girl to compensate for the ascetic life. Then Adil Hussain and I drove to Meerut in Arabella.

The monsoon had rolled back south for another year and I was happy, driving home, or second-home. One cannot feel happy in the rich rejuvenated land, driving home beside a brimming canal, and be altogether an outsider, can one?

SEVEN

# 1932 and 1954

A difficulty about this kind of writing is that I have trouble in looking steadily to one direction and one time. I think of a first Christmas in the jungle. Then I am contrasting the hard-going, if silver-spooned, life of young officers with the life in India of private soldiers (the Jocks, we called them) who were crowded into barrack rooms, with little real liberty and no decent women, a hellish life; and yet they were cheerful, foul-mouthed, the mainstay of our mysterious family.

But then my chameleon mind pops on past Canada and war and prisons to India again, riding in the vast viceregal Rolls-Royce to have a few holes of golf with the Field Marshal. *The dear Lord*, my sister called Wavell in retirement, and he was that in addition to all that he was.

Then I am sole passenger, comfortable in the owner's cabin, riding a freighter to Australia, not idle, writing mad hours to finish a book.

Then back again to be alone again on the front barge, far ahead of noisy diesels, no sound but a light fan of breeze on old man, cold man, Mackenzie river. But that pushes me a few years on to a tent on the sea-ice in a fiendish blow.

Back and forth, and usually linked haphazardly. In a novel one is held to follow the story, however difficult and slow a job it may be.

I mentioned the word family about the regiment and that can have a sentimental connotation, so I will explain what I mean. We, in our early or mid twenties, were certainly just that. We got on together in our casual way, and as far as I know, there was no rivalry between us. That would have come later, at least between those who were ambitious to succeed in the Army.

Above us were a more disparate collection – the Olympian ones, the popular ones, the ambitious ones (some the best of the lot), the ones who were not quite accepted (decent fellows withal), and the ones who were disparaged by every grade of officer and every grade of Jock. It was in general a happy family, a hard family, sometimes an unjust family, with a peculiar pecking order.

The day after I arrived at Meerut, I had a letter from somebody about fifteen years my senior trying to sell me his old car for twice its value. I could not afford the car but he did succeed in palming off a hundred guaranteed top-quality twelve-bore cartridges. They must have been through a couple of monsoons because, without exception, they hung fire for a second, not the best ammunition for shooting a fast jigging snipe, alarming too, the delayed action bang.

He was very much the exception (no one else ever did me down) but I do not want to convey an image of perfection. So we were a loose-knit family, with the regiment as parent, indulgent about youthful peccadilloes, exceedingly tough when toughness was deserved. We were guided with little explicit guidance, kept reasonably in order.

To young people nowadays, or to the young people I know, the idea of soldiering, which means soldiering for war, is abhorrent; and so it is to me. Yet only bigots are not mindful of the human honour that has marched with the profession of arms.

Our first Christmas Patrick Campbell-Preston and I hired the regimental contractor's bus to take us tiger shooting in the Siwalicks, those foothills through which I had driven in September on my way to Dehra Dun. It was an asthmatic vehicle, with a good deal more space than Arabella could provide. Apart from baggage, weapons and general provisions, we carried one turkey, two bottles of champagne and one bottle of liqueur brandy. Our bearers managed us and everything, and the last member of the party was Bacchus, my young bull terrier. So we arrived at Beribara Forest Resthouse, where a shikari awaited us. Bapu had numerous chits (or references) from previous clients, all praising him highly, all discreetly noting that he was a member of a criminal tribe.

I think that the criminal tribes of India were not on the whole very wicked people – not bandits, perpetrators of violence, murderers. They earned their living by honest thievery. Bapu was a charming old boy, far more enthusiastic than my hill shikari. He said that the beat abounded in tigers and that wild elephants also roved in plenty.

Our spirits were already good and they rose still further during a first stroll before the brief evening dusk. Bapu showed us pugmarks in many sandy nullahs, stopped often to listen and to look, small man in his element. Once there was a short sharp call: KYAA, and he raised a finger. *Cheetal*, he whispered. *Sher.* I had been reading Dunbar Brander and other books, so I knew that the spotted deer had called to warn of Lord Tiger on the prowl.

Hearts race, necks tingle, *Sher* (pronounced with long emphasis: *Share*), what a name for the noble beast. But night was falling and we had no torch. 'Don't you think discretion slightly, Pat?'

'Slightly yes.'

We talked loudly on the way back to the resthouse, the subject being the young water buffaloes we must buy or borrow for tiger bait.

Bacchus was pleased to see us. There were still bull terriers in India with square bulldog heads that housed intelligence. But there was much in-breeding and Bacchus was Grecian from tip of nose to top of neck, almost no protuberance of brow, and an abundance of good nature. He was an amiable fool. Frank Weldon, the most gifted escaper I knew in the war, terse, laconic, had another noun for such a person. *An amiable* - - - -, he used to say, but I don't like to write it down.

'There must be at least three tigers in the beat. Those pugmarks were all different.'

'Two anyway. One each would do. *D'accord*?'

'*D'accord*. God, I hope I hear one roar tonight.' But I was asleep if a tiger roared that night.

We were out at dawn, the beautiful fresh time. The country was drying up but there were still a few small pools in the watercourses and muddy places. At one of them the shikari pointed to tracks, indubitably fresh, a monster tiger had passed that way.

And in the jungle were mounds of elephant droppings, still steaming in the cold morning air. We were not allowed to shoot elephants but their presence made the jungle all the more alive.

When we went back for breakfast, Adil Hussain announced that Bacchus had escaped and was last seen at full gallop down the grass road that ran east below the foothills. Bapu explained that the herd of elephants foraged in that direction by day. So the bloody fool was on a pachyderm hunt.

Suitably armed, and with a whistle, I set off after breakfast in pursuit while Pat organized the buffaloes. I walked miles, blowing and shouting, no sign of Bacchus going down or coming back, no wild elephants either, much to my relief. What do elephants do to unshakable-jawed bull terriers? Do they flatten them with a foot? Do they employ a trunk as flail against a tree? Probably the latter. I was sorry about it, the endearing idiot become a bit too much.

I still do not know which is the preferred method because he arrived back at teatime, pleased with himself. 'Bad dog,' I shouted. 'You bad useless bad bad dog,' and I beat him a bit. But abuse and beatings are a waste of time with loving morons who think that bad means good and that the stick is an approving pat. He really was as stupid as that.

Meanwhile, Patrick had assembled seven young water buffaloes, shaggy, brownish-black and woebegone, the sacrificial beasts.

'Puir wee craters. I dinna fancy it ower much.'

'Nor me neether, but it canna be helpit, Pat.'

We were both bilingual and often spoke Scotch in lighter moments, or, as now, to make less of a dirty deed that we were squeamish about committing, yet less than likely to hesitate.

The buffalo would be tied in various places in the jungle in early afternoon. Then, probably never alone before in their dim lives, they would strain at the ropes, lonely and fearful until quick death came, or did not come. If the tiger killed it would feed, drag the rest of the body a distance and sleep the day nearby.

The rich man's way, once you had a kill, was to arrange a beat with a hundred men. The poor man's way, our way, was to build a machan or platform in a tree near the body and sit up for the tiger to come back for second supper.

Three nights all the buffaloes survived and three mornings they were pleased to see us, still more pleased to be led away to a bare modicum of fodder. The Hindu peasant is practical in such matters. Why fatten the beast to feed the beast?

'Bapu say one very clever old *budmash* tiger, he chase other tigers,' Adil Hussain translated. 'They afraid of him. But he get hungry. Tonight he kill.'

Tonight he did not kill.

And still the fresh tracks proliferated. It was disappointing but we were not despondent. Unless in love, one rarely was at twenty-one. There were other things to do. We walked the lower jungle seeking spotted deer without success, or seeking jungle fowl with some success. They were excellent to eat, as different from the stringy chicken of the Indian bazaar as a young pheasant is from a boiling fowl. And we clambered among the low jagged hills, hoping vainly for a shot at the small brown barking deer. We knew a lot about shooting, nothing about the jungle; but in those few days we began to feel at home in it.

More than twenty years later, when I was learning the jungles again for *Harry Black*, I went back to Beribara. The silk-cotton tree was in flower that time. Birds squabbled above at the sweet red pods. And red pods were scattered on the ground, blowsy tulips of the forest. The resthouse was unchanged except for two dreadful coloured prints of Mahatma Gandhi and Jawaharlal Nehru, standard issue. I had met Gandhi once, and had disliked but did not know. There were things about Nehru that I did not like but I admired that tetchy humanist, lover of mankind, if not of men. The last time I saw him I was asked to his house, seven years after Independence (perhaps the time I felt most at home in India). Edwina Mountbatten was staying there, and who should walk in after tea but the man himself. He had no small talk, and nor did I. We exchanged polite platitudes about the garden.

On Christmas morning the seven buffaloes were alive. 'Let's give the poor sods a night off, shall we?'

'Yes, let's,' I said. Even if necessary, the live-baiting was cruel and it bothered us, more Pat than me. He was as kindly a man as I have known.

The bottles of champagne went down with turkey and tinned plum pudding. The brandy we shared with increasing dignity and politeness until it was totter off to bed, to be woken at the usual hour with *chota hazri*, morning tea, with a hangover unbelievable to endure in the deep dark fruitless jungle.

We had seen to Christmas rations for the young buffaloes, which went out quite perkily that afternoon of Boxing Day. Pat and I had more or less recovered and went shooting on the lower ground in scrub forest broken often by watercourses. We were walking home up one of these when, as we rounded a bend, I observed an unusual animal, a langoor, would it be, one of the big grey monkeys? I put the binoculars on it. Not a langoor, but our shikari on hands and knees beside a puddle. He was using his right hand with precision and through the glasses I could see what he was doing. 'Hide, Pat.'

'What's all this about?'

'S'ssht!'

In a while I put an eye round the rock and saw him lope away in his grey tattered shirt, out of sight.

'Come and look.'

What he had been making in wet sand were two perfect pugmarks, the left and right forepaws of a big tiger. The rest of the nullah was dry and stony and no tracks would show. It was a craftsman's job.

'Let's sack the bugger.'

'No,' Pat said as we went on again.

'Why not?'

'Because.'

'Because what?'

'Because he's doing his very, very best to give us tiger dreams, which is jolly nice of him.' Patrick C-P, that cherubic, most equable of men, could be quite annoying. 'There's one other aspect too; if we give him the sack, he'll take the boodle. We're leaving tomorrow, anyway. Let's part the best of friends. Bags you write his chitti.'

So I wrote words to this effect: 'In all my experience in the jungles of the United Provinces, I have never encountered Bapu's equal as a tracker. He knows the tiger as he knows himself, and his marked enthusiasm makes even a blank day rewarding.'

I omitted it about the criminal tribe (not having heard previously of such), and we parted with esteem, modest backsheesh, and our belongings. That was our first Indian Christmas.

## EIGHT

# 1932 to 1935

We were fortunate at Meerut to have as successive companions two British cavalry regiments, the 10th Hussars and the Royal Dragoons, both allies of the foot-slogging Black Watch. We dined together, drank together at the club, and generally had a good time together.

I cannot remember that we had anything to teach them, but they had much to teach an aspiring horseman. I had learned the rudiments of riding at Sandhurst. Now, first with the 10th, and then with the Royals who succeeded them, I went to school again and by the time they had finished with me I was fairly adequate on a horse. My second riding master was Harry Scott, no slapdash cavalryman, an austere, rarely-smiling man, handsome as the devil, he put us through it.

The cavalry also toyed with us at handicap polo. We had one first-rate horseman and good polo player, Tony McConnell. The rest of us were humdrum performers, or new to the game. I had an innate disadvantage in being left-handed, as for reasons of safety polo has long been a right-handed game. Thus, head-on at a gallop, or side by side, your stick was always between you and the opposition. That was the theory of it.

I had been taught to write with my right hand; all other single-handed things I did with my left. So that made polo difficult for me. If you play seven fast chukkers of one game right-handed in the afternoon, and five games of squash left-handed in the evening, you play neither game as well as you might.

The Number One in that greatest of games was usually a beginner, and I was the beginner, my job to shadow and ride off the opposing back. The back in more than one case was the lordly Harry Scott, who sometimes rode in a sheepskin saddle on a pony named Winton. It was an unusual polo pony in that it had been third in the Epsom Derby but thereafter had refused to start in any race. Nevertheless, Winton would play polo for Scott and my job was to ride him off the ball. In every case but one he simply ignored me. That one was when I was on the Colonel's chestnut arab.

It was an arab in grace, in gentle spirit, in everything. Playing slow polo, the arab's mouth was perfect; and for the first two minutes or so of fast polo it remained the same. But then his tongue got over the bit. The arab galloped for the ball and no power on earth, not even Harry Scott, could have controlled him. If you have ever been run away with (carted, we called it), you will know what I mean; and this was not being run away with to the pale blue yonder but sometimes crossing under the noses of other ponies at full gallop. I was not popular.

Leave for officers was plentiful in India – ten days' casual leave whenever you could be spared; two months' privilege leave each year; and every two or three years, six months at home.

My second two-months' leave was in 1933 when I flew home by Imperial Airways. It took four days from Karachi. We flew at the end of May in a four-engined biplane of the Hannibal class, along the Baluchistan coast, across to a story-book fort named Sharjah at the mouth of the Persian Gulf. Our cruising speed was 80 miles an hour, if that, and once in strong headwinds we began to fly backwards to where we came from. But the captain changed course and we edged on again. From Sharjah up the Gulf to Kuwait, to Basra (where the heat was fiendish), and to Baghdad, almost as fiendish.

Flying by good old, great old Imperial Airways meant getting up at two or three a.m., and taking off at dawn to escape the bumps and lumbering on to reach the next stop. It was cool at our cruising altitude of some ten thousand feet. Far below, moving north of us and nearer vertically below us as the morning went on, was our shadow on the bare brown desert, no life anywhere at all but us up here and the shadow of us on the bare brown desert. We landed at Gaza, and then the much shorter flight to Cairo. In Hannibal, and two months later, flying back in her sister ship, Hanno, the crew and passengers were a sort of team, a moon's distance from Jumbo flight nowadays. Held up one night at a remote place in the desert, we slept under Hanno's lower wings.

From Egypt we went up the Mediterranean by flying boat, to Crete and Athens and down to Brindisi at the heel of Italy. Anyone who has travelled by flying boat would agree that it was incomparably the most agreeable mode of flight, from the first belly surge and thrust of spray, to freedom, oddly serene above the sea whence we had come, to the first touch again, the lightest tearing rippling touch, sink slower, wallow, stop, anchor out, sailor boys and girls; it was delightful.

From Brindisi we took train to Paris, and flew by Herakles (an advanced version of Hannibal) to Croydon.

It was home again to Rankeillour, to the familiar place and the familiar people of my youth. At the end of July I flew back to India by the same route in reverse, except that Imperial Airways had extended its service to Delhi. From there, it was only about thirty miles to Meerut. Why not finish the job in proper fashion?

Neil Blair and I had been learning to fly Gipsy Moths the previous winter at Delhi. Our instructor was usually Bhagat Lal, a taciturn Hindu, the best teacher I ever had. 'What about it, Bhagat?'

'H'mm,' he said. It was raining like hell. 'The maidan will be flooded, David.'

'Not all of it, surely?'

The maidan at Meerut was a dead flat plain. 'Yes, all of it, surely. But *Achcha, Koshish Karunga*. Okay, I'll have a try.'

I telephoned the mess to locate Neil Blair, borrowed a helmet and got into the front or passenger's seat with my suitcase and bedding roll, tight squeeze. We made the short hop at about Hannibal speed. Sure enough, the maidan was a sheet of water, with some peeping shoots of grass or the like as evidence of monsoon growth.

Bhagat circled, saying nothing through the intercom until 'Have a shot at it,' and we landed with spray and without much trouble in the water. Neil had arrived in his A-Model Ford. Bhagat Lal bestowed his tight-lipped smile upon us and took off like a floatplane.

The next year Neil Blair and I got our six months' leave and went by P&O liner, second-class, to Marseilles, whence we took

Imperial Airways, home and back 1933

An overnight stop in the desert, 1933

Photographs taken by German photographers the morning after the Warburg Wire Escape, August 1942:
The ladder and bridge from inside the camp

From outside the camp

the train. The most desirable girls aboard were travelling first and there was a barrier to cross to forbidden territory, not particularly fazing. Alternatively, they were free to come slumming with us, which they did less often. Then, even now, even always, I hope, the best women like to be chased a bit.

Back at home, Neil and I played golf one morning on the Old Course at St Andrews. After which, it was a twelve-mile roadrace to Rankeillour for lunch. He got away first in his Talbot and I chased him in Father's new black Ford, one of the first V-8s. The early miles were winding so I bided my time, confident of taking him on the long straight after a village named Dairsie. Just before Dairsie there was a Y junction where the road from St Andrews converged with the road from Dundee. It was a meeting place to be taken with caution. Neil did so, but as I approached the junction a black Ford, identical with ours, slipped in behind him. He went through the village, not furiously, but considerably above the speed limit, fast enough to cause the other car to lock on to him.

Beyond Dairsie the long straight stretch, one Talbot doing its best – sixty, seventy, almost eighty – one black police car doing the same, a second black Ford trailing decorously, its driver, me, in a parlous condition of wild laughter. The police car had the edge and gonged him, and I drew slowly up behind.

He was the Deputy Chief Constable of Fife, out for Neil's blood at first, name and all that. But when he saw the innocent one in matching Ford, he saw the joke, a very decent chap. Fife is Black Watch country, and we were home on leave from India. It was a push-over. But he rebuked Neil roundly and laughed and left.

On Saturday evenings my brother Barkie (who was at Cambridge by then) and I would proceed to Gleneagles hotel, thirty miles west, to beat it up. I do not mean fisticuffs but drink and dinner and drink and dance, and home at two or three in the morning to have (in my case) a slightly tipsy game of golf on the approaching course at Rankeillour. Barks was a temperate man in those and all his days.

There was a rule and we never broke it, I cannot imagine why not. When golf in the wee small hours was over, we had to report in. Pull oneself together, open the parents' door a crack, and say *Home, Mum.* Bedtime at last.

That autumn, when the monsoon was over, the First Battalion moved from Meerut to Barrackpore, near Calcutta. Barrackpore was the only place (except jungles) of some charm that I knew in the plains of India. The golf course, dotted with big trees, ran along the banks of the Hooghly river. I played a lot with Keir Wedderburn, the adjutant, who beat me. He said once: 'You'll never play golf until you batten your temper down.'

I paid heed and set about doing that. Another golfing opponent was our new commanding officer, Vesey Holt, not much good at the game but enormously good value.

Colonel Vesey was a copybook, puce-faced, wide-moustached, broad-checked, slightly splashy-looking, tall, genuine pukkah sahib. I am running out of adjectives in failing to describe that remarkable man. He ruled the roost in Olympian majesty, was intolerant and unfair to people who bored him; indulgent to those, young and old, whom he liked. Even then, in his heyday, his complexion betrayed his habits. It gives me pain to say that in the end the bottle got the better of Colonel Vesey. I know about the bottle, friend into enemy.

His vast, open, bright yellow Rolls-Royce, festooned with spotlights (some common rajah must have been first owner), was wholly in character. He drove, his batman in the back, exactly in the middle of the teeming road from Barrackpore toward Calcutta, and then exactly in the middle of the wide street that led to the left turn on to Chowringhee beside the maidan.

I had acquired (doubtless with Father's long-suffering assistance) a big Ford V-8 with a rumble seat. It was a hot machine for those days, a lot hotter than Colonel Vesey's majestic Rolls-Royce. I followed patiently until the devil got the better of me and I nipped past him on the left, inside.

By the time I reached the polo grounds I was all too aware of the enormity of my offence. The Rolls bore down on me and he got out. 'Impertinent young bugger,' Colonel Vesey said, and said no more. A lesser CO might have mentioned impertinence or some-such in my annual confidential report, not Vesey.

In this eclectic account I have written of the fun and games, one long carefree holiday. But it was not so. The humdrum routine of our working life was there always. When on the job – dull and repetitive as it could be and was – we were on the job. Routine work is as good a key as any to making life endurable, and routine work with the Jocks was no hardship. The warrant officers and NCO's bore most of the thankless brunt of maintaining discipline. The officers were protected, somewhat apart. We could be easy and friendly with everyone. It was a society of trust and some affection, but a truly egalitarian society it was not. What society is? But ours was less so.

In the autumn of 1935 I answered an advertisement and went tiger-shooting in Bengal with a professional hunter named MacDonald. He was a Eurasian, an unusual one, because mixed with the MacDonald was Himalayan blood – from Bhutan or Sikkim or other hillman country. He was a big tough fellow and experienced, if somewhat suspect with the authorities for reasons or activities that I never knew about. What mattered to ignorant me was that he knew his stuff.

We took a jungle block and camped below the foothills by a pellucid river where I fished for mahseer without much success. We had a lady elephant with her baby, a month or two old, a playful menace, he used to butt me in the backside. There also soon appeared on the scene a *Mukhna*, a tuskless male, which was in *must*, a condition of sexual arousal and bad temper in elephant males. The *Mukhna* trampled about our tented camp and generally made a dangerous nuisance of itself. In addition to playing fast and loose with us it caused havoc among the jungle people's crops. So I wrote to the district forest officer asking for permission to shoot the beast but the DFO did not bother to answer. Once, armed, I stood behind the low fork of a tree and there was the *Mukhna*, twenty feet away, with trunk half raised, taking my measure. Eventually it backed out and left.

Every night it came to woo the object of desire, who was by no means unwilling. They were diffident preliminaries watched by moonlight through my binoculars, slap and tickle more gentlemanly than between our elders on that first troopship. Bitten by mosquitoes, I gave up waiting for a rare view of elephantine consummation and took refuge on the camp bed within the net.

We left the infant at home and went every morning to view the tethered buffaloes. The mahout with his ankus (a metal prod) rode astride the elephant's neck. There came a morning when she was nervous and had to be urged on, and MacDonald raised one finger: 'A kill.'

During that day they tied the machan up a tree and by four o'clock, tiger wake-up time, I had climbed to wait above a small clearing. The body of the buffalo, partially eaten, lay below me on the left where my double-barrelled rifle pointed, and where I watched.

Nothing stirred. There was no sound whatever. In the glade below me to my right, a fully-grown young tigress lay. She licked one forepaw and then the other. She indolently licked her chops. She was the most beautiful living thing I ever saw. If she were not, how would I see her now? More beautiful in her rippling stripes of black and gold than any shapely voluptuous girl with thoughts and thoughts.

But the tigress was taking her time before eating supper and I was there to kill her. As stealthily as I was able, and I could be stealthy, I raised the rifle inch by tentative inch to bring the muzzles from left to right. It took a long, long time. But then there was no tigress. I neither saw nor heard her come. I neither saw nor heard her go. It would have been a poor sort of pleasure, even in my killing days, to kill the lissome killer.

We soon had another kill, this time by a big tiger, which dragged the buffalo some distance. MacDonald roped the remains securely to a tree and once more I sat up from mid-afternoon, through the failing light, through the quick dusk of India to night, rather lonely on my perch. It was permissible then to shoot by torch or flashlight, a powerful five-celled contraption clamped to the rifle. You could aim quite accurately along the beam. The night limped on until things happened fast. One moment nothing, the next the snap of a broken rope. I switched on as quickly as I could but already the tiger had begun to drag its kill, so that all I saw was the right side of its head, bushy-faced monster held motionless by the light – as all animals are held briefly motionless by bright light out of darkness. I fired at the only part visible, half of its head. The tiger roared, made a gigantic broadside leap, and was gone roaring through the jungle. Soon MacDonald came with the elephant and we went back to camp.

Next morning we had the unpleasant task of following up a wounded tiger, the shikari tracking on foot in fairly open jungle, us on the elephant.

I felt awful that morning, ghastly, no lesser word – dizzy, a pit of shivers, an aching head. But you wounded a tiger, you followed it up, cardinal law, broken only with shame. The jungle grew thicker, the blood trail less, and we went on foot. We followed for four hours until we reached a forest stream, crossed that, cast far up and down both banks, and gave up.

I went back to bed. The doctor diagnosed it quickly as malaria, benign tertia, the troublesome malaria that returns at intervals, most unpleasant and nothing to make a fuss about.

It was only after my leave was over, and I was back at Barrackpore, that I heard that the tiger's decaying body had been found, not far from the jungle stream where we had lost the trail. It was shaming, even if we had tried hard.

Then I became really ill. This time it was what used to be called malignant malaria, the kind that comes only once and can be lethal.

But the malignant variety was over. The benign tertia came back at about two-month intervals. You felt it lurking, until one morning you got the shivers and went to bed, colder and colder until the heat began and mounted to a hundred and five when the sweat began. What a blessed relief, weak, washed-out, and what a blessing, free of fever.

# NINE

# 1936

By the time I had more or less recovered, we were into 1936, and I took my leave early and easy by cargo ship to Japan and back, stopping at ports down to Singapore and up the China coast and on. She was the *Talma* of the British India Line, a subsidiary of the P&O. The total cost for two months, all found aboard, well-fed and cared for, was seven hundred and fifty rupees, or about fifty-eight pounds at the pegged exchange rate.

They were quiet, pleasant months, in a way not unlike other noisy pleasant days aboard Hannibal and Hanno. The passengers were few, and we had the run of the ship. I had an agreeable companion in John Shattock of the Indian Civil Service. We went to the right places in Japan – Kyoto and others. The Japanese have a wonderful way of blending the artifact into the natural.

Once, walking by a river we saw underwater the slowly-swaying bodies of a Japanese boy and girl in one another's arms. Why had the burdens of life been too heavy for those lovers?

The people hissed and bowed all over the place, hating us. The Army was much in evidence, arrogant buggers, hating us without the hissing. I disliked the men intensely except for one named George Inouye, who had been at Cambridge with my young brother. We played golf and went on the town. Sometimes I wonder what sort of a nemesis later descended on George Inouye, friend of the British.

I had one more go of malaria on the voyage, less extreme, it seemed to be easing off.

Back at Barrackpore, Colonel Vesey said, playing golf: 'Do you mean to tell me that you never went to bed with a Japanese woman?'

'Well, I didn't mean to tell you, sir, but not quite, actually.'

'Bloody fool,' the Colonel said with bluff displeasure.

The reason was less bloody foolish than Colonel Vesey thought, or purported to think.

The hill station for the Barrackpore battalion was not at Darjeeling proper but at Lebong, a thousand feet below, part way down a spur which broadened there to be one of the few flat places in those steep hills. We called them the hills although, at seven or eight or nine thousand feet, they were already mountains, lush everywhere in the monsoon but for the brown slash of a recent landslide, nearly precipitous everywhere but for the terraced tea gardens, where flowery orange pekoe – the bright green of the new flush, two and a bud – the best Indian tea in the world was grown.

We lived in the mist, which was cloud, and in the rain. Once it rained nearly forty inches in three days, and another small earthquake shook my tin-roofed hut by night and I sat on the edge of the bed in slippers, waiting for the big one that never came, hearing the far off roar of someone else's landslide.

That hot weather the signal platoon was part of the Lebong detachment. I had taken a long course the year before and my merry men and I laid telephone lines up and down semi-cliffs, communicating by speech and morse code; or we flag-wagged in morse and by semaphore. There rarely was sun for the heliograph, an optical instrument of aimed mirrors. We had no radios. Our equipment was as archaic as every piece of equipment and armament in the Indian and British armies. With what we had, we were very good. If you have ever sent and received the morse code professionally it is in your bones, just as, having learned to ride a bicycle, you never lose that knack. Forty-six years later I ride a moped, not a common exhausting bike, but the morse code can still rattle through my head from A to Zed, or from A to Zee as our friends across the St Croix estuary inexplicably term it.

That was work. In the afternoon and evening hours we drove up the winding road to Darjeeling, went roller-skating at the Darjeeling Club, or visited new acquaintances at their tea gardens. Most of the planters had Austin Sevens with auxiliary gears, miniature vehicles well-suited for the narrow hairpin-cornered roads. My Ford V-8 was not at all well-suited but neither figuratively nor literally did it ever let me down.

It was living in a saturated cloud cocoon. Once or twice that summer in the early morning we could look forty miles north across a single gulf to see the mountain in her awesome glory, the unclimbed awful mountain. She was Kanchenjunga, a plume, a feather of snow from the ultimate peak. I never did climb mountains, nor had the spirit to aspire to. But for me the Himalayas are Kanchenjunga across that one abyss.

Soon the clouds would billow up and she was gone again.

Malaria came back once, a bad one that time. I suppose that the most abiding or absent heirloom of wretched anopheles were four abscesses and four fewer back teeth.

At last the monsoon was in retreat until almost every morning now we saw Kanchenjunga in stark majesty until cloud rolled up from the depths to hide her again.

The battalion sailed from India at the beginning of December 1936. All the times that I have been writing about Indian days, I have had something lurking ahead of me. It is ancient history now. It is the wire escape at Warburg.

# TEN

# 1942

Now it is time to tell about that time. As I have written, we had hoped to wait until late summer when there would be full darkness for the job, followed by a late-rising moon to help us on our way. We had also expected that there would be no guards beyond the immediate surroundings of the camp.

But now we knew that the Deep Field was a certainty, that the camp would soon be moved, and that in August at that latitude there were no black nights. The Commandant had given the Senior British Officer a preliminary warning, *not for two or three weeks* he said about the move. They always played that sensible trick, so that prisoners could gather their few possessions and when the time came last-minute chaos would be avoided. Then the Germans would spring it on us overnight.

With an announcement that the camp would start moving tomorrow at dawn, it would be chaos enough and the place would be alive all night with Germans. Our stooging system would be worthless. Our signalling system – a pencil-narrow beam of light from the assault point to the top of the camp, thence down to the barber shop, dot-dot-dash-dot, F for Fuse – would be impossible. The diversions, grapnels thrown into the wire and jerked for pandemonium at various places round the camp as well as wide of and astride the real assault point, could not be coordinated.

That was why Tom Stallard decided to jump the German gun. We learned that afternoon that a man most of us knew well and liked, John Dupree of the Seaforth Highlanders, had been electrocuted in a tunnel.

It was not always difficult to hook surreptitiously into electric power and the lighting was incomparably better than with rudimentary lamps. But the walls were moist, the insulation chancy, the space confined, and our own tunnel engineers never used it.

The news of John's death was painful, perhaps the more poignant on that particular afternoon because our own risks were not far ahead.

One may wonder, and I still do, how we got away with months of noisy practice over a mock-up fence in the camp music hut. One methodical German with a modicum of intelligence, observing the musical devotion of the same people time after time, would have thought their looks and their circumstance improbably suspicious. Five methodical minutes of search would have shown him ladder, bridge and wires.

But most of the German staff were middle-aged, too old for the Russian front, unimaginative dug-outs. We were young, at the peaks of mind and body, and we were lucky. As to our planning, that was not a matter of luck but of judgment. Not until the chips were down would luck step in. Then, we would pay one way or another with good luck or bad added to the soundness of our judgment. The last preliminary chance we took – building ladders and bridges and hiding them with our packs inadequately in the roof of a hut – it was plain good fortune that they were not found.

Tom Stallard had appointed an excellent non-playing manager to control the extraordinary intricacies of this escape, with authority to stop it when he so decided. But Tom held himself responsible for it and for us. He had drawn a high place on his ladder. He changed the order and put himself last, Number Ten.

We had dressed ourselves variously for escape. We had collected the ladders and our packs. We sat now on a bench, our faces blackened from the stove of that hut. Patrick Campbell-Preston, my partner, was beside me. We were aware, through chinked fingers, of the lights along the wire, of intermittent searchlight sweeps from the raised sentry boxes at either end, one not far from us. Light was the enemy of eyesight. Do NOT look.

The two sentries shuffled on their beats to meet almost opposite us. *Double Red*, a mutter of words between them, *Double Red*. Now they moved apart. When and if they both were at the far end of their beats, we would have the *Double Green* we needed. It would not then be *Double Green* for the men at the diversions near us and elsewhere round the camp who would lob their grapnels over and into the fence to make the loudest diversionary rattle that they could manage. For them it would probably be a *Single Red* and a nasty risk and no bright prospect of escape.

*Left sentry Red, moving Green. Right sentry Red, moving Green.* I heard the reports. It was not yet and it might not be, so damnably involved, so many men working for us without reward of any kind. And word would inevitably be out among the other thousands: *Something big is on. Behave exactly as usual.*

So gramophones played in the distance and voices called, and occasional laughter, not much laughter. *Madness*, the people who knew a bit were thinking. But we, who knew all there was for prisoners to know, knew otherwise: given both sentries *Green*, and no unexpected visitors; given that our key would turn again for darkness; given that the double fence did not collapse, it was no madness but a risky natural. So many *givens* to make one *natural* was another point.

*Left sentry Red, stopped Red.* Why? *Right sentry Red, moving Green.*

We sat on that bench and heavy packs creaked. A pair of young men near me had been talking casually about fishing in Scotland, unbelievable, but they had been. They stopped talking. *Left sentry Red, moving Green. Right sentry stopped Green. Left sentry stopped Green. Double Green.*

'Go.' The manager's single word was terse and quiet behind the hut. Dot-dot-dash-dot, the letter F, signalled up the camp, to be relayed down. Geography and location made a two-way signal necessary.

The lights went out.

> There was darkness and we all stood up. The people in front went through the door and carried the ladder down the steps. It was even quieter than before. Only fifteen seconds ago we had begun to move. Now we had action and the time of waiting had gone. This was reality and clear.
>
> The other ladders came out with us. We all turned and swung into line facing the dim etching of the wire. It was still quiet but on both sides I could hear the rattle of diversions. The diversion men had thrown in their grapnels and were shaking

the wire fence. Already there were the familiar high-pitched screams of disconcerted Germans. We had waited a long time for this.

We went ahead in line. First we came to the trip wire, a few feet back from the main fence. It had been whitewashed so that it would be visible but it was no more than a pale outline as we stepped over.

The front of the ladder went up. The first man of my team raised the bridge. I could see it against the sky. Now that we had been in the dark for a minute or so, things were showing up. I saw the others in front of me, the fence above, and through it the flat plain and the small hut which would guide us when we were over.

The Number One pushed up the bridge ladder. I heard the click of the sockets and then the tingle of the wire as the bridge lay across it. He went up at once, with the second man close after him. The rest of us crowded in order at the bottom. This was the thing we had practised so often. This was the thing we could do with our eyes shut. It was easy. The three other teams were going too. The wire rattled and twanged.

Pat and I were half way down the team of ten. It went fast, faster, perhaps, than ever in training, and each one of us was drilled to be automatic. I do not have much memory of going over; only a climb, a scramble, a grip of the dropping bar and down on the other side. Pat was in front of me. I followed him past the small hut. There were a few shots round about and by this time the sentries were in full voice. The diversions had shocked them but this was something *unheimlich*.

The first fifty yards were easy going. Then we came to a patch of beans. They were high beans; nothing is thicker nor more tenacious. We came through the beans on to a patch of grass and turned left over ploughed fields. We ran along almost parallel with the camp. Pat forged ahead going well, much too well, I was dead tired already and I saw him fading into the dark. Then he stopped and came back. He forgot his English voice and he said in a hoarse Scottish whisper 'Arre ye wounded, Davie?'

I wrote that account soon after the war for a book called *Detour*, and would not change a word of it now.

There had been some random shots about the place but I was

not wounded. 'Tired,' I said, and we went on more slowly to the west. A few more shots, much shouting. It dwindled behind us. The orders were to fan out and we were following our appointed direction – north a little, west a bit, then south on our own heading.

The human sounds soon faded altogether. The sky was clear and the waning moon had risen obligingly. After an hour or so we stopped for a rest among stooks of harvested wheat, perfect cover.

'The Deep Field must have been on the north side, as we thought.'

'Yes.' Some people had been caught, we knew. We wondered what had happened to those people. But this was the here and now.

'That railway line can't be far ahead. Should we head to hit it, or start swinging to meet?'

The railway on our copied map ran due north and south. The luminous needle on our home-made compass pointed roughly right toward Polaris.

'Better keep on west to hit it.'

'You know, Pat, whatever might happen to us ever again, that would have been the best thing ever.'

'Nothing ever could touch it, nothing.'

That was true for both of us. I think that it must have been true and remained always true for all the people who got over the wire at Warburg. We had seen or sensed a botch-up on one ladder early on, the RAF, and then we had heard the order STOP! behind us. We learned later that twenty-eight people out of forty had got over with only one slight bullet wound. We learned much later that three had got home. By posting guards well north of the camp, the Germans had caught some people. But it was the Deep Field that prevented machine gun fire from the sentry boxes.

We walked west again through farmed land by moonlight. There were no buildings, no sign of human beings, nor of life at all until we picked our way through a field of cows that lay chewing the cud, not interested in us, strictly neutral cows.

Up a slope, and here was the railway line. The luminous needle swung to point at my stomach. Walking across mixed country by night is always hard. Following a deserted railway is wonderfully easy. We were quiet in our rubber-soled boots, alert and strong, and free at last. It was more than two years since we had lost our freedom. There would always be some railway line to find and to follow for the two hundred miles that lay between us and the Schaffhausen salient where Switzerland leaned over the Rhine into Germany.

We made famous time into the small hours of morning. We had put fifteen or twenty miles between us and the camp. There were woods below us on the left for daylight cover. Should we stop now and hide? We were tired but in perfect rhythm. Doing even as little as ten miles a night, twenty nights would get us there. It would be easy. But caution! At the first rim of dawn in the east we would hide. Push on until then.

A small cluster of buildings ahead on the right, no lights, no sound in them. We paused and listened. Nothing. We would walk on through.

They must have heard us coming. We were jumped at the wayside railway station. A few minutes later the milk train came through. Not much later we were being driven back to Oflag VI B.

The facts are that we were superbly trained and prepared for escape *from*, and we had proved that. We were woefully ill-prepared for escape *to*. What was more, it made no sense whatever to think that we could walk two hundred miles and more by night through a densely populated country at war. The people who walked a much shorter distance west for Holland made better sense. So did those who hopped on freight trains. So even did those who travelled openly as foreign workers with false papers. Almost all were caught but they made better sense than we did that time.

There was to be another time for Patrick and me, when we made much better sense, still not enough sense, a fair gamble though.

But, if you put your free minds to it, you will begin to understand the myopia of our all-consuming golden purpose within that wire. *Get out of it.* We would. We did, not thinking enough about a long hard journey just begun.

We did soon move, by packed cattle-truck back to Bavaria where our first camp had been. Being a major, Tom Stallard was sent to a camp for senior officers. Our ways never have crossed again. Tom was our leader, not forgotten.

ELEVEN

# 1940 and 1943

*What matters most is that when high summer comes, the sweet red berries will be a feast for every fruit-loving bird*, I wrote at the beginning. The blossom of the *Amelanchier* was out then in May and berry time is here. Robins and others are vying for them on small trees beyond my window.

Our first German camp in 1940 was at Laufen, on the left bank of the river Salzach, which had been the Austrian border. A few miles to the south upstream was Salzburg, near which Adolf Hitler had his mountain den, above which the thunderheads of Alpine summer piled.

Laufen was shorn heads and lice and an ineluctable press of humanity and hunger enough to eat stinking black potatoes, and bad news, personal and warwise. Laufen was where one afternoon I thought that I had found a private place beneath a high wall to work upon the seams of my one and only shirt, real Aertex too, all tattered and torn. Nests of them, whence they ventured out at birth to make pink narrow lines all over me. A private place, I thought, but the oaf in a nearby sentry box cackled in rude jest or even sympathy at my predicament and probably I cackled back about the intimacy of lousy lice.

Laufen was the end and the beginning. It was a first tunnel under the street and up almost to surface in a pigsty. Overhead were sowish grunts and small squeals and the trot of tiny trotters. How to pick up a succulent piglet on the way to a freedom feast remained a dream and became an academic question when they found that tunnel.

The good things about Laufen were stout companions in adversity, weak beer available in the canteen, and even wine sometimes. The more you tippled the raw stuff, the less intolerable a pack of people became.

But alcoholic palliatives for sale were a thing of the past by the autumn of 1942 when we came back to Bavaria to our third prison camp beside the small ancient city of Eichstätt. The camp, which had been a training barracks, was roughly rectangular, as Warburg had been, but in other respects was much different and much better. It was set in a narrow wooded valley, with no far vistas to tantalize; and it was on two levels. On the north side against the hill was a line of stone buildings with paths down from them to flat open ground, quite adequate for the various games we played. In those middle years, Red Cross and private parcels were coming in and we had energy to spare. At the east end on the lower level were the wooden huts nicknamed Garden City, where about half the prisoners lived. Also vegetable gardens which thrived on the world's best manure.

We lived in Block Two on the upper level beside the Lagerstrasse, and in some comfort compared with what we had grown accustomed to. In our block we even had plugs to pull. One particular plug, or its immediate environment, was to be the centrepiece of my existence for the next few months.

A rough estimate about underground activities at Warburg was that fifty tunnels were begun and fifty tunnels were discovered by the German searchers – ferrets, we called them. The essential reason for this total failure was not incompetent tunnelling. It was that when you burrow to make a hole, you have to put the dislodged earth somewhere. You can make a reinforced false ceiling – all the ferret needs is a measuring tape. You can make an entirely convincing false wall under the floor of the hut, and the same applies. You can wander innocently about, allowing the wrong coloured earth or spoil to trickle down inside your trouser legs. That serves only to whet the ferret appetite.

So there were too many tunnels at Warburg and not one escape through them. We had another idea, and got away with it, over the wire in the most dramatic mass escape of the Second World War. I say this without arrogance or conceit. It was a fact; and as a result of that we had become influential practitioners in the business.

At Warburg, we had had another idea. At Eichstätt we also had another idea. It was a very simple one, which we propounded with some earned authority to the Escape Committee, and they agreed to it. A honeycomb of tunnels makes no tunnels. One single tunnel can make an escape.

So it was to be, and the first essential was a trap. More accurately, the first essential gift and chance in this case was a leader who could use his hands. The second essential was an even more masterly engineer. Two essentials and we had them, Frank Weldon and H-B, or Hamilton-Baillie.

The floor of our latrine was made of square ceramic tiles and the first task, as always in tunnelling, was to make a trap. Frank and H-B chipped meticulously to loosen the tiles, not widening the spaces between each. They had them off, they poured concrete, they fitted the tiles back into place, inserted lifting bars and made a pair of handles with slots to fit those bars. Trap made, we were, in a preliminary way, in business. It was a job of not less than exquisite precision. I know, because Pat Campbell-Preston and I were to become the trap-handlers.

It was back in place in the corner of that multiple latrine – three seats and a pissoir, if I remember rightly. The outline of the trap – a number of square tiles, not forming a square or rectangle overall but each tile perfectly unbroken – was clearly visible because of hairline cracks along each outer edge. We plastered these up with a paste composed of boot polish and fine dust, rubbed the seams perfectly smooth and clean, and wetted the floor down with a mop. So long as the floor remained wet the trap was good, in fact invisible. If the floor was dry, H-B's work of genius stood out like a lined hag at a beauty contest.

We were most vulnerable to the enemy until the next stage was completed – and that was excavating a chamber commodious enough to hold people, ultimately a shift of four, with the spoil that they dug. A cosy place it had to be and so became.

The bags which contained the spoil were made of any strong cloth, either stitched laboriously by hand or stitched speedily by machine in the camp tailors' shop. That was illicit use of machinery provided for the legitimate purpose of mending prisoners' clothing.

I remember going once to the head tailor and saying politely and implacably: 'We're almost out of bags. Could you possibly stitch up a hundred for us by tomorrow?'

'You people spoil everything,' he said. It was true. We did, but that did not deter me one iota, although I knew in a subordinated corner of my mind that this good man was entirely, reasonably right. It never occurred to me then, nor has it ever occurred to me until now, that the material for the jute bags he stitched so speedily for us might by some improbable quirk of possibility have originated at Caldrum Works, a factory first built and owned by those plunderers of the poor, the Walkers of Bonnie Dundee.

That is a random turning of the wheel but my next thought is not random. If you gave up escaping as an occupation, which I did for months at a time even in those earlier days, and you learned a language, or studied the law, or economics, you switched totally to considering the escaper fraternity a nuisance, a disrupter of routine, a dangerous lot of maniacs who at their best caused interminable cold parades while the camp was being searched, at their worst could draw gunfire upon innocent people. One could, and did, switch one's mind from one point of view to the other overnight. In a camp of about three thousand prisoners the engrossed escapers might, at any one time, total perhaps a hundred.

As I have said, the beginning was the most vulnerable time because the trap must be open until we had excavated a big enough hole to close people in. We had to have intensive stooging and that in itself, unless most artfully done, was highly suspicious. It may be that more tunnels were lost through too much anxious watching out for Germans than from any other cause.

But once the chamber was made Pat or I could close the trap, paste it, mop it wet, and one of us be ready in our room upstairs to get the shift out instantly if there should be an unexpected parade and roll-call. That was a daylight trick the Germans quite often played. Being creatures of unimaginative habit, they hardly ever, if ever, paraded us for no reason by night; hence our preference for the safer night-shifts when four dummies could be put to bed or bunk elsewhere in the camp.

Elsewhere in the camp was our other idea. After dark, when the chill of autumn and winter justified greatcoats, we would suspend two bags of spoil, weighing ten or fifteen pounds each, from Red Cross braces – or suspenders, as North Americans more logically call them – stroll a few hundred yards along the Lagerstrasse and down to Garden City or the inferior wooden huts at the east end of the camp, and dump our spoil.

The tunnel which we had begun would not be very long – about ninety easy feet under level ground and then a climb, some forty feet in linear distance, up below the camp fence, below the road where the sentries patrolled, ultimately to break in a disused henhouse on the valley side. Given reasonable soil and adequate technicians, level tunnelling through anything but solid rock is easy. If you encounter too large an isolated boulder you can go round it. Climbing round or beneath that isolated boulder is quite another matter. Newton's law of gravity applies to it and to every other boulder overhead.

These difficulties and dangers would come later, and all would be coped with by Frank and H-B. In the meanwhile, we pushed ahead. We were a nucleus team of some thirty people, many of whom had blitzed the wire at Warburg. At first we took our loads directly from the open trap, along the camp to the dumping ground. Later, as we progressed and volume increased, we enlisted thirty-five more carriers and we doubled up on bags by making an attic hide to hold the night-shift spoil. Thus, the chamber below could be filled a second time. It was another risk of discovery, coolly assessed and taken.

That was our third autumn, winter, early spring. In the real world outside, the war went on. We were not ignorant of it. Indeed, our hidden camp radio gave us the BBC news each evening. I never knew the whereabouts of the secret wireless set that someone operated in every camp. It was not my business. We also had the German press, from the *Völkische Beobachter*, abominable Nazi organ, to the *Münchener Neueste Nachrichten* and the *Frankfürter Zeitung*, both of which revealed glimmerings of sanity from time to time, not by what they wrote – they would not dare – but by what they did not write. Whichever side was winning would be the more accurate in its news. Thus, and particularly as the war edged inexorably to our favour, it might be that we had a better-balanced knowledge of it than average private citizens on either side.

We had strong opinions too. In my prison novel, *The Pillar*, one of the characters said about the communiqué after the Casablanca Conference in January 1943:

> 'I don't like this unconditional surrender idea. I think it's thoroughly stupid. The Germans are beginning to realize that they've lost the war; in fact the less fanatical Nazis are probably wavering already. Instead of encouraging them to plot against Hitler, we blithely announce that we won't treat with any German. We're giving Hitler the one weapon he can use to make them fight more fanatically than ever. And apart from the question of expediency, I think it's immoral.'
>
> 'What's immoral about it?'
>
> '*Bedingungslose Kapitulation*,' Adrian said. 'That's a Hitlerian concept of absolutes. We're supposed to be fighting for freedom and moderation. I didn't think they were such fools.'
>
> 'You can't call Roosevelt and Churchill fools.'

But Adrian did and he was right in that case. And in that case Adrian was me. I thought it then, and I saw it come about. Many people in my novels have held views which were the antithesis of my own, but not about unconditional surrender.

That prison novel, *The Pillar*, was about six varied companions and the six-sided pillar of their house. John Brooks in the *New York Times* wrote of it: 'The most thorough and revealing and also the warmest account of military imprisonment in World War II that this reviewer has seen.' I do not like re-reading my own books but I had to have a look at *The Pillar* for these memoirs. It is on the whole a very good book, just as true and readable now as when I wrote it. But it is lost and gone except from some libraries and bookshelves and I am privately embittered on the rare occasions when I think of that.

In addition to our trap-handling which, of necessity, was a monopoly, Pat and I took our turns at working underground. We were common labourers at that, although we could dig as well as all but the musclemen, and revet in easy going as well as anyone but the experts. Frank and H-B coped with any and every eccentricity underground.

I am not competent to write about tunnel engineering but I must quote from *The Pillar*, tell the simple thing, the supple ambience of a shift:

'Do you really need to revet in this clay? It seems pretty firm.'

'No,' said Bob, 'but it gives moral support. The boys never like an unrevetted tunnel. Every dribble of earth, they think there's going to be a fall. It's worthwhile for that reason. You can't dig forwards when you're thinking backwards. That's rather good, isn't it?'

'It's wisdom,' said Adrian. 'It's Socratic.'

'Want to put in the set?'

'Yes, of course.'

Bob came back and lay down to let Adrian pass him. It's quite homelike up here, Tasker had said. Yes, it was homely in this bit of underground property while the camp was asleep and you were doing a job, although it might be midday or midnight and the bright lamp hissing in its niche would soon need pumping, and it was warm and the air was good and you could remember other ones where you had coughed your guts out for need of oxygen, and the clay was smooth reflecting polishy, and the only dampness was small beads of breath moisture condensed on roof and walls, and you were warm, closed in with whispers booming, and the day shift had made five-foot three which was a record so far, and perhaps nobody else in the world knew as much about making tunnels as you did, but Adrian, your pupil, was better already at some things than you were, and you watched him from behind, swallowed up in a thick once-pink vest and a handkerchief knotted on his head at the four corners, and he had the spiling boards in place in the roof and the two verticals not quite vertical because the tunnel was narrower at the top, and they were in the slots on the baseplates, and those sunk, and the roof cross-piece was in place, so that was the neatest trick in all tunnelling, that juggling with six loose wooden planks now sliding the stressing board up between the verticals, putting his shoulder strength into his calloused slender fingers, and the wood groaned as it went home, and now the whole thing was as firm as a house, without a nail in it or a single hammer blow struck but only the application of the triangle of forces, and if anyone watching Adrian should think it was an easy trick to do, let him try himself.

'I never saw anyone do that as quickly,' Bob said; which was high praise because he did not mean just quickly, but well also.

'I'm getting better at it. What do we do next?'

'We'll dig the nine inches and put in the next set. Then we'll extend the air pipe.'

Adrian took the clay-spiker which was a thing much like a gardener's trowel, only flatter with a long handle. He cut a slot laboriously across the centre of the face to a depth of about two inches; then he peeled it off step by step all the way down to the floor, then step by step all the way up to the roof; by which time Bob had filled six jute bags, loaded them on the sledge, pulled once on the bell-rope for haul-away, and the sledge lurched off into darkness. When the single bell sounded again, he pulled the empty sledge fast hand over hand, coiling the rope, and debating with himself whether it would be worthwhile to instal a railway with wheeled cars because the sledges were so heavy that in another twenty feet you would have to have a relay point.

Adrian was working well and neatly, but he was too slight to be a digger; he lacked strength in his shoulders which was a fatal lack not to be compensated for by any degree of skill. Stamp was a rough worker, but he could dig three inches for Adrian's one. Stamp was the most phenomenal digger in the camp except that you might be as good yourself.

'Let me have a go,' he said.

They changed places again. Adrian was panting, but with exertion only because this air was sweet and as strong as at the seaside. Bob churned the stuff out tirelessly, sweatingly, in the most satisfying labour known to captive men, or perhaps to any man. They put up the second set. Then they extended the air pipe. Klim tins had a neck a little smaller than the rest of the can, and made very exact because powdered milk must be kept airtight. So you cut off the base of the tin; the neck of one fitted into the bottom of the next with hermetical neatness, and the result was a wizard pipe. Perhaps some day somebody would congratulate Messrs Klim or whoever made the things; more likely not.

They pumped the carbide lamp to a dazzle, left it at the face, and went back to the chamber. It was about eleven-thirty.

'Thought you'd gone to sleep up there, Bob, you old bastard,' said Stamp. 'Me and my cobber are frozen to the tits.'

Bastard was his term of endearment. He was tough, foul-mouthed, direct and slightly uncouth like most of his countrymen. But the Australians were good men – the best men in prison.

> 'Go and get warmed up, then,' said Bob. 'And for God's sake remember we're climbing at twenty-five degrees. I'd rather have it short and straight than one of your skew-eyed records.'
>
> 'Muck to you,' said Stamp. He undressed to vest, pants and gym shoes only.

And later that night:

> Now they sat round, the four of them, and ate the night meal by fingers, which is the best way when you are hungry; and it was good; and Keith's coffee from the two thermos flasks was hot nectar; and their breath puffed visibly; and there was a smell of fat-lamp and of earth and of humans mixed up inimitably in the tunnel way; a man's bête noire would be his comrade in the time down there, and a stranger would be known to him.

In all our tunnels until that time the worst difficulty had been air supply – the further you went, the harder it became to force good air to the face, self-evident. But our engineers solved that one in beautifully simple fashion. They hitched the air pipe circumspectly to the chimney of a room stove, kept a good fire going and the air, instead of being forced in diminishing quantity to the face, was drawn strongly back from it and up the chimney and good air filtered forward all the way along the tunnel. Of their many inventions and improvisings, that was the most ingenious.

We worked on through the safer winter months. Each evening after dark our small burdened army walked their bags of earth to Garden City where the Germans searched, finding hide after hide of tunnelled earth, perhaps fifty tons of it. Sixty great-coated figures evening after evening – why did they never stop just one of us? They never did because they lacked imagination. To which might be added that we were cool cats, as innocent and unhurried as be damned.

It may be that through an innate and inculcated tendency to understatement, I have given the impression that we progressed easily and inevitably without much tension toward our goal. But in fact we spent our waking lives in tension, beset by numerous near-disasters. Out there, people were fighting and dying in a war. In here we worked away in comparative safety, trying to make up for what we were not doing. Far too much sentimental twaddle has been written, and is still being written about the noble prisoner. Put your hands up, unwounded, as I did, and how noble are you? But we were calm for trouble; there is no doubt of that.

By the end of winter we had almost finished. I quote again from *The Pillar*, where a similar tunnel failed:

> Spring came at the beginning of April. That was a time of great hopes, with North Africa nearly over, with the turn coming in the Pacific, with the eastern front rolling. But for Bob and Mark and the others, it was a time of immediate hope. It was a time so sweet with anticipation that you said to yourself: My God, I hope the war doesn't end before we get out. If you lay now a short way back from the face, you would hear the muttered thump of sentry-boots pass overhead. You were not yet out, but you were outside. It was a premonitory murmur of delight to be felt underground, and to be remembered afterwards when you saw that the lime trees had broken to the freedom of new leaf; and to be remembered always.

Now it was made except for the final step before breaking out. We closed the tunnel up and waited for escaping weather. So long as Pat and I went about our latrine duties, which were not entirely savoury – I mean that evacuation must go on despite a great future cause of evacuation – so long as we kept the place in good clean running order and that floor wet, all was well.

It was soon after we had closed the tunnel and were idle, walking many miles each day to a physical fitness that we might never reach again – it was then that a bizarre thing happened. Someone wrote a note and slipped it into a letter box at the *Kommandantur* gate at the west end of the Lagerstrasse. It stated explicitly that a tunnel started from the latrine in Number Two Block.

The reason that we knew about this was even more bizarre. The note was handed back to us by one of the *Sonderführers*. They were an odd breed of English-speaking Germans, neither officers nor other ranks but something cadet-like in between, probably unfit for active service.

That peculiar incident was described by Jerry Wood, a Canadian who compiled the book *Detour*, from which I have quoted my own short piece about the wire escape. Jerry was the best of enthusiastic men but I think that his description was inaccurate in some respects about that note and was incomplete about the after effects of it.

He was certainly right about the note's existence because I saw it, and with Frank and others laboriously compared that writing with the writing on every prisoner's letter home. Ninety-five percent of PoWs could be ruled out. Still, there were some odd characters about, and we narrowed it down to a few people and drew a blank.

The notion that a German sympathetic to the prisoners might have written that note seems nonsense to me. It certainly reached the security officer because the ferrets searched our latrine more than once and found nothing.

What Jerry entirely omitted to say was that a few days after the mysterious note had been handed over and kept a while and handed back, a massive search of Oflag VII B took place. I seem to remember, but cannot be sure, that in addition to our own Wehrmacht guard company, SS troops from a convalescent home nearby were involved.

It was an intensive and extensive search, starting early and continuing all day, with strongest emphasis on Number Two Block. But they searched vainly everywhere while the prisoner population remained paraded on the lower level. The key to the wire escape had been negative darkness. The key to this attempt was positive wetness.

As the afternoon went on we became increasingly aware that the floor of our smelly latrine must be drying out. Once it was dry a further, even a cursory, German inspection meant certain discovery.

That danger was compounded when some bright spirit pinched a German officer's cap. Reasonably enough, they did not like that and the mood grew ugly. It was obvious that, whatever other unpleasantness might ensue, the search would not end until the cap was found.

I therefore broke ranks, such as they were, and sought out Jack Higgon, the SBO. These letters need explanation. The Senior British Officer in any camp was usually not the most senior in rank but a level-headed man who could manage people and who stood up for prisoners' rights, thus earning their respect, which often meant the respect of our captors also.

He was Major Jack Higgon of the Welsh Guards. 'Look, Jack – get that bloody cap back, or we're going to be well and truly buggered up.'

'Right,' he said, a man of few words.

The cap was mysteriously restored to some obvious place within five minutes. The German Commandant, a fat excrescence and *Parteigenosse* or Party Member named Blätterbauer, stopped screaming and the parade was dismissed.

Granted some more luck, we would soon be giving the bulbous Blätterbauer something to scream about.

TWELVE

# 1936 to 1938

The battalion sailed homewards after its long service in India at the beginning of December 1936, and we were at sea in the Indian Ocean when the King abdicated. His brief reign had been of no moment to us, and if he could not do his job without having at his side the woman he so explicitly and embarrassingly loved, then let him get out and get on with it.

Our journey home was to be broken by short service in the Anglo-Egyptian Sudan, with headquarters at Khartoum. Aden, as we rounded the corner into the Red Sea, was rather less hot and no less imposingly awful a rock bastion than ever, less unpleasant than the narrow sea itself, including the venomous sea snakes that I saw from the railing that time.

We landed at Port Sudan, and made acquaintance with the admirable Sudan Railways, climbing through barren Red Sea hills to Atbara and on to Khartoum. I came to know only the northern regions of the Sudan, and those not well – the rocky hills, the desert, the varied peoples whose demeanour made so pleasing a change from the generally subservient atmosphere in India. The small Sudan Political Service was a model of excellence for the still-great British Empire. The Defence Force was good. Everything was good except the climate.

There were a few dangerous senior officers in the regiment, but only one killer in my recollection. The first time I encountered him was when, as a second lieutenant quite newly arrived at Meerut, I was summoned to the battalion orderly room to be rebuked for some misdemeanour, and drove in my T-Model Ford down past the row of company offices, raising clouds of dust. While I waited outside to be summoned by the adjutant, there arrived a figure on a bicycle. He was Captain N. M. Ritchie, Neil Ritchie, the killer. This pale-eyed monster reduced me to pulp in half a minute for having the temerity to dust up his company office. He mounted his bicycle and rode back to the settling dust. The lethal ferocity was something that I had never before encountered and hoped never again to encounter.

In the Sudan I soon learned that I was to be posted as adjutant of a detachment at Gebeit in the Red Sea hills under a Brevet-lieutenant colonel. The term Brevet requires a quick explanation. If an officer had passed the Staff College, and showed unusual promise, he was upped a rank, captain to major. If he was a particularly outstanding specimen, he could even be upped by two. The detachment commander to whom I was to be adjutant was Captain, Brevet-Lieutenant Colonel N. M. Ritchie.

It turned out, however, that the lion had changed to be quite a lamb. Having recently visited North America on leave, he had met a girl and now love swamped his being. From his room along the way, I heard again and again the tunes of those times – *Smoke Gets in Your Eyes*, *Night and Day*, and so on, the best tunes ever, not only for the lovelorn.

It certainly worked wonders with our killer in his off-hours, and mellowed him considerably at work. He was still ruthless, breaking inefficient NCOs without the least compunction.

Gebeit was in an elevated plain, below higher hills, or jebels, of broken lacerating rock. Among them lived, in addition to ibex, a proud nomadic tribe of Hamitic origin, the Hadendoa, commonly known, for their bushy hair, as the Fuzzy-wuzzies. They were remote people, having no truck with us, but occasionally, riding their camels in procession, they would pass by. At Gebeit there was low vegetation in which lived dik-dik, minute antelope no larger than hares, a giant tree cactus called euphorbia, with milky ooze, and further up the plain in desert country were ostriches, warily wild. It was an inhospitable place of character and I liked it.

Our MT section consisted of two vehicles – half-ton trucks or pick-ups, they would be called here, with open backs. They rode on the new oversized balloon tyres, excellent for desert driving when they held their air but eminently puncturable.

One afternoon the MT corporal, an incompetent and clueless individual, took off without permission and without a reserve of water in the general direction of the Red Sea. By nightfall he had not returned. So my batman, an Englishman of sterling worth named Jackson, and I set off to track him.

The tracking was easy enough, the three-thousand-foot descent of the desert escarpment was not. We found him at midnight, thirsty and punctured, at a disused Red Sea port named Suakim, some forty miles away. We returned to Gebeit at dawn with two vehicles and one corporal under arrest.

Thinking the evening before that he would be near at hand and easily found, I had not bothered to report my own departure, decidedly delinquent of me as things turned out. And the atmosphere at the Colonel's quarters was decidedly not reminiscent of dreamy tunes.

'Where have you been?'

'Corporal Smith took off with one of the vehicles. He is under arrest. I eventually caught up with him at Port Suakim.'

'What do you mean you eventually caught up with him at Port Suakim?'

'I mean exactly what I say, sir.' It had been a long hard night and I was tired, and I had brought the MT back safe if not sound, hence my reply was terse, but no offence intended.

The first time had been unbridled ferocity about a cloud of dust. This time it was quietly said, bridled ferocity. 'I have heard that you are an impertinent young officer.'

'Sir!' I had been rightly pleased with my exhausted, if delinquent, self, and he was being unfair and I was very angry.

For two or three days we glowered; and then, glowering across the tennis net, we suddenly and simultaneously laughed, a good way to make friends.

At one end of the line of officers' quarters for those few months lived the slightly mellowed Neil Ritchie; in the middle myself and Jack Monteith, a good and trusty officer, if ever there was one. At the other end lived the highly unusual Archie John Wavell, only son of General A. P. Wavell, who was already a legend in The Black Watch, and indeed in the British Army. I came to know Archie John long before I knew his father, except to meet the future Field Marshal once at a regimental dinner in London, and to be the recipient of that kindly grunt.

Archie John was unusual in numerous ways, of which I mention a few. First, in a trimly dressed lot of soldiers, his uniform was invariably a baggy mess. He was a gentle young man, chronically untidy. Second, he was an out-and-out intellectual. Some of us were well-read, but the classics, the modern recondite, any writing of quality, were what he lived for. Third – and this one especially bothered the more conventional among us – he lived day and night behind closed, curtained windows. In a hot climate that made daytime sense, but in the cool early mornings of Gebeit it made no sense at all. Everyone liked Archie John and nobody understood him. So it was to be all his life, all his saintly life, one might say.

Leave in the Sudan, three months each year, was even more generous than in India. I went down the Nile to Cairo, thence home by flying boat. The Empire Class had just come into service and were a great improvement on the older biplanes. At the end of my leave I flew all the way back to land on the White Nile, just upriver from Khartoum, and just before, a minute or so before, a dust storm arrived. Those sudden violent storms, called Haboobs, obliterated everything, forcing their way into every house, into every nook and cranny.

The Empire flying boats of Imperial Airways – how imperial everything was and how few people, if any, foresaw what in a few years would become of the greatest empire that the world had known.

I never gave that a thought, although even then I had begun to ask myself questions about where humanity was headed. That winter I was taken on as a temporary underling aide-de-camp to the Governor General of the Sudan, Sir Stewart Syme. One Sunday he sat on a sofa in the drawing room at the palace while we waited to walk across the palace grounds to make a nicely-judged imperial entrance to evening service at Khartoum Cathedral. Casual talk was not particularly easy with him so I tried out the subject I had just been thinking about.

'Don't you think, sir, that mankind's ingenuity, inventions, I mean, are getting out of our control? I'm not saying it very well.'

He looked quite shocked on his sofa. 'No, David,' he said, 'I don't think you are, and I'm sure they're not. Well, it's time to go.' And off we walked and that was that.

Syme must have been a sound administrator, having risen through the Colonial Service to be a Governor, and now a Governor General. About the important side of his affairs I knew nothing. As a person I found him all right, if not particularly likeable, without much original thought in his narrow head. The real aide-de-camp was Johnny Gifford of the Sudan Defence Force, seconded from the British Army, a large and amiable man who rose in the war to be a fighting general. In those days we became casual good friends and after those days we did not meet again.

It was the custom that the Governor General dined once with the officers of the British regiment stationed at Khartoum. Our barracks were on the other bank of the Blue Nile, low and limpidly blue in the winter season.

The temporary ADC was in attendance that evening. 'I hope Vesey is sober,' said the Governor General, not unreasonably, because my Colonel had lately arrived two courses late and a sea or two awash for a state dinner at the palace. But Colonel Vesey's code would require of him that as host he would be stone cold sober and he was, leaving no doubt, however, in anybody's mind that the recipient of the honour was less The Black Watch than the Governor General of the Anglo-Egyptian Sudan.

A guest night was a grandly dignified affair, with the pipers marching, the military band outside, the toast to the King, and in this case two additional toasts mutually proposed. The Pipe Major played the pibroch, slowly pacing at his lament, to which we listened in silence. He halted, gathered his pipes with that hollow clunk, took the silver quaich from the Colonel's hands, raised it, said *slainte mhath,* 'a health to you, gentlemen', downed the dram of whisky and smacked his lips with ritual smack. There were a dignity and splendour.

The evening ended early with appropriate thanks. The Governor General took the right back seat of honour in the state car and I sat beside him and we started home.

It was then that things went devastatingly wrong. Instead of turning right to follow the bank of the Blue Nile downriver to the bridge, the chauffeur turned left to weave across the desert.

There was a moment's inaction here behind, and then His

Excellency Sir Stewart Syme went for the driver's throat. Syme had an ungovernable temper (of which I had heard and seen minor evidence playing golf). He now set about throttling his drunken chauffeur to death. The effect of this was to put the accelerator pedal to the floor and we swung perilously towards the great Blue Nile.

I hauled Syme off his victim, leaned forward to switch off the racing engine and we lurched to a halt. I told Syme to get out, disembarked myself, and opened the driver's door. He toppled to the desert where Syme again attacked with kick and punch. 'Stop that, and help me put him in the back.'

Large dead-drunk men make heavy burdens but we managed it. 'I'll drive, you sit beside me.' All that pummelling and heaving might have given the Governor General a heart attack, fortunately not, but it took the stuffing out and he sat in subdued silence while I drove him to his palace, an unusual ending to a state occasion. It may be my imagination, but I fancy that after that he looked at his temporary aide-de-camp a trifle askance.

That cost the driver his job, and I reported the mess staff for outrageously plying the poor chap with drink. Johnny Gifford shook with laughter and made me recount events all over again. He found the driver less vulnerable employment elsewhere. We were a happy sort of ship under a captain we did not sort of much admire.

In 1938 we sailed through the Suez Canal (in my case, for the fourth and semi-final time) and along the Mediterranean to Gibraltar where most of the mighty Royal Navy had gathered to ride at anchor. How magnificent they looked, the pale grey battleships of the Mediterranean Fleet, the dark grey of the Home Fleet. Battleships, battlecruisers, such an assemblage of battlewagons, a multitude of lesser fighting ships, invincible. Who could think otherwise?

I was posted to our regimental depot at Perth where recruits did their basic training. Life at Queen's Barracks was busy for the warrant officers and NCOs who trained the recruits. But the few officers had little to do except supervise and had ample time to fish and shoot. For me the depot was especially good, being less than twenty miles from home at Rankeillour.

But my restless foot soon itched again, this time for Canada where Patrick Campbell-Preston was finishing two years as aide-de-camp to the Governor General, Lord Tweedsmuir, better known as John Buchan, whose stories of true-blue high adventure I had been gobbling up since childhood. To be ADC in Canada was the prime red-carpet job for unmarried officers in their twenties, and I finagled all that summer to take Patrick's place. The allure was not to serve the famous John Buchan, it was plain Canada, that immense and wonderful land of rugged legend.

But just as, with Patrick's help, the job was being delicately arranged, the threat of war lowered over Europe and by the end of summer it looked as if my Canadian dream would come to nothing. But Neville Chamberlain signed away Czechoslovakia at Munich and flew home with his piece of paper, with peace in our time, having grasped the nettle danger.

My personal relief at war averted was immense and it was a relief almost universal in Britain. Only a few doughty people opposed the Munich agreement. And who knows? The year of peace that Chamberlain gained may have been the year that saved us.

I barely had time to get to Anderson and Sheppard in London for my viceregal tailcoat and other gilded trappings, and I was off on my travels again.

THIRTEEN

# 1938 to 1939

We sailed up the St Lawrence early in October, the magical time of year in eastern Canada, a kaleidoscope of colour as the great river narrowed on our way upstream.

Government House in Ottawa was, and is, a charming place, a big (in Canadian terms), unostentatious house set in its own tailored parkland. Rideau Hall was its proper name, which we never used, calling it GH among ourselves. The surroundings reminded me vaguely of home if on a much tidier and grander scale, and I liked it very much. Indoors, although the house was about five-fold in size, it was not so very different, with a strongly added measure of formality. However, it does seem ludicrously archaic now, but in British country houses in the 1930s one still put on a dinner jacket every evening, Sunday supper being the sole exception.

At GH the ADC's room, facing the front door and stairs, was the general gathering place where people popped in and out, a place of common politeness and no stiff formality. From there, visitors to the Governor General would be taken along the corridor to his study. But then, if people came for meals as they usually did, we would repair to the drawing room at five minutes before the appointed hour and await Their Excellencies, the guests manoeuvred into a neat row for presentation.

After that, the meal would be announced and the small spare figure of the Governor General, dutifully followed by his wife, would lead into the dining room. He always went first, even if it was a family-only affair, and that always offended me a little. By way of contrast, during the Royal Visit in 1939, the King invariably stood aside to follow the Queen.

Tweedsmuir was the least pompous of men but he did dearly love his honorific plums, a critical comment about a complex man.

There are so many things of praise to say about him. It was almost the last year of his life, spent in constant discomfort with an ulcer and other ailments. His diet was entirely bland, things like scrambled egg or slops, and after meals he would have to prop himself lopsidedly along the sofa. He said to strangers, 'The doctor makes me stretch out like this,' but beyond that necessary explanation he never mentioned his health, or he never did to me, not once in our many walks and other times together.

He was a brilliant and amusing raconteur, the best story-teller I ever met, and his visual memory was astounding. He could read one page of almost anything for the first time and remember it word for word. He was infallibly kind and good company with people, young and old, never speaking down to them out of an encyclopedic knowledge and profound intelligence.

That it could also be inaccurate butterfly knowledge, especially about the natural world, was paradoxical and as transparent as were his other harmless, if irritating faults. 'Oh, he's a great friend of mine,' he would say to someone, when you knew that you had introduced the great friend for the first time to him the day before. He was also a name-dropping snob of unparallelled quality.

About the novels which had brought him fame, he was shy and diffident and never would discuss them. He was proud of his historical works, which he considered to be his real métier. He wrote the fiction in his minute hand and dictated it to Mrs Killick, his faithful secretary for many years. Added to this remarkable fluency of mind was his ability to switch totally from one concentration to another. I liked and admired him for many things, most of all his fortitude.

We were a small staff at GH – Shuldham Redfern, the able Secretary, who had come from the Sudan Political Service; Eric Mackenzie, the comptroller of the household, a tall and hardy Guardsman; Willis O'Connor, permanent aide-de-camp and amiable factotum; Joan Pape, the lady in waiting. Last came the younger generation, Robin Scott in the Navy and myself. Robin had already served a year when I arrived.

Of these few people, including Lord Tweedsmuir himself, I would say that Robin was the most gifted human being. It was said of him that he was the best sailor of his generation. I cannot speak to that but I can well believe that it was so. He went down with his destroyer *Greyhound* off Crete in 1941.

Our working life could hardly in the ordinary sense be dignified with that adjective, being largely a matter of social triviality – getting the seating plan right, which could be of dangerous importance in a stone ivory castle, properly named Rideau Hall. Was, for instance, the unmarried sister and official hostess of the Belgian Minister Baron Robert de Silvercruys, doyen of the diplomatic corps – was she accorded the precedence of the wife of such, or was she not? Or if protocol required that arch-enemies be seated together, what the hell did you do about it? Robin always knew what to do about it. Speeding unflappably and selflessly, he always knew. His mind moved like quicksilver, his body fast, and he never hurried. His memory was as good as John Buchan's. At a grand function, holding his list, he would line up sixty or seventy strangers for presentation, pocket the list, and without fail get every name right.

For big events we were both on duty. Normally, one ADC was in waiting, the other free as air to take off wherever he willed to do whatever he willed. The fall of the leaf that year was no less beautiful than it has been in all my other years, but it was new to me and there was a different strong hardness in the air such as I had never felt in the varied climates I had known.

But let us suppose that it is morning, I am ADC in waiting in the office and the telephone rings.

'Ah, Captain Walker, is that you? Good morning, King here.'

'Good morning, Prime Minister.'

'I trust that you are well, and enjoying our autumn days.'

'Loving them, thank you, sir.'

'I wonder, Captain Walker, would you do me a favour and convey my duty to His Excellency, asking whether I might have the honour of a brief audience at eleven o'clock, if entirely convenient, would you be so kind?'

'H.E. said that he would be free all morning, so I'm sure that eleven would be fine.'

'*Fine*, that splendid word. Only in such usage do you reveal your proud Scottish heritage, Captain Walker.'

'Well, thank you, sir.'

He really did talk to me like that, as if the aide-de-camp in waiting was a Super-Excellency, and he, the Prime Minister, a humble suppliant.

He was always the same to me, except that when I met him at the front door he was less formal than by telephone, the most agreeable chubby little man to escort along to the Governor General's study.

Only once did I see another Mackenzie King, at the front door also, when he happened to be leaving and his Postmaster General happened by ill luck to be arriving. The unfortunate man must have committed some serious crime because Mackenzie King dressed him down ferociously to a stammering jelly and then was himself again, or his Captain-Walker-himself to shake hands with deep respect and get into the car with that fat old beloved dog of his.

Our job, at the foot of the ultimate social ladder, was to see that things ran smoothly, that visitors, the more and the less noteworthy, were made to feel welcome, but most importantly to serve the Governor General himself. That was no hardship. Indeed, our many duty walks with him were enjoyable interludes, either in the grounds of Government House, or outside our gates in Rockcliffe, the exalted suburb of Ottawa where we lived. Or sometimes we would go further afield to walk in the Gatineau hills. In none of these outings was there a detective escort.

The best-loved member of our small company was Lady Tweedsmuir, who subordinated her life in every way to that of her husband. I think that the new wings of hospitals, the ladies' teaparties and so on, the numerous small tasks which a Governor General's wife had to undertake, were burdensome to her. She endured all that with grace and no complaint, and was very good company to slip in to see in her own room next to the study, especially when the bossy Joan Pape was not in evidence.

For myself, I loved Canada from the start, revelling in the sea-change which happens to every reticent Englishman (I use that word generically, and this once, because no self-respecting Scotsman admits to Englishman) who comes anew to North America to experience the kindness and hospitality of its people, all its people. That friendliness derived in some degree, I suppose, from the frontier not so long ago. On the whole, and among the privileged, English-speaking Canadians were more conventional and literal-minded than the British. One soon learned, for instance, not to say in light mood the opposite of what one meant and expect the real meaning to get through. The nuances of British speech were absent. But I found nothing dull in Canada except the newspapers, which revealed no graceful feeling for language, seemed laboriously respectable and almost exclusively concerned with money matters.

But there were things to wonder about. Why did the leading citizens of Montreal, almost all of British extraction, speak no word of French? Why was the French language hardly ever heard at Government House? Why was it that we – speaking English, of course – felt most at ease with our French-Canadian friends? But the answer to that is easy – our ways of thought or mind were more deviously akin.

French-speaking, English-speaking (Francophone and Anglophone still rile me), it made no difference. We were happy with everyone in the small circle of what one might call the GH League, and were made welcome outside it too.

In spare hours and days during that first and only viceregal autumn, I rode with the Ottawa hunt, played golf and went to parties. But soon – it would have been by mid-November, when the last leaves (except the hangers-on, like beeches and oaks) had fallen and been gathered by a gardener-army – soon and suddenly winter arrived, and with it yet another new world for me.

Despite his frail health, Lord Tweedsmuir still enjoyed travelling. In fact, he aspired to be the most travelled Governor General in the history of that office and he was well on his way to winning. During my abbreviated year we covered the whole narrow dominion east and west, except Prince Edward Island, in suitable luxury, our two coaches hitched to the stern of a common lethargic express. The best trains in Canada did not exactly gallop. The engine hooted sonorously far away, long-long-short-long at every open crossing through the night. A melancholy, nostalgic sound unlike the hoot of common locomotives that I had known elsewhere, reminding me, for some reason or no reason, of that lovely poem which begins: 'From the lone sheiling of the misty island mountains divide us, and the waste of seas.'

Then we would be detached and shunted to a siding for the duration of our stay at that particular honoured city. It was much later, in March when spring in the east was already hinting, that on our way to Victoria where the daffodils were out we made an intermediate stop for some function in Winnipeg. We were duly shunted to our siding, clouds of steam enveloped us without, and within we enjoyed ultimate comfort.

'Twenty-five below, gentlemen,' said Percy, a jolly black man and a special favourite in our crew of three. With that nippy comment about fifty-seven degrees of frost, he passed on through. We put our noses out amid billowing steam. It was indeed bloody cold.

'Winnipeg,' Robin said. 'The only thing I know about Winnipeg is that it doesn't quite rhyme with guinea-pig.' Of his many private *bon mots*, that may have been the best. No doubt he knew more about that excellent and vital city than anyone among us but the Governor General himself.

But to go back to November, Canadian winter had arrived and now settled in earnest, nothing earnest for us about it, but the greatest fun. There was skating somewhat staidly to do one's duty with the old folks. I had never learned hockey in Scotland in my youth but had had only occasional free-for-alls with ground-hockey sticks and tennis balls. So ice hockey was not for us but when the snow came there was skiing, the nearest thing but one in common life to bliss.

There was also much obligatory social stuff at Government House. I was as much of a bore at small talk as any other bore, but I had asked for it, had I not? So I did my poor best and often struck it lucky. The ones at the bottom end of the dining room table were usually younger and better value.

Coming and going through Cairo I had bought a Leica (much cheaper there), extra lenses and an enlarger. Water temperatures at Gebeit were difficult but at Government House they soon converted a small bathroom for me. So, when not socially engaged on duty, and not possessed in every available daylight moment by skiing, I took up photography with enthusiasm and became quite good at it in an amateurish way.

The Governor General was not at all a conceited man but he

was quite vain in a simple yet endearing way about his image. He did love having his photograph taken – in the full uniform of his office, as an Indian Chief with eagles' feathers, and as himself without regalia, his unusual cranial bumps camouflaged or enhanced, according to artistic whim. The photographer was Yousuf Karsh, just then approaching fame. So, with my enthusiastic connivance, we made numerous visits to Mr Karsh's studio in Ottawa. They were among the few occasions when I have made everyone happy – the subject about yet another striking portrait of himself; the artist because the sitter with that most interesting face was also distinguished; and most of all myself. Yousuf Karsh was extremely helpful with tips to a beginner, always modestly offered.

We were entertained often at people's houses where stupid protocol could be forgotten, and we ourselves often took girls and others to our favourite haunt, the Chateau Grill, or to the Hunt Club or across the river to the Country Club. It was there that I took Shirley and Catherine Woods, hospitable to, and liked by, every successive aide-de-camp. We dined well, too well, alas, in Catherine's case, and on the way down some steps outside en route for home she stumbled and cut her chin quite badly.

It was clearly a case for stitches, so I telephoned various doctors, no answer, until I did get through to one who sounded most displeased but agreed reluctantly to deal with the case. It was not a happy visit to his surgery, less because of the nasty cut than because they knew one another with mutually strong dislike, and showed it in a screaming match.

But he did the job efficiently and I drove the Woods home to Rockcliffe. By this time Catherine was drowsy, soon altogether asleep, and we had to put her to bed.

The dress came off with some difficulty, but it was off and she was lying on her front. The brassière, no real problem. But there was still an elastic girdle.

'That thing's too tight,' I said. It evidently was. 'We'll have to haul it off her.'

Shirley, across the bed, stood stiffly to somewhat unsteady attention and said: 'David, there is no other man in Ottawa whom I would trust to altogether undresh my wife.'

He was not helping, so, with some efficiency considering my inexperience at forcibly undressing women, I stripped the thing back and along and off and went home soberly to my much-needed if slightly whiskyfied bed at five or six a.m.

I was in waiting that morning and duly presented myself, clean, shaved and properly dressed at half past nine to accompany His Excellency through the small door by his study for the customary short morning stroll.

He glanced at me and a second time, quite shiftily, which was out of character. 'David,' he made himself say, and drew breath, which may have helped him to draw in a whiff of mine. 'Do you sometimes drink too much?'

'Well, not often, sir,' I said, and we went for our walk.

I think that I am right in saying that it was the only time he was ever known to bring himself to rebuke a member of his staff, and that by question, the best the gentle man could do. Rather hard, though, I thought and have thought since, to be the only man in Rockcliffe to be trusted to strip a chap's wife and then to be asked an unfair question, all in one morning.

Shuldham and Ruth Redfern lived at Rideau Cottage, the Secretary's house in Government House grounds. It was a great home from home for us and was to become even more so for me when the unexpected happened. In the meanwhile, and later too, I think that their small son, O'Donnell, aged about six, was my best pal in Ottawa. Among other entertainments we flew model aeroplanes called Frogs together.

In some degree it was the smallness of the viceregal staff that caused us to be a family, much less inclined to squabble among ourselves than are most families. In fact, we never squabbled and the senior member of the hierarchy, Shuldham Redfern, chipped in to help at official functions just as much as the junior aide-de-camp, myself. But with due regard to our entirely differing roles and responsibilities, we were all on equal terms. In part this may have been because Robin and I had been about the world a bit and although we accorded proper respect to the eminent, of whom many came our way, we were not the downy-cheeked devout automatons, popping up like jack-in-the-boxes to light some woman's cigarette, such as I have observed on rare visits since to GH.

Also, I think that I would be right in saying that Government House was much more the hub of the Canadian world in those less complicated, less contentious days than it has since become. The eminent visitors ranged from Stanley Baldwin, rather a ponderous old chap with his comfortable wife, to the incomparable actress Gertrude Lawrence, who seemed to take to me almost as warmly as I took to her.

The colder the weather, the more electrically dry the steam-heated air of that large house became. If you shuffled your shoes all the way along the carpet you built up a smashing static charge. Choose the right victim, usually a woman you did not greatly like, and the courteous handshake was loaded with a shocking spark. Alternatively, it was a trick to play on a girl you rather liked. It certainly was not a trick that Captain Walker played upon the Right Honourable William Lyon Mackenzie King. There was also an old-fashioned gas jet near the dining room door and the taller of us (not me) could light the gas by nose.

And so we worked together, even enjoying, with some reserve, the more formal functions that came our way. One of these, at the beginning of January, was a Drawing Room, to which were invited the chosen upper-ten to dip the head and bend the knee to Their Excellencies.

I happened to notice a slim dark girl who made her two curtsies with singular grace and elegance and passed on by.

'*Who's that?*'

'That's Willa Magee, Allan's daughter,' said my confrère, not without a quizzical glance.

Colonel Allan Magee was one of the honorary aides-de-camp. He had served through the First War with gallant distinction, and nowadays was equally distinguished as a barrister in Montreal.

Later on that evening I spotted the Colonel's daughter alone at the far end of a buffet table in the ballroom. I looked at her and she chanced to look round at me and I edged along in my full dress uniform to meet Willa Magee. She was too strong-boned to be merely a pretty girl, but she was a girl most beautiful to me, my girl.

# FOURTEEN

# 1943

After that peculiar letter, giving away the starting point of the tunnel, and after the ensuing abortive search, we waited for escaping weather.

There were rumours of a Deep Field again, of extra sentries posted beyond the periphery of the camp. We watched every night and saw nothing. All we could do about that possibility was to fan out as soon as we had climbed the hill from the narrow valley. The Deep Field seemed, for various reasons, to be unlikely.

A much more ominous and persistent rumour was that the whole Landwache, or Home Guard, of southern Germany had been alerted about the chance of a mass escape from Oflag VII B at Eichstätt.

Our copied maps, run off by some gelatine process, were as good as could be hoped for, double lines for major roads, single lines for secondary, dashes for paths, dots for tracks; railways shown; and streams and bridges. Our first great obstacle would be the river Danube to the south.

In the early evening of June the third, Frank Weldon and H-B, Patrick and I, and one or two others met at the foot of the slope below Block Two. There was a rising moon, with cloud, and things looked right. We had discussed everything that could be discussed *ad nauseam*. There was nothing now but a decision, Frank's to make. 'We'll have a go,' he said.

Those may be the only spoken words heard by me in the Second World War that I remember *verbatim* with certain accuracy. They were Frank – laconic, sane, pragmatic Frank.

After that, I remember getting dressed upstairs with the others, doing my best to seem calm, which I was far from feeling. And I remember meeting Jack Higgon on the landing half way down. He had come to wish us luck. Except for one long airless wait underground, there is a total blank in memory about the tunnel crawl, the hill climb, the avoidance of deep quarries, the circling of Eichstätt to the west. Then I remember an open bridge across a stream, and nothing more until Patrick and I lay on a bed of stones at the top edge of a downward sloping wood, a most uncomfortable way of spending sixteen hours or more of daylight.

We slept fitfully, with muttered grumble. We ate our staple ration, a compost of oatmeal and chocolate, and made a few brews on the smokeless heater, an ingenious invention. It consisted of one round can within another, with a space between them and holes at the bottom and the top. You fed it small slips of newspaper and, by some magic which I never understood, it brewed smokelessly with dispatch and remarkable economy.

Once a male blackcap arrived to warble in the shrub above my head. I remember that because it was the only time I have ever seen a blackcap. And suddenly, in the afternoon, there were human voices over to the left above us. But it was random speech, men and women chattering at work, and they came no nearer.

Now at last the second night was coming. The human talk had long since ceased and it was peaceful. Nothing moved in the tidy woods below our shelter. Waiting and watching, we held that advantage, soon to lose it.

As dusk was falling we edged downhill, still cramped from interminable terminated inactivity, stopped again. It was a low-lying meadow with a track running across it, and on through woods again, south-west by compass to aim for the Danube east of Donauwörth, our general direction good.

To walk by night through forest, even a neat German forest with a rising moon to lessen darkness, was impossible. We must have a track to follow and we found one, a minor rutted track, so far so very good. Pat led me, or I led him in line astern, taking turn about to keep the leader just in sight.

We went on like that for some distance, for an hour or two it might have been. Completely alert, meeting what one has to meet of an ever-new unknown, one has no thoughts except for that. But in one's head, or in my head, there plays a hackneyed tune or verse, like *My Cutie's due at two to two, She's coming through on the big choo-choo; or Tiger, tiger burning bright In the bloody forest of the night*, with variations of that night's signature tune.

It seemed so easy, and it was until they heard us, must have heard something, although we were padding quietly – two short sharp voices, not the idle voices of people filling in time at forced labour in the afternoon but the hard voices of men on the hunt.

Leading at that time, I saw their torchlights sweep about as they came our way. I slipped off the track and lay on the forest floor on soft pine needles. There was no cover between the trees. The excited mutterings came closer, on to something, on to us.

We had done our good best, and how good was that best with an army searching for us? The Landwache rumour was very evidently true. Face down, I saw the sweep of his flashlight beam. It swept across pine needles a yard from my eyes and swept away. The hunters turned and went. The hunted lay and then came together.

'Quite a close one, Davie, eh?'

'A whisker, Pat.' Looking out of my window on a sunny morning, I see that bright beam sweep short across the darkness.

'What now?'

'Wait. I think they're going.' The voices dwindled, no longer suspicious, into nothing.

'We can't blunder through these bloody woods. Keep on path.'

Agreed about that, we followed the track on and down to where it met a narrow road. We waited again and nothing, nothing. Or was that the dim shape of a darkened cottage? Thought not, could not be sure. We crossed the road, a wire fence, over that with one solitary maddening twang. The enemy came running back and we ran on.

Ahead, beyond open ground was a wooded spur, narrowing down towards us, a road on either side of it, meeting at the foot. We took the left road uphill and they were not close but hot after us with shouts, so we crossed over the wooded spur to the other road and ran back down to turn back up – up and across and down and up, a demented game of hares and hounds, and still they did not shoot.

To the left a tall crop in rows, peas or maize or raspberries or something. We took to it, last resort, and lay down panting. It was hopeless.

Not so, our dimwitted pursuers faded off again. If they had had a dog, not even a dog trained to follow scent but simply faithful Fido keen to make new friends . . . We were exhausted, too tired to move. Any dog would have homed on us, but there was no dog and the Heimwache might be old weary men who had been running. *Pflicht ist Pflicht*, duty done, they would have earned their Schnapps.

Our breath came back, not old weary men, but very thirsty. We finished our water bottles. It was a well-watered land, this Germany, there would soon be a brook for replenishment.

Patrick and I moved down the field and found another track, its general direction south. There were still hours of darkening night to go as the moon dipped into forest. We walked on, undisturbed, the track veering to and fro and gradually up. The hachuring on our map showed only a minor watershed. Still no spring, no trickling stream. We and the land were dry until we came upon one small puddle on the rutted track. Pat and I lay down and drank a few mouthfuls of it, down to the last muddy grit.

We topped the hill as dawn was hinting, as the grown forest ended and sapling woods began, good hiding places everywhere.

Short of starvation, we knew all about hunger. We had never picked blades of winter grass for sustenance, as the skeleton Russians did, staggering round our Warburg camp to the delousing hut, a horrible memory always to haunt. But about thirst we had never learned. We probably knew more about hunger and less about thirst than any combatant of the Eighth Army or Rommel's Afrika Korps.

We had a good parched gummy taste of it now. A little later Patrick went off from our hiding place on a water search, came back and shook his head. Apart from that unceasing lack it was a pleasant day in the bare shaded canopy of young beech trees, with undergrowth beyond to hide us, sleep and waken to be nagged again, to watch. The mice were most confiding.

My father who, at least in peacetime, did not much frequent the kitchen, used to say, forbidding traps: 'Mice are guests in my house.'

In our woodland house that day, they were not guests but friends, chasing each other and nibbling our few crumbs, quite fearlessly at home with us. Two of them played a game of 'I Spy' over the toe of my rubber-soled boot. It was most endearing. Also, a roe deer fed this way, looked at us, sniffed our scent and came on closer to within ten or fifteen feet. Then it turned its head to some real danger and was instantly gone. Our huntable team of five was down to four, two mice, two men. It was a new experience for me, this fellowship of being hunted. What had alarmed the roe deer? We were alert but no hunter came.

We knew our position. Two miles or three away across arable land was a stream, crossing our general direction, with a watermill marked on the map.

We had walked many dry miles and had lain for many dry hours. We did not walk well across the easy land on that third night. Escape was the insubstantial dream beneath thc nightmare need for drink.

Still no babbling brook, still no splashing mill, until at last we were on it, at it. I took off my pack to kneel at the brimming stream for the blessing of a drink and fell into deep water over my head, rather too much water now for comfort or survival but I managed to climb out. We laughed. It was not unfunny.

We had learned that map by heart. Upstream, still west and some miles on, was an *Urwald*, virgin forest, ancient woods, forest primeval, whatever in this case *Urwald* might mean, darkly sinister in anticipation.

The night grew overcast and heavy rain began, soon to make Pat as wet as I already was. Famines and feasts and thirsts forgotten, it did not much matter being soaked to the skin, with canvas packs still fairly dry.

We found a shallow place to cross the stream and by dawn were at the fringes of the *Urwald*. How many dawns? Three only in this sort of life within a life within a lifetime.

The rain had stopped, the clouds peeled off and the sun was already warm when we found our hiding place. It was a small green open glade within a tangle of tall trees, deadfalls and underbrush. People think of virgin forest as being mighty and upstanding. Some are, perhaps, as for example the immense and long-lived stands of sequoia, or such few as still have not been plundered by man. But most virgin forest is a mess. Some trees survive to splendour, only to become decrepit, eventually die and fall and others take their place. As a result, the forest floor is an obstacle course.

But our glade was perfect in the sun. We filled our pot from the rivulet nearby, brewed up by smokeless heater, took all our clothes off including white underwear, and laid them on bushes to dry out.

It seemed entirely safe but one of us must keep watch. It was during my turn to be sentry that movement caught my eye. Across the far side of our glade, not thirty yards from us, not even twenty possibly, beyond the brook, there walked a man. He made no sound. He was a man middle-aged or old, in a green uniform, presumably a forest ranger, with a badger bristle on his hat, a gun on his shoulder. He crossed from right to left, looking straight ahead, oblivious of white underclothes on bushes, of us naked on the open ground, and he was gone. Had he seen us? How could he not have seen us? Was he a spectre of my fancy?

'Quick, Pat!'

We gathered everything and hid. But he was no figment of a tired imagination. A few minutes later he passed again from left to right, taking the same woodland path to wherever he had come from. We did not understand how his attention could not have been drawn to us. I do not understand it yet, unless the answer is the simplest of all simple answers – he felt sympathy for fugitives from the hated Führer. Ridiculous but possible. More probably he was too lazy or browned-off to look about him.

We had made one rudimentary mistake. I passed our lesson on in a cloak-and-dagger novel I wrote (*Cab-Intersec* in the United States, *Devil's Plunge* elsewhere). The case manager is a beautiful girl with a long, long nose, Mary Dunn by name. Harry Ambler is the case.

> 'It is lovely,' she said.
>
> 'Where shall we go?'
>
> 'By the brook?'
>
> 'The noise of water robs your ears. Never lie up near running water, Dunn.'
>
> 'This is a picnic luncheon, Ambler.'

'Figure of speech. Max Vyan and I nearly got caught that way by a forest guard – never heard him coming.'

'Oh, I see.' She could be curiously respectful. 'Would up the field be better?'

All our things were dry by now. We moved into deep cover further on, clambering over fallen trunks and through dead branches, one more battle, not unmindful of another possibility – that he had gone for reinforcements to deal with desperadoes.

But nothing happened and we lay in some comfort with one new discomfort. The chills, the soakings, the concentrated diet – so different from the soup, potatoes, bread to which we were accustomed. In escaping across country, stomachs were always the first things to go and our insides were no exception. Diarrhoea meant dehydration but there was plenty of water to counter that, if not to quell stomach aches. We were all right, though, good for any distance at walking pace.

The Danube crossed our route five miles to the south. There were road bridges, all of which would be guarded. There was also one footbridge, faintly marked. That could be a possible crossing. Or there were boats. We might find an unshackled boat, or somehow break its chain.

The thing to do, therefore, was to head for the river, move westwards upstream, and if no boat, that footbridge, and if no bridge, keep on.

There had been rumblings all afternoon, not of bombs (I recollect no distant bombings or air-raid warnings in that time) but of thunder. The storm gathered swiftly and broke with violence on us in our *Urwald*. We sheltered as best we could.

The storm passed over, and the late sun shone and set and we struggled wetly out of that forest which had shielded us but which we did not love so very much.

The roads and paths or lanes between us and the Danube were etched in our heads to be remembered easily and exactly – first a lane, marked by dashes, and then not much further on, a single line secondary road. They ran parallel, separated by half a mile or so, for some distance until the road turned sharply left down to a hamlet at the river but the path went straight on to meet the bank of the Danube further west.

Our choice was obvious. We had discussed it in daylight with the map. Leave the *Urwald*, the edge of which was marked, strike south across open ground, reach the lane, turn right. What could be simpler? We had had good reason to know that they were hotching for us. We were still free so they must still be hotching, but even if they had an army of old men and Hitler-*Jugend* on the watch they could not cover every path or lane in south Germany. We knew that too, because only two nights ago, our second night, we had been chased and then had walked a long way unmolested. And last night we had not been near the roads and paths of human habitation.

We stopped often to watch and listen – nothing. I noticed that Pat was lame and asked him about it.

'Only a blister,' he said, and we went on.

It took us longer to reach the lane than we had expected, but here was a line of trees and here it was. Stop, listen, nothing.

The trees began it, the same thing that had happened to me at the end of the ghastly retreat in 1940. That steep-roofed house with a gabled window, so positively, absolutely real. But not. It was two leaning trees, sky for the window. That silent waiting man, not a man, a bush. That church spire reaching high to a cross, clear and sharp against the sky. But it too was a tree. And so they went on, the tired fancies of my mind.

But it was open astride the lane again, no more night visions. It was wide for a lane, wide enough to take farm vehicles, smooth enough for cars, straight on and on, all as it should be. We went over a rise and were at a sharp left turn before we saw it and they jumped us.

'*Hände hoch*!' The torchlight held us while they looked us over, calling. Two more men came, and the four men marched us down into the hamlet. There was some prodding but I told them in German to stop that, and they did. Speaking German usually worked, although it could be a hazard if good enough to conjure up spy-thoughts. Mine was fluent but not of that order.

Our immediate port of call was the Burgomaster's house. They were middle-aged and elderly country people. The weapons – from rifles to hammer guns – did bristle but that settled down, quite decent people, especially the Burgomaster's wife, who gave us each a slice of angel cake. Once, on the line of march through Belgium or Holland in 1940, a German soldier had cut off a piece of his sausage ration and given it to me. Now, three years later, a German woman did a kindly thing. She was what we would call in Scotland a *decent auld body*, good old soul. It was a change, a small bounty of kindness after this time, and we were grateful for the lovely light slices of home-made cake.

It was warm in the kitchen and an excuse to unzip and take off the plain navy blue jacket which I had bought for golf in the 1930s. It was the best thin double Grenfell cloth, and reversible, which the Germans had not noticed. When it arrived in a clothing parcel, they painted a red triangle on one side with a white O below it, either O for officer or O for bullseye, I would not know which. Anyway, I peeled it off and pulled the sleeves through. That worked for me on all three escapes and it was never painted on the other side or confiscated. In earlier years it had not mattered but by the summer of 1943 to be caught in legitimized prisoner's clothing was a sound insurance.

Two of our captors went off prisoner-hunting; two remained to guard us until a policeman arrived and we were on the road again.

The mistake had been mine because I had been leading. Either I had crossed the lane, missing it altogether, or the lane marked so clearly on the map no longer existed. It was the road that we had followed to its turning. I should have known that it was too good a road to be that missed or mythical path. But excuses do not hold, least of all in escaping.

Patrick was very lame by now. I explained that to the rustic policeman, who paid heed, sent Pat first and kept me next to his pistol. He did not badger us on our walk of a few more miles to a high-walled, blank-faced building at the end of night.

This prison was not like the coolers we were used to – a row of cells with a lock for each one. This was the genuine article, a bunch of large keys, a barred gate to be unlocked and locked behind us by the jailer or turnkey, a word known to me but not thought about before, another clattering ringing gate, systematically down through the bunch of keys until the last one was turned on us in quite a big cell with a deep mattress on the floor.

# FIFTEEN

# 1943

It was the end of that escape, the beginning of the most improbable incident of my existence.

One weak electric light in the ceiling of our cell, one barred narrow window far overhead, a paleness of dawn beginning to show in it. I took off my boots which had come in a parcel from home, stout rubber-soled marching boots to take me quietly to Switzerland, Goddamit. Patrick's second boot was giving him trouble and he did not have the strength to struggle with it. I took the laces out altogether and eased it off but there was still the blood-encrusted sock, stuck to his heel from the achilles tendon down. 'We'd better leave it till we can get some water.'

'Tear it off,' he said, and his whole body stiffened as I did so, revealing not a blister but a totally skinned heel, side to side and top to bottom, red and bleeding, bloody awful would not describe it. For at least two nights my tough friend and partner had walked as that swelled and burst, saying *only a blister* when asked about it. I tied his heel with a handkerchief.

'God, that's better,' Patrick said. We had a blanket each, a pillow, sleep forever.

It was mid-morning when the footsteps thumped, the key-ring jangled and the lock turned over, obsequious manservants had brought breakfast – one with two slices of bread for each of us, one with two squares of margarine, one with mugs of acorn coffee steaming hot.

Our waiters wore striped convict garb. They were emaciated, with faces of that ashen colour, or the absence of it, which means no daylight ever. They looked terrible, and terribly pleased to see us, gabbling their pleasure in streams of German.

'My goodness gracious,' Patrick said, which about summed up the situation.

'My friend says thank you many times,' I said, tucking into good honest German bread, even moderately fresh. 'I also.' But I pointed to Pat's bloody heel. 'He is wounded.'

Tutt-tutts of sympathy, an order barked by the neanderthal guard to one of the trusties, and very soon a medical convict arrived to minister, which he did well, bathed it, a powdered lint dressing, elastic tape.

'You are officers?' asked the guard. Even he seemed pleased to see us.

'Yes, we are captains. *Es tut mir leid*, it does me regret that I am so dirty.'

'Come, then, Herr Hauptmann, please,' he said to me. The common convicts were sent packing.

I put on boots and my red-triangled jacket and went with him through barred gate after barred gate after barred gate. It was a slightly funny feeling, funny peculiar more than the other.

He was a small man at a table, an officer, although the uniform and shoulder tabs were different – the SD *Sicherheitsdienst*, Security Service, which ultimately meant the Gestapo under Himmler.

'I understand that you speak German.'

'Yes.' What did I call him? 'Yes, Herr Kommandant, I speak German, but not very fluently.'

He was expressionless and quite polite, taking down my name, rank and number, and then he jumped into a question: 'What acts of sabotage did you plan to commit?'

Our belongings were spread separately and neatly on a longer table – packs, icelandic sleeping bags, groundsheets, underclothes, food, soap, a safety razor each, my small pocket knife with a single blade two or three inches long. 'We are escaped Prisoners of War, headed only for freedom, Herr Kommandant. You can see that.'

'Headed to join a group of saboteurs,' he said, but without much evident conviction.

'Headed west to cross the Danube and to Switzerland.'

'Hopeless for you,' he said, not pursuing sabotage, it seemed. 'Fetch the other one,' he told my guard.

At a widening of the corridor beyond our cell were stacks, stack upon stack, of small white flat-bottomed boats, or they may have been sleds, destination the Russian front. Where else?

Speaking broad Scotch, I told the gist of my interview to Pat. They would need a special interpreter for that one.

'Och ay, mon,' he said, departing.

It had not been relief from the long trail awinding that had made our cell seem so comfortable. Not a thing in it but the soft mattress and the pillows, a latrine seat in a corner. Even now that we were rested out it was as much as, or more than, any recaptured prisoner could hope for. But we were in a German penitentiary, at the very end of Herr Himmler's leash. I felt rather lonely for the hidebound Wehrmacht. It was a month or so ago that the warning had been issued: *Gegebenenfalls*, under certain circumstances, *Entfluchtete Kriegsgefangene*, escaped prisoners, *erschossen*, would be shot. That recollection lurked.

Pat soon came back. 'The interpreter was a striper, used to be a barber in Chicago. Murder, rape isn't in it by the looks of him, what a monster.'

We discussed the situation, drifting again into Scotch, not sure about bugs or spyholes, but the accent would beat any German except that Parcel Hatch Goon back at Eichstätt who had grown up in Glasgow and spoke more outlandish Glesky Scotch than we could. We were not despondent, indeed quite cheerful. The disappointment at being caught again was annoying, just another burdened failure. Our future, out of the hands of the Wehrmacht, which paid some lip-service to the Geneva Convention – the only certain thing about our future was its uncertainty.

The fears did lurk, unspoken, not much and not for long. We were akin in a muddled untroubled sort of way to the roe deer lately whose fears were not anticipatory but immediate when a fear-moment came.

We lived in our cushy cell, visited with bowls of soup, *ersatz* coffee, any excuse or no excuse, streams of convict visitors, always the same bottom-of-the-barrel emaciated types and usually different ones with different guards. The fact is, or was, that we were the pets of the place, prize exhibits of that penitentiary where nobody had seen the likes of us before. Nor we of them, the ghastly side beneath the madly amusing side.

They were the lowest dregs of Herr Rosenberg's Aryan myth or trough. Thinking logically, one would have thought that Nazi Germany would have seen to their extermination, got rid of the degenerate seed. More than probably it did but some Aryan convicts still survived to make funny small white boats or sleds for the next Russian winter. The worst of all paid us several visits, Patrick's interpreter from Chicago, the friendliest of dreadful little men, his smattering of Chicago English matching the loving rest of him.

'Ask him what he's in for,' Pat said in French.

'*Mon ami*, in some circles one does not pose that order of a tactless question.'

We had last shaved in the *Urwald* and were bristly, which offended us, as is the way with soldiers. But being also penitentiary pets, we would like to look our best. Not only did they bring those materials – water, soap and our bluntish safety razors – but they took our clothes bit by bit for brushing up.

It was on the second morning or the third – time did not seem to have much meaning except stomach-time in that hospitable place where we were quite well fed in a basic way, double their starvation rations, I feel sure – that we were told of departure, through clanging gate after clanging gate and so on to that Commandant's office, no sign of him but our belongings still meticulously laid out. We were ordered to pack quickly. The honoured-guest atmosphere had disappeared and we went somewhat glum in spirit, putting a good face on being the prisoners of whatever there might be ahead for us. The roe deer were alert to danger and could not flee.

Outside our *Zuchthaus* penitentiary hotel were four common soldiers from the guard company at Oflag VII B, a most welcome party. The corporal of the escort was well known to us by sight, if not personally, as he must have been known to every observant prisoner because he wore a bright russet wig, the most flagrantly obvious of toupets peeping squarely below his helmet. He held a piece of paper, which he read to us: *Beim geringsten Fluchtversuch wird so fort geschossen.* I remember it because of a key word:

*geschossen*, which means *shot* in the sense of *shot at*, in contrast to the other past participle that I have quoted, *erschossen*, meaning executed by gunfire.

With one guard on each side and two guards following, escaping to be shot at made no sense on an open country road in daylight. As to that penitentiary where we had been so weirdly welcome, we did not know its size or location or anything about it. As we came to a wayside railway station we met a small procession, shuffling along in file with one armed guard. They were four – a man, a woman and two children, each one tied by the wrist to an old frayed rope in a sad short line, not Jewish in appearance but German peasants. What crime in this horror Germany had father, mother and the little ones committed? Were they headed for our *Zuchthaus*? That small crocodile is a pathetic microcosm of a memory, entirely vivid.

And so we returned to Oflag VII B, or to crammed quarters outside the camp. I seem to remember that we were numbers 58 and 59 to be brought back. I am not sure about that but I know that ultimately they caught all sixty-five of us, unshot and unharmed, except that Peter Greenwell fell into a quarry and broke an ankle. Someone wrote in *Detour* that, on the credit side, we had put 60,000 members of the Home Guard to work to do the job. I daresay that, with every pair of German eyes and ears on the alert, the number of our adversaries was a good deal larger than that. But they had won. To employ the terminology of a few years later, our rocket, so brilliantly engineered, so meticulously laboured on, so well and truly ignited to a perfect lift-off, had fallen in a fizzle.

The ending of the fizzle, however, had not come yet. We were marched through the town to climb a hill nearby. On top of that was an ancient castle, the Willibadsburgschloss, once the seat of the prince bishops of Eichstätt.

We were kept there for about a fortnight, ten days of which represented our more or less statutory cooler sentence for escaping. We were grossly overcrowded, which was no new experience, but a latrine seat over a hundred-foot open drop provided a novel kind of updraught to one's bottom.

The senior among us was Cecil Merritt, who had won a VC commanding his Canadian battalion in the gallant Dieppe raid,

Mountbatten's baby, perhaps the European war's worst bungle. There was an ominous aspect in that waiting time because ten or twelve people were segregated by name, if not in fact, for having escaped in civilian clothes. I would guess now that we were kept waiting while Himmler, the Reichsführer SS, made up his mind as to whether or not we, or the chosen among us, would be *erschossen*, an effective way of putting a stop to escape attempts.

We had a small exercise yard, walled in, with an open side that led to an SS convalescent home along the hilltop. The Wehrmacht officers and guards were particularly obnoxious. The SS, on the other hand, to whose quarters we were taken for minor medical treatment, were fighting soldiers recovering from wounds, men of our own generation or younger, belonging to a miscellany of Waffen SS units. At the end of our imprisonment, still nearly two years away, the American Army advanced to free us. But in my novel, *The Pillar*, the camp was evacuated westwards to meet the Americans.

> Then they came to a detachment of SS troops with tractors and two long guns. 'Eighty-eights,' Keith said. They had drawn to the side of the street to let you pass. They were children with tight, exhausted faces, but they were fighting children below their skull and crossbones which was also the badge of some British cavalry regiment. Didn't the Jesuits say they could make anything out of anybody if they got him young enough? The *Waffen SS* . . . They looked at you without hate and without despair. They were going to die for the Führer and enjoy it.
>
> 'When I see Waffen SS,' Peter said, 'I can't help remembering those chaps who escaped in 1943 and were shut up afterwards beside an SS convalescent home. They said the only kindness they'd ever had from Germans was from them.'
>
> 'That's the Aryan myth,' Adrian said. 'It wouldn't stop them shooting you with efficiency and without the least compunction in the back of the neck, you and a million Russians and God knows how many Jews.'
>
> 'I know,' said Peter. 'But it ought to be said. You have to remember everything.'

Peter spoke of the few pros amid a multitude of cons, but he spoke for me in that. It may be that as our indifferent interpreter, trying to explain common ailments to the SS doctor who spoke no English, I saw more of them than most of us did and my impressions of them may be too favourable. But there was an odd sort of comradeship between us and them on the top of that hill, much more the same kind of animal than were we and our German Army staff. That Adrian in the book was also right – if ordered to do so, they would have shot us without compunction – did not detract from a certain equality of respect between us.

In my four years and ten months and a few days extra as a prisoner – that life within a life which was nevertheless the truest time of my life – I knew positive kindness from Germans three times only: a soldier's sliver of *Wurst*, a slice of angel cake from the Burgomaster's wife, and a biscuit or two from the Waffen SS. Take it or leave it.

When our few remaining possessions from Oflag VII B arrived in cardboard boxes, we knew that we were on the way again and to some camp. Otherwise, why send our meagre baggage?

But first another search. It went on and on, and no booty until they found a round-pointed pair of scissors, longer than nail-scissors, but perfectly innocent cloth-cutters. *Konfiziert*, said the most unreasonable, bloody-minded camp officer. The owner protested via me, and I protested vigorously, getting nowhere, then too vigorously, getting ten days in some cooler somewhere. They were not ordinary scissors but of case-hardened steel. With handles attached for leverage they would have cut through barbed wire very nicely and were well worth arguing for. But I argued badly.

So we left the Willibaldsburgschloss, an easy shamble down to Eichstätt station and a train journey which ended below a fairy castle floodlit on a hill.

# SIXTEEN

# 1939

*Later on that evening I saw the Colonel's daughter alone at the far end of a buffet table in the ballroom. I looked at her and she chanced to look round at me and I edged along in my full dress uniform to meet Willa Magee. She was too strong-boned to be merely a pretty girl, but she was a girl most beautiful to me, my girl.*

Ten years after that I wrote:

> Geordie and Jean sat side by side under the pine tree, not saying a word but eating their ices and happy together, each knowing now that the other felt the same. It was love – bright as a diamond, warm as the evening sun, soft as a fluff of dandelion floating in the air, sweet as the heather honey.

Geordie was a small boy who grew big enough to win the shot-put at the Olympic Games, and Jean and he had known one another all their lives in a Highland glen. Willa and I met at a gilded affair when she was almost twenty-six and I twenty-eight. The one first memory would be lost in childhood, the other sharp from that time on, and yet no different in a simplicity of truth – the diamond, the kindly sun, the dandelion and the heather honey.

In a New Year message to the Canadian people John Buchan, Lord Tweedsmuir, spoke with prescience of war. If there was to be an irony for us in that the happiest of peaceful days raced by to an ending not far off, we paid small heed. Life was here and now – skiing, dancing, talking and not talking, with laughter and quiet in the ways of love.

For me there were no doubts from a first moment on, which was not quite to banish thought of hurt elsewhere.

I will not write more of our beginnings.

Meanwhile, Canada was preparing for a big event, the visit of the King and Queen in May. To begin at the end, one should say that it was a smashing success from start to finish, across the dominion to the farther shores and back and briefly to the United States.

Everybody was a busy bee, not least at Government House. Lord and Lady Tweedsmuir were their eminently sensible good selves. Shuldham Redfern wrote speeches and oversaw the lot. Eric Mackenzie comptrolled meals and rooms and the household in general with a Guardsman's aplomb. Willis O'Connor and Robin Scott made ticklish table plans and I helped them over the minutiae of royal occasions in Ottawa. My wife is keen on scrapbooks and she must have had from me one page, being amendments to an original printed draft.

The following appears in my handwriting (more legible in those days):

> 11.05 a.m. at the conclusion of the ceremony, His Majesty will drive to the Speaker's entrance of the Senate. The King will change into Morning Dress in the Speaker's Chambers. Her Majesty's car will join His Majesty's procession to the Speaker's Chambers as the procession passes the South door of the East Block.

It would be my guess that, so far as is possible, the pronoun third-person, singular or plural, is avoided about royal personages. But in our original draft, a loyal subject had evolved something like this: 'After the King has changed into morning dress, He will . . .

Mr Broderick, a civilized and entertaining man on the secretarial staff, said: 'With deepest respect to the Divine Right of Kings, I reckon that even His Majesty doesn't rank that capital H. What do you say, Captain Walker?'

'Even the monarch himself bows to Our Lord above. I'm heartily with you, Mr Broderick.'

Ths firm of Broderick and Walker made that decision without consulting any of the higher-ups. As I have said, everybody was a busy bee in preparation for great events. The busiest bee of all was unquestionably Mackenzie King, who became obsessed about a constitutional point. Who should greet the King when he stepped on to Canadian soil at Quebec? Should it be the Governor

General, the King's representative and titular head of state for him? Or should it be the Prime Minister, First Minister of the Canadian Crown?

The answer was fairly obvious. It should be the Governor General, who would then slip into a sort of limbo while the Prime Minister accompanied his King across Canada. But Mackenzie King worried that bone as his fat old dog would have worried a bone in puppy days. His immense little mind was adamant, and cables criss-crossed the Atlantic until he won his point.

So the Prime Minister met the King and Queen at Quebec and accompanied them to Ottawa, where they stayed for three days at Government House. About this storm in a teacup Lord Tweedsmuir behaved with his invariable urbanity. What mattered were the King and Canada, not himself.

Those three days were a succession and procession of state dinners, garden party, Trooping the Colour and so on, at all of which functions the King and Queen were the marvels that they were, a sovereign couple for the world to see, yet alone together.

I saw them from afar, even if at close range. But once the King and I were actually alone. It was soon after they had reached the comparative peace of Government House and he wanted to find his study which was, in ordinary times, Lord Tweedsmuir's.

We went along that corridor, so familiar to me, and I opened the door for him. 'It's too damned hot in here,' he said, going to the nearest right-hand window to remedy the situation. But the thing would not budge. 'It's unsnibbed all right,' he said. 'Let's have a shot at it together.' We each took a handle and up she came.

He was a plain and ordinary man. I do not mean plain by lack of looks but plain in himself, and growing more sure, with only a movement of cheek muscle that might reveal the stress of the burden that had been thrust upon him. He was our plain and lovely King, and his Queen was lovely both ways.

I was mad as a hatter about Willa Magee, yet do not deny that, when those lambent blue eyes looked down the luncheon table to consider in a kindly way the junior aide-de-camp, my heart made loyal flutter.

The staff who accompanied them, men and women, were the most unpompous people imaginable and marvellously kind to us. If the King ordered, which he sometimes did, short and sharp, they jumped to it. But the atmosphere was carefree in those few days before the long expedition. A family party would improbably and fairly accurately describe it.

Each evening, another state dinner over, the King and Queen would sit alone at a small table by the fireplace, have a late cup of tea together, and bid us goodnight.

There is perhaps a bit of hair to be let down in such a circumstance, even among the hierarchy of a royal household. Some of them, for example the secretaries, ladies in waiting, and equerries had specific jobs to do. Others such as the Queen's Lord Chamberlain and the Lord in Waiting held titular offices which seemed to involve few specific tasks. As to who was senior to whom could not seem to matter less among themselves; the best measure of quality in a staff.

On one of those evenings the drawing room door closed behind the King and Queen and immediately the Lord Chamberlain, the most exalted of the lot, plucked a bunch of gladioli (grown out of season in our greenhouses) from a vase and advanced upon me, certainly the most junior of the lot.

Solemn as a handsome owl, he held them up and out and then made a stately backward withdrawal, step by prancing step, from the Royal Presence, me. It was like that. He was Lord Airlie to me then. Many years later, when he rented a house to us for a pittance, we came to know Joe and Bridget Airlie well.

They were all good fun to be with, and supremely competent. On another of those few evenings I went out with Michael Adeane, who had been an ADC earlier in the 1930s. We visited the Shirley Woods, whom I have already mentioned, friends of his from times before.

Coming back rather late we were stopped at the main gate to Government House grounds. In those better days, security was almost non-existent but during the King's visit the RCMP did have a man on and he asked politely who we were.

'I am Captain David Walker, ADC to the Governor General.'

'And you, sir?'

'Al Capone,' Michael said without a glimmer of a smile. The policeman laughed and sent us on.

At that time Michael Adeane was an assistant private secretary, bottom of the royal heap in Ottawa. Later, he rose to the eminence of private secretary, and to retire as Lord Adeane. I feel sure that Al Capone still lurked somewhere. The balance and the rapier wits, he and Robin Scott matched one another.

They said goodbye and began the long train journey. I am at pains in these personal memoirs to keep them so, and not fall out of my depth into affairs of state as I once did into a mill-stream. But I allow myself one digression:

In her book, *John Buchan*, Janet Adam Smith wrote that there was some Canadian criticism about the Prime Minister being the first to meet the King, 'and when Queen Elizabeth II visited Canada in 1959, it was the Governor General who met her and handed over his responsibility as her representative. On this later visit, too, the Queen was accompanied across Canada by a succession of Ministers.'

Not so in 1939; Mackenzie King went every inch of the way, popping out at each stop to be the first to greet Their Majesties. And, being his own Minister of External Affairs, he also accompanied them to the United States.

While the tour was going on, Lord Tweedsmuir made himself scarce and we went salmon fishing on the Grand Cascapedia. The spring run was late that year and all we caught were slinks, or mended kelts, fish that had spawned and were on their hungry way to sea again. They were no good to eat, so we released them, but it was a good introduction to salmon fishing, if only from a boat. I have never much liked boat or canoe fishing, which is necessary on the larger rivers like the Cascapedia and the Restigouche. I much prefer to wade or fish from the bank. I was soon to catch my first salmon, wading the Metis, a fresh-run twenty-pounder.

At the end of the tour, we went to see the King and Queen off on the *Empress of Britain* at Halifax. They stood alone together on the bridge, waving as the great ship drew out from Canada. It was a noble parting.

Before, during and after these splendiferous events, Willa and I had been quite adroit at snatching moments, and more than moments. Even then – after the Indian and other years and common doings, after passing almost all my days without my name appearing in a newspaper – even then I had ambivalent feelings about the grand life into which I had so avidly jumped. The spurious side of me enjoyed it. The genuine side of me looked down upon myself in it. I lacked Robin's apartness of spirit from himself.

All that splendour would soon be over with a proper vengeance. In the meanwhile we were madly happy and our affairs moved inexorably on according to the fashioned book. Our engagement was announced at the end of May, and our marriage was to take place in Montreal on July the 27th.

It took place in grand style. My own parents did not come because their youngest son, Barclay, was to be married at home in August so the Tweedsmuirs stood in for them. Robin Scott was best man to me at St George's Church, and Willa's father and mother gave the reception at the Ritz.

Oh, my God, it was a shindig, and almost everyone who was anyone was there, from the doyen of the diplomatic corps, Baron Robert de Silvercruys to Sergeant John Gray, MM, of The Black Watch Association of Toronto with his increasingly merry cohorts.

There was one reluctant absentee. Not only did he give us a most handsome silver bowl but he sent this telegram:

> Please accept my warmest congratulations upon your marriage and my very best wishes for your future happiness as I have already said to each of you I regard the marriage an ideal one may I say again how sorry I am not to have found it possible to be present at todays ceremony.
>
> W. L. Mackenzie King

All that was but a backdrop to our simple happiness. We sailed next morning in the *Duchess of Bedford* from Montreal.

So far I have written of Willa only as the Colonel's lissom and devastating daughter, but if I, as a young man of twenty-eight, had been here and there and done this and that in a few far places, so, as a young woman of twenty-six, had she. Her first important job was to be postmistress on a world cruise of the *Empress of Britain*. No doubt that employment was initially fostered on the old-boy-net by a paternal string-pull through Sir Edward Beatty, king of the CPR. But she soon justified it by becoming the most efficient and best-loved postmistress in the history of the Canadian Pacific Steamships. Her particular ally during that long voyage was Paddy Malone, the Master-at-Arms, whose prime tasks were the maintenance of peace and good order. Paddy saw to that, but it soon became secondary to a more important task – the protection at all times of his young postmistress. If she went ashore, Malone saw to it that she was suitably escorted. At sea, if a young officer sought to dally with the postal service on the boat-deck beneath a tropical moon, who should loom sternly up but Paddy Malone.

Later, I was briefly to be the pet of a German convict settlement. Much earlier, Willa had been the remarkably competent pet of the flagship all the way round the world. That was in 1934.

Her next job was private secretary, social secretary, plain secretary to Lady Marler, wife of the Canadian minister in Washington. She was as good at that as she was at everything, whether the social whirl or the common task.

In Washington she became friends with younger diplomats – among them Michal Vyvyan of the British Foreign Service, much later to be a Tutor at Trinity College, Cambridge. Also among them, Charles Ritchie of the Canadian Legation, her colleague, and therefore Ritchie could exercise a certain one-upmanship on Vyvyan. I came to know them both and like them very much, each totally unlike the other except for an abiding devotion to Willa Magee.

After being Ambassador all over the place, Charles Ritchie retired and has since published three volumes of diaries, which have not yet been so widely read as they will be. He is perhaps the best diarist of this century in our language.

Charlie brings me to the expression of a final thought about Mackenzie King, Prime Minister of Canada for some twenty-two years in all; brilliant, unctuous, tough, sentimental, devious, a spiritualist, he manipulated Canada to increasing stature as no one else could have done. The sad thing about that tubby little man is that none of the gifted people who served him liked him for himself, not one to my knowledge. Charlie Ritchie wrote to me:

> One night in 1976 I was sitting up in bed reading aloud to my wife excerpts from the private diaries of W. L. Mackenzie King which had just been published. I accompanied my reading with guffaws and such remarks as 'The old monster' and 'Do listen to this rubbish.' Then a peculiar thing happened – the bed on which we sat slowly subsided, the front legs collapsed and we were precipitated on to the floor.
>
> I had not a moment's doubt as to the cause of this phenomenon. It must have been Mackenzie King himself. He who believed so fervently in communication with the Other World was there brooding resentfully in the spiritual stratosphere and had administered this sharp rebuke to his disloyal former subordinate.

But we were sailing on to Scotland and by the time we reached Greenock war was less than a month away. Perhaps we sensed that but I think not. It may have been bemusement and seeing the same people at the same old place with a new dimension added. And if meeting all my family and a good many other strangers was an ordeal for Willa (as indeed it was) she revealed that not at all.

My father and mother, my elder brother Willie and Bluebell and their three children; my brother-in-law Thomas Rennie in The Black Watch and Huldah and their two; Barkie just to be married to Margie Pilcher; my formidable Aunt Isabel Walker at Pitlair – that they were an easier lot of people than most to meet for the first time does not detract from the demand it must have made upon her. But we were together, and mostly at Rankeillour, which she loved from the start just as I had loved it from the age of twelve. Not least important, she got on famously with the people who were the backbone of the place, like John Keiller, the keeper, companion of our boyhood; like Irons, the head tablemaid; like all of them.

Scottish country life in August 1939 continued in the same old way. On the 12th we shot grouse with the Nairns at Pitcarmick as I had done so many times before, George Nairn having been my only other boyhood friend at home. On the 15th Barkie and Margie were married, as well-blest an affair as our wedding had been. Things came to fruition as Nemesis drew near.

The younger aides-de-camp in Canada had never been married men. They were wedded off, usually to Canadian girls, and left. But the War Office did not want me back. So a precedent was to be established by the married outcast, who would rent a house in Rockcliffe. We sailed from Southampton in the *Empress of Britain* on August the 19th. The *Empress* was home ground or ship to Willa, just as Rankeillour had so miraculously become home ground to her.

I know that this will be hard for anyone to believe but it was not until the 23rd or 24th, nearing Canada again, that the bolt of *WAR* did strike into us at last.

I will not dwell upon those final days in Ottawa when Robin and I decided to go. We did not go in the crusading spirit of those expatriates who had hurried back not to miss the fun of the First World War. We went because it was our bloody duty. But even that nightmare was touched by the light fantastic. Willis O'Connor had a bright idea, which was that in the event of boarding by the enemy at sea, we should not be a sailor and a soldier but have civilian identity. I do not remember what false passport Robin was given but I was a salesman of ladies' underwear. I lost the thing long ago but there on my oath I was, a purveyor of brassières with a legitimate false passport.

Goodbye to Willa. Goodbye. Goodbye. We boarded the *Empress of Australia* and were in the Gulf of St Lawrence when Britain declared war on September the 3rd, 1939.

SEVENTEEN

# 1939 to 1940

The German U-Boats wasted no time in going to work. On that first night of war the liner *Athenia* was torpedoed with heavy loss. We crossed the Atlantic, forging at full speed from zig to zag, and encountered no enemy. But the conducting of our voyage was unusual.

While bringing the King and Queen to Canada in May, the *Empress of Australia* had been held up by fog off Newfoundland, a worrisome delay for any captain but for this good senior officer it was a trauma from which he did not recover. Now, as we thrust on through fine weather, much too fine for comfort, with columns of smoke on the horizon that must be sinking ships, and once close by an empty lifeboat bobbing in mid-ocean, the captain had had it. He sat, he simply sat in his cabin with gin and tonics talking to his parrot.

Fortunately, Robin was there to take command in all but formality. He conferred with the chief officer, a competent man, worked out our complicated changes of course in his mathematical head, made all the captain's decisions and brought us safely to British shores. It was a case of thank God for Robin Scott, and goodbye to Robin Scott.

During that first winter, war went on in a devastating and dramatic way at sea and in a very small way by air. Our few bombers flew time and again to ultimate destruction, pinpricks against the Kiel canal. While we trained recruits at the expanded Black Watch depot, Sandy Innes, bomber pilot, came home on leave to Perth. He was cheerful but he knew it, one could see that in his face, and he went back to be killed on the next fruitless raid.

Living conditions for the troops were appalling but gradually improved in that long cold winter under Colonel Vesey, who was to command the depot throughout the war.

Willa came over soon by American ship. We shared a gimcrack bungalow for a while with Arthur and Pam Wilmot. Arthur and I had been in India together and he was now adjutant of the depot, later to be killed in North Africa. He asked me to be godfather to his small son, Robert. Other people to remember in that winter were Keir Wedderburn, Archie John Wavell (who was concerned with the early radar defences, and dropped by fleetingly), John Elphinstone, Sandy Barnett, Thomas Rennie, my brother-in-law, whom I saw briefly in London when volunteering for the abortive Finnish expedition. They are all dead. It leads nowhere to be morbid but if one tries to write of one's life one has to mention some friends lost. There were others too.

The women, led by Mrs Syd Innes, mother of Berowald and Sandy, worked indefatigably at knitting comforts, making bandages and so on throughout that dismal winter.

The young Jocks slept at first on pallets on the cold stone floors of Pullar's Dye Works beside Queen's Barracks. The officers worked much longer hours than in peacetime and the married among us were with our wives. It was still very much a man's world, at least for the privileged. Arthur Wilmot and I shared a decanter of port in that bungalow most evenings after the women had left the dining room. For me, it was the incomparable blessing of my wife in the grey dimness of Perth, a railway junction, Bell's and Dewar's whisky, called the The Fair City.

But spring came – crocus time, daffodil time, blossom time. The gean, the wild cherry, was in blossom at Rankeillour when Hitler attacked on May the 10th.

Probably I would in any case have been sent to France but I went before Colonel Vesey and volunteered. This volunteering – was it glory that I sought? Or was it a bug about duty again? Or was it both?

Nobody, even if sufficiently interested to bother, could answer that one, certainly not me. Willa came down to London with me for our parting on May the 18th. It was springtime still, and she was expecting a baby in late autumn.

If I had known the human composition of The Black Watch contingent at the 51st Highland Division base depot in France, I would have done no volunteering.

The *raison d'être* of a base depot was to provide reinforcements, replacements for casualties in battle, a reserve pool formed in 1940 from the frontline battalions. I cannot speak about other regiments but The Black Watch, instead of sending back NCOs of average quality, had made the base depot a repository of the useless. One universal solution – if he was a thoroughly bad sergeant send him to the base depot. I do not remember the officers, if any, nor much about the Jocks, some of whom were new young soldiers, and only a composite faceless image of a sergeant, dim-witted, slovenly, not a punch or a bite among the lot.

I think that I joined the base depot near Rouen, whence we drifted south-westward through and with the refugee chaos that was northern France in the late days of May – Dutch, Belgians, French, riding high and wild-eyed in their packed camions, peasants with few possessions in overloaded carts – demented chaos on the run. We had reached Le Mans, the motor-racing place, when I volunteered a last time. It was an escape in desperation from those cast-offs. I volunteered to Norman Hudson, known to me slightly in Indian days. I have no idea how he got there, nor what later happened to the base depot.

I felt an immense relief to be going forward to our First Battalion, to be free of the demoralizing horror of retreat. But the notion of bold advance was not to last for long.

The 51st Division had spent the winter on the Saar, attached to the French Army, and now, while the last of the British Expeditionary Force were being evacuated from Dunkirk, they fought on with the French, having been moved to the Somme to Abbeville near the coast. It was to be retreat again, not in refugee disorder but in withdrawal night by night.

There was a pattern to those nights and days. At dusk, or soon after, the German attack would peter out and our orders to move back would come. After the Somme, the rivers which made our defensive lines were all small and all flowed across our front from right to left toward the sea. So we would march ten miles or so, reaching the inconsiderable stream that was to be our next defence line as dawn was breaking. The Jocks could rest a little, waiting for breakfast. The company commander, after the CO's orders, would site his platoon positions, the platoon commanders their sections, slit trenches to be dug, then sleep for them until the enemy began arriving.

I was too tired to be hungry but managed an egg, a slice of bread, a mug of strong tea, and it was time to go round the platoon positions. Thus, perhaps one hour's sleep before the inevitable motorbike and sidecar came into view beyond another shallow valley. Soon then, the shelling began. They ranged unpleasantly on us and sometimes our shells whistled comfortingly overhead. After that it grew with machine gun stutter and rifle fire and mortars as things became hotter and nearer in another late afternoon of glorious weather to the end of day. The enemy, in our part of the line at least, were not particularly aggressive. They advanced by day and stopped for a good night's sleep while we withdrew in another bad night's march.

For me it was gathering exhaustion, earned fairly enough, but I had not encountered fear before. It was something new and shameful to be much afraid.

There were abundant rumours, the most persistent being that the Germans were using gas against the French along the line. What line? We did not know, or yes, we knew that another piddling stream winding below those woods would be this line to defend today.

But a few things stand out. One morning I was with Nogy Dundas, the second-in-command, and someone else, sitting in a hut with mugs of tea laced with whisky produced from somewhere, warm encouragement. Probably we were waiting for battalion orders. We heard the drumming of multiple machine guns overhead and the louder slower thump of cannon fire.

We went out to watch the dogfight. But it was not a common dogfight, one fighter trying to get on the other's tail. They were one Spitfire and one Messerschmitt, meeting head on in ferocious single combat, sweeping wide to turn and drive head on to meet again, each pressing home against the other, tilting, tilting at six hundred miles an hour or whatever, tilting not in the sense of deviating at the last split second although they must have done that. I suppose that it happened and was watched many thousand times in war but I saw it only once. My war was short.

They were still at it, gone from sight, not sound, so we went in and sat again. The next thing was a banshee scream, a thousand banshee screams, whatever they may sound like, to end in an earth-consuming crash. One companion and I got up from the floor, ashamed of ourselves because the third of us, Nogy Dundas, had not stirred in his chair. He did stir now, went out, returning soon with his pistol to the head of that Messerschmitt pilot who had parachuted. The remains of his plane nearby accounted for the banshee crash.

In the last days leading to our surrender on June the 12th, General Victor Fortune, commanding the 51st Division, had received orders and counter-orders, which latter, as everyone knows, lead but to confusion. And in retreat, the further down the unit or formation, the worse the muddle. We would start for one line, be ordered to another, changed to a third, and blunder on to that.

I remember nothing of those days and nights until our last day of fighting, which was June the 11th. We were to form a perimeter a few miles from St Valéry, whence the division would be evacuated by sea. That was clear enough, as clear as anything could be in withdrawal. My company positions were on a downward narrowing slope, headquarters at or near a farmhouse.

True to form, the German motorbike and sidecar appeared on the open horizon of the hill beyond. They were out of range, except to artillery fire, and, true to form again, they almost at once withdrew.

It has often been said that the French Army in 1940 showed little fight but in my solitary meeting with them in the line, that was far from being the case. Immediately on our left, perhaps a hundred yards from the farmhouse, were the remains of a dismounted squadron of Cuirassiers. Under their commander, a square-faced major, they had fought for many days across France, and the survivors fought on as hard as ever.

In his history of the regiment in the Second World War, *The Black Watch and the King's Enemies*, Bernard Fergusson wrote of that day: 'Some dismounted French cavalry arrived under a veteran major with a gallant heart; and in this penultimate position of the original Black Watch, Frenchmen and Scotsmen lay side by side and fought . . . casualties mounted; the old French major had his arm blown off, but insisted on being carried round his position to encourage his men. We do not know his name.'

Surely that must have been my major, although he was not wounded in the time we were together, when he gave me heart to fight. It was that Frenchman who showed me at last, high time, that the frightened me was not entirely me. And perhaps more effective than the strong Frenchman was the anomaly of observing that there were others far more afraid than I was myself.

In a shed behind, a young soldier crouched in a corner, crying, the boy was crying hopelessly, cravenly. I could not force him out. But a man much senior to him in age and rank also dithered. I forced him out and returned to the farmhouse where Bill Bradford, the adjutant, had come to see me. We ducked, wincing at one another as the shell arrived, a near one, near as a whisker. I laughed and so did he and went away.

A mad moment to laugh at no laughing matter, and yet it was a true laughing matter, and I ran down across the small meadow to our forward platoon unharmed, to lie beside a Bren-gunner in a shallow slit trench behind a bank.

To our right front, across the low valley, was a wood. It was from somewhere there that they must be directing shellfire and a machine gun at us.

'Where is he?'

'Canna see 'im, sirr.'

I put my binoculars on to that wood, searching the top, nothing, the middle, not possible from a dense canopy of grown trees, the foot of the wood, along it, back along it, along it again, and what was that? It was a leafed branch weaving slowly, so slowly in no wind that it hardly moved. Why so stealthily back and forward in no wind? Then I got him, the helmeted enemy behind his slowly moving branch. Not a wise enemy – if he had stayed entirely still, I would not have seen him.

The Bren-gunner beside me went on with random bursts at likely places.

'Gimme the Bren.'

But he did not give me the light machine gun, for the toes of his boots drummed and he was still, shot through the head.

I took the Bren, put on a full magazine and gave the lot to that slowly weaving branch. The branch and the helmet subsided and were still. No more bullets came from there. I suppose, looking back after these forty-two years and a few months more, that I killed him or them, my only killing in the Second World War, and that at long range.

But I did find out something that afternoon, a small thing, yet not small for any fearful man to find. A brave Frenchman helped me but I think that it was the other thing. How paradoxical to gain a mite of strength from weakness more than one's own. It was not, and is not, much, but there it is.

We moved out and back at dusk. I had never attacked in war, nor would I ever.

It had been eight days, or nine or ten, during which my total hours of sleep may have been fifteen. That is a guess like almost everything in that exhaustion. We were in trees a last night, a haunted city of mind, the cathedrals and the lofty towers, the greengrocer's shop stacked with vegetables that was a deserted barn, the broad street that was a lane that became too narrow to blunder on into again. To be night-blind was another deception of oneself, a failure that could not be fought.

Next day, June the 12th, the division surrendered. That morning I met John Elphinstone by chance and we walked together to St Valéry, one close shell to put us in the ditch, then no more firing as we reached the town. We were both shocked to see on our right, on an open space like a garage floor, crème de menthe bottles, other bottles, all kinds of bottles, at which drunks were drinking from the neck, boozy-happy. It made us feel prim, not our kind of thing at all, and then a nasty little German hounding us on to the long road of captivity.

In that same book Bernard Fergusson, himself the most gifted and one of the most gallant Black Watch officers of our generation, wrote:

> . . . The Navy was powerless to take off what little remained of the Division, and early in the morning, acting on orders from

> home, General Fortune had been forced to surrender to the German General whose troops had surrounded him, whose name was Erwin Rommel. The one, beginning from a moment of abasement which might well have dispirited the bravest heart, was to win renown as the undefeated captive. The other was destined to enjoy high triumph, and to end in disgrace and suicide.

What Bernard wrote then, and later, about General Victor Fortune did justice to the gallant soldier who was to set an example to all British prisoners for the rest of the war. His health deteriorated but he declined repatriation, insisting upon staying captive with his men.

But Bernard would not have intended thus baldly to dismiss Rommel: 'to end in disgrace and suicide'. At that time Rommel was recuperating from grave wounds. Whether or not he was involved in the plot to kill Hitler in July 1944 is beside the point. It is not beside the point that he was the one man whom the German people would have followed at Hitler's death. In disgrace with the ultimate monster, Hitler, certainly yes. But he was murdered, swallowing the pill to save the lives of his wife and son. That is what Bernard would have meant to say about a great tactical commander and chivalrous enemy.

It was all over and the column straggled, passing death in the covered huddle of two Frenchmen behind their anti-tank gun, passing a German tank on the top of which a black-uniformed officer pointed here and there issuing orders with those barking screams so peculiar to Germans. I was to have plenty of time to learn to despise Teutonic screams but I never have quite understood why Rommel in that victory or in any other or in defeat should have been a screamer.

Many years later in Scotland I said to John: 'Are you sure it was Rommel on that tank?'

'Of course it was,' he said. John was never sure about anything unless he was sure.

They marched us remorselessly through France and Belgium and to the Rhine where we were crammed on to boats to go up river, and to move by cattle truck to a final first stop at Laufen on the left bank of the Salzach, which had been the frontier with

Austria. But I have written enough of that. It was old prison history three years later when another train journey ended below a fairy castle floodlit on a hill.

EIGHTEEN

# 1943, and on, and back

I am wary of writing about Oflag IV C, Colditz Castle in Saxony, which has been written of so much. The word mystique does not appear in the big Oxford dictionary, nor in my favourite stand-by Webster in two volumes, but it is in all the new lesser dictionaries and is perhaps exactly the word to describe the particular ambience or legend which has grown out of that particular prison camp.

When we reached there in the summer of 1943, there was the Old Brigade, many of whom had been at Colditz since early in the war, and there was the New Brigade, sixty-five of us, fresh from our tunnel which had been a brilliant success and a total flop. Many of us had also participated in 1942 in the Warburg wire escape which was anything but a flop.

The Old Brigade were splendid people, gallant and rambunctious, who fostered that legend or mystique. They were the glamorous Bad Boys and revelled in it. This is a generalization and inaccurate about many of their daring small company, but it is essentially true. They christened us the New Boys. Old Boys, New Boys, Bad Boys – Boys is the rather tiresome keyword. Many of them were the eternal Boy. Most of us were men of thirty, or more or less, common ordinary people, by that time greatly experienced in methodical planned escape, not at all interested in glamour, or I cannot remember any of us who were.

In some ways the Old and the New were poles apart but we were invariably polite to one another. If you did not like someone, you avoided him. But quarrels, in my recollection, were unknown in prison. We could not afford to quarrel.

Pursuant to that was a wonderful simplicity, denied to free men and women in ordinary free life – we had a common and blameworthy enemy to blame for everything. There were some shifts between the two groups, mostly from them to us, but essentially we were disparate entities and so remained.

The physical place, what was it like? It was a complex of high buildings surrounding a small courtyard, around which we walked and walked, and sometimes sunbathed in the summer and played games – their violent stoolball game, our tamer but very fast passball variety of game. We had counting parades in the courtyard morning, noon and night. There was also a small park nearby in a hollow; a rustic, not unpleasant shady place. Proceeding to and from the park was a formal affair with a touch of menace. Formed up in the courtyard, we would be counted and recounted and eventually let out through the main gate to be escorted to the park.

In all other camps the guards would move on either side of a prisoner column, their loaded rifles slung. Not so at Colditz. There, they held their weapons in both hands in the way that one would hold one's rifle when ready to shoot at a deer glimpsed in a woodland ride. They did not, in fact, aim at us but were instantly at the ready for a pot-shot. It was mildly disconcerting until one got used to it.

And so through more barbed wire to be free to walk in that green place. To walk and walk and walk, and to sit and talk in the shade of acacia trees, a pleasant fine tracery of leaves above. And there were birds to watch and listen to, a comforting pastime to me then and ever since. I cannot remember what we talked about, or each within our private selves did not talk about. If the war was exciting with new Allied success then it would be another surging hope of home by Christmas. There was always the unknown waiting for our private captive selves. We were not morose. Cassandras, if any, if ever, got short shrift. The stiff upper lip is a great thing to hide behind. Try letting it loose and see what happens. I remember the long oval of that quiet park with some affection, yet it is spoiled for me by one horror that I must later tell.

When we arrived at Colditz there were still some officers of other armies – Polish, Belgian and Dutch – but they were soon moved away and until the very late days of the war we became predominantly an English-speaking camp – people from Britain and the Commonwealth, a few Americans and Frenchmen who had been parachuted into the Resistance forces all over Europe, one or two splendid Czechs who had flown for the RAF, two or three Jews, of whom one, Simon Hacohen, later became a prominent Israeli, a wonderfully acerbic, witty man. I said that our lot did not aspire to glamour. But some of those older originals were certainly glamorous, Czecho, the fighter pilot, was nothing if not. Bush Parker, the Australian, could pick any lock in to or out of anywhere in Christendom; what was he but glamorous? I frig around with that word – who revelled in it, and who did not? But almost all of us had earned something in dull prison days.

One man, and there were many, who would have spurned any such phony appellation had the next top bunk to me when first we reached Colditz. Lights-out time would arrive and the blackout screens could come down and at last fresh air could filter in to disperse the fug. Through the window bars I used to watch, as he watched, we watched through the floodlit bars, and once or twice, a few times, never speaking of it then or after, we would see a white owl fly past along the castle walls.

I imagine that the owl – a barred owl or a barn owl or whatever owl of medium size – was not white but rendered so in appearance by the floodlights. I watched him watching it. He was John Arundell, Lord Arundell of Wardour, one of the most ancient Catholic families of England, and I had heard somehow – not from him, I think – that when an Arundell saw a white owl it meant death for him.

Colditz had been established early in the war as the particular camp for those who escaped or were otherwise troublesome. Once there, you were there to stay. It was supposed to be impregnable, from inside out, as it were. But the escaping record – eight people who had reached home or a neutral country – was the best among officers' camps in Germany. However, by the time we reached there in 1943, the place was more or less sealed-in. It was the only camp where there were more guards than prisoners. It was the only this, and the only that, it was indeed a very special place for me and everyone in it, and has so remained.

There were two successful attempts at getting out in our time, both at the beginning of 1944. Mike Sinclair, the most determined escaper of the war, and John Best got clear away and were caught near the Dutch frontier. The last was a brilliant lone escape by Bill Miller, a Canadian. He was never heard of again.

I have mentioned Himmler's warning in 1943 – *Gegebenenfalls wird erschossen*, under certain circumstances would be shot. That put a stop to escaping for almost all of us. If the odds might be ninety-nine to one *against* getting out of Germany, and if the odds might be, as the enemy became more desperate, ninety-nine to one *on* being shot when recaptured, the odds were somewhat loaded. So, perhaps ignobly, we stopped trying. Our assessment and apprehension were monstrously borne out in 1944, when the great escape of RAF fame and tragedy took place from Sagan and over fifty of them were executed.

In my off-times from better things since 1940, I had set about learning German, at which I had spent an hour or two a week for one year at school and remembered nothing. But I learned it basically now and went on learning, and, having an ear for speech, came to speak *Hochdeutsch* quite well. Even now I can still talk simple German without thinking. French was another matter. I had been learning it off and on from the age of eight but it has never slipped easily through my mind and tongue. Yet I loved French poetry of the easier sort, Baudelaire or Verlaine and so on, just as I came to love German lyric poetry, Goethe and Schiller for example, and best of all the simplicity of the forbidden Heine, who was a Jew, hence a non-poet in Nazi Germany. It is that kind of truth-destroying bigotry which makes me dislike the human species.

But I had a good French friend at Colditz, Jean-Claude Tiné, who almost brought me to talking French. Meanwhile, I taught German to John Arundell, sporadically and impatiently. He was always late or he forgot. With what marvellously mannered courtesy the apology would be pronounced, in mockery, of course, of my hidebound concern over such trivialities as time and place.

The next language I attacked was Spanish, much to my liking, and in a few months it was up to my French, if not in vocabulary

Fishing with John Elphinstone on the Jupiter River, Anticosti Island, about 1965

The King and Queen in Ottawa, June 1939. Robin Scott in naval uniform in foreground, on D.H.W.'s left

Willa in the spring of 1939

D.H.W. in 1943. Charcoal drawing by John Watton

In the corner of the Chapel Room at Colditz
*Left to right:* Patrick Campbell-Preston, John Arundell, Jack Fawcus, Colonel Staymer, D.H.W., Peter Dollar, Colin MacKenzie, Douglas Bader

Dinner with the Baders in the 1960's
*Back:* Peter Dollar, Martin Gilliat
*Front:* D.H.W., Douglas Bader
Photograph by Thelma Bader

certainly in speech. I never did have any feeling for Spanish poetry.

There were things about, or hanging over, Colditz, which made it an uncomfortable place to sit out the war. It was the *Sonderlager*, the Special Camp, the *Straflager* as we called it, punishment camp; and if the enemy, desperate in defeat, should seek a target among prison camps, Colditz was the obvious bulls-eye. We thought of that and did not speak of it.

But there were good things, and the best of them was that we were not overcrowded. There was room to move in our living quarters and we even had dining rooms. There was also a row of disused cells below where one could go and work alone. When I served my last cooler sentence of ten days, it was not there but down in the town of Colditz, presumably escorted by a guard or two guards at the ready-ready.

The first days of a cooler sentence were not lonely days. It was purest bliss to be alone, to be away from the maddeningly familiar quirks of friends, messmates, sleeping room mates. One was spared, for example, the sonorous, rhythmical monotony of snores from Jack Fawcus, the steeplechase jockey, a decent mate, if ever I had one, but my God, the rumpus through that often-broken nose. Desperate one night, I took a boot and lobbed it at his snores which stopped for a minute or two, my only physical assault in prison.

But I was in the town cooler, still four days to go. Now it was not the food that I missed so much. It was the company of my maddening people, who would soon drive me deeper within myself that I might escape them, from the one to the other. I, who had been bored paralytic with them, longed now to see them again. More than most people, I have had to live my working life alone, yet needing the relief of trusted companions. It has always been thus for me since prison days, just as it has been that crowds discomfit me.

Apart from visits to the Colditz cooler, I also went to the town a few times otherwise. I had some gold crowns in my mouth and these progressively fell out and were replaced by a German dentist with stainless steel.

But those too have gone long since. My wife did not like my

steely smile. I had a soft spot for them myself, enjoying the rather raffish *gospodinish* Soviet air. But one yields in such matters, and no steel teeth remain among the dwindling few.

I remember three German officers there, no other officers or men. There was Prawitt, the Lieutenant-Colonel Commandant, Oberst-Leutnant Prawitt, a remote hatchet-faced individual who, with retinue, would go the rounds during our periodic searches. I never spoke with him except once on a final day. He may deserve credit for the gentleman's agreement, peculiar to Colditz, that if you were caught at an escaping attempt and stood still, you would not be shot.

The second one was Hauptmann Eggers, the security officer, who spoke excellent English – smooth, foxy, competent, a bit too smooth, we had nothing much against him but we did not like him.

The third was Hauptmann Püpcke, who took most *Appels* or counting parades, a large Teutonic essence of a German. He rarely smiled and apparently spoke no word of English. A solid, stolid, typical officer of the enemy, we should, almost by definition, have disliked him. On the contrary, without a single exception to my knowledge, we liked Püpcke very much.

Once, only once, he appeared on morning *Appel* the worse for wear, his face blotched with lipstick, he weaved a bit, solemn as usual; but this time solemn as a boozy owl. Someone called: 'Good old Püpcke,' and we cheered him as he tottered out.

Our affection for the seemingly-so-wooden Püpcke may seem irrational but there it was, a soft-spot for old Püpcke. I spoke with him only on two occasions, once when I acted as interpreter at a routine meeting between him and Wully Tod, the Senior British Officer. There were others more senior but Colonel Tod was our SBO and much revered. In fact, he had been posted there as the only British officer who could control unruly Colditz, and he did. That time, Püpcke was indulgent about my interpretive inadequacy. It was not until the night that the Americans had reached the other side of the Mulde river, down there below us, that I met Püpcke again under topsy-turvy circumstances and he did not fail me.

So much for the Germans, but I have been writing about the

few I knew by name. We saw more of the common run of sentries, most of them corrupt in the lesser ways of a brisk onion/cigarette trade. There were also periodic searches when we were all turned out except for one prisoner representative in each of the larger rooms.

I happened to be the senior in the Chapel Room, so-named because it was directly above the camp chapel, and as German-speaking Room-Führer of a sort I was the one who stayed to guard our possessions, legitimate and otherwise, against the searchers.

The stratagem was easy, so easy as the war wore on to sure defeat for Germany that invariable success was nothing to boast about. One was amiable without being matey. One mentioned, perhaps, that this long war was a burden for them as it was for us. That was quite enough to do the trick. One after the other they would stop tearing straw mattresses apart to find hacksaw blades, or searching the floor or the tiled stove where maps, compasses and other contraband were hidden with consummate skill. One by one they would take the bait, until I was surrounded by German soldiery asking me, pleading with me, a common prisoner of theirs, why we were not fighting shoulder to shoulder against the Russian *Untermenschen*, sub-men. I did not yield. I argued with them in a kindly rather lofty way about ideological matters. It always worked. They gathered round to listen to the sage, their lost brother of the Aryan race.

Then the warning would come and they would all flee back to tear the place apart and in would stalk Oberst-Leutnant Prawitt, Hauptmann Eggers and his other minions, a formal call to see that searchers sought assiduously.

One thing that the Germans were quite human about was the distilling business, at which our experts were highly skilled, using as basic source German jam, dreadful red stuff made from dyed beet pulp. I have a clear recollection of Prawitt at one search going to someone's locker, opening it, taking out a small bottle, smelling it and saying *Verabregierungsmittel*. I never asked anyone but I took that to mean in our less convoluted language: *Means of blowing-off steam*. He put the bottle back. The enigmatic Prawitt may have meant just that, or so I thought. Anyway, they never interfered in the manufacture or consumption of our rot-gut hooch.

That these memoirs are personal is self-evident. I have hardly mentioned the long march of war which we followed intently and intensely; nor the classics; nor the philosophy, Berkeley and Hume, easy enough to the superficial searcher, but what was Whitehead getting at so far above my head? Nor the real anchors of our lives so far away, so near and dear to us alone; nor the political balances that we tried to weigh. We were not dunderheads. We were more or less intelligent vain strivers after truth. We were cynical idealists. Some of the Old Boys may not have been that. Most of us New Boys were. But old and new we shared a watchword: It was *No Bullshit*. How rude that may sound. It was not so for us. *No Bullshit* perfectly expressed our disdain for phoney pretension of any kind.

The Russians took back Smolensk. The Allies fought hardly and bitterly in Italy while we fought nothing and grumbled about and tricked our common enemy, the Goons, and among our few close friends came to know one another's characters better than husbands may know wives.

I have a personal thing to write about. Willa, back in Canada, had our first child on November the 30th 1940, a sturdy infant called Patrick David, godson to my escaping partner and friend since Sandhurst days, Patrick Campbell-Preston.

Late in February 1941, a senior German at Laufen had sent for me. He was decent about it, handing me the cable telling me that Patrick had died at the age of two and a half months. Our healthy baby died in his pram without any warning. It was so terrible a thing for Willa. I suppose that in most troubles one is sorry first for oneself. But I sat then in a crowd of people, a body-touch-body press of people, and I cried in silence, watched by some stranger, he watched me crying helplessly, hopes lost. We did not know one another then or later but he watched me crying. I hate the memory of Laufen.

# NINETEEN

# 1943 to 1945

It was not long after she had lost her child that the Women's Division of the RCAF was formed and Willa was among the first recruits. I had known, as even a lover may know, that she had rare gifts. We had shared cheerful fun and some gifts in bed.

I did not know until I learned of it then, and more so later in our many years together, that she was an organizer, an administrator, a leader of unparallelled ability. She rose in meteoric fashion to head the Woman's Air Force of Canada. All that energy, that patience when patience mattered, that implacable will which enabled her, being also a most appealing woman, to twist stuffy male air-marshals round her little finger. She came to command seventeen thousand women, scattered across Canada, and flew to see them all. She then gave it up to cross the Atlantic to London when V bombs were flying and to wait for me at home. That is the story, and for Willa, Patrick David still lies beneath the story.

In those days I lacked a photograph that did justice to my smashing wife and kept on asking for one by prison letter. A very handsome likeness did at last arrive but it was not of a wife, it was of a female aeronaut with the three bars of a wing commander (wing officer was the correct equivalent in rank). The others suitably admired, winced faintly with impeccable good manners, and instantly christened her the Air Vice-Marshal, which title she was to retain for the rest of the war. In a charmingly vicarious way the Air Vice-Marshal was their own.

She was not, however, mine. I wrote to state with loving acerbity that I had not married my woman for a uniform but for many other reasons, not least her April the Third suit, and would she please go at once to Mr Karsh? Eventually there did arrive a masterpiece by Yousuf Karsh, my old mentor. He did not hint by gossamer or tulle at the birthday suit, that would not have been

Mr Karsh's form at all. He took Willa in a tweed jacket, smiling, the very girl I married. I have just been looking at her above a bookcase in my workroom, the same photograph that was on the wall beside my bunk at Colditz.

We knew that it was coming. The whole world knew that it was coming. At long last invasion came on June the sixth, 1944. The Allies fought it out to the eventual breakthrough. They fought and rolled on; we waited and did nothing but cram ourselves with knowledge, and spice ourselves with yet another rumour of yet another breakthrough and hunt the trash cans for bad potato peelings. We had been hungry in early times. We had been well-enough fed in the middle years by Red Cross and private parcels. But now the parcels became fewer, became occasional, and ultimately ceased. The Flying Fortresses took Germany apart by day. The Lancasters took Germany apart by night. Now again we were becoming hungry, not yet very hungry, never to be reduced to the desperate starvation of the concentration camps, assaulting human pride. I would say that, on the whole, the sins of the Wehrmacht against us were of omission, not commission. Compared with the barbarities perpetrated in Japanese prison camps, we suffered nothing either at Colditz or elsewhere.

Except for the worsening but not yet serious hunger, and except for one incident of vital importance, prison life went on as usual. That incident was the attempted assassination of Adolf Hitler on July the 20th, 1944. For a few days, for a week it might have been, our Germany wavered. The guards slouched at their beats and turned their backs on Colditz Castle.

But Hitler lived on and Hitler spoke huskily to the German people. Then, unbelievably, the grip of terror tightened on them. Every man (and woman, I suppose) took a new oath of loyalty, and the evidence of that was the Hitler salute to every soldier. One morning when our counting parade was called to attention, Püpcke did not salute hand to cap as a soldier does but his right arm went stiffly up and out, his plain face expressionless, yet suffering. We saw that, knew it, and we jeered our ringing mockery in the castle courtyard. I do not know how many Allied lives and German lives were the price of Unconditional Surrender.

It was during that summer and the last heavy winter that I began to write, a few verses only, mostly bad. After the war I was going to write, I did not know what, but I was going to write. Only my Irish mother had ever thought that I could, or had ever, in her diffident way, encouraged me.

The Blackbird

When the first threads of evening fall
Through the young valley and down on the river,
When the late sunlight fires the castle wall,
And only the aspens shiver

Then he who runs through heavy prison days
Reads in the bold-billed blackbird's chortle
Harshness and melody, inconsequent delays
And peace for the doubtful mortal.

The burden of prison days lies on my few verses. It was fiction that I was to write later on, and very successfully in the second league of success, never the first league. But often I wish that I had learned to write austere spare poetry, which might have been the true thing for me. Yet how does the spare poet earn the boodle to pay the bills?

Earlier in this book I mentioned Douglas Bader. Now he is dead. At Colditz he shared a small room with Peter Dollar and most days I used to pop in to see them in between learning this and learning that language, philosophy, economics, or what-have-you. Douglas was always sitting on his bunk, with one leg off or both. He worked incessantly on those tin legs, one below the knee, one a little above. They were unusual, even unique in those days – I think I am right about this – in that the ankles were articulated both forward and sideways. He worked with his set of tools, loudly, abruptly, cheerfully talking with an 'Old Boy' every second sentence.

He worked to good purpose, fine-tuning his extremities for the next excursion with his room-mate. The only denizen of Colditz who was allowed parole-walks (with one companion) was, you can guess, Douglas Bader, and for some ludicrous non-reason – that he could not exercise properly in the courtyard, or for some other improbable reason. They would return from those walks, laden with eggs and onions and other booty of fair tobacco trade.

He was a perennial nuisance to his captors, and in being a nuisance to them was often a nuisance to us. Sometime or other, I would like to write about the other Douglas Bader, quiet and alone, without the bragadoccio that may in part have been a defence against being the most instantly recognized man in London, or here or there or anywhere; which fame he also did enjoy. *Oh, come off it, Douglas – Fuck you, old boy.* There was more to him than that.

The war rushed and dawdled on. We would cross the Rhine and it would be over. We did not cross the Rhine. There was Arnhem, a valiant failure. There was hunger, getting worse. There were the V2s now, Hitler's ultimate *Vergeltungswaffen*, weapons of revenge? Not so. There was the Battle of the Bulge, that incredible last effort which was to be the last. Often the armies of the air flew over us by day. Almost every night the air raid sirens, the searchlights sweeping far away over Leipzig, over Chemnitz, over Leuna where they made synthetic fuel, the thunder-rumble never near but present. The sweeping searchlights would narrow to a point, then the brief flame of a bomber gone.

For me, there were my companions, to be endured and trusted.

Our mess was a proper hotch-potch, nicknamed the 'House of Lords'. There were the common non-lords, regular soldiers like Patrick and Martin Gilliat in the 60th and myself, and the younger ones – Colin Mackenzie, Seaforth Highlander; Phil Pardoe, 60th; Charlie Weld-Forester in the Rifle Brigade. There was Jack Fawcus, steeplechase jockey, healed broken bones from top to toe, champion snorer, his skin ailment aggravated by some stupid doctor's arsenic treatment. Jack was eventually repatriated, as he should have been long before, and when he got home the grand little not-exactly-brilliant man coached Willa and Frances Campbell-Preston about what they could expect of Patrick and me. There was Micky Burn, taken in the St Nazaire commando raid, one-time devout Catholic, now equally dedicated Communist. Michael Burn was the most fluent speaker I ever heard. The words flowed on from him as he expounded Marxism. Some people, not without reason, considered him a dangerous menace. He came to see us at our small hotel in London this spring, Micky unchanged except for the Communism, long learned at sordid first hand and abandoned. Willa had never met him before and she was enchanted by him. He and I had not seen one another for the thirty-seven years that might have been yesterday. Micky wrote a good prison novel, *Yes, Farewell*. Then there was our other Communist but of the parlour variety, Giles Romilly, highly intelligent, a wayward type much disliked by some. I liked Giles well enough. As a matter of fact, I liked them all, and am not by nature a liker of all. Giles was a nephew of Winston Churchill and hence became a member of the *Prominente*, pronounced Prominenty, the small band of hostages who were gathered at Colditz, to be taken away just before the end, and all to survive, largely due to our indomitable semi-lord, John Elphinstone, who was brought to Colditz in that last year. Only he and Pat had been my friends in times before, Patrick by ten years the longer. I say semi-lord because John was one of a small band of heirs to Scottish baronies, who were called *The Master of*. The *Prominente* aspect was because John's mother was the sister of the Queen, now that champion woman whose age goes with the century, Queen Elizabeth the Queen Mother. If there were more like her it would be a better aging century.

I have already mentioned the last Lord Arundell of Wardour. If the Pope cared to accept the recommendation of a failed Presbyterian like me, he should look into the beatification of John Arundell.

Our final lord was Charlie Hopetoun, who got to Colditz by tunnel but also became a *Prominente* because his father was the incumbent Viceroy of India.

Everyone liked Charlie. He became involved in the writing end of the Colditz theatrical world, in which I had no part. My singular experience with the drama had been as a small boy at my preparatory school in Scotland, when I played a French toddler and had this one line to speak: *Bébé veut du chocolat*. Acting was decidedly not my thing. Chocolate still is.

But Charlie, who had been good-time-Charlie-Boy always to me and others, thought and thought and thought too much, and evolved a circular meaning to life. It explained everything, that circular philosophy, and it almost did to me. I wish that I could remember because, if the truth of life is not a perfect circle, then what is it? Charlie tried to explain an evolvement of his philosophy to me when we went for a walk in London three or four years ago, still making sense if I could understand it.

Most of us became a little unusual, or more so, some not at all as the never ending war clamped on us. For me it was music. I had never gone beyond *D'Ye Ken John Peel* or a *Wee Deoch and Doruis* or anything without semi-tones on my cheap accordion as a boy. I had never listened to classical music and privately suspected that the love of it was affectation. But one evening at Colditz I heard something in the easiest of all, Handel's Water Music, vaguely appealing somehow, was it not? I wound the portable HMV and listened again.

Every night from then on I wound and listened to the easier things, wound and listened to Haydn, to Mozart, Brahms, Rachmaninoff, Chopin and others – nothing superficial or frivolous like Strauss. Then I came to Beethoven, not much to his First, Second or Fourth Symphonies, which were Mozartian, nor much to the programme music of the Pastoral Symphony, but to all the others, gulping them in, obsessed by music, and only the hard great Toscanini recordings would quite do. It became life to me – the symphonies, concertos, overtures, the chamber music. Not knowing a note, I ate up Beethoven, even coming at the end to the last quartets, to the mysterious haunt of the Cavatina. There was Beethoven and there was Sibelius, and all the rest were incidental except one to whom I took a violent dislike – Tchaikovsky. I could not endure his treacle. He made me ill. If it were to happen to me now again, I think that J. S. Bach would be my companion. But Beethoven suited the mood and stored passion of that time.

I was music-mad and it saved me. I lost that pure passion long ago. I still love the *pizzicato* in the Fifth Symphony of Sibelius, the refrain that comes once and does not quite come again. Or the best of all for me – the third movement of Beethoven's Ninth Symphony which does the other thing. It grows to an ultimate entire perfection.

The gusty tumults of November sweep
Wild guardians of the Saxon keep,
And night's dull fingers creep
Upon the sallow day.

The floodlights chisel casement bars and play
And weave on trellised walls and sway
To captious rainsquall's lay,
And windows spatter.

The heavy-footed sentries clatter,
Clip metronomic clop of matter,
And fancies scatter
About the errant mind.

Gone with the storm the superficial rind
And tentative and slow the knives unwind
All but the core is blind
Beyond the vale of sleep.

The music was at night in our dining room by the dim light of a fat-lamp, wherewith to get the records in right order, until twelve or one or two a.m. while the bombers droned. Only at Colditz did PoWs have dining rooms, and in ours I was again the so-called Senior by Army Rank which meant nothing in the most total democracy known to man. Next to us in that room was a mess of three French Canadians – Guy Vandelac, Jean Roy and Roger Marchand, taken at Dieppe and team-mates in the Eichstätt tunnel, so different from us, so much the same. It was entirely mutual between the lords and non-lords and the French Canadians.

Some people, like Patrick and Martin Gilliat and Colin Mackenzie, never changed, but most of us became a little mad in this way or in that way. We were all totally sane in abiding by our golden rules – first, if you dislike a chap, avoid him. Second, never quarrel; get up and leave, but never quarrel.

One afternoon in September 1944 Colin Mackenzie and I went down in the usual closely-escorted fashion to be let loose in the park. As I have said, it was a pleasant enough place to be, roughly oval in shape, the one longer side being higher than the other. We walked anti-clockwise, as always, in ones or twos, a fine autumn day for an unhurried stroll. We were on the upper side, a sentry above us outside the fence. Sentries were not people; they were an inevitable part of our existence, to be ignored. But this sentry shouted and we looked down across the park at the reason for it. A lone prisoner ran at the wire below us, climbed it hand over hand in the face of the sentry there, who brandished his revolver not firing it, then firing it as Mike Sinclair was over and running downhill toward the river, shots going off all round. He ran on out of sight, more shots, then silence.

Colin and I were too appalled to duck at the crack of bullets. We stood there and then walked down to be counted, less one. A *Feldwebel*, or sergeant major, arrived at the column. He said one word: *Tot*, as absolute a word as *Dead*; not *tot* as in child but *tot* as in smote.

Mike Sinclair had escaped more often, more determinedly, more ingeniously than any other prisoner in Germany. He was caught at the Dutch frontier on his eighth attempt. But he was killed at this ninth vain escape.

By day in that last year or more, I went to my private cell below and took a course by correspondence with the Chartered Institute of Secretaries and passed everything except one or two of the final exams. Mercantile law and things like that seemed to be in my alley. But few people have passed accountancy with flying colours not understanding a word of it – double-entry, balance sheets, I did not have and never would have a clue about them, but I learned them by rote and received high marks from my indulgent examiners, eighty percent at least.

The other thing which I did for the last six months of war was to plunge for eight or ten hours a day into a language entirely new to me. English, French, Spanish, German. I had the training in Latin to help me. But I had never learned Greek and the Cyrillic alphabet was unknown to me. Under Laurence Pumphrey (my maestro also in Spanish, I think) I learned, attacked would be more like it, the Russian language and basically had it buttoned up, I mean really buttoned up in essence, spirit and vocabulary. After the war we were instructed to report our qualifications and I reported this with some well-earned pride. In a further intensive six months I could have become a high quality interpreter. The nitwits at the War Office evinced not the remotest interest, thank God. What a fate that would have been, even worse than being a chartered secretary. I was not a Mike Sinclair to do or to die. I was blessed by the music, obsessed by the work, and did survive.

# TWENTY

# 1944 to 1945

I wrote a short story about those days, or nights. It was never published except in a collection entitled *Storms of Our Journey*, but it tells truth enough. The English Milord we have met. Pierre was as near as might be perhaps to my friend, Jean-Claude Tiné. But the Adrian of *Jam Hooch* was not the Adrian of *The Pillar*. In that book, quite a different kind of man became obsessed about music, not knowing a note. So it might be said that there were three of us. Bob, the practical one, came from nobody in particular but from all the practical ones who made our lives bearable.

## JAM HOOCH

Bob poured the red stuff into the container on the stove. Plop, plop, plop, it went, like thick soup. It was still working a bit so the bubbles frothed and the smell of ferment was sour and heady. Then he hammered the lid on tight, tested the water cooler and sat down to wait.

It took a long time but you couldn't be impatient. If you stoked her up too much she would boil and spew out muck instead of clear drops of eighty or ninety per cent stuff that went pouff in your mouth. So he waited. Waiting was no trouble; it was that anyway, wasn't it.

The gramophones were in full swing. Two concerts tonight, one on the top floor and one across the courtyard, and the whole place a jangle of classical stuff which left you cold even when Toscanini and Sibelius or whatever they called themselves weren't having a competition.

The container was hot now. She'd be coming off in a few minutes. Bob closed the draught so she would take it quietly, and turned on the water. People came and went. *Hullo, Bob,* they might say, or they might say nothing, and he would glance at them in the light of the fat-lamp or not.

But here was Pierre. 'Does she come?'

'She hasn't started yet. Any minute now.'

Pierre sat on the table, dangling his bare legs. *'Maintenant nous parlons français.'*

'Not now, you fool. Can't you see I'm busy?'

Pierre gave him French lessons. They started every month or so and did it for a couple of days and gave it up till next time.

'Here she is.' The first volatile drop swelled on the lip of the pipe and trembled and fell into the bottle. It was a long delay before the next, but less for the next and the next and the next until it came in a steady trickle

'*Ça va bien*,' said Pierre. 'How many will we have?'

'Six good ones, I hope. That'll be enough for the four of us.'

'Tomorrow night?'

The Lord came past then on his way to bed. He had been doing his exercises along the passage, so he was sweaty, and his Norman features more carved out than ever in the shadows.

'Tomorrow night, did I hear? Ah, hooch, divine hooch, intoxicating essence of fire! Tomorrow did you say?'

'Yes, tomorrow.'

'May I be of assistance? May I take my little trick?'

'No,' said Bob. 'You're more trouble than you're worth.'

'Goodnight, then, Maestro. A good night's sleep before the party. *Bonne nuit,* Monsieur le Froggy-wog.'

'Goodnight, English Milord,' said Pierre.

'He's getting so damned thin.'

'He is ill. He mortifies himself to death.'

'Do you think so, Pierre?'

'*Oui.* I know it. He is a saint, that one.'

'Why the hooch, then?'

'That also could be a penance.'

'Beyond me,' said Bob. Fifteen minutes a bottle. It came off about that speed. There were nearly two now. You never had a moment's rest once it got going – the stove to keep right, connections leaking, the whole gangling contraption of pipes to watch, and a sample spoonful every now and then.

'*Licht aus*!' from down below. They hadn't noticed that the courtyard lights had gone out. Bob went and pulled down the blind. He was the practical one. He did everything.

Here was Rudi the snoop, come up to see about the light. But he saw the blind was down now, so he just stood and shuffled his feet.

'What d'you want, Rudi? *Was gibt's*?'

'*Nix neues*,' said Rudi. '*Hab' ein paar Zwiebeln*.' He tapped his trouser leg. '*Licht aus*,' he added absently.

'We want his onions, Pierre?'

'Yes,' said Pierre, face closed off. He sat looking at his feet.

'Let's see them. I'll give you five cigarettes.'

'*Nee. Schokolade.*'

'Give him the cigarettes, Pierre.'

Pierre put them on the table beside Rudi and went back and sat down.

The air-raid alarm went off, three long ones for Be ready.

'*Deutschland Kaputt.*'

Rudi sighed. '*Yaw*,' he said.

'Buzz off now, Rudi.'

'*Licht aus*,' he said again, and went away.

'Not a bad Goon, old Rudi.'

Pierre said nothing. The real alarm came then, wailing frenziedly about the castle and down the valley. You got a shiver of dismay even though they were your own planes; and you could feel the fear going across the continent. The first one came, and then the second and a steady stream, the noise of one dying as the next came up, regular as drops of hooch coming from the still.

'Sounds like Dresden.'

'Good killing,' said Pierre gently. The time went on.

'It's weak now. I'm going to stop.'

Bob doused the fire and took the still to bits. Then he emptied the big container into the sink. If it had been smelly before, it was double stinking now, hot and putrid and the virtue gone from the brew.

Pierre stayed with him till he had decanted the spirit. It was cloudy with a hint of green about it. Hooch made from German jam wasn't bad when you got used to the taste. Vicious, like absinthe.

The planes had stopped passing, and so had the rumble and tremble of bombs. It was one o'clock.

'Bed.'

'Yes, bed,' said Pierre. He yawned.

They went through the dining room. Adrian was still there with his fat-lamp and his hands shaded across his forehead.

'What are you working at now?'

He looked up and back at his book. 'Russian,' he said sourly.

'We've got six bottles for tomorrow night.'

Adrian's face lit up, like opening a door he kept shut. 'Six! That's wonderful. You're a hero, Bob.' He closed the Russian grammar.

'Too bloody right, I'm a hero.' They went to bed.

Bob lined up the six bottles and the four small mugs on the table.

'Where's his Lordship?'

'He's still doing his exercises.'

'Do we start?'

'Better wait a minute. He's hardly ever late for hooch. Pierre says . . . ' But Bob stopped himself.

They were in the reading room at the top of the building. It had windows with thin bars over the courtyard and windows with thick bars opposite. They were all open, for this was October and still mild. The moon came in from outside but you couldn't see it properly because of the floodlights. Those floodlights, you hated them, but you got so you missed the latticework on the ceiling when they went out for an air raid.

'Mind if I shut the courtyard windows?' said Adrian. 'They're playing Tchaikovsky again. I can't stand that perverted treacle.'

'One sounds as bad as the other to me. Oh, here he is at last.' The Lord came bounding into the room, panting from his exertions.

'Am I too late? Have I missed the boat? May I still sup with Lucullus?'

'Here you are, boys – a bottle each and two reserve.'

They poured themselves drinks. Some people took it straight and others watered it. Whichever way, the first mouthful was unbelievable but the second was better and by the third you felt the glow.

'There were two SS officers in the *Kommandantur* today.'

'It's only a matter of time,' said Adrian. 'We'll wake up one morning to find them in charge.'

But even that anxiety was dulled, was fading into hooch and plenty more.

'I congratulate you, Bob,' said the Lord after one cupful. 'What bouquet, what full rich body!'

'Is it as strong as usual?' Pierre looked at Bob.

'Strong as usual? Christ, it's strong. It burns cold. Don't you think that's strong enough?'

'I pull your leg,' said Pierre, and everyone laughed, including Adrian; the cool friendly light of the moon and the warm hostile light from below outside the bars lit up their faces with the bones strong and happy.

'It'll be over in a month.'

'I'll believe that when we've crossed the Rhine.'

'But they're finished. No more fight in them. You only need to look at the sentries to know that.'

'These ones are a lot of useless dugouts.'

'You're a bloody awful pessimist, Adrian. What do you think, Froggy?'

'*Je ne pense plus*,' said Pierre. '*J'existe.*'

'We shall storm the bastion,' said his Lordship, turning his cup high so his Adam's apple stuck out. 'We shall win through thanks to Bacchus.' Talk on, talk on.

'He was damned attractive in that last play.'

'She was, you mean.'

'He or she, depends which way you look at it.' They laughed and then were quiet for a minute. The gramophone had stopped down below. The Lord poured the last of his bottle.

'*A quoi penses-tu, Pierre?*'

'Do not *tutoyer* me; that I implore you. Even with my father there is no tutoying. It is a vulgarity.'

'What are you thinking of, then?'

'I am thinking of women, of real women.'

'Why so sad?'

'One must be sad to think of pleasure. One must be in Hell to see Heaven.'

'You talk a lot of cock.'

'Yes, that is what I talk.'

The music had stopped beyond the closed windows with thin bars over the courtyard.

'I'm going to get a gramophone,' said Adrian. He got up and went out.

‘Adrian is crazy for music. So much is not good.’

‘Remember Johnson. That was the way he went before they took him to the loony bin.’

‘I think it helps him,’ said the Lord. He sighed, which was not a thing you often heard him do.

Adrian came back. He put it on the next table and held the records up to the window so he could see the numbers. He had them in the right order when the floodlights went out.

‘Here come the bomber boys.’

‘D’yever think of them being shot down while we sit and get sozzled?’

‘Yes, I think of them being killed and the Goons they kill.’

‘Of that I think with pleasure.’

‘What are you going to play, Adrian?’

‘The Seventh Symphony.’

‘If you think I shall sit in reverent silence, you’re much mistaken.’

‘Talk away. I just want Beethoven to get drunk with me.’

‘Let us now broach the reserve.’

‘Pierre says you drink as a sort of penance.’

The Lord laughed for several minutes, but at the end of it you weren’t any the wiser.

The full air alarm went off. It was a splendid place to hear it up there, the first and then the second, all the alarms vying in frenzy, wailing up and down the valley and over the hill, and the river placid in the moonlight. No unease in hearing it now. The boots clattered down below and Germans shouted at one another with the usual venom, and some bloody fool fired a shot.

‘Here they come!’ The periodic disconcerting murmur of engines out of tune.

‘Let’s look. I’ve never seen one yet.’

‘The moon travels fast. It sails about the heavens.’

‘His Lordship’s drunk.’

‘*Zurück vom Fenster*!’

‘Shut up, you bloody Goon!’ But they got back from the window. Adrian couldn’t have timed it better if he’d tried. The last movement of the symphony and the sound of bombs came together. He leaned back in the corner. His face was white and tortured happy; he turned the last record as neatly as if he had been sober. You could see the ectasy streaming through him.

'I like silver Mozart,' said Pierre. 'Beethoven too elemental. But he tells them. He tells the Third Reich.'

'See what you mean. C'mon. Let's punish the last bottle.'

'Christ have mercy upon them,' said the Lord loudly.

The music finished its wild riot. ''potheosis of the dance is nonsense. Conquest and retribution'sh what it means.' Adrian got up and weaved towards the door and through it without touching.

'He all right?' They looked at Bob.

'Yes. Only being sick.' They listened to Adrian in the lavatory. He was quiet after a bit but he did not come back.

Pierre leaned his elbows on the windowsill. His Lordship pushed the empty cup away and folded his arms and closed his eyes. Bob sat on at the table. The hooch was strong in him and wonderful.

'Why are you crying, Froggy-wog?'

The tears were pouring down Pierre's cheeks, welling in a glimmer of moonlight.

'I cry for my country, for that and everything.'

The Lord was fast asleep and he began to snore, a wasted man snoring through his mouth below the beaky nose. Adrian was being sick again outside.

Bob finished up his hooch; but he did not move. He was the practical one, and these three people were his children.

Meanwhile, that courtly and selfless enigma, John Arundell, mortified his flesh and was dying of tuberculosis when repatriated, the last Arundell of Wardour.

Reading this manuscript through and revising it many times (which I always have to do before transferring the cramped written word to a tape-recorder), I see that the chronology of that last year is jumbled. It could be straightened but I think that a time-confused account is more true of those tangled days and months when no certainty but hunger was a certain prospect.

Jam Hooch was dreadful stuff but it blew our steam off. In richer days at Colditz we used to ferment from raisins and other dried fruit and sugar and distil that to potable whisky, even coming, for a short time, to the civilized ritual of a drink before dinner in the Chapel Room.

But that reminds me of a distasteful thing, the only occasion when I did have to command, if only in a formal sense. The Germans had tried to slip a stooge into the camp, an officer of the British Merchant Marine taken early in the war who, it later transpired, had been a member of Oswald Mosley's Fascist Party and had broadcast on the German radio to Britain. I would not know why they thought it worthwhile to put him into Colditz, where he was given a vacant bunk in my room. We knew too much about who had been where for how long with whom, and there were unexplained gaps and contradictions in this man's prison story. He was a haunted, spent creature, anyone's tool, yet he could be dangerous. I therefore reported to Wully Tod who ordered me to arrest him.

I put on uniform – our normal clothing at Colditz was hardly that – and summoned two officers of his own rank, Phil Pardoe and another. 'Get dressed up,' I told them and when they came back, I said: 'Put Purdey under close arrest.'

Meanwhile Colonel Tod required to see the Germans and told them to take him out of the camp, or else. They did.

We saw him no more but after the war he was tried for treason, sentenced to death and ultimately reprieved. I never did like the idea of executing people for their beliefs, however misguided.

As luxuries became sparse and vanished, it had to be Jam Hooch, enough of that to have an occasional, say a monthly, binge with consequent appalling hangovers. Which brings me to the Australians. They were a rough tough lot, not the most appealing of people when things were good. But when bread was to be measured and treasured by the millimetre it was quite another matter. They were champions in adversity.

I remember one time when two of them – Johnny Rawson, who once got as far as Jugoslavia before being recaptured, and George Boulding, whom I never saw after the war because George wrapped himself round a telephone pole back home down under.

Anyway, Johnny and George came to see me, curiously respectful and ill-at-ease. 'Davie Boy!'

'Yes?' But I knew damned well what it was. I had perpetrated a shoddy trick – borrowed two bottles of top-proof Jam Hooch and repaid in weaker stuff. It had been on my conscience and I did not wait for them to say their piece. 'Dead right,' I said. 'I apologize.' I had one spare extra, which they accepted and asked me to share. Yes, give me the Australians – Jack Champ, Rex Baxter, the woolly and trusty John Rawson, sometimes a bit much to take, George Boulding, Mark Howard (originally English) and the others. They were a good hard breed from a good hard land.

Before I come to the end of Colditz days, I will quote part of a poem that I wrote to Willa at that place.

Here in the dawdling night
In the dim-lit murmuring room
The ceiling is touched with floodlight
And memories loom.
And the west wind below the castle wall
Sweeps in the trees and the owls call.
Ah, My Love, let us fly together
Through the night
Through the cold
Through the winter weather

It was in March, when we were suffering nothing worse than extreme hunger, when it might be said of us, withal, that we were enduring – in March I learned of Thomas Rennie's death. He was my brother-in-law, whom I had introduced to my sister Huldah in 1931. He was taken with our old 51st Division at St Valéry, escaped on the line of march, reached Spain and home and fought the whole war through. He was commanding that same Highland division at the Rhine crossing. Thomas was a legendary front-line general, killed by a mortar bomb on the last day that death might have come his way. Bernard Fergusson wrote: 'There was never anybody like Thomas Rennie'.

That last month was trouble as Germany collapsed. Orders came that the *Prominente* were to be moved. There was a possibility that they might be hidden in the castle but John Elphinstone, who was the senior of them, took command. He talked about it alone with Patrick and me at our table in the dining room. We knew that there were SS troops nearby. And we knew that, as John said, if they were hidden (which for a short time would be possible in a maze of Colditz attics) all hell would break loose for them and for us. They had been offered hiding but John told us what he had decided: they would go. No one might ever guess, before or after, the core of steel that was in John Elphinstone, so reticent a quiet man. One might have said, perhaps one did say, I would not know, that with hostages such as the *Prominente* their only value was to be alive. They would therefore live. In a sane world that would be true, and even in this case it would be true up to a final point. That point was that Adolf Hitler tried to take Germany down with him. They went, and John saved the lot of them in the end.

A few days later, the air raid siren screamed its warning for a thousandth time, a last time, and there was no all clear. The radio people said that they could hear tank crews talking Russian and tank crews talking American English. We were in the middle of the pinch, still being counted by good old Püpcke, and down in the town the Germans still Heil-Hitlered one another. They went on doing it and doing it, the devil's terror at their heels, until to raise one's right arm stiff and straight at forty-five degrees was to invite a bullet. Then they stopped as if by magic and not a soul had been a Nazi sympathizer, far less a Nazi.

The tank crews talked and Micky Burn and I made a bet. He bet, wishful thinking, that his Communist friends would relieve Colditz. I bet, wishful thinking, that the Americans would be first. Micky, that rare Communist, honoured his fifty quid a few weeks later.

On the last day it already seemed a certainty that I would win my bet when tanks came into view from a westerly direction, hulls down with long snouts peeping, not yet firing but an air of menace. Then the Americans ranged on the castle, the most prominent object, and scored several hits on top. It was nasty to be shelled again. I lurked at the foot of the chapel stairs until there was a lull, more than a lull, an end to shelling.

The rumour was that Douglas Bader had been hit, later modified to nearly hit, as he stood at a high window to watch the fun. I asked him about it this spring, 1983. 'Nowhere near me, old boy,' he said. 'I did fall on my backside, though.'

A curious silence settled on the day. We knew that the Germans had had orders a few days before to evacuate us to the east, that the SBO had refused to move, that they had yielded, and that was all we knew, or I knew.

The night of April the 15th came and Colonel Tod sent for me.

# TWENTY-ONE

# 1945

I knocked and went in. He had Martin Gilliat, the adjutant, with him. Martin was a member of our mess, as I have mentioned, the wit of our mess, as I have not. We had been over the wire and through a tunnel and had spent most of five years in one another's company off and on. Colonel Tod, the taciturn Scotsman with a slightly bashed nose and Martin, whom you might take for a smoothie unless and until you knew more about him – they were very different men with a thing in common: both unflappable.

Wully Tod sat in his chair. He looked exhausted, the same gruff kindly man, exhausted as well he might be, having forced the Germans to yield about evacuating the camp, which they had had orders from on high to do. I knew that, and knew nothing much else.

'Hullo, David. Have a seat. Martin will explain.' He puffed out his cheeks in a way he had and sat back.

'The Americans are due in at the crack. The Colonel wants you to go outside and be official welcomer. Colonel Duke is sending an American along but you will be in charge.' Florimund Duke was an admirable *Time-Life* man who had been parachuted into Hungary or somewhere and had found his way, or it had been found unpleasantly for him, luckily too, via the Gestapo to Colditz.

Martin was being unusually terse, for him, something else on his mind not revealed, trouble not revealed.

'Okay, Martin. Anything else, sir?'

'Yes. You look like the spaniel's dinner in those clothes. Try and dress yourself to resemble a Black Watch officer.'

'Right, sir.' I would take anything from Wully Tod but was not best-pleased about the spaniel's dinner. In fact, I was dressed quite smartly for imminent release – my blue and white checked shirt, my tie, my fur-trimmed waistcoat. Smart as anything, if not soldierly.

'Oh, and David!'

'Sir?'

'Guard company confined to barracks, officers in their mess, all arms locked up. The place is surrendered before they come in. Quite clear?'

'Yes, sir.'

'Püpcke will meet you at the gate. No one else gets out except you and the American. One last thing.'

'Sir?'

'In a preliminary way, you're in charge of the situation. Don't get shot, and see fair play.'

'Right, sir.'

I shaved because it was already tomorrow, put on a khaki shirt, a tie, my one and only pair of Black Watch tartan trews, battle-dress jacket with a captain's pips, all crowned by my TOS or tam-o'-shanter, khaki bonnet with feathered Red Hackle which was our emblem.

So much, so little had happened in that long time and it was almost over, climax coming up. I should have been excited but was not. Yet a small selfish flicker of a plot was hatching, how typical.

A Hullo and a Hi exchanged with the American, a tallish lieutenant not known to me, a New Boy, he must be, as I once had been, that juvenile terminology. Püpcke and I saluted one another army-fashion; the seniority had changed, the formality not.

He led us through archways, possibly over a quondam moat, I have forgotten, quite a long way through the agglomerated interstices of the medieval castle to a final archway before an open bridge. On the left in the archway was a door, a small room with two bunks in it. Püpcke standing to usher us inside.

I stopped a moment before going in. A light at the far end showed a fair distance of open bridge, a good thing. People were more likely to come in shooting round blind corners than across open bridges. But how would they come at the crack of dawn? A jeep, a scout car, a rumbling tank, on foot, or how? 'Herr Hauptmann,' he said. 'They will come over the bridge. There is no other way.'

It was unreal, more unreal than all the dim realities which had been going on and on for ever to no ending that had nearly ended. My small plot was real, though.

'*Hauptmann Püpcke, wir möchten* . . . We would like something to drink, please, not too much and not too little, perhaps a quarter of a bottle of Schnapps.' I was explicit about it because Martin and I had been scavenging for blackened potato peelings lately, and drink gallops to the hungry head and I had to see fair play.

Püpcke looked surprised. If there were still unknowns for us, what about the unknowns for him? A small smile crossed his plain, worried face. '*Ja wohl, Herr Hauptmann*.'

He came back with a bottle and two glasses, a dark bottle one quarter full. It was pre-war Grand Marnier, the best of liqueurs, not common Schnapps.

'Thank you very much,' I said in English, and continued: 'I shall be in the bottom bunk. Wake me as soon as you know they're coming.'

'*Ja wohl, Herr Hauptmann*,' he said and went away.

'You seem to like that Kraut.'

*Krauts*, they said, and *Goons*, we said, and I did not like either word although sometimes I said Goons too. Mostly, I said Germans and mostly disliked them. We sipped our sweet strong nectar, pre-war nectar, pre-madness nectar. 'Yes,' I said. 'I do like him. Most of them have been buttering up to us lately, not Püpcke. He never changed, except to be a bit more testy, bloody-minded, whatever the word, a decent chap.'

'All goddam Krauts to me,' he said. 'Look what they done.'

'I know,' I said. We finished the drink, even shares, prison fashion, no effect on me that I could feel.

'How long have you bin in the shaft?'

In the shaft, *Kriegsgefangenenschaft*, he must have been in a while to pick that one up. I wished that they had given me one that I could like, or given me to Colonel Duke though that would have stolen my tiny thunder, but what the hell. I worked it out. 'Four years and ten months and four days coming up,' I said to annoy him.

Did not annoy him, worse. 'Jesus!' he said. 'That long! I'd be climbing the wall.'

'Try climbing the bunk,' I said.

He looked in a hurt way at the Limey sonuvabitch I was, and climbed.

I got into the easier lower bunk and strong drink swooped in. *Pie-eyed*, my bunkmate would say. *Pissed-up*, I might say, and closed my eyes but that would not do at all. The Grand Marnier world swam round and round, round and around the rugged rock. I opened them again. Three hours to the crack of what, of five a.m. at dawn, or whatever.

I simply must get to sleep, closed them, still swimming, warm and woozled, stopping, stopped.

'*Sie kommen gleich.*' Coming at once. I was up, eyes rubbed, TOS on my head, shook my bunkmate awake. No noise of a vehicle, they must be on foot. 'Stay in here,' I said to Püpcke and shouted at the door: 'Hullo! Good morning! How d'you do?'

'Come on outta there,' a voice called.

Welcomer-in-chief, still groggy a bit, taking no chances. 'Good morning,' I bellowed again, stepped out and was looking at the business end of a tommy-gun, not at the crack of dawn but in full early daylight across half a bridge.

'Hi!' he said, knowing at once that I was nothing German, weapon from both hands to left hand, both parties rather relieved, I know for myself and think for him. We shook hands, as in 'Doctor Livingstone, I presume'. He was festooned with weaponry, a fresh-faced young man hardly out of his teens, point of the advanced guard, a vulnerable position.

'Okay, you guys,' he called back over his shoulder to two more men covering him from the far end of the bridge. 'Come on over. I've gotten myself a Scottie here.'

They came over, pleased to meet his Scottie, but their own lieutenant, Scottie's assistant, they totally ignored.

'Would you listen a moment?'

'Yeah, listen to Scottie.'

'The camp guards have surrendered, all disarmed, soldiers in barracks, officers in their mess. But there's one officer in there I want to take care of.'

'You wanna take care of a Kraut officer? Hell, Scottie, we'll do that, a real pleasure.'

They homed on our Grand Marnier lair where Püpcke must be lurking.

'No. You misunderstand me. I mean look after him, he's quite a decent chap. Put him in with the others is what I mean. Leave it to me.'

'*You misunderstand me. Leave it to me.* This Scottie with the fancy talk, givin' us orders, must be a goddam officer.' They viewed me with less favour. 'You an officer?'

'Once upon a time I used to once was be,' I remarked with some brilliance and was at once favourite Scottie again, even if goddam officer.

So Püpcke went in with his fellows. Jeeps were now arriving and the outer regions began to swarm with Americans. 'Will they miss you if you come in for a cup of coffee?' I asked my liberator.

'Hell, no,' he said. 'I done my stuff. Sure, I'd like to, Captain. That's right, isn't it? I didn't kind of notice much before.'

'Yes, that's right, but David would do fine.'

'Okay, Dave. Lead us to the coffee.'

'It's not quite the kind you're accustomed to. Our finest brew, though. Liberty brew.'

We went into the courtyard through the door, which was closed behind us. 'Where have you sprung from, David?'

'Sent out to meet them.'

'Were you now, you lucky sod?'

'Well, for crying out aloud,' he said in there in my alien courtyard, almost empty in the early morning, not asking me any questions, not one. How lucky the lucky sod was in my liberator, whose name is lost to me. For the next two days he was to be an honorary member of our mess. Now he laid weapons away and drank our best acorn coffee as if it was the real thing, a polite college boy soldier, pleased to meet my mates and they to meet him.

'Did you hear about Wully Tod?' Pat said, aside. 'His only son was killed months ago, Martin says. Never told a soul, or he might have told Martin, I wouldn't know.'

'And he didn't change, not one iota.' I saw poor old Wully Tod, sitting back in his chair, exhausted. 'Fortitude, Pat. The King once sent us a good message about fortitude. Remember?'

'Yes, I remember,' Patrick said.

But I heard a rumpus outside below, a good deal of shouting. *See fair play*, Wully Tod had said. 'Stay for breakfast, won't you? Only bread and margarine, I'm afraid. I have to go.'

'But you guys are hungry,' he said, glancing at us one by one, so polite, as Americans can be with such an endearing diffidence in their politeness. 'What say I go along with Dave and rustle up some rations?'

A popular move and we went down and out again and separated. Being free again in a sort of a way was nothing much, a bit too much. I walked on. On the left, Eggers, the security officer, was standing, or was stood, back to the wall at rifle point, no other Germans visible.

'Captain Walker!'

'You shut your trap.'

'Let me speak to him. What's the matter?'

'Captain Walker, I am separated from my comrades through no absolute fault of mine.'

'Colonel's orders, hold the bastard, Captain.'

'Where is the Colonel?'

'Command post there!' One of them pointed across the way. Colditz Castle was more of a maze outside than in.

'May I speak to the Colonel?'

'He's giving out orders. But sure, have a try after.'

The Colonel was allotting positions on the ground east of Colditz, his war not over yet, or he had a touchy ally to encounter soon.

'Oh, hullo,' he said, when his officers had gone and I had saluted at the open doorway. 'Do anything for you?'

'This German officer outside. He seems to have got separated from the others.'

'Yes, I kept him. We were sent as a spearpoint to get those prominents, the hostages, and he admits he went with them in a bus to some place, Königstein. Says he had to go or it might have been the SS.'

'I think that's true, sir.'

'You got anything against him?'

'No, sir. He's not a bad chap as far as I know.'

'I sent the others across the river.'

'Would you like me to take him down to join them?'

'Well, I guess so, if you want to.'

'Not particularly, Colonel. I wouldn't mind walking in a straight line again, though.'

'I hadn't thought of that,' he said. 'You bin in long?'

'Since 1940.'

He looked down at his map with the black crayoned circles on it. 'That Scotch hat of yours. You're The Black Watch Regiment.'

We say it without the *Regiment* appended. 'Yes, Colonel,' I said.

'A famous guy of yours, two-star general, major general, killed lately. I met him once, always wore that hat.'

'Yes, sir.' But I did not speak of Thomas Rennie.

'I'd better send you an escort with this fella.'

'No need, Colonel. The last thing he'd want to do is to escape.'

'Okay,' he said. 'And get yourself something to eat some place. You look like you need it.' The Colonel stood up and shook hands across the table, and to his adjutant or whatever he said, 'Tell 'em to hand the prisoner over to the Captain.'

So it was arranged and Eggers preceded me along and round and down and along and out, past a house on the left that had been blasted, like a million other blasted houses in this blasted war. Eggers showed signs of being ever so loquaciously grateful but I walked in silence, marched him in silence to the bridge over the river Mulde and across that bridge and to the other end where a body lay spreadeagled. It was the body of a boy of about fourteen, a Hitler *Jugend* band on one arm, a flattened *Panzerfaust* beside him, like our bazooka we called them, didn't we? A primitive weapon to fire at tanks. The face of the child was palish green where it was not bloody.

An American corporal stood at the end of the bridge, a hulking truculent type. 'Hullo, Corporal. Where are the other German officers?'

'What's that to you?' He did not like me, pushed me out of his way and frisked Eggers roughly.

'Are you in radio communication with HQ up there?' I looked across the sluggish river and up at that place and back at him.

'Sure,' he said.

'Get on to them, then, and ask if I'm acting under your Colonel's orders.'

'Oh well, okay,' he said, backing down. 'In there!'

I opened the door and went in with Eggers. They were packed tight in a windowless room, all staring, blinking at me – Prawitt, Püpcke, some whose faces I knew, some not. They looked as if they had been manhandled – a bleeding cheek, buttons torn off, one of Prawitt's shoulder straps hanging down. Supplication. Had I ever looked like that? But my weasel-faced captor had been unknown to me. Prawitt held out a paper.

'Captain Walker, it is our safe conduct from the SBO to honourable treatment as prisoners under . . . '

'I can read, Captain Eggers.'

I do not remember all the contents of that paper but I remember exactly its intent, which was a request to the commanding officer of American liberating forces that the German officers and men, comprising the guard company of Oflag IV C, be accorded full status as Prisoners of War under the Geneva Convention, that the Commandant had been ordered to evacuate the camp, which order the Senior British Officer had refused to obey and the Commandant had yielded. His conduct and that of the guard company under his command had been honourable. They had been unable to prevent the removal of the *Prominente* by bus on April the 12th, for which removal they could not be held blameworthy.

The letter was signed by Colonel Tod as SBO, and by a Brigadier Davies, senior officer in British Army rank.

The intent of the letter, our undertaking, or *quid pro quo*, was entirely explicit. We had given our word. But these people had been herded into a black hole, no longer black with door half open.

It was ironic that my prison sheet, which I had seen, bore an attached red card: *Deutschfeindlich*, hostile to Germans, German-hater, a badge of distinction that might have been an uncomfortable distinction under other circumstances of, say, an SS selection board – and here I was, a sort of last straw to which, or to whom, they clung.

'May I have this paper?' I said to Prawitt.

'*Ja wohl, Herr Hauptmann. Freilich.* Certainly, of course.' He thrust it at me.

Was it some old lag's league that the German-hater should be entrusted so eagerly with a piece of paper, an undertaking to safe sort of conduct that he might tear up and throw over the bridge into the river Mulde? I do not know what it was but I felt some outrage on their behalf.

Outside was the glowering corporal. 'I'm going up to the camp and will be back. In the meanwhile please see that those German officers in there are not molested and let them have some air.'

'Say,' he said. 'Are you some kind of a collab . . . ' But he stopped at that.

'God damn and blast you to bloody hell. Where is the radio?'

'Okay, Captain,' he said quite meekly. 'I'll leave the Krauts alone. Say, Captain, what is this old dame goin' on about? Somethin' to do with that dead little bastard?'

The old woman was torn with grief, streams of tears and dialect German that I could not well understand but I got the drift. 'That boy was her grandson, and the undertaker lives across the river. She wants to find him.'

'But I have to stop 'em crossing over. No Krauts is my orders. Those little bastards, worst of the lot. Hell, the day before yesterday, was it, they killed two of our guys before we crisped 'em in a bunker.'

'I know,' I said. But I knew nothing, protected all these years from war, from the flame-thrower that would do the crisping. *Collaborator*, he had almost said. I could not look again at the child's body. 'Hadn't I better take her across?'

'Oh well, okay, Captain, you're the boss.' My explosion seemed to have made me another buddy.

'*Komm mit*,' I said to the old wailing woman.

She vanished somewhere after the bridge and I went on up and through and into the strange place to seek Colonel Tod, who had lost his only son and told nobody until it was over.

I found him at a table with some others and produced the paper which he had signed. 'Sir, what about this?'

'I know,' he said. 'But Davies is senior. He says we signed it under duress.'

It was not Davies, some bouncy squat British brigadier, dropped into Yugoslavia, who had defied the German general's order to evacuate the camp, knowing that SS troops were near. It was Wully Tod who had forced Prawitt to yield: Wully Tod, respected by them as he was revered by us, had done it.

'Sir, if we signed under duress, so did Prawitt act under duress.'

'I know,' he said again. 'I'm sorry, David.'

That shoddy little brigadier whom I hardly knew and disliked – why did I not find Martin or Douglas, or any of the strong ones of whom there were plenty, and go with them to Davies, to confront him, to threaten him? But I did not. I did no such thing and I do not know why not. And yet I wonder now, I wonder: might Wully Tod have gone and blown the head off Davies?

I went out again and down again and stopped on the bridge across that mouldy river to think on the morning that should have been a singing and dancing for joy sort of morning. I thought of the great Wully Tod, bereft; of that damned corpse I still had to pass; of this damned unasked-for responsibility thrust upon me, and I had failed again. And what did it all render down to on this freedom day? I was sorry for myself.

We had two watchword phrases. One, as I have said, was *No Bullshit*, straight, vulgar and true. The other we might ourselves have originated, or might not. It was *Colonel Self-Pity*. Usually we said it inwardly, when we caught ourselves at it. *That's Colonel Self-Pity*. Or sometimes we said it at large, not often.

'Colonel Self-Pity,' I said aloud, alone, and laughed at myself, troubles gone.

'Whatever happens,' I said to Prawitt, 'hang on to this.' I gave him his paper. 'Keep it, I mean. Translate that, Captain Eggers.'

He did so. *Auf Wiedersehen*, I said with civility, without enthusiasm.

Great clicking of heels by the ex-enemy and floods of thanks as if I had done something, rather than nothing. *Auf Wiedersehen*, until we meet again. But I never did meet any of them again.

There is an improbable postscript to this. Reinhold Eggers was released by the Americans in August 1945, returned to his home in the Russian zone where he was arrested again and held prisoner until 1955.

Freed then, he went to southern Germany where he spent the rest of his life. He wrote to me among others and met some of us in Germany or London, including Douglas Bader. I had several letters from him in his quaint English and replied once or twice.

Eventually, he wrote a book which was translated and published in 1961 in England, *Colditz, the German Story*, and he sent me a copy. I read bits of it, having by then more or less had my fill of Colditz.

It was only a month ago, when I was bolstering a shaky memory of those last days, that for the first time I came upon his inscription on the fly-leaf.

*David Walker*
*der mich am 16.4.45 in sehr ritterlicher, nobler Weise durch das eben besetzte Colditz führte, meinen Kameraden und mir sehr viel Unannehmlichkeiten ersparte und vielleicht das Leben rettete, in Dankbarkeit und zur freundlichen Erinnerung an seinen langjährigen Wächter gewidmet (Oflag IV C Colditz/Sachsen 1939–45)*
*Sigmaringen, Weihnachten 1961*
*Reinhold Eggers*

Roughly translated, this means: '. . . who very chivalrously and nobly escorted me through Colditz on 16.4.45 when it had just been occupied. In doing so he spared me and my comrades much unpleasantness, and perhaps saved our lives. Dedicated in the warm and grateful memories of his long-term guardian.'

It is open to question whether or not I helped them much, if at all.

## TWENTY-TWO

# 1945

For the next two days of April we dipped into American K Rations, which were distasteful battle-fodder to them and bliss to us. My liberator friend, honorary member of the mess, was often with us. He was at the age of devouring romantic poetry and I gave him a fairly treasured possession, *The Oxford Book of English Verse*, that Willa had sent me years ago. He asked me to write to his mother in Philadelphia, which I faithfully did after reaching home but received no answer from Mom.

What else happened while we champed at the bit? We went for walks in the countryside, wherever we willed to the west, dull country if I remember aright. We ate largely and slept long and drank a bit and were not very happy about the looting habits of that overfed army – every Kraut wristwatch and appealing knicknack in the neighbourhood was liberated with shouted abuse, no worse than that. They sure did hate the goddam Krauts.

I realized a compelling reason for it too when I saw a few living skeletons from an SS camp of Hungarian Jews nearby. But the guards had escaped. If I had had one of those monsters before my little gun I would have shot him stone dead without compunction or pleasure, and I would now still. Does the beast in humanity grow worse, the highest of animals more wicked?

We, in our fabled Coldtiz Camp, were lucky. How assiduously decent people have set about making legends of it. It was no more than a common prison camp, in many ways better, in some ways not. We might never go to Colditz reunions. We might never speak of the place except to a few friends who had shared it with us, or as briefly as possible to outsiders asking questions. Yet, as I have implied or said before, Colditz has remained with me as nowhere else did. Through a glass darkly I see it still.

In those days we wondered about John and Charlie and the others, of whom there was no word.

In those days the Colditz glider was produced from its attic hiding place and assembled complete in the courtyard. It was a stubby-looking job, a two-seater machine. The designer was Jack Best and with him throughout construction was Tony Rolt, ex motor-racing driver, whom I knew well. At the beginning I had had a humble part in it, sawing and planing spars; and then gave up for the Russian language.

The plan was not short of fantastic. It involved dismantling part of the wall of the topmost room overlooking the valley. It involved an adequately strong rope, a launching slip, a colossal weight, a trigger at the glider's tail, a tremendous acceleration imparted by the falling weight with the same effect as catapulting a plane from an aircraft carrier. The experts said that it was aerodynamically sound and would work provided the demolition could be done.

When they had finished manufacture and had hidden the glider in a false wall in the Colditz attics, Tony Rolt asked me to manage that escape but I declined the job, which would have been a double fulltime job. I was deep into Russian then. 'I'm a candidate for a seat in it,' I said. That was phoney in one respect; the war was nearly over and they shot anyone who escaped. It might not have been phoney in another respect – being catapulted in a sound glider with a sound pilot was my kind of risk. But I had not earned a seat and would not have taken it even if I had. Three years earlier, yes. So the finished glider was on display and never flew.

There was still no word of the *Prominente*, to rescue whom this armoured spearhead of Patton's armies had been vainly sent, not to liberate us common herd.

But only two days later we were loaded into army trucks, the whole lot of us who were bound for England, and whistled westwards at high speed. We passed evidence of a war still going on – a battery of guns firing shells into Leipzig – whistled past that and on, and the black drivers whistled up the German girls, and to an overnight stop at an airfield and into Dakotas for the positively final hop. I was an airborne parcel, special delivery. It did not occur to me that since 1940 I had had no decisions whatever to make for myself except escaping decisions, which were decisions of a sort, and pass-the-time decisions like learning this or reading that.

We were disembarked at some airfield in the south of England, not far from London, a receiving station of which I remember that my personal particular individual parcel was herded towards a militant woman who held a small dust-shooting sack and instructed me to open the top buttons of my shirt.

'Madam, I'm not lousy,' I said in offended protest, clean as a whistle, devoid of vermin.

'It's only DDT, the miracle powder, to destroy any possible contamination,' the adamant female said, inserted the nozzle and squeezed her bag like a bagpiper's bag and shot me full of pinkish stuff, not an unpleasant sensation on the whole, decontaminated from top to bottom with her wizard dust.

I was free now, on my absolute ownsome to find a telephone. The queue was long and I had no money and I wandered about like a lost sheep seeking whom he may devour, and the evening came and I had some supper, free on His Majesty. I had not paid for anything; I did not have anything to pay for anything; and I had forgotten how to pay for anything.

Perhaps Patrick and Colin Mackenzie were in the same boat with me. I do not remember. John was not there, and where was John? But I went strolling. The nightingales were singing here in England in the dusk. The nightingales bubbled and sang most beautifully as night fell on England.

I did at last reach a pay telephone but what did you say? In Canada it used to be a *collect call* or *reverse the charges*, and here you had to put tuppence in for the operator. Where was tuppence?

'Could you lend me tuppence?'

'Here, take it,' he said, whoever said. *Cupar 108*, I remembered that; and it was done, and I was home to her voice again. Yes, I was fine and she was fine, and Father and Mamma and everyone were fine. And I knew about Thomas, did I? Yes, I knew.

'Where are you?'

'Near London somewhere. It's too late now. I'll catch a train tomorrow.'

'I'll meet you in Edinburgh at the hotel where the station is. Just ask for me at the desk.'

'But why Edinburgh? On to Cupar Fife and home.'

'No, Edinburgh, darling, please. Then home.'

'All right,' I said. 'Fine evening down here. *It's a braw bricht moonlicht nicht the nicht*,' I said, to make her laugh, it always used to and it did. 'The nightingales are singing.'

'Oh, are they? I never heard one sing. I'll go right outside and listen.'

'No nightingales in Scotland. To-whit-to-whoo, you might hear an owl. Or even a cuckoo in the daytime. I'm plain cuckoo.'

'You don't sound different, not one little bit.'

I was very different but did not say so. I was happy, though, and said so; and it was goodnight.

Next morning we were to be organized in queues again about leave and rail-passes. But Micky Burn and I were not for being organized again. It chanced to be Micky who came along with me to Lloyds Bank, 6 Pall Mall, where he humped his kitbag. 'I'll push-on,' he said. He had a Communistic gleam.

'Remember me to the Comrades,' I said, and he laughed and we parted, understanding one another very well and not at all.

Extracting twenty pounds from that soulless barn of a place was not easy because of a frozen account and my father's power of attorney, but they yielded. Funny feeling, real money after the bogus, meaningless *lagermarks* of prison. Everything funny queer feeling. 'Where to, mate?' said the taxi driver.

'King's Cross, please,' I said. How often in my life before I had travelled by Flying Scotsman behind the green engines of the London and North–Eastern Railway, my old same world.

I had endured that woman's dust and listened to nightingales with such delight, and more delight to Willa by telephone. And I had managed the bank and the taxi driver, same old kind of taxi driver, tipped him handsomely out of my manifold riches.

But at King's Cross station, another vast domed crowded place, small me, I was bitched, buggered and bewildered with a ticket to buy which I could not face up to buying. I put down my kitbag and sat on it.

'Are you all right?' someone said. He was a captain too, a real captain, spitted and polished, he had no problems.

'Yes,' I said. 'A bit bamboozled by all this.' Crowds and crowds and crowds of free busy people milling about.

'Where are you going?'

'Edinburgh.'

'No problem,' he said. 'All you need is a pass.'

'I don't want a pass. I want a ticket, top quality, third class.'

'Come on, then,' said the kindly chap. 'A bit strange to you, is it?'

'Yes,' I said.

'Long time no see? Been overseas?'

'Long time no see,' I confirmed. 'Been overseas.'

'Let's get that ticket.'

So I bought my ticket to Edinburgh. 'The trains are chaotic,' he said. 'Just watch that board. Are you sure you're all right?'

'I'm fine,' I said. 'Out of practice.'

'Cheerio, then.'

'Thank you very much,' I called after his receding back and I sat on my kitbag and watched the board.

We sped to the north. It was no flyer, this Scotsman. We slowed up and stopped at all sorts of places and drew out smoothly to speed again. British trains always draw out smoothly to speed again, busy, clunk, clatter, busy, clunkety-clunk, not like any other trains; not like furnace first class in India; not like narrow small neat ones in the Sudan; not like packed cattle-trucks in Germany where one poor chap was so shy that he never could manage to piss for a day and a night and a day through the small crack where the sentry stood; not like the big lumberers in Canada, crying their warnings in the night, long-long-short-long, *here I come to you*, open crossing, *here I come*, so far away and sweetly sad in the empty land.

This was busy-busy, clunk, busy, clunk, inimitable too, not like any other trains at all, at all anywhere; and I sat in the corridor on my kitbag, standing now and then to let people pass.

How green England was between the stations, and the leaves were out in England now, the beeches as pale as lemony silk, busy,

busy, crossing the points, busy clunk, speeding North for Home.

Let us fly together
Through the night
Through the cold
Through the winter weather.

That flight had been a fancy of the mind; but now it was springtime in the afternoon.

# BOOK TWO

## *The Leaf on the Birch*

# ONE

# [1945]

The last time I saw Wavell was on December the second 1949. We were in a well-travelled New York taxi cab, sharing it with his well-travelled luggage which had accompanied him on many journeys. But the bags and the man still held together, a bit creased and battered, strong as ever. He had nothing to say and I had nothing worth saying, so we sat without speech.

We were nearing the Battery and the liner *Mauretania* when a policeman stopped us and a long traffic jam piled up, with us as leaders of the queue. 'Some bigshot, I guess,' said the taxi driver.

We sat in silence, awaiting the arrival of the bigshot. Eventually there crossed our bows a large and explosive motorcycle escort, a police car or two and then a dignified Rolls-Royce. The hold-up of common mortals was explained; and here sat Wavell in a humble taxi, and there passed in exalted state another field marshal.

Wavell smiled that wry grim smile of his and said, 'There goes Monty.' Neither rancour nor envy dwelt in him.

That train trundled into Edinburgh at five a.m., by which time hours meant nothing at all until I was lost in sleep while Willa went seeking food, and, being Willa, tracked food down at the American Red Cross and came back to waken me with the only room service available.

The hotel was awful but we waited because John Elphinstone's mother was coming to see me that afternoon. She was a composed and quiet person, like John himself. I told her that we had had no word of him since the night that the *Prominente* were taken from Colditz, when he was well and strong in spirit. I knew that John would be all right, not knowing that, and Lady Elphinstone knew full well that I did not know that. But be confident, be sure, and I tried to seem so.

Next day we left for home, really home. We went to Rankeillour when I was twelve, and I had returned now twenty-two years later, soon to leave again. It was only when I was thinking about this particular home-coming, the best of them all, that it occurred to me to make a rough estimate of time actually spent (or nights slept) at the place I loved best on earth. The total, from school holidays on, might be about three years. What a fuss about nothing. Not so, though, not so.

There were new young plantations, and some old trees had been felled. Father and Mamma were exactly themselves, five years older. John Keiller, the keeper, was exactly himself, not looking a day older. In the house, apart from changes like having most meals in a cell-sized pantry halfway along the cold stone passage to the kitchen regions, nothing had changed, not even the ice in the refrigerator. My first gin and tonic tasted more than a little peculiar because the ice in the tray was still of 1940 vintage.

We lift the long window in the smoking room and step out through, Mamma with her garden basket and secateurs, Father with his walking stick of cherry wood, Willa and I with whatever and one another. Outside are the lawns, somewhat wartime unkempt, and beyond are the same wire fences, ugly necessities. Then, all the way round from south–west to south and east is rolling parkland, with single old trees dotted here and there and cattle grazing or chewing the cud.

Astride and behind the house is a semi-circle of woods. A blessing about Rankeillour was its duality of open park and secret old forest. Beyond that enclave lay open farmland stretching north for a mile or more to the foot of the Mount, an inconsiderable hill with a tall chimney on the summit, monument to a Hope of Rankeillour who had been killed in the Peninsular War, a landmark for miles around, never a thing of beauty and less so now that the beech forest which framed it has been ruthlessly stripped and it towers up there, a preposterous lingam in the staid kingdom of Fife.

But we were strolling to the garden a quarter of a mile away, past the big holm oak. It is in the shrubbery near the oak that I found, for a first and only time, the nest of the long-tailed tit. It is not a rare bird but by no means common, seen occasionally in parties, tiny birds trailing tails from tree to tree. But this is a pair and they arrive in turn, tails following along, to feed their young in a down-lined nest with a side entrance, the cosiest home you could imagine. They are shy of the stranger, yet come quite soon to accept the stranger's presence, not one with me as were the mice and the roe deer in German woods. It was, and is, an innocent private thing. We go towards the garden, down one of the mossy paths where Barkie and I raced on our bikes. It is not all noble woodland. To the contrary, there is much dull laurel, some rhododendrons in bloom but they are the common mauve *Ponticum*, and the feathery *Cryptomeria Japonica*, the one and only, a favourite always. Through the gates across the back drive and under the climbing tree where we used to smoke Father's excellent small Havana cigars aloft, past the beginnings of the Green Drive to the door in the high sandstone wall.

My mother is not quite the same in herself. She has always been a retiring, self-effaced person, with a subdued Irish wit. But she has had three sons away at war, and her son-in-law lately killed. I sense her burdens of which she cannot speak and nor can I. There is her in me. Inside her beloved garden, however, now largely in mundane vegetables, she grumbles forthrightly about what a shadow of its old self the garden will be in summer. 'I think I'll just potter,' she says now, dismissing us from her lapsed demesne.

Father heads out and up the Green Drive, or the Green Avenue we called it too, once the main drive to an older Rankeillour Hope but long since grassed over to adjoining parkland. Willa and I have to walk smartly to keep up with Father's long-legged stride at nearly seventy-one. Ditches are absolutely his thing, and his absolutely pre-eminent ditch runs east and west, draining both ways. We leave Green Drive to follow Ditch, which is fenced. Father stops every now and then to inspect the cross-flow of subsidiary drains, while I, who am not at all ditch-dotty, watch for the waterhens, moorhens, flying clumsily from their obvious nests and away along super-ditch, and I climb the fence to collect eggs. It is prime egg time, a few in each nest, not incubating yet, delicious hard-boiled eggs in salad. So I give them to the wife to carry in the impromptu bag of my handkerchief. She is as dutiful as all get out in such matters, and everyone is happy, whatever shadows of sorrow or anxiety may lie below. Everyone is or everyone was, everything is or everything was, the one as true as the other.

And so south for home again. The woods near the house have not been butchered, thank God. Father leads the way, knowing about him and me and the line of beeches, smooth-faced giants. Barkie and I carved our initials on one of them when we were young. But shame on us, we could not find B.C.W. and D.H.W. when we sought them again. John Keiller led us to the tree at once.

In those ten days at Rankeillour, we are there, and we were there. My elder brother Willie was still in Europe, commanding the Fife and Forfar Yeomanry, but his wife Bluebell and their three children came; and Huldah and their two children came, Huldah brave and composed, too brave maybe. Barkie and Margie and their children came. Barks had been stationed at Gibraltar where his stomach went wrong, and after ulcer operations he was invalided out of The Black Watch. He was the same Barks, thinner, less light in spirit, perhaps because of the discomfort that he never mentioned.

People do not often pay me compliments, no wonder; and anyway, they embarrass. But I have never forgotten two in those particular Rankeillour days. When I was young *Self-control, Davie*, Mum used to say, and for good reason, as near as she would come to rebuke. But now, on one of those days, she was sitting at the window in the smoking room and she smiled and said to me, alone, 'You did learn self-control.' It was true for then. Willy-nilly, I had had to button my temper down, think first, speak then.

The other one was from Barks, and if I remember aright it was said in family public, just Willa and Margie and the parents. My young brother looked me over coolly, levelly, even coldly – what was coming? – and said, 'Twice the man.'

I knew that I had lost along the way to both compliments, of which the second was the one to cherish. But it was true that, for that present, *No Bullshit* put *Colonel Self-Pity* in his place. The latter words would have been very well understood by Mamma, the former would have horrified her. Funny thing, I cannot and do not tolerate the metaphorical use of the four-letter word for ordure or excreta. It is a dirty symptom of these dirt-encrusted times. *No Bullshit*, although long unspoken, remains quite apart.

Willa and I also bicycled the two miles over to Pitlair to see Aunt Isabel Walker, who was worth a guinea a minute. She had given her earlier life to looking after Grandfather, an invalid. She was by far the best-read member of the family, the only true intellectual, with a sharp tongue and a darting mind. She spoke fluent if garbled French, German and Italian with a strong Scottish accent. With the exception of me sometimes, for our relations could be stormy, she liked men very much and during the latter part of the war had a Polish colonel billeted at Pitlair, lucky fellow. She doted on her Polish colonel (a suitably cultivated man) in the formal way that was also her way.

She had been at a finishing school in Switzerland with Mamma and I suppose that my mother had come to stay at Pitlair, the germ of the romance, of a marvellously tranquil marriage. They must have been friends once. They observed the polite proprieties now but had nothing in common except gardening, about which Mamma had far more knowledge and artistic feeling.

Home again, but Willa and I could not be alone together even at home. We needed and wanted to be alone. Then neighbours of ours in Fife came to the rescue. The Jock Hutchisons offered to lend us a cottage in the Perthshire highlands for the first three weeks of May.

Before I describe that halcyon time, I should mention that while I was still a prisoner Willa had been hunting all over the rural place for a house to rent when I came home.

One day at Rankeillour the telephone rang. 'That you, Willa? Vesey speaking.'

'Oh, hullo, Colonel Vesey, how lovely to hear from you.'

'What's this nonsense about you trying to rent a house?'

'Well, it's not nonsense, and I am.'

'My dear girl, the war in Germany is nearly over but don't you realize that there is still Japan? Don't you realize that David will get about two weeks' leave and be posted back to duty?'

'No, I don't, and I will rent one.'

'Don't be a fool, Willa. Have you got some petrol? If so, come to lunch tomorrow.'

'I haven't got any petrol, Vesey, and I can't come to lunch tomorrow.'

Colonel Vesey, king of the depot all the war, lord of all that he surveyed except in the end of himself. He was right and she was wrong and very angry but came to forgive him.

To get to that cottage above the headwaters of the river Tay we had to have a car. Bluebell lent us an 8-horsepower Ford which had been laid up in the war. They were generous to us, they had always been most generous to me, and I applied my mechanical ineptitude to changing plugs and so on and got the sturdy little thing going, registered, a small petrol ration, and we were off, by Perth and Dunkeld and up the broad winding river to Aberfeldy and on past great larch trees to Bolfracks estate, past the stone Druid circle, below us that mammoth Taymouth Castle, seat of the Breadalbanes, now a hospital for Polish wounded, still climbing on gently to the head gamekeeper-stalker-ghillie's cottage where the lordly McKerchar emerged in his knickerbocker suit of bold Bolfracks tweed and fore-and-aft hat, which he doffed. I had known him slightly on grouse-shooting days before the war. We shook hands. 'I'm glad to see you again, McKerchar.'

'The Major looks well,' he said, unbending. He had promoted me to major for reasons best known to himself. And the third-person could indicate pleasure or displeasure, in this case the former.

'And Willa – this is Mr McKerchar, my wife.'

'It is a grand pleasure to meet Mistress Walker,' he said with enthusiasm. 'The wife has a cup of tea for Mistress Walker if that is Mistress Walker's wish.'

'I would love a cup of tea,' Willa said. *Mistress Walker*, how charming that old-fashioned Highland address.

So we all had a cup of tea. 'The river is low to be in right ploy but worth a try. I would suggest meet here at twelve noon, Major.'

'I haven't a salmon rod, McKerchar, and no flies. I do have a trout rod.'

'We have the two rods ready, and mebbe Mistress Walker would fancy a go at the trout?'

'I would love to, Mr McKerchar.'

'Twelve seems a bit late. What about the morning, McKerchar?'

'Before twelve noon would be a waste of the Major's time.' The third person meant that the Major should do what his mentor commanded, and the Major always did, or tried to.

McKerchar opened the gate for us and we began the stiff climb to Tombuie which was at about a thousand feet, not far below the tree line. It was a simple isolated cottage, without much more than ample bed and chairs, a fireplace, a temperamental paraffin stove. It had all the comforts that we could need, and all the peace. The hill burn tumbled by. Tombuie abides with me as perfection.

We slept late and went out to kindly weather. Hitler was dead in his Berlin bunker, thank God, and that war, a galaxy away from us, was over; and word had come that John Elphinstone and the others were safely home. At the appointed hour we got into the old Ford and freewheeled downhill until Willa had to get out to open a gate, then on again. Coming up was expensive in petrol. Going down cost nothing but wear on Willie's brakes.

The maestro awaited us to row across the river – Jock Hutchison had the fishing from boths banks on that stretch – and walk to the hut where the spliced rods were kept. *Grant's Vibration*, they were called, eleven feet and thirteen feet or so, cumbersome two-handed implements, to the chosen of which he tied a fly – a Blue Charm, a Silver Doctor, a Thunder and Lightning, a Jock Scott, any of those or other good names. *Bright weather, bright fly* was the general dictum but I was not consulted. 'Just easy now, Major, one step down at each cast, and fish a short line meanwhile till I get back.' Then he would take Mistress Walker with my trout rod and his scarce flies – he did not fancy our small selection – and set the Mistress to fishing for trout.

McKerchar knew only one fish worthy of the name, the salmon, and he was fully determined that the Major would get a fish. 'A wee thing more line now,' he commanded on his return, and I stalked the river and he stalked me. McKerchar taught me much, how to draw in and shoot spare line, how to mend the line – that is, apply a small last twist and present the fly head-on to current, and one very clever trick for freeing a hook snagged underwater. 'There is some improvement in the casting,' he accorded after several fruitless days.

During all those meanwhiles Willa would fish away, often losing the only flies permitted to her – caught in a branch behind – and fish faithfully on with no flies at all; and then give it up and read a book.

A tempestuous woman, as I was coming to know, she was, and always has remained, a model fishing wife, perfectly content to sit beside a river while I flog it vainly.

I learned much from McKerchar and caught nothing, either in the big long pool, a dull stretch of river; or in the Piper's Pool, where the river took a sharp turn below a ruined cottage. There was a sad story about the piper who once had lived in the cottage. But it was a merry pool with runs and hidden rocks and likely lies, fished from a shingle beach. No good.

Back again to part again until the next midday hour. McKerchar had the dignity of a biblical prophet: he was always right, but then he always was, and a very human and kindly companion to us.

Up the hill to Tombuie in the evening sun to behave in a way of which McKerchar would not approve, safe from McKerchar to get slightly pickled and often more than slightly, dance to the wind-up gramophone and sing Scotch songs and make love again, and have plenty to eat some time or other, and rest awhile, even listen to news on the wireless about events and people of no importance. We also played a game, which I strongly recommend to the irresponsible athletic. You strip off such valuables as there may be from the furniture. The course is ready. The game is to circumnavigate the room without ever touching the floor. It is a beautifully simple bruising game for nincompoops, a game that most of the happy-go-lucky have played at one time or another; yet not many have been privileged to play it at a lonely shepherd's cottage, high up amid the bonny purple heather, not purple at that season. The day ends with a brief roaming in the gloaming and a famous old song to match it below the high hills and above the glen, and a final drink of which His Majesty McKerchar, lifelong teetotaller would not approve, and so to bed, of which McKerchar, being an earthy chap too, would certainly approve, and sleep it out and off before a far appointment, rain or shine, with the master at twelve noon.

The road, or track, that we climbed to Tombuie was a private one but up there near the cottage it joined a third class public road from Kenmore which went on over the bare moor and down south to Amulree. It was not high country, fifteen hundred feet or so, but a good road to walk on the Sabbath Day when salmon fishing is not allowed but trout fishing is. I had some casts of tiny hill-loch flies. Above the cottage there was one more gate to open and close because of the highland cattle which were supposed to live up there but were never in evidence.

We turned to look west across the narrow ribbon of Loch Tay to the massif of Ben Lawers, nearly four thousand feet, the highest of these hills but a heavy conglomerate, imposing enough, not beautiful. To the north, beyond the spreading valley, tall Schiehallion stood alone.

'I think that's the loveliest mountain I've ever seen,' she said.

'Ay, it's bonny,' I said, to please her. 'Mebbe just a muckle hill, though. Not four thousand feet to make it a mountain for the purists.' Snow-capped Schiehallion was indeed lovely, not grim in its awful purity like Kanchenjunga beyond the abyss.

But we walked on to the hill loch, stopping for me to put binoculars on birds, most of them familiar like the larks up here on the open moor or down in the Lowlands. But the wheatear was a hill-bird, new to me. I was learning birds. They were to be my companions from that time on.

Far behind us and below us on this Sabbath morning the bell of Kenmore Kirk was tolling for peace after silent years. All the bells of the island were tolling for peace.

We fished the rest of the morning without even a touch, along the reedy shore, which was difficult for Willa, along the wall of the dam, which was easier. Not a rise to a fly, not a single ring of a feeding fish anywhere on the loch. 'I don't believe there are any,' she said.

'It's loaded with tiddlers, not in the mood. Let's have lunch.' During lunch I spied the hill with the glasses and saw a party of red deer higher up in a corrie, a narrowing glen. I searched for those highland cattle above us or below us but saw neither brown hide nor shaggy hair of them.

A pair of larger birds flew in turn, crying and wheeling, sad and lonely or not, as your mind might tell you. 'What are they, darling?'

'Curlews – whaups, we call them.'

'*Woe is me*, the curlew cries. Or *let's have some fun*, the curlew cries. Gosh, I love Scotland. I never want to live anywhere else.'

She loved my country and so did I. But her country called me back.

We fished again vainly until, of a sudden, the rise began. Spreading circles of feeding trout pocked the whole loch. They rose avidly to Willa's flies but she was not quick enough and I took over. *When you're into a fish, Major*, he kept telling the beginner, *you will see the line check. Do nothing, Major. Bide your time until you feel the tug; then set the hook, a wee jerk, just firm.*

Of that stealthy hooking I was ignorant, having caught only numerous kelts and one fresh-run twenty-pounder in times before in Canada. At fly-fishing for small trout I was fairly expert, with quick reflexes. They boiled, you struck in that split-second. I caught seven before the trout stopped feeding and we went home to Tombuie. Were they mythical, those highland cattle?

Why it was that for a year or more after the war I never fired a gun, and ever since then have had a reluctance about extinguishing warm-blooded life, or any life at all except for the pot and except for the fish, I would not quite know. About fish to eat, I never had the least compunction except a small one at the sharp knock on the head. A half-baked carnivorous mammal, and yet not all is fraud.

They were quarter-pounders, or a little bigger. My job was to clean and Willa's to fry on that paraffin stove, and still enough hard-sought booze before and after.

We were content at Tombuie but time grew short and I had not even touched a fish. The spring salmon jumped silvery clean, up and over and in, out there on the way to the loch. 'Patience,' said the pundit. 'The Major will take a fish yet.'

'Mr Bobby is a sad loss,' he said to me once, about the elder of the Hutchison sons, killed in The Black Watch. There was much thought in that patriarchal head. He never asked me about my dull prison years and I never talked of them, perhaps hardly thought of them. I still dream of them, though, occasionally. Even now, more and less than forty years later, I still dream of no end to it.

The fish took quietly as he had said it would. I bided my time and set the hook. 'Good,' he said. 'Be firm,' he said. 'Keep a tight line, but if it wants to run let it go. The Major is doing fine.'

Thus calmly encouraged, I played that fish coolly. Then it made one long run, all the line and half the backing, and it jumped, a big fish three feet out of the water. 'Point doon, Davie!' screamed McKerchar.

But Davie, the Major, knew that one too, having been warned a dozen times never to let the line be airborne all the way from jumping fish to rod, a sure break. I dropped the point smartly.

The Major's wife shook with silent laughter about the collapse of feudalism if the rod point was up and the chips were down. I suppose that it took half an hour to tire my first Scottish salmon and bring it to the gaff. Poor fish, I thought with the subordinate part of me.

It was over twenty pounds on McKerchar's spring scale. 'The Major did himself credit,' he said.

'Thanks to you.' We were greatly pleased with ourselves and one another.

Tomorrow morning would be goodbye to Tombuie, one more climb in our chugging steed. Up there, we switched on the radio and who should be speaking to the people whom he had led through dark days to victory, defiant in the dark days, magnanimous in victory. Those rolling lisped cadences could have come from no other man on earth.

I turned up the volume and stood at the open door of the cottage, listening to Winston Churchill, before me the hills of truth and legend. 'Willa, come here.'

She came, and we looked together at the closed gate above the cottage, and there, in a row, heads over the gate, were the highland cattle that we had never seen. Gentle as lambs, entirely belying their ferocious looks and mighty horns, the shaggy creatures were magnificently intent, entirely motionless, listening to Winston Churchill. When he finished speaking they turned and went back up the hill to disappear as usual.

## TWO

# 1945 and 1946

Colonel Vesey was right in dissuading Willa from renting a house but wrong about the amount of leave I would get. It was not two weeks but more than two months before ex-prisoners like Martin and Patrick, Phil Pardoe and I were sent on a refresher course at Dunbar in south-east Scotland. Wives were not allowed but they were having none of that and came.

I remember nothing about the course except learning to fire a bazooka, a frighteningly wayward rocket weapon for infantrymen to shoot at tanks. I was thoroughly estranged from weapons of war.

In the meanwhile we stayed at Rankeillour and went, as usual, for walks. Not quite as usual, though, because it was only then, so belatedly, that I came to know my father better. In earlier days he had seemed rather a forbidding figure who lived entirely by rote – up on the dot, breakfast on the dot, in the car on the dot, to be driven by Thoms, the chauffeur, who had been with us since the First World War, into Cupar Fife to catch the eight fifty-two for Dundee and Jute Industries. In his small leather attaché case were a thermos of *café au lait*, dutifully prepared by Mamma, and two Rich Tea biscuits. Then another day's business, of which he never spoke. He was involved in the manufacturing side of things, the practical tactual aspect. To him, larger financing was finagling, vaguely suspect. In the evenings he came home at the same hour by the same train, to exercise himself and dog on the standard weekday walk round the roads, which meant half a mile of front avenue, along the main road, back avenue, a mile and a half in all. Time for a bath at exactly the same temperature by thermometer, change for dinner at which he drank one sherry glass of whisky, in two halves, diluted with soda water in a claret glass. After dinner, his Weinberg cigarette, his small Adey cigar, half an hour's reading and then along to the business room to keep the estate accounts, to make out pay envelopes meticulously for every employee.

How dull and hidebound it all might seem, and no doubt his life was that, but his patience about my slapdash ways was extraordinary, encouraged by Mamma, I have no doubt. Routine is a comfort, though. It was a comfort in prison days; and as I was to learn soon enough, it was to become the backbone of my writing life. I could write nothing unless under the burden of routine, an alien load to bear on one's back, to escape from to blow off steam. The vivid imagination that would enable me to write novels had perils within it. In all the mornings in all the years I never wrote with a drop of drink in me. But in times off the job, things gradually changed. A soothing old friend tippled down to be a sodden enemy. Coke (the liquid variety), if not quite the real thing, is no bother, with cigarettes for one residual vice.

But Father needed no safety valve. He was the routine man *par excellence* and in those later years I came to admire and like him very much. There was only one thing about him that bothered me always. The grazing and the farms at Rankeillour were rented out, so Father was not involved in farm administration. He was, however, a country landowner and the shooting was ours. He was too reticent a man, I think, to have the light personal touch. For instance, the partridges nested in hedgerows which, as the war went on and agriculture grew more intensified, became narrower. Instead of chancing upon the farmer and making a friendly verbal request for more partridge nesting-room, he would write a letter. The same applied about more important matters like mending fences and cleaning out the silted burn to improve drainage along the march with his neighbour. Instead of easing things by casual talk and then writing the necessary letter for formal agreement, he always wrote first. It made for unnecessary heavy weather about things trivial and important alike.

In his politics Father was, as you might expect, a true-blue Conservative. Indeed, I think that he never could quite bring himself to forgive Winston Churchill for switching parties. Having lived on the other side of the tracks and having had plenty of time to think, I had moved in my sympathies or beliefs quite strongly to the left and on our walks, which we both enjoyed, I worked on Father. I never converted him (I was not entirely converted myself) but I certainly did persuade him in his late years that the working man's point of view was to be respected, even if suspected.

No such success with Colonel Vesey. Glaring at me across a dinner table he said, half in choleric joke: 'If you say that, you're a traitor to your class.' His very words, not exactly original, and I happen to remember them, spoken with blunt amity to take some edge off.

At the end of the Dunbar course (or while it was still in dreary progress – dreary workwise, I mean, companion-wise and wife-wise after hours it was fun) I was offered a job, and no doubt whatever, on the old-boy-net, a hackneyed term but I know no other.

Neil Blair, with whom I had been in India, lost a leg while commanding our First Battalion and was now chief instructor at the Staff College at Camberley. My job, thanks to Neil, was to be PA, personal assistant to the commandant, which in practice largely meant PA to Brigadier Julian Gascoigne, the assistant commandant. I was a local acting unpaid lieutenant colonel, no more a colonel than my eye, entirely ignorant of a staff officer's duties and of higher command. I did not know about them and saw a personal threat in learning about them.

I took the night train south on August the sixth, and in London next morning read about the atom bomb. The news horrified me, *appalled* might be the stronger word for my feelings about that barbarity. Most people seemed to exult about it and few, if any in the company I was now to frequent, shared my opinions.

Much later, in a novel *Where the High Winds Blow*, I let David Dorrien, a somewhat bibulous British artist, express them for me:

> '. . . It was certainly the most fateful and possibly the worst crime in world history.'
>
> 'Not worse than Hitler and the Jews,' said Anna. 'Surely, David.'
>
> 'Worse in its ultimate effect. Hitler incinerated the Jews out of an unmentionable pagan philosophy of the nordic *Übermensch*. But we incinerated a few hundred thousand human

beings without warning of any kind while singing "Onward, Christian Soldiers". It just as simple as that, which is very simple.' He looked about for contradiction.

'But, Mr Dorrien,' said Bob Carter moderately enough, although his colour darkened, 'bombs were dropped on London and Berlin, and dropped to kill. I see no difference between one large bomb and a thousand smaller bombs. Furthermore, all Western leaders have agreed that Hiroshima shortened the Pacific War by at least a year and saved many thousands of our boys' lives.'

'Nonsense, *our boys' lives*! Don't you know that they had sued for peace before Hiroshima?'

If they had demonstrated the bomb by dropping it, with suitable preliminary fanfare, on an unpopulated island (which was what Oppenheimer himself and a few others of the scientists had wanted), and if the Japanese had not then at once surrendered, I would have been wholly in favour of dropping the spare bomb on a city. But they had achieved their miracle of manufacture. Human nature being what it is, the temptation to use their monster toy was irresistible. Yet, let us not forget what the British deliberately perpetrated on the refugee-jammed city of Dresden, forty miles from our last prison camp.

But leave the loathsome subject and, all in the same boat, laugh if we can at the simpletons who preach limited nuclear warfare.

The job at the Staff College was unimportant but not without interest. Among the instructing staff were some brilliant officers and very civilized people who knew the things of which I was fully determined to know nothing. And among the students were some of the best soldiers in the British Army who had been too busy fighting all the war to take a Staff College course. They were an impressive lot, of whose confidential reports I was the custodian. That did involve responsibility of a sort, and sometimes the unenviable task of telling people in mid-course that they had failed, gallant people, two of whom I knew well from earlier days. To be the bearer of bad news was hard but someone had to do it and they used me.

I was also president of the mess committee, PMC, which meant ensuring that the food was adequate and the drink sufficient. There was a competent Mr Mitchell to look after all that and I had nothing much to do except put in a word or two now and then with the makers of Coates's Plymouth gin, famous Navy tipple. The quality of the famous Navy tipple had deteriorated in wartime but it was still gin and Coates our most reliable source of supply. You could obscure the raw tang somewhat with tonic.

I enjoyed my nine months at Camberley. First, Neil was there, one of my few pre-war friends with whom I had shared those carefree Indian days. He had lost his leg high up and the stump gave him trouble. With one artificial leg he was much worse off than Douglas Bader with two, just above and below his knees. Neil and I used to grumble during our first hot weather in the plains. Now, with real trouble, discomfort and pain not a peep of a grumble came out of him. He and Betty had one of the Staff College bungalows, their two remarkably gifted children, Jamie and Lavinia, with them in the holidays.

I hunted down a modest flat in Camberley and Willa soon came to join me. Towards the end of the war there had been Cassandras who warned that, until they regained full health and vigour, ex-prisoners might not be able to father children. Such did not prove to be the case with us. We had wasted little time, if any, and she expected a baby in mid-January. War was finally over and in its place there was uneasy peace, Mr Attlee Prime Minister, Mr Truman President, two-thirds of the triumvirate gone, only the terror Stalin to rule the roost.

Uneasy was the word for it, not for us. Willa still had the boring business of rationing to cope with but our spirits were high and nothing much mattered.

My working life was pleasant too. Apart from showing people their confidential reports, which could be both easy and burdensome, and running the mess, which was nothing, the centrepiece of my job was Brigadier Julian Gascoigne, the assistant commandant. He was a Guardsman who had had a distinguished war record fighting in North Africa and on up through Italy, an Olympian type, reminiscent of Vesey Holt. He lived in the country nearby, arriving rather late and leaving rather early in his open sports car which was the apple of his eye.

I think, although I cannot quite remember, that my job involved the timetables of work, which were intricate, but there was always Neil to turn to when I was flummoxed. About such incidentals Julian did not much bother his head, unless things went wrong, in which case he raised hell.

He soon expounded to me his philosophy of soldiering life, or more particularly, of higher command. First, the dim-witted, get rid of him. Second, there is always a niche to be found for the moderately dull and industrious officer. Third, the able and hard-working officer can rise to quite high command. But fourth, the cream – he is the brilliant, lazy officer who makes other people do the work. He is the one for the top of the tree.

That he saw in himself the cream was fairly obvious. That he may, on occasion, have taken work home is possible, if most unlikely. But conceit was not the word for Julian. He was supremely self-confident and looked it and behaved it, a large man, immaculate as Guardsmen tend to be.

A likeable thing about him was that, provided he respected your wits and yourself in general, he did not in the least mind being stood up to or contradicted. In common with the successive Commandants (Philip Gregson-Ellis and Dick Hull) he tried to persuade me to take the Staff College course myself. That would have meant D. H. Walker with the magic letters PSC. Passed the Staff College. It would also have meant entrapment in the Army for some years at least. So I declined politely. I expect that I said I wanted to leave the Army, which at that time was almost impossible for a regular officer. I do not think that I told any of them what my intention or fixation was.

Anyway, that set me apart from military ambition for myself and it tended to raise me above my somewhat nebulous job. Julian drove his directing staff not mercilessly but too hard, and the ultimate sufferers were the students. I felt strongly about it and told him that people who worked habitually until two in the morning were not fit for much. It was his own philosophy too, as applied to common mortals – the able and industrious. Eventually he called a conference of the directing staff, and said: 'I want to discuss working hours. David says I drive you too hard. What do you think?'

They thought just as I did and said so, and as a result the workload was eased and the DS on the whole viewed me with favour. Popularity is always agreeable but not in that case spuriously achieved. Julian, right or wrong, was not an easy man to argue with.

Basically I agreed with him, and still do, that the brilliant and lazy officer who drives others to do the work is the one for the top. That is why, when I first heard that Mr Reagan was a lazy man, I thought that he might be just the man for the Presidency. Now I am inclined to reverse that opinion, being by no means sure that he is also a brilliant officer.

Apart from the teaching staff work, which was carried out in small study groups or syndicates and was no concern of mine, many interesting things did happen at the Staff College. There were the demonstrations on Salisbury Plain or somewhere, when we saw the latest British tanks (Centurions, perhaps), the helicopters, the fighter aircraft diving vertically with a load of rockets to streak ahead and obliterate a copse, the proximity fuses which caused shells to explode mysteriously and lethally before they reached the ground. I enjoyed watching war magic from a safe distance.

Then there were the distinguished visitors, people like Averell Harriman, to address the Staff College. Inevitably, of course, there was Field Marshal Montgomery to lecture us like a lot of schoolboys, no smoking permitted, five minutes during which coughing was allowed. He was an immensely cocky little man but immensely staunch and sure. His pearls of wisdom fell, or were shot out, not once but usually repeated in staccato fashion.

Fools like me might dislike the man on sight but fools like me could not but admire him. I cannot remember whether I was introduced to him that time but his observant eye must have spotted me. I was having a glass of gin before lunch when who should come to sit beside me on the ante-room fender but Neil Ritchie to whom I had been adjutant at Gebeit in the Sudan. Neil's rise in North Africa had been meteoric and he was commanding the Eighth Army against Rommel at El Alamein, the last closed gate to Egypt, when General Auchinleck took over from him for no good reason in the field. Almost invariably generals who have been relieved of command in crisis disappear into oblivion. But not Neil Ritchie. He rose again to be a successful corps commander from D Day on to the end of the war. He had gone far and I had gone nowhere and it was good to see one another again. But he was the bearer of a tentative invitation to become one of Montgomery's liaison officers, fairly junior people who were the Field Marshal's errand boys and in general his eyes and ears. That meant entrapment too, a prime reason for declining. A second reason, not less compelling, was my conviction that I would be a misfit in the personal entourage of this cocksure, ascetic wonder-man.

The next time I saw Montgomery, and the only time at close quarters, was in January 1961 at lunch with Billy Collins, my publisher for many years and his at that time. Willa and I had taken our four sons out of school in Canada, spent the first part of the winter in Scotland and now were in London en route to a Swiss chalet. The boys were sent out to Lyons Corner House or somewhere with instructions to report back in due course to St James's Place. Meanwhile, we had our excellent luncheon (one of many before and after that) at Billy and Pierre's charming flat above the office. Lunch was over when word arrived from below that the boys had returned.

'Four of them, indeed! Send them up! Send them up!'

Our sons trooped in, ranging in age from just fifteen down to nine, Giles, Barclay, David and Julian. 'Fall in now, tallest on the right, shortest on the left. Tallest on the right . . . '

They duly obeyed, unaccustomed to military drill. He was being kindly after his fashion. He was a kindly man, I think, rapping out orders like a machine gun.

He started his inspection at the right of the line, tallest member. 'So you come from Canada, over here for the winter. Good country, Canada, good country, that. But Britain's better. Britain's better, I expect you agree.'

'We like it here, but we like Canada better,' Giles said, spokesman for the parade. He was a very shy boy, and Willa and I were immensely proud of him setting Monty to rights, inspection over.

*

Willa's time was near so when I went south after Christmas she crossed the Tay to stay with Barkie and Margie near Dundee, handy to the nursing home and to her eminently gifted doctor, Margaret Fairlie.

Giles was born on January the 17th 1946. I did not get there in time for the event, thank goodness, but tottered off a sleepless night on the train to find that all was well. The modern fashion of expectant fathers being present at the birth is in my view both vulgar and a quite gratuitous strain upon them. As one eminently sensible young woman of our acquaintance told her husband: 'I have a job to do. Now go away and let me get on with it.'

But there he was, a healthy baby beside his happy mother. So many things to be happy about, to counter a past sorrow for her.

As spring came, we were allotted one of the Staff College bungalows in the grounds, very much of an improvement over the flat in a Camberley street. Willa was wholly busy with Giles and replacing curtains and so on. In my spare time, which was not in short supply, I gardened a little and watched birds a lot, sometimes alone, homing by sound on the modest and elusive nightingale, stealthily on hands and knees until I could put my binoculars on the plain brown bird in undergrowth, singing so gloriously for love and spring.

Could it be that a whole year had passed since the nightingales were singing on a first night home from Germany?

So life was pleasant for us at our gimcrack bungalow, with our small smiling son, now so amusing for a father to be with. And my job was amusing too amid military things which I was determined to escape, yet serving an entertaining if most exacting master. I had Julian buttoned up in so far as that was possible. The Staff College was a thinking centre of the British Regular Army and it had me trapped.

Then a letter arrived:

*Personal and Confidential*

VICEROY'S CAMP,
INDIA
(Simla) 10th May 1946.

My dear Walker

We have not met for a very long time, but I have heard of you occasionally. I am writing to you because I shall shortly have a vacancy on my staff here for Comptroller; and I understand from Colin Mackenzie of the Seaforths that you might like to be considered for it.

I do not know at all how you are situated at present and whether you would be available to come out if I decided to offer you the vacancy. It would be open at any time now, since my present Comptroller is due for demobilization and wishes to go home as soon as a successor can be found.

I understand that you have done a good deal of service in India, and know the conditions well, and I hope that you have some knowledge of the language. I have asked Colin to enclose in this letter a short note giving you information about the pay and conditions of the appointment.

Since the matter is urgent, would you please either write at once by air mail or send me a cable saying whether you would like to be considered. In present conditions I cannot give any guarantee at all about the length of the appointment, it entirely depends on the progress of the Indian Constitution and developments out here. It might come to an end quite suddenly or last for a year or two.

Yours sincerely
Wavell

Lt-Col. D. H. Walker, The Black Watch,
Staff College, Camberley.

I do not remember that Colin had written ahead to sound me out. Perhaps he did. I do remember that I jumped at this chance of escape and took the letter at once to General Hull (Dick Hull, later himself to be a field marshal), the Commandant, my titular chief. He read it, a cool, composed man, and said, 'What does your wife think about it?'

'Well, sir, I thought she would want me to speak to you first.'

That was casuistry, although I knew for almost certain that Willa, despite being just settled into the bungalow with our infant son, would be no less keen than I was myself. That turned out to be the case.

So yet once more we were on the move. For Willa, it meant the drudgery of packing all over again what she had so recently unpacked. It also meant a chance for her to take Giles to meet his Canadian grandparents and other relations across the Atlantic and then, provided conditions were stable enough in that uncertain land, to join me in India after the hot weather.

For me, it was a crucial step on my way to freedom – from a nerve centre of the Army to the least militaristic employment that a regular officer could have. It meant leaving most congenial companions, in particular Neil Blair. He and Neil Ritchie were, and have remained, my only non-prisoner friends with whom I keep in more or less regular touch. It also meant saying goodbye to Julian Gascoigne to whom I had become attached. I suppose that, in our sometimes mettled relationship, he may never have given thought to the self-confidence that he was helping me to find again. On the other hand he may have. I remember Julian with strong affection.

He rose, as brilliant lazy officers may do, not to the ultimate but high enough. We never met again and the last time I heard from him he was Governor of Bermuda and had taken up scuba-diving at the age of nearly sixty, typical Julian.

The comptroller of the viceregal household (known as CVH) had a grandiose title, reminiscent of the Grand Vizier. In fact, he was no more than a glorified housekeeper, if possibly the most glorified housekeeper extant, with three or four hundred servants for whom he was theoretically responsible, down through an excellent chain of command. I am not conversant with Buckingham Palace but I expect that I had the edge on them in numbers of employees.

Under CVH was the comptroller's assistant, an Englishman, the man who really made things work. Unfortunately, Mr Haslam, who had occupied that office, died suddenly a week or two before I reached Delhi early in July. His regretted demise was to make my sinecure job into a battleground, to which I shall return.

But I should try, at this long range, to examine the motives that made me so keen to go back to India. First, and probably overriding everything else, was the hunch that this high-sounding comptrollership would be my stepping stone to escape. I knew that, having a one-track mind, I would never write, or more important, find out whether I could write, until I could make writing my sole occupation.

But I should not make too much of that at that time. There were other reasons as compelling or which perhaps took precedence – there was India itself, where I had already lived for nearly five years, the same endearing infuriating country, even if so different now that independence drew near. And there was Colin Mackenzie, eight years my junior in age, a messmate at Colditz, that peculiarly ageless place, Highland laird and all that, an impregnable unchanging man from then to now. As with all our few prison intimates, we took on casually and easily exactly where we had left off.

By good fortune Colin was the only member of the viceregal establishment present at Delhi when I reached there. He was deputy military secretary, dealing with tours and all non-domestic aspects of the situation, a worthwhile job. The Viceroy, Lady Wavell and the rest were up in the hills at Simla.

During those days I got to know whichever of my immediate Indian subordinates were at Delhi – they were a Muslim, a Hindu and a Sikh who worked together in harmony with extreme efficiency. We got on well from the start and they served me with impeccable loyalty. Indeed, I became fond of all the household staff, from them down the ladder to the most lowly.

This short interlude also gave me a chance to learn a little about the Lutyens colossus of reddish stone that was the Viceroy's House. It was a monster, the interstices and convolutions of which I never did learn. What I speedily learned was that my air-conditioned bedroom, a good thing, was three hundred and fifty yards by gloomy corridors from my un-airconditioned office.

So Colin went about his DMS business and I went exploring, and we met in late morning for a swim at the azure viceregal pool, a queen among swimming pools to paddle about and drink gimlets and have a cold lunch. Life was not exactly hardship.

Willa has kept some of my letters from that time. In one I wrote aptly enough that the Viceroy's house put me in mind of a mixture between the Hampton Court maze and infinity. But if the house was a confusing monstrosity the gardens, where fountains played at the moment for only the Major and the Major, were beautiful in their formal Versailles way, and in particular the sunken garden with its wealth of scent and colour. The maker and guardian of all that was the august and portly Mr Reader.

Heat never bothered me much, and not at all when one could sleep in coolness, but it was clear that the new comptroller must arise and go unto the hills to make his number. I took the overnight train to Ambala and then to Kalka, whence a diesel-engined railway bus climbed the fifty miles to Simla in about four hours. It was a wide beast on a narrow gauge and, being fearful of heights, I did not much enjoy overhanging precipices, pleasant as the gradual arrival of coolness was.

It was a very different journey from the only other one that I had made to Simla with Neil Blair, from furnace heat before the monsoon broke in 1932.

At the other end this time was the legendary figure on the hilltop. I do not think that he headed my list of reasons for coming back to India. His son, Archie John, was a sure old friend whom I had not seen for years. His wife, the Vicereine, Countess Wavell CI, was said to be dynamitish. The man himself, enormously admired by all who served him, was an enigma.

They said that he never spoke except about business, or socially except when the mood took him, which was rarely. They said that he was given to emitting cryptic grunts, which was true, as I soon found out. So many things were half-true about that simple, brilliant, complicated man in whom there was no vestige of conceit. Even the simple, the brilliant, the complicated were half-true.

Viceregal Lodge at Simla was a comfortable, dowdy country house, much more to my liking than the grotesque if magnificent palace in Delhi. I had to meet all the staff, from George Abell, the private secretary downwards, new people never easy for me although they were an unpretentious agreeable lot. I liked them, perhaps in particular George Abell.

But surprising as it may seem, the easiest of all for me was Wavell himself. I quote from one of my letters to Willa, written soon after I reached there.

> . . . I am going out with H. E. and George Abell this afternoon to play golf. The course is about 15 miles away. We go there by car. There is also a small approaching course round the grounds of the Lodge. It is a good little course. I had two rounds with H. E. yesterday afternoon, and a walk round with both of them in the evening. They are rather sweet together. He walks along with a wrinkled brow apparently deep in thought but really taking everything in, while she chatters without stopping. He has a good sense of humour and a whimsical grunt which indicates that he is thinking of a joke or is going to make one. He keeps catechizing me about escaping. I have talked more about that in the last two days than in all the time since I came home . . .

I had entirely forgotten that he ever asked me about escaping. I have rarely talked about it in all these years, old hat to me, but I suppose that it is a subject that interests people, even great warriors.

## THREE

# 1946 and 1947

To later generations, except students of history, Wavell is a remote figure, if a figure at all, a general who had some smashing success in North Africa early in some old war, and then was beaten, shunted off to India and Burma to be beaten again, to be made Viceroy of India until the glamorous Mountbatten came to finish the job at which Wavell had failed.

So it may be helpful to insert a brief description of his life up to the time that he became Viceroy.

In the 1930s Wavell – always called Archie Wavell – was being talked about as a coming man in the British Army. As a gifted writer he was already well-known beyond military circles.

What had this man done and what would he go on to do?

As had Wavells for over four hundred years, he went to school at Winchester where he won a scholarship and showed rare promise in the classics. Indeed, when he applied to join the Army class, the headmaster wrote rather tactlessly to his soldier father protesting that the military life would be a waste of his talents. But the Wavells were soldiers, and a soldier Archibald Percival Wavell became.

He joined The Black Watch in 1901, served in South Africa and India, learned Russian, fought through the First World War and rose to be a brigadier on Allenby's staff in Palestine. Later he was to write a history of that campaign and a life of Allenby, books of distinction written with the lucid grace and economy that were his hallmark.

And so Wavell wrote of what had been, thought of what would be, and through the years between two World Wars he rose step by step, a forward thinker in a reactionary, economy-haunted army.

He was promoted to his first general officer's command in

1935 – that of the experimental 2nd Division at Aldershot. It is interesting that this man, so direct of thought, ever seeking the shortest way to truth, should have been the master of deception that he proved himself against his luckless opponents.

But Wavell was destined for much bigger things than outwitting other British generals on manoeuvres. Just before the outbreak of war in 1939 he was appointed to command all our forces in the Middle East. The next summer the Germans overran Europe and Italy came into the war. With very large forces in North Africa facing a small and wretchedly equipped British and Commonwealth Army, Mussolini envisaged speedy victory and a triumphal entry into Cairo. But such did not transpire.

On February the 14th 1941 Wavell issued this special order of the day: '. . . The Army of the Nile, as our Prime Minister has called us, has in two months advanced over 400 miles, has destroyed the large army that had gathered to invade Egypt, taking some 125,000 prisoners and well over 1000 guns besides innumerable quantities of weapons and materials of all kinds . . .'

He had accomplished this, one of the boldest and most successful feats in the history of arms, with O'Connor's striking force of some 25,000 men. Field Marshal Rommel, himself a great tactical commander, wrote, in assessing British generals: 'The only one who showed a touch of genius was Wavell.' And Rommel carried Wavell's *Generals and Generalship* all through his own campaigns in North Africa, a fair tribute from an enemy.

But Wavell's command did not extend only to Egypt and the western desert. It embraced the whole of East Africa, where he mounted attacks against the Italian-occupied territories, switching forces from one front to another with consummate skill, effecting in a few months the destruction of the Italian empire.

This was the apogee of Wavell's success. But trouble came soon. There is no space here to discuss the reasons for the Allied landings in Greece, for the German thrust down through Jugoslavia to Greece, to the capture of Crete, to the driving back of Commonwealth forces by Rommel in the desert. Suffice to say that Wavell, with inadequate forces spread by necessity far too widely and too thinly, was unable to stem the German tide. It may well be, though, that his delaying actions in the spring of 1941 saved the whole war. Hitler secured the German flanks in southern Europe but, in doing so, he was forced to postpone his attack against Russia by six weeks, just failed to take Moscow and suffered the disasters of the following winter.

Meanwhile Wavell, the lightning conqueror, was not only harassed by the enemy but increasingly harried by Winston Churchill, the other man of the affair, the man ultimately responsible for the whole affair. To state the matter baldly, they were incompatible and neither understood the other. Churchill mistook Wavell's refusal to anticipate the deed with extravagant promises, for half-heartedness about the deed itself. Time and again he failed to understand that it was Wavell's nature to act first and let the action speak. Equally Wavell, irritated by the Prime Minister's incessant badgering and interference, was at fault in cloaking his intentions from the man responsible for more than one theatre of war, for the whole conduct of a war.

What might have been – that fascinating speculation. What might have been if Wavell had come to high command two years later than he did, with the full flood of Allied war production at his disposal?

As it was, the victim of the half-war that we lost, a half-war that no man could have won, he was sent to India to be commander-in-chief, soon to be involved in another lost cause – defence against the Japanese assault in south–east Asia. It has happened so many times in history that the first leaders are expendable and are expended, but never before perhaps that the expended leader was found to be inexpendable. Wavell fought on against adversity, not yielding to it, not complaining about it, sowing the seed that would yield harvest to others.

But in 1943 his life as an active soldier ended and he started another life as Viceroy of India. Winston Churchill disliked him, never forgave him for certain blunt ripostes, and treated him scurvily; but he knew Wavell's quality well enough to make use of him again.

Lady Wavell was to stay on in Simla for the rest of that summer but the Viceroy and most of his staff soon went down to Delhi. I had already had intimations that all was not in harmony as between the Vicereine's ideas and my own. Our trouble arose about the vacant post of comptroller's assistant. And about the filling of that post our opinions were diametrically and adamantly opposed.

It was a well-known and sensible adage among comptrollers that if you wanted to have a contented Viceroy you had better have a contented Vicereine. The best-known precedent had occurred in the famous case of Lady Willingdon, a strong-minded woman with a passion for the colour mauve. She bullied and badgered her comptroller about things in general and in particular mauve walls, mauve slip-covers, mauve this and that until he decided upon one last mauve thing. He arranged that Lady Willingdon's personal lavatory paper should be of that colour. He had had enough and took that fatal step and lost his job. A noble defeat, I would call it.

The contretemps with Lady Wavell was much different, if not much less ominous in its later stages. The comptroller's assistant had always been an Englishman. That made sense because, so long as the British remained, the catering was predominantly European and Lady Wavell did like her food. Therefore it must be an Englishman. I knew that India would be handed over to the Indians within two years at the most and I held, with equal determination (and in common with everyone else) that the job must go to an Indian.

This difference of opinion had become evident when I was still at Simla. She wanted the guiding hand of a trained *maître d'hôtel*, which skills I myself certainly could not provide. She was a very intelligent woman and must have seen, as the rest of us saw, that it had to be an Indian. But Lady Wavell did love an argument, and the more she argued the more adamant she became and the more interminably she argufied.

This contretemps deepened and grew at long distance between the Vicereine in the cool Simla hills and CVH in hot humid Delhi. I had the right man too for comptroller's assistant, the senior in my officer, Abdul Hakim Butt, an admirable fellow.

But it dragged on and on, as things did with her, and still nothing settled. Eventually, I went to talk to George Abell, the private secretary, who was busy with important things, not storms in tea-cups, and I said to George in the private freedom that we enjoyed, 'There's only one person who can crack the whip and I'm not going to ask him. I don't presume to suggest initiating divorce proceedings, George, because in that case she and I would both get the sack, but about this, George, it's her or me.'

George laughed, and Abdul Hakim Butt was duly appointed and I went to Simla to try to patch things up. It was *de rigueur* that we bow in royal fashion at first meeting each day and also shake hands after separation.

I duly lined up in some trepidation, held out my hand and bobbed my head. 'How d'you do, Your Excellency,' I said.

Lady Wavell's hand came forth, palm down, permitting me to touch the tips of her fingers, and she turned her head to present a perfectly expressionless plump profile, *retroussé* nose and all. She must have been very pretty when she was young and slim. It was a glacial non-welcome.

Fortunately Archie John, their son, happened to be staying at Viceregal Lodge and it must have been his influence, egged on by Father, that caused the thaw. At any rate, we were soon on speaking terms, and then amicable terms, and so remained.

Years later, after she had lost her husband and her son who were the centrepieces of her life, Lady Wavell and I met quite often, usually in London at the International Sportsmans Club, and became fast friends, truly a redoubtable woman. She wanted me to write a life of the Field Marshal but I knew that I was not competent to do that, for at least two reasons: first, I had a lamentable lack of feeling for history; second, I knew next to nothing about the art and conduct of war. I did write a short character sketch of Wavell as I knew him, which she read and approved, with many highly cogent comments.

So back to Delhi, to our bachelor existence, which centred in spare hours on that superb swimming pool. As I remember it, we were essentially a triumvirate, Colin Mackenzie, Charles Rankin and myself. Charles was the assistant private secretary, the junior man on the political side of things, a barrister by profession. He was exceedingly good value and talked incessantly about anything and everything, coming inevitably to his favourite topics which were India and women. About the former he had Colin and me sitting at his feet, or at his bare toes. About the latter he was knowledgeable too. Between Colin and me in age, prematurely grey, a smallish, good-looking man, the girls did collapse before Charles in droves. But he was in voluble despond at that time, the unthinkable having happened, he had recently been jilted, which served but to encourage Charles to lay down the law about those adorable devils of the other sex. It took the Viceroy to sum the matter up with an inimitably pithy comment – that in his opinion Charles was suffering more from an injured ego than a broken heart.

Colin was also in love at that time, awaiting the arrival of Anne FitzRoy from Africa, and I was wifeless until Willa at last got a passage to reach India in November.

All this might lead one to think that we were a despondent trio, roughing it beside and in the pellucid waters. But such was far from being the case. We had a high old bachelor time.

There was Philip Mason in the Indian Civil Service who, as Philip Woodruffe, had recently published a good novel *Call The Next Witness*. Later, under his own name, he wrote a definitive history of the ICS, that honourable service of the plundering raj, and *A Matter of Honour*, an account of the Indian Army. And there were the young ADCs on the staff and others. Best of all were the Indians who enlivened many evenings, two brigadiers, one Hindu and one Muslim, who had fought in Burma.

I had come as a stranger to India before I was twenty-one and had remained essentially a stranger all those pre-war years. But it was different now. Now they knew that we meant business about leaving India and now we all foresaw the horrors that might be ahead, and now there grew a bond of brotherhood between us. It was something new to me, and no less true because it happened in and near the rarefied atmosphere of the Viceroy's house.

The other social aspect of my life was Art, with a capital A. Billy Henderson, my predecessor as comptroller, was an artist who did much, perhaps more than anyone else had done, to foster painting in India. A particular ally of his, and the driving force behind art exhibitions at the Viceroy's house and elsewhere in New Delhi, was Roy Chowdhri, a Bengali artist, as different from those brigadiers as a roly-poly pussy-cat is from a panther.

I wrote to Willa just after arriving that July:

> I was going to my future office this morning when I met a well dressed (in Indian clothes) Hindu chap of about 32 who was introduced to me as Billy's artist friend, Roy Chowdhri by name and a leading artist himself. He it was who had persuaded Billy to start the exhibition. I was much taken with him, a most jokey, jolly sort of chap. We became so pally that I had qualms afterwards in case I might have chummed-up with a charlatan. However, it appears not. He was disarmingly frank. He said he was devoted to Billy; they had so much in common because of their art. 'Of course,' he added, 'it is a good thing to get someone in the Viceroy's house to sign letters begging for funds. You get so much more that way.' He then said that he must have me on the committee for the same reason.

So, on the committee I went, signing letters as required and attending exhibitions. A hazard at those was Roy Chowdhri's manifest affection. It had never been my practice to walk hand-in-hand with males above the age of four or five. But whenever my hand next to him was spare, he would grasp it in his and we would go linked through the exhibition. There was nothing queer about it. We were brothers in art and he loved me very much, especially when I signed those letters. Nevertheless – and how ridiculous of me because the most heterosexual Indians hold hands – it was not quite my kind of thing and I sought occasional relief in dodges like a nose-blow, or a quick shift to a following position the better to study some *objet d'art*. But most of the time we went hand-in-hand.

As the monsoon dwindled and fell back and as Lady Wavell's return from Simla drew near, I became familiar with the job. The administrative side of it was no problem. The senior members of my staff knew all the routine backwards, depending upon me only to take responsibility. Having had by then a fairly varied experience of managing affairs and people I was quite good at that. I was also useful in helping over menus, at least until Lady Wavell came back. Thereafter it became a balancing act between indulging her excellent, if extravagant, tastes in food and observing a certain austerity. We should not feast while India hungered. It was not so long since my own hungry days and I was a bit of a prig about it but we did ourselves by no means badly.

Her Excellency was of slothful habit, never stirring her stumps until late morning. But that was no bad thing, enabling one to get the work done.

In at least one aspect of my job I was a total flop. Both my immediate predecessors had been unmarried and both had had their own quarters in the house. Both were people of exquisite taste in interior decoration and similar matters. They enjoyed discussing rare cloths (*stuffs* is the word) and silk brocade and so on as much as Lady Wavell did. My own taste was good enough in its way, favouring the plain, eschewing the ornate, a few quick looks made my mind up for me. I simply could not endure fingering fancy staffs hour after hour. But they enjoyed it as much as she did. Hence the flop.

Meanwhile the Comptroller's house was readied for a wife and infant, back from Canada, waiting at Rankeillour for passage to join me, waiting through delays, unexplained postponements, gathering frustration.

It was a bungalow of modest size with a delightful garden, improved still further because – ever with an eye to the main chance – I wooed the support of Mr Reader, lord of all gardens. I remember best now the eucalypts that bounded it, the gums of Australia, planted in warmer climates all over the world, graceful trees to bound a garden.

I wrote to Willa:

> My bearer is quite a good man. He is a Muslim, by name Umr Din (pronounced oomaar Deen). Like all Indians very sentimental about babies. It is one of their pleasant characteristics, they genuinely dote on children. He was much impressed by Giles's picture and said *Baby Sahib bahut achcha wallah* (rough translation: Baby master, jolly good type). I expect this was said to please me, which it certainly did. He sends you the most profound messages of devotion.

And later:

> Umr Din brought his small son, aged about four, to see me today. He arrived without warning, a very serious young gentleman in khaki shorts and a smart checked shirt, really a sweet little fellow and not very shy at seeing me. We shook hands gravely. I then gave him 8 annas (about ninepence, not a

very princely present) which he grabbed exactly like an English child and made off. However, Father stopped him and made him Salaam me, returned with equal gravity.

While I was settling in at the bungalow I still took most meals at the Big House. There were usually people staying or people in for lunch or dinner. The Viceroy did not talk much on such occasions, those famous silences about which far too much has been made, but they were trying for women on his blind side and his good side, left and right alike.

It is as a soldier that Archibald Percival Wavell will be first remembered. As I have said, I did not know him in those fighting days but only at the end of his time as Viceroy and during a partial retirement after that. Nor was I concerned in the political problems that beset him during his last Indian year. They were intensely complex and none of the Comptroller's business and I had only a sketchy knowledge of them at the time. But in essence he was trying doggedly and patiently to obtain agreement between the political parties and to prevent, if possible, the partition of Hindu and Muslim India, trying also to dissuade the British government from too precipitately leaving India to the blood bath that he foresaw and that later came about. During that year his very impartiality made him increasingly unpopular with the leaders of the opposing factions; and during that year he progressively lost the confidence of the British government.

Now it happened that we played golf on more or less equal terms, so through the monsoon and the winter of 1946-7 we would mount the juggernaut Rolls-Royce that was the Viceroy's state car and be driven to New Delhi golf course to play a few holes. He was only a fair golfer but an enthusiastic one, a stickler for etiquette and rules who played to win, and he did not always concede the doubtful putt of fifteen inches. But two can play at that game and he would address the short putt with a grunt of displeasure. He grunted also for fun, for doubt and for agreement. I never got nearly to the bottom of his grunts.

Sometimes he talked nineteen to the dozen; sometimes we proceeded in the total silence which bothered some people but suited me well enough as I have never held that the human tongue wags to best advantage when it wags eternally. He did not talk often about current Indian affairs. The early morning ride, the hour of golf, the occasional shoot – these were his physical release from burdens such as few men have had to bear alone. The burgeoning fate of four hundred million people went with him always. Small wonder, when one considered that a few months after he left India half a million or a million or even more people were slaughtered in communal riots. Nobody knows how many.

What did we talk about? Often of friends in The Black Watch, which was the anchor of his soldier's life. Often of books and writers; of our families; of his early Indian days and mine; in short, of cabbages and kings, and a warm and witty raconteur he was when in the mood. He talked best *à deux*, or with a few people. But between him and an audience there seemed to dangle an awkward curtain of reserve.

All his life he had been a lover of poetry, with an unusual gift for committing it to memory. The many poems that he knew by heart gave him comfort and companionship in peaceful times and crisis alike.

In an introduction to his anthology of verse, *Other Men's Flowers*, published in 1944 when he had recently become Viceroy, he wrote: 'It amused me lately to set down in a notebook – mainly with a view to discussion with my son, who shares my liking for poetry – the poems I could repeat entire or in great part. I have now collected and arranged the poems I set down. I did it with no idea of publication, but my son and others have suggested that the collection might appeal to a wide circle.'

His anthology did have a wide success and became a *vade mecum* for many travellers on life's journeys. There is little modern poetry in it and little blank verse which, as he wrote, commits itself less easily to memory than rhyme.

But the selection itself, and his own comments interspersed throughout the book, are perhaps as good keys as we could have to the mind and character of that many-sided man – simple in heart, complex in taste, witty, scholarly, above all intensely human. Here are a few of those comments: 'I have always dated some decline in English character from the time when tea replaced beer on the breakfast table.'

In his preface to the section he called 'Love and All That', he wrote: 'Some fall in love in season or out of season; for them there is no cure, nor do they often desire one. Perhaps an Elizabethan, who first shocked and then amused his royal Mistress, phrased it most succinctly: "It is better to love two too many than one too few".' And again, in the section 'The Call of the Wild': 'The dog, man's most intelligent and responsive friend in the animal world, has inspired little real poetry, while that foolish quadruped the horse has been the subject of much. Swift, in the last part of *Gulliver's Travels*, endowed his horse (Houyhnhnms) with superhuman wisdom and intelligence, the last thing that horses have ever had, in the view of their riders anyway. Beauty and speed have nearly always been preferred to solid worth – this is the reason for many divorces . . . '

I have two copies of that book. One is signed on the title page: 'A. P. Wavell, alias Wavell F. M.', typically laconic. The other is the memorial edition, given to me by his son Archie John, the second and last Earl Wavell.

Archie John was an idealist, a more fervent idealist than his father, and he wrote in his introduction: 'Jogging home from one of the early morning cavalcade gallops across the plains behind New Delhi, I posed some over-earnest questions about the possible revolutionary change of society in England when the war was over – and his eye twinkled as he began to reply:

It may be we shall rise the last as Frenchmen rose the first
Our wrath come after Russia's wrath, and our wrath be the worst,
It may be we were meant to mark by our riot and our rest,
God's scorn for all men governing. It may be Beer is best.

---

No wonder that with this resource of mind, he could bear with patience the rebuffs of the Council table.'

Archie John concluded by describing a last moment of foreboding on the night before the Field Marshal died: '. . . I took down from the shelves of the library of the Nursing Home a book of verse for solace, and came upon this poem by Francis Brett Harte:

Came the relief, 'What, sentry. Ho!
How passed the night through thy long waking?'
'Cold, cheerless, dark – as may befit
The hour before the dawn is breaking.'

'No sight? No sound?' 'No, nothing save
The plover from the marshes calling
And in yon Western sky, about
An hour ago, a star was falling.'

Archibald John Wavell was in his own very different and perhaps unrealized way as remarkable a human being as his father. He was killed by the Mau-Mau in 1953.

So that was how I came to know Lord Wavell – not the soldier and statesman, simply the man. I saw him hardly at all in the action of his work; and knew him far less well than many others who had been his lifelong friends. But if you are a man's companion in time of stress you cannot but take measure of his quality.

He lived by a code, a composite or component rule of which was: 'Take the blame and don't complain.' His code was a simple one, as any code of honour worth the name must be. Indeed, I think he was in the good sense a simple man, with a brilliant mind that saw the short way to the truth. But his straight-thinking intellect was not that best equipped to cope with the devious simplicities of Mahatma Gandhi; nor with the lustered orotundities of Winston Churchill.

There are people who have said that Wavell's silences reflected not deep thought but the absence thereof. Most of them, I have noticed, are those to whom silence is an unnatural condition. And I have no doubt that he did let his mind ride easy. Only psychopaths think all the time. But I am sure that the stricture is in general untrue, and once again for a simple reason: the woes of India were directly reflected in the woes of the Viceroy of India's golf. When things were particularly awful, so played he. But he blamed himself for his bad golf, not Mr Jinnah or Pandit Nehru. I often wished that he would blow off steam and scream at them or the world or me. But no. It would have done him harm, not good. It was so burdensome to see that once or twice I tried to miss short putts so that the poor man could win at something, even golf. Try to hole it, you miss by a whisker. Try to miss by a whisker, in the ball goes. Some irony there about golf, and things.

Bernard Fergusson, who served Wavell for many years, wrote: 'His standards were high, and he did not shrink from rebuke; but his personal relations with us were indulgent and comradely, like those of an understanding and nearly contemporary uncle.'

I do not recollect being rebuked about my job because house-keeping was something of which he was totally unaware. But he did not suffer second-rate thought or slipshod comment and I was chided for that, chided not by a nearly contemporary uncle but by an equal. Which was remarkable. It was humility.

And yet this word humility needs qualification. He was a humble man in the sense that he had no conceit whatever, nor small pride in what he had accomplished. But there was a grand self-confidence and sureness in him. He took the blame himself for things that went wrong and did not bother to talk about the things that went well. However strong and gifted he might know himself to be, he never thought of himself as other than a common human being and was totally devoid of the vanity which is tiresomely prevalent among lesser men who have achieved large things. A majestic humility, certainly, but he could strike back in a way that was hardly humble.

On one occasion Mr Attlee, the British Prime Minister, sent a message complaining that it was unfortunate that the Viceroy's policy differed so greatly from that of His Majesty's Government.

Wavell cabled back at once in these approximate terms: 'It is impossible for the Viceroy's policy to differ from that of His Majesty's Government since His Majesty's Government does not have a policy. That is my complaint. Wavell.'

The truth of the matter is that he was tough – as tough in spirit as he was in body. And if he knew physical fear, he put that weakness down where it belonged. As an aircraft passenger he was a wholly imperturbable Jonah. When, during flight, the pilot reported that one of the engines was on fire, Wavell said, 'Well, let me know if there is anything I can do to help,' replaced his monocle and went back to working on his papers.

Eyeglass or monocle, the word conjures up a vaguely foppish

image. But set in Wavell's right eye (the other had been blinded at Ypres) in that square furrowed face, the image was anything but foppish – appraising or amused or bored, but hickory tough.

He gave me few orders but once I had to give him an order, on the only occasion I ever saw him angry. We were playing a weekend round against, I think, the Sikh brothers Malik, both excellent golfers who gave us strokes and usually a beating. We had reached the first green and Wavell was bending, stout legs apart, to line up his putt when a ball trickled slowly through between his feet. We had been driven into by the party next behind us. I would not care to remember the words the Field Marshal used but his outraged golfer's ire was, to say the least, impressive. He turned and strode in fury, putter in hand, to deal with the offender, a callow youth. Wavell clearly meant business and it occurred to me that it would hardly do for the Viceroy of India to commit assault and battery on the New Delhi golf course so I went to do the job verbally myself. Wavell growled at me but withdrew obediently, good soldier that he was. I wonder now whether I was wrong. Perhaps I should have let him blow some superheated steam and that young man's head off.

One morning early in 1947 he sent for me and I walked a quarter of a mile or so through the cavernous corridors of Lutyens's pink elephant from my office to the Viceroy's study. 'Look at this, David,' he said, and gave me the letter which a King's Messenger had just brought to him from the Prime Minister. I do not remember the exact text but it was a coldly discourteous document which I can paraphrase as follows: It had long been apparent to His Majesty's Government that its views and those of the Viceroy had moved apart. Accordingly, he would be replaced by Admiral Lord Mountbatten. The letter was signed by Clement Attlee.

Three years later the London *Times* obituary said: '. . . Wavell's supersession by Lord Mountbatten came as something of a shock, which was not lessened by the curt and ungenerous terms in which the change was signified to the world at large. It was characteristic of the man that he kept silent and made no attempt to put his views on the matter before the public.'

Once over a trifling affair I had seen his temper roused. Once now over a great issue I saw him moved to show emotion. If the change was signified to the world at large in curt and ungenerous terms, it was signified in grossly churlish terms to the recipient himself. But, just as he made no public complaint later, so that morning he made no private complaint in his study. He had shown the letter to George Abell; and he showed it to me, not as his comptroller but as his friend.

There ensued a few weeks before the secret was out and then intense activity about the change-over. Lord Mountbatten was bringing a much larger staff and the preparations therefor gave even comptrollers a lot of work. When yet another list of the future Viceroy's entourage was shown to Wavell he noted in the margin: 'The Battens Mount,' a characteristically dry comment.

But Mountbatten came and the handover was done with amity and goodwill, for the two men admired one another. With his empirical talents, his swift decision, his dazzling presence and last but not least, his gifted wife (whose beauty and charm were as delightful as her energy was formidable), Mountbatten drove through to the handing over of power in India as no other man could have done.

FOUR

# 1946 and 1947

To go back to November, Willa and Giles arrived at Bombay and we took the train north to Delhi and to the comptroller's house, that gem among bungalows, all spic and span for mother and small one. Even the nursery walls had charmingly fanciful sketches, contributed by Haro Hodson. We had our own servants in viceregal livery – from Sadiq Hussain, the butler or head-waiter, to Mohammad Yakub, the chaprassi or messenger, and to Mithan, the sweeper, each one to his ritual task. If grand luxury ever had a miniature lap, we lived in it.

Nor could a memsahib escape ritual tasks – the locked cupboard, the daily apportionment of food to our Goanese cook and household supplies to others. I helped for a few days, then left Willa to it, saying: 'If in doubt, ask Maud Currie,' who was most helpful, a veteran of many Indian years, wife of Douglas Currie, the military secretary.

But Willa did not have to ask much for assistance. Day after day the dhobi, or laundryman, came with a long face to say that another light bulb in his house had broken and would the memsahib give him a replacement? After rather much of this, Willa announced that she would like to visit the dhobi's quarters. That was duly arranged and she made her formal inspection with retinue, only to find that there was no electricity in the *dhobi's* house. To her surprise, they all, including the culprit, were delighted to have such a promising memsahib to referee traditional games. That settled light bulbs only.

The winter of northern India had come, with its mild days of sunshine and cool nights, cold enough occasionally for a skim of ice to form, as I remembered from camping in times before. For us, it was a climate of perfection. For the Indian peasant, huddled shivering in one cotton blanket, it was less so. Colin and I used to go on a bit about our Indian brothers' plight, Willa says, and then raise a lordly hand for more whisky and soda.

After so many abbreviated games of golf with Lord Wavell I was playing quite well and reached the semi-finals of the Delhi championship. We each had an *agi-wallah*, or fore-caddie, whose job it was to wait ahead to seek the ball that had wandered from the fairway. My *agi-wallah* was named Hukm Chand, a very small boy with a Hindu topknot and with that amazing liveliness of Indian childhood, so early to dim into lethargy.

Whenever my ball went astray Hukm Chand would vanish into the rough, which could mean longer grass or tangled undergrowth further in, or even old ruins of some shrine. Invariably that small magician, Hukm Chand, had found it. Invariably also the ball sat up in a perfect open lie.

At first I was glad about his wizardry and my good luck, and then I wondered and became suspicious. It happened too often and I was certain, looking down at the beamingly innocent culprit, so pleased to please Master. *Mat Karo, Don't do it, Hukm Chand.* My Hindustani, although adequate in practical matters, was not up to explaining that improving lies in the rough was cheating. So I said sternly, *Mat Karo*, and never caught him at it, and the competitive spirit, that scoundrel, flourished with a nag of conscience. Perhaps it was as well that my semi-final opponent, who did not have nearly so gifted an *agi-wallah* but rarely went into the rough, beat me soundly. It was not Hukm Chand's fault that I failed to win the Delhi championship.

The winter rains may have come for a day or two that year. I do not know. I do know that the other clouds gathered over India. The trouble that was to come was in everyone's mind and fear grew in the land. We, the British, did not fear for ourselves. We were probably safer than ever before while the three wicks smouldered on, the Hindu, the Muslim, the Sikh, to explosion point someday, somewhere, somehow.

Wavell never changed, nor lost patience with the interminable wrangling and jockeying for some sort of accord that they wanted and did not want. His patience with Indian leaders seemed inexhaustible. He expected deviousness from them, endured it and could not cope with it. But with the British government of

Clement Attlee it was otherwise. He had the straight-thinking soldier's intolerance of politicians, 'the politicians', too often in inverted commas. Not to understand the inevitable contrivings of partisan political life at home was a fault and it dogged him always.

We met in the early mornings when he led a small cavalcade and raced with it across the plains nearby. Well mounted, that was the exhilarating thing to make a day.

In the afternoons we had our golf. It must have been after he had told me of his impending replacement that I spoke of my own resolve. He would have known before then that I wanted to leave the Army. He would have known that, except for the Regiment, the army meant nothing to me. He understood that, even if he disagreed with it, and liked it too – unto each man his own, provided he means business. And when I told him that to find out whether I could write I must make writing my job, whole and complete, he understood even better.

That was the only time, in my recollection, that I made use of him, my eye resolutely fixed on my own main chance. He said: 'Write the letter and I'll see what I can do.'

A field marshal who was also Viceroy was a potent endorser of applications to retire, and mine was approved.

I kept most of the letters he wrote to me after the Indian days. In one, of April 1949, from England to Canada, he said: 'I have just been reading your story in the *Atlantic Monthly* and much enjoyed it. It is very well and attractively written, and makes good reading. I hope that it will be the first of many. How does the novel get on, and when is it coming out?'

The novel would have been my first, *The Storm and the Silence*, about which he did write later but I do not have that letter. He made a blunt comment about the photograph on the jacket: 'By the way, that is an awful portrait of you on the back-page of your cover, you look too much the budding author and not enough the man.'

In the April letter he went on to say: 'Archie John was here for Easter, and has gone back to his School of Education in Cornwall. The Head Master of Winchester asked for him to come and teach there for a year in place of one of his masters who had gone off somewhere; but the War Office was narrow-minded about it and refused to give him leave, although Winchester were prepared to pay him altogether for a year, and he was also going to run their Cadet Corps. So I suppose he will stop at that dim and tiresome School of Education, where I think he is wasting his time completely. I wish he would get down to writing, like you, but he is so cumbered with the affairs of his Unit that he never has time.'

It was my small second novel, *Geordie*, that Wavell much liked and to which he was to give a tremendous unsolicited fillip.

Wavell always meant business and he was glad that my meaning business had borne some initial fruit. What an ally to have on the New Delhi golf-course, and later, and always.

It was while we were girding ourselves for the arrival of Mountbatten that a welcome appointment was made, that of deputy comptroller, welcome on several counts to me. I badly needed help, so Freddy Burnaby-Atkins was welcome that way. Also he had been a fellow-prisoner and a friend, if not an intimate one. Also he was in The Black Watch, the old-boy-net working wonders again, just as it was to work later when Martin Gilliat, another member of our Colditz mess, was to take on from Colin Mackenzie.

Freddy was (and is) a most endearing man. Everyone loved Freddy who had a propensity for making harmless, if sometimes startling, gaffes. On the evening of his arrival he said to Lady Wavell, with that slight hesitancy of speech:

'S-sorry to mention it, Your Ex, but there's a fly on your eyelid.'

'Don't be a fool, Freddy. It's a wart, not a fly. I've had it all my life.'

But Freddy was no fool, a great help to me and to everyone.

As February went on, the fleeting cold weather was reaching its end. Whenever I did not ride before breakfast I would go bird-watching and Willa sometimes brought Giles along in the pram. The abundance and variety of winter visitors from the north was remarkable. I had one memorable walk with Dillon Ripley, the American ornithologist. There were complications about wagtails, small birds aptly named and confusing to a beginner because of varieties and shades of variety within each species. We were looking at one particular bird, black and white, dipping its tail as it walked about a lawn. The yellow-headed, the grey, the yellow, a shared colour ruled all those out. But the pied or the white? 'White wagtail, isn't it?'

'*Motacilla alba*, yes, that would be the white, but which? *Personata*, not *dukhunensis*, yes, I feel sure. Yes, *Motacilla alba personata*.'

It stands to reason that Latin is the *lingua franca* of ornithologists, of whom I have met few, but Ripley happened to be the only one who identified them first in that language. I remembered the *Motacilla alba* but have cheated about the *personata* by looking up Whistler's excellent (and well-written) *Handbook of Indian Birds*.

Dillon Ripley came back to have breakfast with us in the garden, an entertaining fellow whose talents later took him beyond ornithology to head the Smithsonian Institute in Washington.

There were many formal functions and state dinners at which I was theoretically responsible for the varying diets that ranged from Hindu orthodox (entirely vegetarian) to omnivorous European. By then all pomp and ceremony were burdens to me.

Yet one would be a fool not to admire the true splendour of the Viceroy's bodyguard, a squadron each of Sikhs and Punjabi Mussulmen, magnificent men magnificently mounted, parading as the Viceroy handed over to the Viceroy, a simple ceremony, the more impressive for that.

We went to see the Wavells off at Pallam airport. They were to fly in an Avro York, a four-engined derivative of the Lancaster bomber. The aircraft was loaded and loaded more, and loaded yet more with Wavell possessions, until even the passengers' cabin was crammed to the roof.

The captain was a senior RAF pilot who did not seem perturbed about what must have been an Avro York's record overload, which Colin Mackenzie, who was to fly with them, supervised down to Lady Wavell's last and final afterthought.

So we said goodbye and the York trundled out. I was unhappy about the goodbye and kept to myself the fear that goodbye might also be disaster. He gathered speed, faster, still faster, surely to be airborne now but not. The aircraft was still earthbound as it came to the far limits of the runway and rose sluggishly at last.

Under Mountbatten there was an instant and dynamic change.

As a pre-requisite to accepting the Viceroyalty, he had demanded and got plenipotentiary powers (something that no other Viceroy had ever had), which meant, in simple terms, that although nominally the servant of the British government, he was its master, with freedom to hand over power as and when he decided.

And then there was his royal presence, by right of birth as near to royal as made no difference. And Indians of all persuasions had veneration for the royal mystique. There was his fabulous record as a sailor and commander. There were his extraordinary empirical methods – sit round a table, hear this view and that view and thrash it out to swift decision. There was also his wife, no less glamorous, no less brilliant, no less energetic. They would fly together, or separately, to every far corner of India.

I was with them a bare two months, and hardly knew him, and did not regret that. He was not the kind of man with whom I could ever have felt at ease. But whenever I did see him, *El Supremo*, master of himself and all about him, there would flash across my mind the picture of a destroyer captain on his bridge, turning turtle, all the way round and up the other side, the captain still standing on his bridge. It may have been all the way down and back up the same way again but full circle was the way my mind's eye saw it with some awe.

I did have much to do with Edwina Mountbatten and liked her immensely. It would be some big social affair for us to discuss and for her to decide, and I would get on with it, just as simple as that. Their younger daughter, Pamela, was with them and I became devoted to Pammy, a diffident girl, sweet seventeen or thereabouts.

The Mountbattens had India in thrall. I saw them in action together only once. It was above Simla, at Mashobra, at a small house belonging to the estate, two or three thousand foot higher, where Mr Reader, master of gardens, grew apples.

It was a small picnic, the three Mountbattens, a few members of the staff and only one Indian present, Pandit Nehru. Walking along the path beside him, above apple trees, Willa stopped to look at the high snows and said, 'The Himal*ay*as are so beautiful,' or words like that.

'Him*aa*lyas,' he corrected her in a kindly way, if a trifle testy.

'My dear young lady, you must get it right.' Nehru was an appealing man whom I did not know well but I came to have a soft spot for him, not only indulgently testy like that but explosively irascible.

After lunch we hung about, something momentous in the air, a signal expected from London, I never did know what, but then it arrived and the two Mountbattens walked up and down the small lawn together, talking, discussing quietly just out of earshot.

Mr Nehru sat on a bench beside some infant's pram, holding his forefinger out for the baby to grasp, and his eyes followed them as they paced and talked. He was uneasy, watching them while the baby clasped his finger. They had him mesmerized. I saw it work, that uncanny power.

Later that afternoon, I took some photographs, of which one became reasonably famous. It is reproduced here.

Willa and Giles stayed on at Simla through April's heat and on into May when we sailed for home. We had had an anxious day or two with Giles at Simla. One of the servants, to make assurance double sure had, on the journey coming up, strained his boiled water through a muslin cloth in which bacillary dysentery bugs must have been lurking. It was an unpleasant, wasting disease for adults, as I had found out in 1932. It could be swiftly lethal for babies, but there were sulpha drugs now and he was quickly cured.

In Delhi, Lady Mountbatten, back between whirlwind tours to the sick and starving, said that she would like to visit the servants' quarters.

'All of them, Your Ex?'

'Yes, all of them, David. Or don't you think it's a good idea?'

'I think it's a superb idea.'

No Vicereine before had done such a thing. I passed the word to Freddy, Mr Butt, Kashmiri Lal and Sohan Singh, my captain and lieutenants. The word was enough. Every one of the three hundred quarters would be spotless.

But alone in my office just before we started her tour she asked me a question: 'Should I shake hands with them all, David, do you think?'

She meant the sweepers, the untouchables, I knew very well, and just as well that the hand that had touched the sweeper's hand was sullied for the Brahmin's hand, a taboo that never had been broken. But she had asked me and would do what I said and I had no wise George Abell to consult. 'As it's you, Your Excellency, I would say so, yes.'

'Okay, I will.' And so she did.

Edwina Mountbatten was the only woman I ever served, and what a man to serve that woman was.

The Mountbatten calendars were now on every desk. So many days to the hand-over of power in August, and a day to tear off, and one less day.

It was a gimmick, the sort of gimmick that Wavell would not have tolerated, nor got away with if he had been persuaded to it. I never knew enough to have opinions worth expressing about partition – the division of India by religious majority into a joint Muslim state, West Pakistan and East, the former viable, the latter doomed from the start, divided by a thousand miles of India. Or would Mahatma Gandhi's dream of a unified India have led to less slaughter, or to more? Nor would I presume to judge the precipitate mode of British departure. Some would say a ske-daddle to a holocaust. But one thing is certain – that no other man alive could have achieved what Mountbatten drove through in those few months. He had brilliant advisers, headed by Lord Ismay, Secretary to Churchill's War Cabinet, the shrewdest of men, but Mountbatten did it.

There is an unbridgeable gulf as between my memories of two men, both great, that suitably unfathomable word – the one, whom I knew well, who always took the blame; the other, whom I hardly knew, who was always right. He made a speech in Toronto not long before his tragic death and I heard him by radio, still speaking of the invaluable lessons learned from the Dieppe raid. But I had lived in prison with survivors of that bloody disaster, moderate men, and the only lesson that they could remember therefrom was that Churchill tanks spun their tracks off on beaches. There were plenty of beaches in England where that could have been found out.

The one unqualified stricture that I would make is that our abandonment of princely India, of the Indian states making up a quarter or more of the total population, was shameful. They had sworn fealty to the Crown and had served it faithfully in war and peace. We simply abnegated our responsibility and left them to the untender mercies of Congress to be crumbled and dismembered. That many, by no means all, of the princely states were ill-governed is beside the point. We washed our hands of them and in so doing connived to join the dirty tricks department.

When Willa and Giles and I sailed in May there were still about seventy-five pages to be torn one by one from Mountbatten's calendar. I thought then that it was a final goodbye for me to India. But seven years after Independence, looking for a novel, I went back to jungles and other places familiar to me from earlier times. I bought a secondhand Landrover and drove, entirely alone with a Muslim bearer, up and down and across Hindu India. Without a single exception the people were kind to me and pleased to see me. And so it happened that free India was much more my India than any India I had known before.

# FIVE

# [1954]

This is March the twenty-first, the vernal equinox of 1983. It pleases me, for unknown simple reasons, that in the spring and autumn of each year one day and one night of equal length happen everywhere on earth. I think of the equinox here, and I think of it at distant places, like Holman Island at about 71 north latitude, or like Nareeb Nareeb at about 38 south latitude in the western district of Victoria, Australia. We are all the same today. What is so odd about that? Well, nothing much except to wonder.

This time at St Andrews, or two miles from the town, we do have something unusual. It is the earliest spring that anyone remembers, not that we normally have spring – residual winter jumps on May Day or so to summer. But this time the aconites are out and the buds of magnolia stellata are dangerously swollen and the snow has dwindled almost to be gone. Yesterday's fog helped that. The local saying is: *There ain't nothin' like the fog, not to take 'er down*. It is a good human and natural place in many ways, and the best human place I know for double and triple negatives.

Book One of these sporadic memoirs was based on prison in Germany, flashing back to my childhood, on to India, to Canada, to and fro and out and in, and ultimately to release.

In this second book I began with a near-parting from Lord Wavell, a flash-on (for which term I apologize), and we shall meet again before it is goodbye.

After my last Indian visit in 1954 I wrote a story, taking a few liberties with fact. All that happened did more or less happen on one evening, one night, one early morning; it was free India, no less marvellous, no less maddening than it had always been, yet something more for me.

The Roorkee chair is a survivor of or from the British raj, with long wooden arms to hold one's legs spreadeagled. I sprawl thus in this excellent chair and drink my mug of tea.

All day, driving up from Delhi, circumnavigating bullock carts in blankets of dust and the soulless plains and the shapeless hordes, never a respite from humanity, I have been low in spirit, wondering how I ever was such a nincompoop as to suppose that I could drive a motor vehicle round this country; I should have known better, so very much alone, with only occasional glimpses of reality, like a girl slapping clothes beside the village tank, her bosom straining at its bodice; through Meerut my first Indian home, past winter crops, green and yellow, sugar cane and wheat and whatnot, an endless curve of flatness, past the aforementioned Roorkee, and now the land begins to tilt a little, and with it my spirits, and those are the clouds that hide the hills. The hills, they should be there, they always were, those blessed hills to dream upon from heat.

Yes, they are here, the first small Siwalicks anyway, outriders of the Himalayas, and I and my mug in the Roorkee chair are on the verandah of a forest resthouse which is familiar to me. I have been here before, but even if I had not, I would have been, in this pretty place at the edge of jungle where sal trees will rustle when the night wind blows.

But now the forest is still. I watch the garden, not quite a garden, a cleared place between woods and bungalow. A small dove dips about, and flies with a fluster and a clap to feed again and kroo again, I wrote something like that before, in the future possibly. A bulbul sings, I like the liquid bulbul. And babblers fuss in a huddle in the dust, *Seven Sisters*, the British called them; or in Hindi, *Seven Brothers*, boring either way.

It is nearly five. Sunlight softens to copper on Siwalick rocks. The lovely hour is coming. Just after dawn is lovely too, but with hard day to follow it. Now I shall sit, and if I am lucky, as I used to be in this place, I shall sit until the parakeets cram wheeling dashing in to roost. I am happy for once, the restless beast in me is still, then click in a wink I am bothered about my family at St Sauveur des Monts, other hills nine thousand miles away or something, and thirty below, who knows or cares about Fahrenheit, but are they safe and sound?

Near at hand people chatter incessantly, quietly with shrill cackles. In the jungle tigers are waking up. I wish one would roar. I hope I shall hear one roar tonight when I am safe in bed. It is a top-quality sound. I can hear it again, just thinking of it.

Now I am thinking of old Jim Corbett. I sat at his jungle-booted feet for a few days once in this very place, or I followed those light lazy feet through the jungle of which he was a boss animal. *This is our rope*, he said, stripping bark from a tree by the watercourse, and twisting strands, and lo! a serviceable rope. And he stopped and raised one finger, he had a friendly doggy face, alert, his finger raised. The call came again, it was nearby, *Kyaa*, the light alarm call of the cheetal, dappled deer. *A tiger is walking slowly there*, said old Jim Corbett. And sure enough, we found the fresh pugmarks, still crumbling.

I was brought back from Jim Corbett by the arrival of Hafeez Husseinuddin. His whole name sounded better with a good Muslim roll to it, but for brevity's sake: *Well, Hafeez*, I said.

He was a very thin man, and he grew thinner and thinner in the next two months, my fault, I have no doubt, I bounced him and drove him to emaciation in that blasted car with my driving demon. *Huzoor*, he said now. Your Honour, he explained, we had no hurricane lamp by which to cook, not one plate from which Huzoor could eat, neither knife nor fork nor spoon with which to eat, no butter for the bread, no fat with which to fry.

I had been busy in Delhi, buying the car, trying to get my rifle through the Customs, such a timeless petulance of patience. *It is strict regulation. There can be no upspeeding of proper channel.* But I got the rifle in the end, and a shooting licence, and a letter to the district forest officer, and I had bought all the essentials for roughing it in the jungle, remarkable efficiency. But could Hafeez cook by my flashlight and lend me my flashlight to eat my corned mutton hash off my newspaper with my fingers? *Dehra Dun is not far, Huzoor*, he said, hopeful, never reproachful to your half-wit honour, never.

*Okay, Hafeez*, I said. *Ham ghari-men so fort jaenge.* My Urdu is a trifle idiosyncratic, especially when out of practice.

*Bahut achcha, Sahib*, he said. *Mehrbani.* There, he was pleased with me and grateful.

I take my long jungle flashlight just in case, and I start off in the car. She is a four-wheel-drive job, and on the whole I love her, but for tactful reasons I am calling her the Beaver, not her generic name. 'Dehra Dun, 14', it says on the milestone – say half an hour each way, half an hour to buy the needful, back before seven. But dusk is at six in the Indian cold weather so I shall miss those screaming parakeets, a pity. The easiest parakeets to watch are the green ones, flocks of them. But the best to see and hear are the blossom-headed, much less common, coursing melodiously in ones and twos along the fringes of the forest. I shall also be late for whisky time, a worse pity, my aesthetic sense being subordinate to, if heightened by my whisky. I forgot to buy plates, but not the whisky, one never does.

The Beaver is said to have done only seven thousand miles, all with the right sort of princely careful owner. If so, they were rough-and-tumble jungley miles. She squeaks in every joint and corner, and the play in her steering is one quarter turn, which makes for a nice gamble diving between two bullock carts. The word nice is just too nice except in this particular use, perhaps. But despite her wear and tear the Beaver is in good form this evening. She romps uphill and into the tunnel which marks the pass. It is a reasonable deserted tunnel, not like those machine-gun pea-shooter tubes that terrify me around New York.

And now we are running down into the Doon, a valley between the Siwalick foothills and the Himalayas. It is a good place, neither of the plains nor of the mountains, but a stepping stone. The Doon awaits me in a kindly hour before the night, shadows stretching, it won't be long. I first ran this road in salad days in my T-Model Ford. It was my Doon then and my India, but now it is no India of mine. I last ran this road shortly before Independence when India was only in a residual manner of speaking mine.

But look! I do see green parakeets, a team of ten or twenty, far too swift to count, they hurtle across our bows, the same old parakeets, the same old Doon. Only I have changed from twenty-one to forty-three, too many memories and nothing ever new, unless it is to be some esoteric vice not yet explored.

There is no other traffic, not even bullock carts. The sun is dying as we near the outskirts of Dehra Dun and come to a boy and his herd of goats. He is in a hurry, yelling, dashing and belabouring, a boy of twelve or so, with a flying topknot, and all the vitality they lose so soon. No wonder he is in a hurry at the rim of dusk when panthers prowl. He slept on the job this afternoon, that may be it, and now he is too frantic to notice us behind him. He is thinking of the stick that he will get from Father Bap for tempting providence and panthers.

In bad old days I would have blasted a way through. But now I am a guest of this fair Doon, so the Beaver and I dawdle patiently behind. I am doing my daily good turn too; I fancy that we are a small discouragement to panthers.

Then, as quickly, as unpredictably as my mind can fly across *x* thousand miles, one and all the goats break into a bleating gallop, the devil himself or a panther after them. No, it is stampede for home. They bottleneck to the left, into a barnish kind of shack, all safe, and the boy turns at the door, sees my red face in the gloaming, and shouts the rudest insult. I have tried to persuade myself otherwise, to kid myself; but they hate us, don't they, that's the truth; and honest boys do not pretend.

I hate him for the moment too, it is discouraging. I put my foot down and the Beaver surges. But not for long. I stop altogether to see things beautiful.

Here in the valley the sun has set and we are in the violet time, the interregnum of day to night. Violet may not be the shade but there is that kind of colour in the world. To the north, sunlight climbs past wooded hills and bare, the fulcrumed lever of the sun climbs smoothly to four thousand, to five and six, and metal roofs still shine up there. Then it is gone. Were I able to see the far high snows, which I cannot, they would still be glowing, I think they would.

I wait longer, watching up for the lights of Old Mussoorie where I finished my first leave. Yes, they sprinkle on. This memory is of Mussoorie in the rain. Her father was an assistant medical officer, I think; and the pale sloe-eyed girl and I, we shared a rickshaw home, I know.

But night has come. Out of the violet, out of tired blue, full night has come, and we have come through the Doon to Dehra Dun. Why the Doon and the town were usually spelled differently I do not know, and it does not matter.

Coming though Old Delhi this morning it was sordid awful but now it is worse at Dehra Dun by night. We are not yet in the town itself but squeezing through an outlying bazaar – the miasma and the muck, altercation in a dung-smoke smog, a dingy light or two, questing skeletons of cow and dog. It is crowds and filth and callousness and destitution. It is that fat bania lending sixteen annas at one anna a week, three hundred per cent per annum or more.

Obese stallholders accord me indifferent notice; women glance and look away like startled fawns, quite unappealing; small children stare. I am unwanted and very much alone, but not afraid, they would not hurt a fly.

Then a toddler dashes and I stop with a foot or so to spare. If I had hit that naked eyelid-darkened infant . . . apprehension prickles in my neck and the Beaver and I crawl on and we are through the worst of it.

Ahead there a crossing, an overhead lamp and a policeman. He is helpful but I follow his gestures better than his Hindi torrent. It is simple, though – I see the lights of bigger shops beyond a dark stretch of road. I thank him. He deigns a casual salute and I drive on. Things are better in this helpless hopeless country where every molehill is a mountain unexplored.

We are within shouting distance of those lights but not within their influence when the Beaver packs up altogether. I can see the sheen of tarmac well enough to bring her to a halt on it. It is rather sudden and alarming but I have not lost my head. What I have lost is the Beaver's electricity – the round black button of her starter, her ignition switch, her lights, all dead. It is annoying but not serious. It is the battery connections, stands to reason, the commonest cause of breakdown in this dusty India, this helpless hopeless Hindustan, and I know just what to do. I open her bonnet and, bringing light to the matter with my five-celled torch, I strike the Beaver's battery connections smartly with my spanner. That usually works, but not this time. The next step, using the same adjustable wrench, is to loosen those connections and scrape them shiny with my pocket knife, both the male members of the battery and the female of the leads, and tighten them up again, and nothing happens. I bought a new battery in Delhi. Is it dead totally without warning, surely not, even in this India? I short across the terminals and there is a healthy spark and I have reached the limit of my expertise.

It is depressing. There is naught to do but go for help, seek succour. The sucker must seek succour. That is the caustic corny kind of thing I think of to keep sane.

As I walk toward the lights of Dehra Dun's smart shopping centre, a first touch of cool night comes from the north, bringing a scent, a something from the clean high hills. Wearing my old tweed jacket, my khaki shirt, my whipcord trousers, my sambhar shoes a bit down at heel, I am (in clothing anyway) a dead-ringer for the pukka sahib of days when India was mine. But I am no dead-ringer deep down inside of lonely me. However, I square my shoulders to put a good face on it. First things first, I ignore the ironmongery or hardware with paraffin lanterns and tin plates galore, and go on round the corner. Ah, that is better, I am in luck, a garage and petrol pump, a young man in black coat and clean white dhoti.

Tucking my flashlight between chest and upper arm, I contrive to make the two-handed Hindu greeting, not very gracefully, being restricted by flashlight and lack of practice. As a matter of fact I like the custom, better than that pumping from pudgy office hands that goes on all the time at home. The young man responds likewise and I explain in Hindi, even more halting than usual after a long hard day of it, that my car is broken down along the way.

'So do not bother your head,' he says, 'I shall send skilled mechanics instantly.' He turns to scream orders into the repair shop, and it is true, four men come instantly. I explain the symptoms to him and he translates and some fuses and suitable tools are fetched. 'It is mere nothing,' he says. 'My men will complete repairs in no time flat. So long!'

We set off past the shops and into darkness pierced by my narrow beam. When we reach the car, I surrender our source of light to the mechanics. Keen as mustard, they examine every fuse, trace every circuit verbally and by hand while I hover and shiver and run out of cigarettes. At length silence falls among them, an hour gone by, the car as dead a hulk as ever. It is eight o'clock and suppertime and long past whisky time and I am far from any home. The mechanics are disconsolate. Intervening now, I suggest that we push the car to the garage where at least there is adequate light.

They agree at once and we all push or I steer mostly, walking by the wretched Beaver until these sturdy fellows order me into the driver's seat for better guidance. To cheer myself up I play at being the beauty queen in the float parade, but truth to tell I am not easily cheered. Yet it is some relief to apply the parking brake at the garage.

'At least you are here safe and sound.' The young man in the dhoti listens to his four men and cuts them short with a lordly wave. 'These are not mechanics even worthy of name,' he remarks. 'Merest haberdashers.' He considers me. He is full of thought about me, I know. What thought about me, I do not know.

'I don't think it can be much,' I say. 'A dead short somewhere, that sort of thing.' I turn the key, press the black button a last futile time, and abandon ship. 'A good mechanic . . . '

'It is late,' he says. 'All good mechanics are already in the Land of Nod. Unless . . . '

'Unless?'

'Oh, it is nothing. But there is not the slightest use to kick against the pricks. Now I will take you home to sleep with me, and in the morning, greatly rested, we shall find top-class mechanics.' His eyes are gleaming, in so far as Indian eyes can gleam, the whites so muddy and the browns so turbid, but they gleam.

'It's exceedingly kind of you. But I told my bearer that I would be back by seven and he'll be worried.'

My captor smiles. He is amused by me, I would not quite know why. But I am dogged: 'Couldn't we perhaps find a decent electrician?'

'So be it then. There is one humdinger decent electrician possibly.' He screams to the shadows, and a man runs off. 'Now we should effect introductions in strict Blighty fashion.' He shakes my hand vigorously as we exchange names. Kanji Mal is not his, but that is what I call him, for reasons similar to the Beaver, at which he now stares: 'There is much trouble always with these *Kachcha* vehicles. So while the man is working, I will take you to my house.'

'I wouldn't dream of imposing on you. Isn't there a hotel or somewhere I could wait?' I am very thirsty and very hungry, in that order, and I want to be alone.

'There is no hotel without fleas or other vermin worse. There is my house, or there is also possibly this Doon Club, if you would prefer to go to such a place.'

'I haven't eaten yet, actually.' Not since one o'clock actually, seven hours and a hungry world away. 'So perhaps a quick meal at the club.'

'Come then. It is near. We cannot have you starved to death. So we will take a shortest route. Please shine your torch. This ground is notorious for bad snakes and ditches.'

We set off across a field, meeting no snakes but several ditches. After negotiating another one, he says sadly: 'This Doon Club, I am not so happy for you. There are no good proper meals but only some pieces of fish and little things.'

'Can one get a drink?' There, I have said it, even if good Hindus never touch the stuff and cannot bear its mention.

'Drinks!', he cries. 'Come with me for drinks. Come now at once. We will forget this club.'

We go back across the ditches to the lights we came from, and along a street and, wonder of wonders, into a bar where two men are drinking and eating on stools at the counter. *Do bara peg*. The doubles come. I have been allotted a stool at the end, and Kanji Mal has interposed himself between me and the others. 'Here's cheers, old chap.'

'Good luck,' I say. Thank God for you, I think to my whisky and soda, dropping fast. I ask the barman for a tin of Players, holding out money.

'On my account,' says Kanji Mal, pushing back my hand, indeed holding it affectionately, surely not at my age, but my hand escapes with its rupees.

'Same again, Kanji Mal?'

'Same again with certainty, but all drinks and smokes are on me absolutely, it is my privilege.'

'Do let me share.'

'Even-Stevens is out of question. To us Hindu people, stranger is first duty. Should I be sponging to first duty? *Ec aur bara peg sahib kiwoste*.'

My host and I exchange toasts again. I do not understand it.

'You are not happy, then?'

'Very happy,' I say more heartily than I feel, too heartily. 'Are you?'

'My happiness is yours,' he says.

His is mine and mine is his, he owns me totally. 'You speak English very well.'

'I attended English school Mussoorieside.' He pauses and adds: 'I was at one time solitary Wog.'

That word is abhorrent to the likes of me, but he says it loudly and rather proudly. I think he is being funny at my expense, I am not sure.

He orders us more whisky, but soon I plead for food and we are eating curried mutton balls and rice and Bombay Duck and so on, not excluding red-hot chillis. 'It is to your satisfaction?'

'My utter satisfaction,' I reply. His turn of phrase is catching on to me, or I am catching on to it. 'A feast fit for any king,' I say. Apart from the chillis, which are more dynamite than I can manage much, it is a delicious curry. Kanji Mal eats chillis one by one, alone. I admire him for that, say so, and he is very pleased.

We finish our curry and have stewed mangoes. The two other people at the bar – a Sikh and a Dravidian man with a pock-marked face, a Madrasi probably – wear European clothes and therefore must speak English but they are talking Hindi nineteen to the dozen until a rare silence falls and Kanji Mal, staring at me as usual says, 'I love you.'

Now replete, content, caught in his web and not to be outdone, I say, 'I love you too.' But since I have never said this to fellow-man before, the winsome aspect gets the better of me and I emit a snorting giggle. The Sikh and the Madrasi laugh heartily, so we are now splitting our sides, all buddies together except Kanji Mal whose feelings are hurt.

'You pull my leg,' he reproaches me.

'Certainly not. How could I help loving anyone who is so kind to a perfect stranger?'

'This is not true love,' says Kanji Mal but he is mollified and I have scored a point. 'Now let us have more drinks, some Napoleon brandies would you fancy?'

'Many thanks, but I really must get back.' With all my intake of good food and drink, the Beaver has dwindled into her proper perspective; but she beckons me now, repaired and ready for the road. 'Do let me share the bill.'

'For us the stranger is first duty.' He is adamant.

The garage is not far along the street, and the Beaver is no less dead than she was before. A night watchman reports to Kanji Mal, who says, 'This so-called electrician worked in vain. At best he is useless type. Tomorrow at crack of dawn we will get one crackerjack mechanic. Now we go to my house for sleep together.'

I know that this is a plot. I know that Kanji Mal has from the beginning been fully determined not to have my car repaired until he has had me at his house. All this generosity – is it the prelude to dark crime? I have quite a lot of money in a small way in my pocket. But he does not seem dangerous. In fact he seems physically harmless; and if he loves me more than I am used to, it is purely. He has trapped me, and I resent it, and he reads my thoughts again: 'If my humble home does not meet with your approval I can drive you to the Forest Resthouse, so why not, I will drive you gladly.'

Then either I shall be stranded there alone, or I shall be landed with you there, Sri Kanji Mal, drinking whisky the whole night through. I must yield, and I do so with as good grace as I can muster: 'If you are really sure it won't be a nuisance to put me up, I would be delighted.'

'The sheer delight is mine,' he says, and beams. 'Come then. We take my car.'

It is a small old two-seater. I do not know whether he is rich or poor, a failed BA or a PhD, he has me guessing in every respect, and underway, he says, 'I trust that your rest will not be disturbed. My daughter of two years, she is dangerously ill. It is too bad. She is perhaps sick unto death, who knows?'

I protest with such protest as remains in me that he must not even dream of having me to stay, and . . . But he interrupts me: 'Do not bother your head. There is no smallest danger of infection.'

'I didn't mean that.'

'With us,' he explains patiently, 'the stranger is first duty. If we do not take stranger to our bosom, then what shall we be but mice, not men?'

He wins; he always does, and I sit beside him in the Indian night thinking of my paternal panic if one of our offspring were to be dangerously ill, perhaps sick unto death, who knows, even might be now for all I know. I shiver.

'You are cold, then?'

'No, no – just a little chilly.'

'Yes, it is parky *in media nocte*. Do you like our Indian sweetmeats, they are very warming?' He puts on the brakes and skids to a stop at a vendor's stall. It occurs to me that Kanji Mal's driving may be just a little whiskyfied.

'Might I have a mild one – you know, not too strong and spicy?'

'You shall have mildest possible.' He orders one for me and one for himself; and then adds grandiloquently: 'Gold-leaf, *sahib kiwosti*,' and thinks again, and his command is high and shrill: 'Double gold-leaf.'

I eat my sweetmeat, wrapped not once but twice with purest gold. It tastes very good, and I like gold too. 'Delicious,' I say.

'For you only best with double gold-leaf is good enough; for me most pungent sweetmeat, since I must not advertise fumes of alcohol. My father is most orthodox. You will not drop hints of whisky?'

'Don't worry.' And I think for a moment that we do belong to the same human species.

It is quite a big house. He puts finger to lips and we tiptoe in. He shows me to a room, a charpoy, a warm quilt, a pillow, Hindu paintings round the walls. Bed, a simple thought, a simple close to a confusing day. 'Here is your bathroom, merely Indian style, you will not mind too much?'

'Of course not,' I say.

'There is no other smallest thing you want?'

'Nothing,' I say. I yawn, and he catches it. We yawn and smile like anything, *en rapport*. 'How can I thank you, Kanji Mal?'

'Do not, please. It is first duty. Now sweet dreams!'

I am in bed. There are voices somewhere in the house. Then the wailing of a child, harsh whispers, muffled wailings, silence. Has his first duty to the stranger impelled him to strangle his sick daughter? It is so awful a thought that my charpoy shakes to cruel silent laughter on my first night in a Hindu's house, an orthodox father's house at that. I am quilt-wrapped and cosy. With the eye of my improbable mind I see a giant bamboo clump in the forestry gardens at Dehra Dun. I see it from another time when this was still just my India, the graceful complex of bamboo tree. Then I see the parakeets in needled flight and I remember, shameful memory, that twenty years ago we used to shoot green parakeets for fun because they gave good and difficult sport. I dislike myself and I am going to sleep.

It is after eight o'clock when I awake from my first sound sleep since reaching India. I feel good, and repair to my bathroom, Indian style and slightly strange. I have a shower but cannot shave, which is a bore. Most ex-soldiers have a fixation against stubble and I am no exception.

Kanji Mal arrives to lead me to the breakfast table. He is constrained, much less his loving self than heretofore, perhaps mourning his daughter, I do not like to ask. He slips out and I breakfast hungrily on curds and figs, chupatis, tea. No Hindu could find fault with my eating habits. I am sipping tea and looking at my shopping list when he returns with a small child in his arms.

'Is this your daughter who has been so sick?' I ask. Or is this another one you did not strangle? I do not ask.

'She is quite salubrious again, thanks be to holy God. It was some little tummy trouble, nothing.'

'Oh, I'm so glad.' I smile in a kindly way at her but she clutches at Father and hides her face.

'It is doubtless the ruddiness of your complexion, of which she has never before encountered the like. Now this paper – is it a list of articles you wish to purchase? So let me have it and I will send one man to market for you.'

He takes my list and his daughter away. I hear the barking of orders as I finish my tea. 'Let us go while the day is not too far spent.' He seems as anxious to get me out of his house as he was determined to inveigle me into it. Perhaps I have committed some *bêtise*. More probably he fears to expose me to his orthodox father, or vice-versa.

There is a cold-weather mist about the Doon but it is burning off. Knowing them, I cannot hope that the car will come to life again before afternoon, or come to life at all, a hex on the old bitch.

We round the corner and there she is, ticking over by the petrol pump. 'What was the matter, actually?'

The man explains to Kanji Mal but it is technical language, double-dutch to me. 'Some small thing, actually,' says Kanji Mal. 'Nothing to crackerjack mechanic like this chap.' He does not intend to tell me what actually the small thing is and I do not press the matter. The mechanic has not only mended her electrical guts but has tightened up the steering.

There now arrives panting a man with my shopping list and every item. Kanji Mal checks list against purchases. 'All optimum quality,' he says, 'at wholesale price.'

The prices are extremely low, far less than I would have had to pay myself. 'I'm most grateful,' I say, and so I am, ever sheepish over thank-yous. I pay that modest sum and now ask him for the repair bill.

'It is five rupees *in toto*.'

'But look, Kanji Mal, at least six men have worked at least six hours – that's far too little. Couldn't I add something for their work and overtime?'

He smiles at me. His eyes gleam momentarily. 'No bakhsheesh in these days.' But a telephone rings from his office and he says, 'Excuse, please.' I take advantage of his absence to hand out rupees, which are accepted cheerfully by these trusty fellows.

So all that may be paid is paid and it is time to take leave of my benefactor. 'Thank you,' I say, and make myself do better: 'No one has ever been so kind to me in all my life.'

'It was my pleasure.'

'Will you come and have drinks and dinner with me at the Forest Resthouse?'

'Most gladly,' he says. 'I will send messages as to day, if suitable to you.'

But I have my built-in barometer too and I know that Kanji Mal will never come for drinks and dinner with me at the Forest Resthouse. We shake hands all round and off I drive for temporary home. I have not gone far when a piteous beggar sways before the Beaver. *Bakhsheesh, Sahib. Main Bahut ghareeb admi, Bakhsheesh, Lart Sahib.* I give the very poor man a rupee, untold riches, conscience money for his terrible appearance, for my sins, for strange kindness shown to me.

I drive on. At the outskirts of the town I pass a tonga. The driver is whipping his skeleton pony mercilessly. In the days of my India I would have stopped that. But now I put on speed. Cloud has gathered over the Siwalicks. As I come out of the tunnel rain begins. These are the small winter rains, familiar to me and well loved by me.

Hafeez Husseinuddin was standing at the resthouse. He evinced no surprise whatever that I had taken some seventeen hours to accomplish what I should have done in less than two. And I was inclined to feel that he had not been altogether beside himself with anxiety about my welfare in long absence. He murmured his satisfaction with my purchases, or with those that had been made for me.

Now it is night again. I am comfortable in my sleeping bag and I am listening to jungle noises while a light rain splatters on the roof. Some of the sounds I know, and some of them I do not know, and my thoughts are wandering here and there and back to Kanji Mal, a winner all along the line.

Yet, stranger though I am and must remain, this India is more mine than any India of mine before. Thank you, Kanji Mal. Down in the jungle a tiger roars, as I have been hoping. Near at hand a night wind stirs the sal trees, as I have been expecting.

## SIX

# [1947]

Except for later airport halts on the way round from Australia, that was farewell to India, land of heartless loving muddle, ever dear to me.

But we are back in 1947 and freedom has arrived at last. It is the sort of pipedream that arrives to jerk one to the truth.

That autumn we rented Bolfracks Cottage from the Hutchisons, from the same Jock Hutchison who had given us Tombuie and Mr McKerchar and one salmon soon after I came home from Germany. It was not up the hill but low at the south side of the river Tay and what is in Scotland called *back-lying*. The sun never reached cottage, or fussy little garden, from mid-November until February.

The sun did still shine at us occasionally when we went there in October. We had an outhouse machine to chug away for light. We had a paraffin stove. We had a fireplace. We had our newly-bought small ancient car. That first night in October – it was at about 4 a.m. – the telephone rang and went on ringing. I left wife and warmth and went to answer.

'Hullo.'

'This is the *Daily Express* from Glasgow.'

'Oh, yes?' Still two parts asleep, equal parts bamboozled.

'Is that Bolfracks?'

'Bolfracks Cottage, yes. What is it?'

'It's about the murder, sir. Can you fill us in?'

'Don't know what you're talking about.' Murder. *Murder*?

'There's been a murder at Bolfracks estate, near Aberfeldy, is it?'

'Yes, it is, and I don't know anything about a murder. This is Bolfracks Cottage, I told you, not the Big House.'

'It was at a cottage, the murder was.'

'Not this one,' I said. 'Why don't you ring the main house number or the Aberfeldy police? What kind of a murder anyway?'

'A lady's been murdered, sir.'

'Try someone else,' I said and hung up and thought fast. I did think fast but even in my heyday was a poor dissimulator. Murder, by God, not funny at all, authentic murder too, no doubt of it.'

'What was all that about?'

'Wrong number, someone from Glasgow wanting old Jock.'

'Funny hour to want old Jock from Glasgow. What time is it?'

'Four or so. Go to sleep, darling.'

'Can't. Kick, kick, kicking all the time.'

'Very good sign,' I said; and soon Willa slept again but the night dragged on for me. She was expecting the baby in November, and I had my shotgun.

Before breakfast I went down to the cottage gate, black cars passing, and one stopped, a businesslike policeman.

' . . . we got here yesterday afternoon,' I explained after terse introductions. 'No, no sign of anyone in the night, nothing except that telephone call at four or so. Can you tell me the gist of it?'

It was that the head shepherd's wife had been murdered yesterday at the Tower Cottage up the hill. He was away all day at Perth about the sheep. His wife had been due to clean at the Big House because the Hutchisons were expected, but when she had not arrived by afternoon a gamekeeper went to the Tower Cottage and found her body. Wages for the other shepherds had been at the cottage and they were gone.

'Can I help?'

'Not now, Major, thanks. The murderer is still on the loose. Maybe up yonder.' He jerked his head to the hills to the south. 'Maybe far away by now. The best you can do is to watch after your wife and bairn.'

'Right, Sergeant. I'm here if you want me.'

I was going to start on my unknown writing pilgrimage that very morning but instead I told Willa what I knew, armed myself and prowled the small place – the copse above, the garage beside us, took the car key out. The whole bijou joint thoroughly cased, I took Giles, now a jolly child coming up for two, in his pram, snibbed windows, locked Willa in and went for a short walk along the road by the river.

Just upstream from us was a *haugh*, a low-lying field that flooded in spate but was dry now, a widening between road and river bank. The police prowled that bank, perhaps thinking that he had swum the river, not very likely. But the main search by police and volunteers was in the low wooded hills and on the high bare moors to our south, and master of the situation, by right of a lifetime's knowledge and consummate aplomb, was McKerchar with stalking rifle.

Our small boy and I went perambulating along the side of the wide valley. When last would tragedy like this have struck upon this valley, a respected woman murdered in cold blood for a few pounds of wages? Peering cars kept passing. The ghoul does lurk in all humanity.

My police sergeant's car was tucked in along the road, a stern sergeant with a row of campaign medals.

'Move on, please,' he said to passing cars, ignoring questions. Good doctors are hardened, yet they say it kindly. Good policemen are impassive and polite until. The traffic moved on and there was a lull.

'You're a braw wee laddie,' he said to Giles. 'What's his name, Major?'

'Giles,' I said.

'Hullo, Giles,' he said. 'Is Giles a Scotsman, Major?'

'Ay, he's a Scotsman, Sergeant, Scotch as you are.' Not quite true, he was on both sides totally half Irish, but no matter.

'Here's tae us,' said the friendly sergeant.

'Wha's like us. I think we'll go back now. Say ta-ta to the Sergeant, Giles.'

'Ta-ta,' Giles said, not a bit shy of him.

'Keep to the right, against the traffic. I doubt he's over the hills and far away by now. But ca'canny, Major, a day or two.'

'I will,' I said.

'Nice man,' Giles said, going back, going home, I suppose you could call it, but that cottage never was home for me.

'Nice to you,' I said. 'He wouldn't be nice to me if I was bad.' And Giles laughed like anything.

Archibald Percival Wavell, F.M.

At the Viceroy's House, New Delhi
*Seated:* Field Marshal Wavell, General Sir Arthur Wauchope
*Standing between Black Watch pipers, left to right:* Nigel Noble, Archie John Wavell, D.H.W., Jack Monteith, Freddy Barnaby-Atkins

The Mountbattens with Jawaharlal Nehru at Mashobna, 1947

D.H.W. in the Arctic, 1956

I unlocked my wife, kept my eyes open for a day or two, and that was the end of factual that.

Some weeks later the murderer was caught in Aberdeen. He was a Polish soldier and the story went that he had been told by a comrade of a tower with hidden treasure. The comrade meant a treasure in a tower at Taymouth Castle, that enormous seat of the Breadalbanes, now a convalescent home for Polish soldiers. But another tower was visible, the Tower Cottage, we could see it.

But now to work, free as air to work – free of nannies, schoolmasters, parents, COs, Your Excellencies, shells, Germans, hunger, Staff Colleges and Viceroys, free at last to be a slave all on my lonesome. Freedom, just you try it, love it, hate it and yourself, and want no other non-existent thing.

It was to be fiction, not to fall plumb into the lap but striven after. My first step was to take a correspondence course, which I gulped down in short order. I knew already, it was in me then for always, that there is no teaching of that thing. No one can teach you to bring fancied character to life, nor to write dialogue, nor to deny yourself digression's trap, nor to learn the poetry of the right word true, nor to stick it out to the hard sharp end, humble, arrogant, complete. I never did learn to do all these things. I aspired to them and sometimes nearly won. But they were in me.

From that correspondence course I learned basic things, the minor complexities of specialized punctuation, the major importance of begin and plot and end. Let us forget the middle everyone goes on about. Most of all I came to learn, and not from a correspondence course, that plot springs from character. It was Stuart Rose of the *Saturday Evening Post* who first put into words for me what I must have known instinctively already, with two books done before he said it. I took that course, and from it what my demon held worth absorbing.

I wrote and wrote. All that winter I wrote frightful tripe, not quite all of it tripe, a few hundred thousand words written with the absolutely wrong intent of being bought; and sometimes, once in a while, with the intent of truth.

They went out to most magazines in the British Isles, a quarto envelope; inside, a half-sized stamped addressed envelope to me. And they all came back, once or twice (once even from *Chambers*

*Journal*, a distinguished magazine) with a few words of encouragement: *not this, but try us again*. The stories were awful and I began to learn what I could and could not do. I could do action, that I knew.

Once a week or so that winter, the postman came with my brown envelope and one time he said, the decent Postie said 'It must cost ye an awfy puckle stamps.'

An awful lot of stamps, it did. 'Ay,' I said, not in the least down-hearted, disappointed, yes. 'Ay, yon's the truth of it.'

My demon raged but only in that. Common fanaticism is alien to me, as alien as any other bloody ism, communism, fascism, narcissism, evangelism, or what-have-you, with an exception that does momentarily occur: it is witticism. I do occasionally, if in the mood, say funny things, on the spur of the moment only. Trying to be funny is no laboured use to me.

That was every morning, six days a week and often seven; and in the evenings, teatime before whisky-time, I would work out tomorrow's session of the current *magnum opus*. Already I was into the routine from which I never deviated in working time in all the years.

But that was no more than half-waking life, also broken into during working hours by thoughts about Willa and the baby. Her time was near. The sun no longer even peeped upon us over yonder hill and I wore my flying suit, wartime surplus bought to fend off the chill. It was so damned cold, forty degrees in that living room and that armchair.

In the afternoons Willa and Giles and I went for toddles, mostly on the flat haugh below us. Or I would stuff him into my old army pack and we would climb the hill, Giles very happy saying birds' names after me, I happy enough, writing forgotten, totally forgotten unless in the last stages of a job, up through the twisted hill birches and by the poor hill farms, as deprived of sun as we ourselves, and on to the beginnings of the heather hill. How sweet life is with a beloved child.

It was coming to that point when any day or hour or minute we must take off for Aberfeldy cottage hospital, two miles away, and the car battery was on the blink. From about the fifteenth night of November on I got up at three-hour intervals to start the thing. If not totally chilled, it would grind and go. Down through the frigid night with torch to dinky garage, would she start? Too long an interval of sleep and she was dead as mutton. It was worrying, and about things near and dear I am a frightful worrier. Midwife D. H. Walker, God, the thought. Was I too broke or too mean to buy a new battery? That is not like me. They were still hard times, the right battery not available, it must have been.

Meanwhile I fussed, and it rained and went on raining. Writing – what was writing?

I met Dr Swanson at the garden gate. He was our doctor, our obstetrician, he was to be.

Should I move Willa to the hospital now?, I asked him. He looked at me. His glare was icy, another fusspot softy father in the making. His gateside or bedside manner was anything but kindly, more like the bobby, cop, policeman I had told Giles to his great amusement who would be bad to me if I was bad. Dr Swanson said gruffly, 'Keep your hair on.'

Wonderful country doctor, everyone said, and so he was. In the wee small hours of November the 22nd, Willa said: 'We'd better go,' totally calm and packed up and ready, my woman, wife, for better or for worse, to love and to cherish, to obey and to neglect.

I had ventured out in the rain each hour that night to start the bloody little thing. It started like a bomb and we were off, some woman in to look after Giles.

'We'd better hurry,' the wife, ex-commander of seventeen thousand women remarked to the retired short major, and it poured with rain.

'Go home,' ordered Dr Swanson. 'An hour or so yet. I'll telephone. Dinna fash yersel,' he added, with some indulgence now. *Don't worry.*

I went home and went walking in the rain, and went down across the haugh which was flooded at the farther end where the right bank of the river Tay was lowest. But I heard a melody of calls, a trumpeting that grew, and the great white birds were circling low. They circled me alone. They were the whoopers, the true wild swans of wilder places, unafraid. They splashed in to land on the shallow water of the haugh, alone with me, I alone with them, and I went home.

'It's a boy you have,' said Dr Swanson by telephone. 'And they're both just fine. You can come when you want.'

One and one make two, Had I wanted a girl? Later it was to be two and two, making four and a first boy lost. A girl to spoil and to make fun of me – I would have loved to have a daughter, but we made four more boys and would not swap them. A girl would have been a comfort to Willa too, so many damned reticent males without relief. *Quant à moi* (I am writing in France now) I would have fussed my head off about a daughter out with loathsome lustful youths.

He was christened in the Presbyterian church at Kenmore where the long loch ends and the river begins, beyond McKerchar, below Tombuie. He was christened Barclay James after my young brother, after Willa's elder brother who had died in boyhood.

I was learning to write. You cannot be taught the things that I have mentioned but there is much to learn, and indeed to lose along the way as the mind dulls and the store runs out of stock, the inventory depletes.

We were soon *en famille* again, with a monthly nurse, a *nurse from the month* they call it or her, of whom I remember nothing except that she said disapprovingly that there were rats, and I said nonsense and saw one on the bird-table. Or do I remember a *nasty repeat*, catchwords for the afterburp?

Small babies bore me. I like them when they smile at me, self-love, of course. As for the rat, I soon murdered it.

That cottage was fearful cold in my flying suit. People came to see us and we made forays to Rankeillour to show off the endearing Giles and the second Barkie to his grandparents.

Rankeillour had a huge furnace in the nether regions tended by Drummond, the forester, and kept at precisely 61 degrees by behest of Harry Giles Walker, elder statesman now, fully retired to prowl his ditches, quite resigned about his second son's predilection for parlour socialism, indeed pondering a bit himself but a good deal bothered about the wayward one's intentions. Accustomed as we were to huddling for warmth, we found the central heating at 61 degrees Fahrenheit drily intolerable.

There was a shadow now on home. It was the change that was

happening to my mother, who spoke ill of no one, or almost no one, an angelic woman, and I mean that adjective, angelic all her life. But she was no longer quite herself, still gentle, but mildly carpy in comment now and then. Her mind was gradually being deprived of the strength that blood may bring. She had one companion, then another, bitches both of them who gave her nips of gin. All she had ever drunk before was a health wine called Wincarnis. I have to write of this slow eclipse, and have no more to write.

Meanwhile, my elder brother Willie had succeeded to the chairmanship of Jute Industries, the conglomerate successors to Harry Walker and Sons, and to the Coxes and other big jute family firms. Willie had the larger view of business which Father and Barks both lacked. Willie was a top-quality executive, admirable in labour relations, able, unconceited, a thoroughly decent chap to boot and a materialist in all things. We have nothing in common and never have had. I do not think that he ever read a novel, except perhaps possibly (I do not know) my small book *Geordie* out of familial piety. We played golf together and shot together and could talk of nothing but the practical together. As I have said, he and Bluebell were always most generous to me. I think he quite liked me until the bottle grew on me; but that was much later; and now again we may share affection.

The sun shone again on Bolfracks Cottage and its tidy garden. People came to see us. Colin Mackenzie, of course, the impregnable one. And Bill Bradford who had endured near-miss shells with me on that last day of fighting. Bill borrowed my grey top hat. I could not envisage myself ever wearing a grey top hat again. It was a relic of red carpet days. Anyway, Bill borrowed it. When I asked him about my grey topper a few years after that, he simply laughed and expropriated that top hat. Archie John Wavell came to stay, still absorbed with his stupid Army School of Education of which his father and I shared a very dim view, which I never dared to express to him, nor perhaps did his father.

He was telephoning London one morning when outside the window beside him, Giles fell out to dangle inverted by harness from his pram. Archie John went to do a thoroughly inefficient job of undangling Giles while the telephone dangled on, to which he ultimately returned to continue an expensive conversation. I liked him just as much as I liked his father. He was a little younger than me, and in the ways of the world perhaps much younger to me than I was younger to his father.

Meanwhile, the writing on and on, the Postie's knock with another one, until the first miracle occurred. *Harper's Bazaar* bought a story for eight guineas. I was saleable. I was a pro. I was perhaps happier at that moment than in all my writing life to be. It took me a week to write, a week to churn out, how easy it would be, eight badly-needed guineas a week to come, and much much more when due fame arrived. It was so simple. My first triumph was the beginning of so much to come. But not another single penny came. A few words added to the rejection slip did sometimes mention a paper shortage, and I was thinking.

Meanwhile, apart from the writing life which became much the worse for once being better, two things of importance happened.

The first one was that the Bolfracks gardener, who came for an hour or two each week, and his wife who burned the toast and cooked a bit, quite a comely woman, childless, took a hate on us. We, as smartly, took a hate on them. It was her mostly, I think, in cahoots with the monthly nurse, and two against one in the women's league in an isolated place are lethal, even against Willa, who is the toughest nut in the distaff business. I am not being prideful when I say that no one else who ever worked for us took a vindictive hate on us. He or she would not have lasted if he or she had. We were amiable and reasonable enough and greatly experienced in dealing with people, we were what we were, not putting on the dog. They had us trapped.

But the nurse soon went, leaving two against two, leaving us slightly hamstrung because of the Hutchisons who thought the world of their paragon gardener and his wife and had been so good and generous to us. Was she jealous of babies? God knows. Did she work on her ratty husband in the long winter nights? Perhaps. I disliked them so much that, for the only time in my adult existence, I invited him to accompany me round the back beside the electricity-engine and I said: 'Do you want it, or don't you?' He did not, and became almost civil thereafter. Even McKerchar chose once to volunteer about the gardener's wife:

'An exceptionally fine woman.' I remember those words precisely, blandly said without preliminary.

He was himself an exceptionally fine-looking old boffer which might have had something to do with it, but that is a bait you never rise to.

'Oh, yes,' I said, adding a Wavellish grunt to shut him up.

That was the hateful thing for us peace-lovers, except love-hating with one another from time to time. Then the wonderful occurred. Her name was Helen MacGregor, granddaughter of the registrar of Aberfeldy who wrote Barkie's birth certificate. She was a short, highland-faced, taciturn, squarish girl. We came to call her Ella, and we have loved her ever since.

One afternoon when we all were out, the paraffin heater in the children's room went berserk, every wall, the ceiling, the cots soot-blackened. Ella said not a word but laughed and got down to it with Willa and scrubbed the whole small place clean while I was elegant baby-sitter in the living room.

But all was not embryo slavery in the winter days. I took times off to go hind-shooting with McKerchar. We went high in fine weather and in foul, and then low as snow drove the beasts down the bare wild hills as the rut was ending and the wasted sperm still lay about the ground, the mad lust of the stags now over. The hind population must be kept in bounds, the worthless young stags – switches, they were called – once with bad antlers, always so, each spring to be dropped and grow another set in velvet and to harden up. McKerchar and I were mates up there. I was *Major* to him but never the third person now. The weather was capricious, fine, cold, sometimes hellish in the blizzards as I learned the hill from him, as the snow buntings sometimes, rarely, flew by us in small parties on the hills. We crouched below rocks for me to have a smoke. He showed me the bare flat ledge, favourite perching place for the noble peregrine, and on it a bare unbaited trap. I did not object aloud to what appalled me. It was his job to do that cruel thing. It was John Keiller's job, my good old friend, to set traps for weasels and stoats in the dry stone dikes of Rankeillour in the Lowlands. But the rare peregine falcon was worse. McKerchar was a Highlander in his element. I was a common Lowlander, although not quite, because in among us were the Neishes – my grandfather was named William Neish Walker – who are a sept of the MacGregors, who are a clan within the clan of Ross. So Ella MacGregor and I might have been senior and junior cousins a hundred years or two or three ago.

McKerchar did ask me now about my prison days, and he taught me many things as immediate days grew shorter with the bitter wind. But these were occasional times when we stalked, selected, killed, gralloched and dragged the dead beast to a handy place for the pony man. Mostly I wrote my head off.

I was hatching a plot to take Willa back where she did not want to go. Ever since she first came to Scotland she had loved my country beyond her own. But just as I longed to write decently, so did I long for her great empty land, from Ernest Thompson Seton onwards it had been my land in my wandering mind. I did not say a word to her until I produced the emigration papers and said:

'Canada, that's where we're going.'

There were sound excuses for an aspiring writer to go on about – abundant paper, markets and so on. Father protested too. He wasted no time in finding out that I would be allowed a bare £5000 capital to last me four years, added to the £154 annual pension from His Majesty, regular officer retired with seventeen years' service, not a princely sum but I did not blame our plain and princely King. It was impossible, *with a nanny too*. 'You can't do it, David.'

'Yes, I can, Father. That's what we're going to do and you're going to come and stay with us.' That idea did spark his eye, a romantic, my father, dour and forbidding as he might appear. He had been abroad in his youth, at Heidelberg University and once to Petrograd; and in between the wars he and Mamma went on Mediterranean cruises. I think that all his life he pined for the derring-do that he never did. But what he did do in the summer before he died was come to stay with us in Canada.

The Field Marshal and I exchanged letters during that winter. He was pleased with me for doing what I meant to do. Little did he know, and not for my bottom non-existent dollar would I have shown him those terrible effusions.

But he wrote in the spring to say that he was coming up to Scotland to play golf, and what about it? He did not need to ask.

We could play golf at what had remained my one and only club, the Royal and Ancient, of which I am a very senior member, even senior to Willie who later I watched whip the ball round his neck as he played himself in as captain of the Royal and Ancient, a bad shot for a fair good golfer, bad luck, Willie. The most pessimistic caddie got the ball and the golden sovereign.

The Field Marshal and I played on the Old Course which is really and truly the only course for us, although the New Course is good too, without appeal. The former favours hookers of the golfing variety, the latter slicers, and it was on the New Course that I once in my life (that was in 1938) played well, beating David Blair in an Army competition at about the twentieth hole. I should mention with suitable modesty that David Blair captained the British Walker Cup team after the war. He was not yet good when I beat him, and I was not bad that day, 74, I think.

Though Wavell's partial retirement was no real retirement – a host of honours, duties and engagements were piled upon him – he no longer bore the weight of great responsibility and I think that his last years were very happy ones. He missed his early morning rides at Delhi but he did not miss the panoply and pomp, which I think he had endured rather than enjoyed. So the erstwhile proconsul bought his own bus ticket and played much better golf. The man who beat me usually at the Royal and Ancient was precisely the same person, if more carefree, as the man I used to beat in Delhi. Later in 1948 he wrote: 'I played rather well but have always had one disastrous hole in competitions. I had the big handicap prize at the Senior Golfing Society at my mercy, and I only wanted two fives at the last two holes for a net 72 (a net 74 won), but took seven and eight.' No alibis, you will observe.

He probably liked golf for the exercise, the skill, the competition, the companionship, the pitfalls, the banter of gamesmanship. But he did not bother to analyse his likes; nor his dislikes, for the matter of that. If he considered someone pompous, bogus or a bore, he said so in private with bluff acerbity and forgot him (or her).

Willa has a recollection of those days. She and one boy of two years and one of six months and one field marshal were at the members' parking place outside the Royal and Ancient clubhouse. Her arms were occupied with children and he was manfully struggling to put our folding pram into the back of our decrepit car.

'Sorry, Willa,' he said. 'I'm hopeless at this kind of thing.' He was, too. The last time she had seen him he was flanked by the splendour of the Viceroy's bodyguard, handing over India to his successor.

We went once or twice to lunch with my sister, Huldah Rennie, who had spent the long war at St Andrews and lived on there after Thomas was killed. The old boy was shy a bit and talked a bit (just as he later did one day at Rankeillour), and ever afterwards Huldah had a name for him: *The dear Lord* she called Field Marshal the Earl Wavell of Cyrenaica. He was the dear Lord too, among all the things that he was.

We were playing the seventeenth, the Road Hole, over the railway sheds if you were so bold, and I was, playing well that day, one up. He took the safer left-hand route, not having my distance, and when we met up again on the fairway I told him about Archie John and Giles dangling from his pram and the trunk call telephone dangling, forgotten while horrified Archie John did his bungling best to go to the rescue. It was after the folding pram incident at the clubhouse.

'About prams at least, you're totally hopeless, both of you,' I said.

The old boy bust himself with laughter, he bent over double and positively cackled and dropped his eye-glass which I retrieved. It was the only time I ever saw and heard him cackle.

I lay up just short in two, had an easy pitch and muffed it, over on to that road, quite hopeless, and it was all square.

At the eighteenth he hit a good one but I had outdriven him, over the road and on a bit, and then a pitch and run with my number four to land before the dip of the Valley of Sin, run through it and up to lie six foot from the pin. My opponent was short and missed his putt and I put mine in for a three. I pipped him. The warrior grunted a compliment.

'Thank you,' he said. 'Too damned good for me today.'

Once Wavell days were over my opinions about golf were

ambivalent – the best safe game in the world, or a waste of time potting at a small white ball? Anyway, he paid for my gin and tonic, and we went to take lunch off Huldah.

'In my opinion,' he had said about Charles Rankin, 'Charles suffers more from a wounded ego than a broken heart.'

'In my opinion,' her dear Lord said to her, 'David's venture to Canada is the sort of Mad Hatter's tea party that appeals to me.'

There, I had his blessing, and everyone else, which was everyone else, stopped muttering darkly about the Mad Hatter.

We paid up in sterling for the Atlantic, for CPR tickets, even meals, all the way across to Vancouver, British Columbia. Willa needed nothing but her passport. I needed the two boys on mine and I endured every kind of bureaucratic rigmarole, and so did Ella MacGregor. We spent our last night in Liverpool at the Adelphi, which Jack Fawcus used to beat up after riding in the National.

We slept at that renowned hotel and on sailing day Allan Giles Walker woke up dead lame. He had no temperature. His right leg would no more than let him hobble and fall down and hobble, so intolerably precious to us, what did Canada matter, or anything matter?

The hotel doctor, a short grave man, came at once and examined him and did not know. Had he been exposed to polio, the dreaded infantile paralysis? We said that to the best of our knowledge not. In the end the doctor bore part of it for us.

'Go,' he said, 'if the ship's doctor will let you go.'

The ship's doctor asked the same question, and let us go with our burden of anxiety.

SEVEN

# In 1948

We sailed in June 1948 in a Duchess liner of Canadian Pacific Steamships. The greatest travel system on earth, the CPR could still rightly call itself, but not for much longer. Both Empress ships were sunk in the war and had not been replaced. The rot of a proud institution was beginning.

It was rough all the way across, and we kept Giles in bed until calmer waters. But his leg was improving. *Periosteomyelitis*, the ship's doctor diagnosed. That difficult name, he explained, meant a swelling or infection of the bone sheath. It was yielding to antibiotics and we should not worry.

We did worry, though, perhaps the suddennes of it the worst thing for us. But by the time we had taken on a pilot at Father Point and were steaming up the narrowing seas of the estuary for a brief stop at Quebec, Giles limped much less badly.

And so to Montreal on June the ninth, and soon to a specialist who confirmed that diagnosis and prescribed a pair of boots until the patient was entirely cured.

We had planned and paid right through to Vancouver but our own immediate plans had changed, or had been changed for us. Every summer all her life, Willa's family had moved from home in the sticky heat of Montreal to the cooler Maritimes, and always to St Andrews in New Brunswick. Her mother was a Smith, a notable seafaring family from Saint John, sixty miles east along the coast. Hence, the Magees went to the summer resort of St Andrews, at which they had now rented us a house for three months.

Our tickets west would still be valid later. Meanwhile, the prospect of a rent-free summer was most appealing, as was the chance to see Willa's family again.

Giles had altogether lost his limp but we still kept the boots on him and did not let him run about or play with his first cousin, Peter Breese, who was a lively boy. He did seem all right, though, and we decided to ask Dr O'Neill's opinion.

Dr O'Neill was a rough and ready country doctor, and much more than that. He had a continental reputation as a diagnostician. People came from all over North America to learn the best or worst from Doc O'Neill. He examined Giles's leg and said: 'There's nothing wrong with him now. Take those darned boots off and let him run.'

'But, Doc,' Willa said, 'you should have seen him – he couldn't even stand, and that's not even three weeks ago.'

'Why not get a second opinion? Goldbloom is here at the hotel. Do you happen to know him?'

'Yes, I do,' Willa said. So she wrote a note to Dr Goldbloom, one of the most renowned pediatricians in eastern Canada, staying at the Algonquin hotel. He agreed to come, provided that medical ethics were observed and the referral came from Dr O'Neill, who should also be present.

That was arranged, and where the Doc had needed a couple of minutes to make up his mind the famous pediatrician took at least twenty over a meticulous examination.

'You may run off,' he said to the patient. 'I mean run, run, run.'

But Giles walked, and limped and forgot to limp.

'I entirely concur with Dr O'Neill. Your son is cured. But in my opinion you have impeded that recovery.' He then, with utmost gravity, delivered the punch: 'In my opinion you are both suffering from a guilt complex.'

Dr O'Neill did not bat an eye except for a hint of a wink, or was it? But two days later he met Willa and enquired bluffly after her guilt complex. If, instead of the fashionable gobbledigook, Goldbloom had said that by too much cossetting we had made Giles worry about himself, he would have been dead right and no doubt that was what he meant. But guilt, with complex added, in common people's understanding of those words, was a bit much.

We settled in to the house on Montague Street and I settled down forthwith to get on with the writing struggle. A worse thing happened. I did not pour out the stuff; I was stuck altogether for anything to write. I had written enough by now to know that dramatic action was a thing I could do well. But what dramatic action when there is none to find? Four hours each morning tucked away upstairs in a corner room while the family went out to spare the author from disturbance and to swim at Katy's Cove, a fashionable bathing beach where the cold Fundy water was trapped to make it warm. At the end of the morning, a sheet of paper with a few fruitless words on it.

St Andrews was an unusual place, a small town of some fifteen hundred people, first settled late in the eighteenth century by those who were true to King George III, the United Empire Loyalists. It had remained more or less static in population since early days, first as a garrison town and then, at the beginning of this century, it became a summer resort for the builders of the CPR, the Van Hornes and the Shaughnessys. They led the way, making themselves a spur railway to it. After them came many others of the affluent, from Upper Canada and the United States. Their houses along the hill were capacious mansions, always called summer cottages.

One might think that, wealth being the power it is (and nowhere more absurdly worshipped than in North America), the town would be a playground for the rich – to be preyed upon and slumbered from in their winter absence. A little more examination, however, would reveal that St Andrews was far more complex than that, for it had four or five distinct elements of population. First, the indigenous merchants and working men and women, whose chief means of livelihood did come from the summer people; second, the sardine or herring fishermen, an independent tribe who had nothing whatever to do with summer influxes, except of fish. Third, there was the Marine Biological Station, the scientists of which were another group apart, serving the town in many ways yet not accepted as real St Andrews people. Fourth, there were the tourists who drove in to stay there overnight, spend little, and push on to Nova Scotia. Fifth, an increasing number of city people who came to retire at the sweet little place – *if only the world could be more like St Andrews*, what I call the St Andrews Drool – but most of them found our long, capricious winters intolerable and took off to Florida for respite.

I suppose that no other small town in the world has accepted so much largesse from benefactors as has St Andrews and yet has retained its self-respect. No one in the place kow-tows. St Andrews has always treated me the same whether gloomy with a book on my back or in more cheerful mood. And I am grateful.

But I was writing about not being able to write. If the Mad Hatter had not been quite so mad, I would have given it up. My brother Willie wrote to offer me the well-paid chairmanship of the Jute Industries subsidiary in New York City. *No, thank you very much, I'm just getting started properly with writing.* It was a flat lie. I was not getting started with anything workwise at all. Even Willa, who had never questioned my gift and purpose, not for one moment, said, the fruitless summer nearly gone: 'Darling, what *are* we going to do?'

'It'll be all right,' I said. 'It's coming,' when it was not.

In spare time in the afternoons – the idea of more than four writing hours at a stretch was, and has remained, impossible for me – I learned the trees and birds, and got to know Willa's family better. Her father was a most respected and kindly man, ever a little distance between us. There were two people especially. First, there was her mother, not unlike my own mother in her selflessness, but in the best sense much more worldly. She was my favourite woman just as, when he came over each summer to stay with us, she became John Elphinstone's favourite woman. The second one was Willa's sister, Nora, who had been married soon after us in 1939 to William Breese. Nora was marvellously casual and light-hearted in those days, slave to the egregious William.

He was American, his father having been killed serving in the British Army, the Horse Guards or Blues, in the First World War. William's mother (most people called him Bill, or Billy but I have usually called him William) took him with her on a cosmopolitan round of the best hotels. He grew up to be a rare man with rare causes, sometimes rarer in his ways than I could comfortably stomach, but an endearing man too when not infuriating.

William was a gangling six-foot-four, with a brilliant eye for a ball, a Wimbledon tennis player. The only times that I ever obeyed him explictly and altogether were when, two years in succession, we nearly won the St Andrews doubles championship. I was a fairly good squash player and exceedingly nimble, a dirty cutter of the ball at tennis. I did exactly what he ordered me to do by secret signs – two fingers in the left-hand trouser pocket meant cross over at the net, that sort of thing. We got on entirely on the tennis court, and mostly, in a weird way, off it.

But this is not about William Lawrence Breese, it is about my life and the beginning of a job found late. We were broke and getting broker, and I had just decided that I would have to give up drinking whisky when the idea for a story came. It was a story about a man marooned on a haugh, a low-lying field beside a river, suddenly flooded by the break of an ice-dam further up. That story came quite easily and, being me, I sent it off to disappear within the intestines of the *Atlantic Monthly*, the most distinguished magazine in the United States.

September came and Labour Day, the first Monday in that month, when the summer colony, habitually as by rote, took off. Our lease was finished. We should be on our way to destitution in British Columbia. But something more arrived.

I got the idea for a novel, or three ideas, one on one on one, and all indirectly from before. The first was a young man who killed a handsome woman by mistake in heedless passion. He fled across the bare hills in winter. I had learned the bare hills in winter with McKerchar. Much more important, I had learned what it was to be the hunted one. The name for my hot-headed young man was Tam Diamond. It was the right name for him and it came to me by chance from years before at Lebong, down the hill below Darjeeling.

A private soldier whose name was Diamond (I don't remember his other name) was a bad hat with an ungovernable temper. He was standing at attention, bare-headed, before his commanding officer, charged with some serious offence again. Losing that temper, he committed the unforgivable and tipped his commanding officer's table over on him, ink and all.

It was a general court-martial and I was deputed to defend Private Diamond. I wrestled with the *Manual of Military Law*, and went to see him in his cell. He was a blue-eyed, fair-headed man, an honest-seeming man, and I took a liking to him, as I think he did to me.

At Strathcroix, with the coast of Maine beyond, mid-1950s
*Left to right:* Barclay, Willa, Giles, David, Julian and D.H.W.

Strathcroix 1983

Willa and D.H.W. at the old surface well, Strathcroix

'But you did it, Diamond,' I said, meaning that upset table, 'and I don't see how I can possibly get you off.'

'I know, sir,' he said, well-spoken and resigned. 'Don't worry, sir.'

The deed was not in question, but some hearsay evidence was. A man in the next cell swore that Diamond had spoken of what he would do later to the fucking bastard's table. I protested and was over-ruled. It really made no difference as to guilt, but hearsay *fucking bastard* as a description of his commanding officer did not help and Diamond got three years.

So I made the Tam Diamond of my novel such a man as the real Diamond might or might not have been, a straight chap with rage to explode in him.

Diamond chopped wood for the bowl of soup the young woman gave him on his way, and then it happened, not in temper but in passion, and she fell to hit the back of her head on the pointed knob of the coal-box. No jury would have found Diamond guilty of murder. But it was not the rope that my man Diamond feared. He could not endure the certain prospect of a cell, shut away from the open world that he loved.

So Diamond fled to be hunted across the Scottish Highlands to an inevitable finish. I knew personally, intimately, what I wrote about, except the killing and the cold of night. He was Diamond to me, towards the end he was Tam to me, poor Tam who did not yield.

It was a simple story, interwoven. I called it *The Storm and the Silence*, and typed it up on the old Remington portable which I had bought in Delhi soon after I first reached India in 1932. Willa read my story and loved it and cried about it. She has been the first reader of everything that I have written.

The job was done while other things had happened and not happened. The fall colours came and went. Before the Breeses left, William wrote to two of his Harvard contemporaries, Paul Brooks and Craig Wylie, who both worked as editors at Houghton Mifflin, to say that he had a brother-in-law who was writing a novel and would they consider looking at it? Houghton Mifflin are among the leading publishers in the United States. This was a great service for which I remain grateful to William Breese.

Classmates are classmates, especially, it seems to me, at Harvard. Most importantly, it meant that the manuscript was assured of a reading by an editor, and not allotted, like the thousands of unsolicited manuscripts, to a preliminary reader.

So that happened and I wrote it fast. A minor thing that had not happened had been any word from the *Atlantic Monthly* about my story of the flood. But Houghton Mifflin and the *Atlantic Monthly* were both in Boston. I must therefore descend on Boston.

By then we still had enough to pay Ella's wages and to feed ourselves, but the first year's £1250 were disappearing fast. I had to get there. How to get there?

'Take the Greyhound bus,' Willa said hardly. 'It costs half as much.' I was about to take that bus when rain began in earnest. At St Andrews-primeval there were various streams running down to the sea. They were underground streams by now, perhaps always so, but one crossed below Montague Street. Our cellar, never quite dry, was flooding. The water rose to exterminate our coal-fired furnace. I waded about, up to my gum-boot knees, could find no outlet to open up and called for help to Mel Bartlett, father, and Herman Bartlett, son, whose plumbing shop was just up the street from us. They said that the only hope was a sump-pump.

That was embarrassing because our absentee landlady was Miss Edith Jones, a retired English nanny of limited means who could ill afford an expensive sump-pump that ran twenty-four noisy hours a day to keep an underground river within bounds. It was a thoroughly unsound remedy, even I knew that.

But poor Miss Jones yielded and we got our sump-pump at the expense of a higher rent, which we now paid. It did occur to me that to be wading knee-deep in a flood boded ill for my flooding story.

I caught the bus on election eve, November the 1st 1948, and rode the night through to Boston where I carried my battered aluminium suitcase from the bus terminal and booked myself into the Statler hotel at five dollars *per diem*.

The first thing was that story, a hopeless quest, but I had come a long way to take on any hopeless quest and I telephoned the *Atlantic Monthly*, asked for an editor, got a helpful girl and explained myself.

'Poor you,' she said. 'All that way on a bus. The story's title, could you tell me again?'

'*My Strong Lambs*,' I said, and told her when I had sent it. Not a good title I had come to think.

'Can I reach you anywhere, say, in about two hours' time? It's probably hopeless but one never knows.'

I gave her the Statler number and my room, a haven of luxury after that bus.

'If you could make it in two hours or so, I think I'll have a lovely sleep.'

She laughed and said, 'What part of England are you from?'

'I'm not. I'm from Scotland.'

'Oh,' she said. 'Scotland. That's something else again. Good-bye.'

It was not like me at all, bold and brash, and what the hell. I slept with dreams of flooded haughs and basements and the telephone rang.

'Mr Walker?'

'Me,' I said.

'Mr Weeks has a very busy day but he could spare you five minutes if you could come right now.'

'Mr Weeks?'

'Yes,' she said. 'Editor.'

'Can you tell me the way?'

'It's easy, no distance . . . '

'Coming,' I said. 'Thank you more than I can say.'

I took my black brief case, which my mother had given me to go with me on my first travels. It is here beside me at the end of the morning in a French hotel. In it on that other morning were two copies, original and carbon, of *The Storm and the Silence*, no doubts about that title, also the carbon copy of *My Strong Lambs*, not happy about that title.

I walked up the one-sided street – on my right a pleasing expanse of park, on my left the buildings of the street, and into the modest *Atlantic Monthly* office. Was it possible that an *editor* was actually fitting *me* into his very busy day? I was told that Mr Weeks had visitors in his office but would be down in a minute and would I please wait in the ante-room?

Soon a man's voice spoke with the nonchalance of command.

'Yes, Mr Weeks,' the girl out there said. He must be some senior kind of editor, the slim man who came in, the typed manuscript of my story in his hand.

'We like your story,' he said, after brief preliminaries. 'It reads as if you know that country.'

'Yes,' I said. 'My own.'

'Our price is $250,' he said. 'All right?'

'Very much so,' I said. I make him out to be abrupt but he was not. He was possibly a little more suave than my kind of man. I do not know, because I never saw Mr Weeks again except from a distance at a funeral long after that, still lean-faced with the marks of the years.

'Have you written much else?'

'Just a novel. I had an introduction to Houghton Mifflin and I'm on my way to them with it.'

'Good luck, then,' he said. 'And if they don't want it, you might let us have a look. We and Little, Brown are together, you know.'

I knew Houghton Mifflin and Little, Brown, the two Boston publishers, and I knew the famous *Atlantic Monthly*, but not of the link.

'Well, of course,' I said. 'Thank you very much, Mr Weeks.'

He came to the door with me and pointed across the park. 'Straight up to the top, turn right down that short one, Two Park Street on your left, you can't miss it. Oh, and Mr Walker, if you get a chance afterwards, you might find the common and public gardens agreeable to walk across. We shall make things formal in writing to New Brunswick.'

'Many thanks again,' I said, over-thanking as usual, out of thanks. *Sold a story to the Atlantic Monthly*? It was unbelievable. Now take it slow, take it quiet, be your cool, hot-headed self and keep your hair on. One string to the bow already. Hand it in, leave your telephone number and go away.

The ground floor of Two Park Street was rather blank except for an antiquated elevator with a sliding mesh door and a coloured lady of uncertain years and diffident mien.

'Which floor, sir?'

'Might I see a secretary?'

It clanked shut and we lumbered up and I met a nice secretary at a desk. The atmosphere, the ambience was unhurried, no frenetic rushing about as one might expect in these United States. The air was of a distinguished club.

I was on-high inside. Therefore *ca'canny*, no pushing was the order of the day, more cunning too, if I had rightly assessed this old-fashioned club. I introduced myself and explained about the letters to Paul Brooks and Craig Wylie.

'Mr Brooks, the editor-in-chief, has somebody with him but Mr Wylie might be able to see you. He's upstairs in the trade department. Shall I ask him?'

'May I just leave this envelope, if you would be kind enough to see that it gets to one of them?'

'Why, of course. How can we reach you?'

'I'm at the Statler,' and I told her the room number. The merest hint of a flinch at the thought of this poverty-stricken English author at the five-buck Statler. I went down in the elevator and out, thinking soon that I had not been cunning in my diffidence but bloody stupid. I would sit vainly in that hotel room for the two days that I could afford and take the bus back to New Brunswick. No, I would not. I would play diffident today and go at them tomorrow.

Following the suggestion of Mr Weeks, I walked across Boston common on election day in 1948. It was grassy and open, a wonderful place for the smart and tatterdemalion human world to stroll within the rumble of the city. The American elms were magnificent, upthrusting trees, far more beautiful than European elms. I crossed the street to the public gardens where on the left was a broad specimen of the American beech, not a patch on a dozen Rankeillour beeches; and on the right was George Washington on his charger. I lifted my hat with proper alien respect to the memory of General George Washington, soon on to the Statler and took the elevator up. It was tea time by then, I must have had a hamburger or something somewhere for lunch, and on the way I said to the elevator man:

'Mr Dewey, the Republican, seems to be favourite.'

I couldn't care less who won, President Truman or the other, but I was still a little light of head and talkative after the *Atlantic Monthly*.

'You'll know better when the working man gets out to vote,' he said sourly to me, an Irishman not liking my Limey accent.

I ordered tea, triple strength, still not strong enough for a decent British army brew but better than the usual American wish-wash. Past five, nearly six and they had not telephoned from Houghton Mifflin. What a half-wit I had been, sleepy again, I snoozed.

'Hullo,' I said.

'There's a Mr Wylie here, enquiring for you. May I send him up?'

And so I met Craig Wylie, a tall American, dressed in the same sort of tweed suit as my own.

'You can't stay in this place,' he said. 'you're coming home with us.'

I protested, bamboozled again, and went. The Wylie station wagon was even more decrepit than our third-hand Jeep. We headed out of the city, in and out and under and out in a westerly direction, arriving at a big house in a suburb called Weston.

His wife was named Angie, and she knew the Breeses and laughed about Bill, ever a topic of conversation. They had numerous children – Moira, Kate, Andy and Meg (she was also called Piglet), the smallest one then.

'. . . don't be so stuffy, Craig. Call him David, for God's sake.'

Children and I on the whole get on. The stuffy reserve that I have with most grown-ups does not apply. So, with whisky, I read to Piglet on my knee until it was bedtime for Piglet.

Then dinner and a glass of wine and more whisky after dinner while Angie darned socks.

'I'm not a bad darner,' I said, so I was darning in the Wylie family.

'How in God's name did you learn to do that?' Craig asked me.

'Willy-nilly when I was a prisoner.'

'Were you sent down for a stretch, David?' Moira asked, the almost grown-up one. I liked them all, but perhaps Moira and Piglet became my favourites.

'In a manner of speaking, yes.'

'He was a Prisoner of War, you stupid,' said her father.

'Stupid yourself, Daddy. A pity you weren't a Prisoner of War, then you might be some use.'

It was all good at home with the Wylies by some miracle and just as bedtime began to beckon, I said innocently to Craig:

'I went to the *Atlantic Monthly* today. Met a man called Weeks.'

'*Ted Weeks*, the editor. How come?'

'Well, I sold them a story.'

'Did you, by God?'

The writing had not come up before then, not a word about it except to thank me for the manuscript and no further comment.

'He seemed a decent sort of chap, a bit smooth perhaps.'

Craig laughed and we went to bed, and I knew very well that I had planted a seed that would germinate right off tomorrow. Some editor would start reading.

He went to the office and I stayed with Angie, taking children to and from school and shopping and going for a walk and so on, and I bought a bottle of bourbon whisky, called by everyone in the United States *berbun* except by one Craig Wylie who called it *bourbon, comme un français*. He always did.

It transpired on our walk that Angie's brother, Harry, had fought in the British Army in Italy – the Green Jackets, which meant the 60th or Rifle Brigade, the *crème de la crème* – which made it all the more confusing, and I was thinking of the book. She made me a real cup of English tea, so she knew that one too.

Craig came home earlier that evening and he got me a drink of my *bourbon*, a funny taste which I was taking to, but mostly I was on edge about the book. Would he keep me on tenterhooks, play the sphinx?

But he said:

'Dorothy de Santillana was free, so she started straight off on your book this morning and came into my room and said: *Listen to this.* It was the first half page, I expect you remember it, David.'

'Not quite precisely,' I said, 'if she changed one word, I would know. But my memory works the wrong way round.'

'Oh,' Craig said. He seemed disappointed, and so did his family.

'I have the carbon copy in my room.'

'Please read it to us,' Moira said.

I fetched it and read: *'In the autumn evenings the hills are a deep and murky blue, and the stranger will think: these are gentle hills, warmed by the west wind and the mild sun. There is no violence here. But to the Highlander that colour tells a different story. "Murrky," he calls it, and the abrupt "u" and the hard-rolled "r" hint at the true character of the place; for the steep moors are not always peaceful.*

*'See them when the blizzards come from the north; or see the spates of springtime tumble down the gullies. Then you will know that that there is a harshness in the beauty. But then you will no longer be a stranger.'*

The Wylie family were absolutely silent, until Meg or Piglet said, 'That funny word about the blue, could you say it again?'

'Murrky,' I said.

'Can you really talk Scotch?' young Andrew asked.

'Ay,' I said. 'Ut's ma ither langwidge. I was raised wi' yon.'

'It's reading time, David,' Piglet said. 'Just put it into Scotch.'

'Scottish, darling,' Angie said.

'No, Scotch, we say, when we mean it like that, or Scotch whisky, too, otherwise Scottish.'

'Gosh, you're funny,' Moira said.

So I translated a children's story into the broad Scottish dialect which had been the second language of my childhood. It is a memory of sentiment with the Wylies – sentimentality too – a stranger at home in a foreign land. Nothing quite like that had ever happened to me. And they were not semi-English. They were utterly American.

'Dorothy took it home to finish gobbling it tonight. Then Paul Brooks's turn. Then mine. How long can you stay?' Craig asked.

'The day after tomorrow I must get back. That is, I mean, if you can endure me for so long.'

'Why not come in tomorrow and meet the others, and we'll have some lunch?'

'Sponging,' I said, which they ignored. 'I don't want to talk about it while you're reading it.'

'You won't,' Craig said. 'But Dorothy will have finished; you can talk to her. Dorothy is our fat girl, you'll get on.'

'Dorothy who?'

'de Santillana. Her husband is a professor of philosophy at MIT.'

'How do you know that Dorothy and David will get on? That's enough to make them loathe one another.'

'Because first, she's crazed for his book, three-quarters way through, and second, she'll take to him.'

'Fingers crossed,' I said, and we went to bed.

Back next morning to the club to meet Paul Brooks, diffident and a bird-man, so that was all right, and Dorothy de Santillana who was charming and plump and that was all right. And to lunch with Craig at the Tavern Club, two dry martinis each, those were the days, and on the way home that evening Craig said:

'Paul's finished it. He and Dorothy are both on, with what you would call *knobs on*. I'm only the new boy. I get paid less than the truck driver. But I'll be on too, bound to be, from what the others say.'

'For God's sake take it,' I said and was quiet, thinking of the battle that the last year had been. 'I mean, I trust you. That's all that matters.'

'It's a hell of a life you're in for,' he said; and was quiet too in the noisy rattle-trap, and then he said: 'You should have an agent.'

'Who?'

'Strictly speaking, we're not supposed to recommend agents but the one for you is Diarmuid Russell, Russell and Volkening in New York. His father was Æ, the Irish poet.'

That sounded like more big literary league, out of my depth.

'Is he a straight-thinking sort of chap? I'm not an intellectual. I only begin to seem to feel that I can write fiction somehow. An intellectual wouldn't do me.'

'Highly intelligent, entirely intuitive, incapable of dissimulation. That's why I would say Diarmuid is the man.'

They did take the *The Storm and the Silence*, which was published first in the United States and later by Jonathan Cape in England.

As for Diarmuid Russell, I sent him what I thought was the best of what I had written the winter before in Scotland and in his first letter to me, he wrote, typed out untidily himself as his letters would always be: *I cannot say that they are all exactly bad.* It was a rough beginning to the most solid of trusts and to differences of opinion. Diarmuid had marvellous instinct, or intuition, which could be wrong and was much more often right. He was an honest, uncompromising Irishman through and through.

The wonder had happened – being rich now, and a fearful spendthrift, I bought Willa a present and still had enough to take the bus home. Letters of introduction opened the jungle gate a crack for me, a crack, no more than that. You did not buy books because of classmates. Yet fiction was an easier jungle to penetrate in my early days than the tangled, prolix, perverted jungle that now pertains. Poor old world out of hand, and too well we are confounded.

My jungle path was far more straight, but it was hellish thorny, as I was to find out. Craig Wylie warned me.

EIGHT

# 1983 and earlier

There are always new sidetracks if one goes far enough along that jungle path. This one is in the hinterland a few miles from Cannes, and the track leads from hooting bedlam a hundred yards or so away to our sequestered cottage at a small hotel. It is a perfect place to write, a decided improvement (or so one hopes) on Strathcroix where the tractor is mired or the furnace has fused, or there is some excuse. Here, there are no excuses, and Willa has climbed to the village of Mougins to have her hair done.

In the afternoon we venture out in a midget hireling, a small Fiat, an excellent car of which I am the chauffeur. I am getting quite good at it and can hold my own with any hurtling Frenchman of similar dimensions provided only that I know the way. Alas, that is not often, for the road direction signs are execrable. One has to admit that they could hardly be otherwise in this hilly, rock-strewn countryside. We have lost our way again and in a trice fifty angry horns are hooting at our heels. Draw off where possible and bicker a bit, but we usually get there somehow. We even got somehow by auto-route and numerous *centre de ville* signs to Vence and the Chapelle du Rosaire, decorated by Matisse at the age of eighty, a small shrine of exquisite simplicity. I dislike being the tourist that I am but that was worth it.

I always lose ourselves in the climb to Mougins, one kilometre only, but I have the ten or so kilometres to Cannes fairly well buttoned up. We bombed it there the other afternoon to park the car beside the railway station in a parking complex – standard method, you pull out the ticket from the slot, the bar lifts to let you through and you wind up and round and round to the fourth floor where there is a space. What could be easier?

We repair on foot to the railway station to check about our tickets to Marseilles and Paris, where I did not want to go but

Willa loves Paris; and if we must go I intend to go by the fastest train in the world. Our enquiries about booking baggage ahead lead nowhere much except to another bicker, and we give it up and now walk, crossing the Rue d'Antibes, passing shops of extreme elegance and expense. I have had unanimous instructions from the next generation: 'You mustn't miss the topless, Dad.' I am not particularly keen, bosoms being but bosoms, two by two, and I know perfectly well that even the hardiest of belles would not bare herself to this chill wind. I am right. The *plage* is truly bare.

The one thing that catches my fancy is a head and shoulders bust of King Edward VII amid a grove of palm trees. There is a simple inscription on the marble plinth:

A S.M. LE ROI EDOUARD VII
HOTE FIDELE DE CANNES

*Faithful guest of Cannes*. I am touched by it, and so is Willa, a better Cannes in good King Edward's day, it must have been.

We decide to go home and walk again to the parking complex where the *ascenseur* takes us up to the fourth floor and the car, all so familiar to us sophisticated people. Now we have to go down and round and down and put our ticket into a slot and pay whatever it tells us to pay. We go down one flight, or is it two, and my eagle eyes, rendered eagle again with long-distance spectacles, read *Sauf pour véhicules à voie rapide*, and a clear way to an exit. I am not sure whether *sauf* in this case means *except* or *only to*, but I risk it anyway and come to the booth before the gate where it tells me to put in my ticket. I see nowhere to put in my money, but never mind. Ticket goes in and rolls back out. I put it in again and it pops back out, something wrong, something very much wrong to the crocodile of hooting cars behind. Things are utterly hopeless, but a kind Frenchman explains that we should have paid first in the nether regions somewhere. I manage to find a corner to tuck the Fiat into, crisis averted. Willa stays with the car and I take the ticket down to pay and have it stamped. It keeps rolling back out at me because the counter machine indicates that I am two francs short but in the end the ticket returns without asking for more money.

It was the fourth floor, wasn't it? But on the fourth floor is neither car nor wife. Of course not, you idiot. That was where you parked and descended from. Which floor, then? I try every floor, safely by *ascenseur*, or dangerously against the tide on foot, total failure. In the end I go back to the pay place and appeal to the man at the *bureau de change*, a decent chap who by this time considers me to be some sort of joke, and I have an inspiration. I say, 'I remember seeing *Sauf à voie rapide*.'

'*Ah, Monsieur*,' he says with a jolly yet sympathetic laugh. 'It is the third floor.'

I get into the crowded lift. Things have become so awful that I think they have become not unfunny, so, inhibitions entirely vanished, I say to my grave companions in meteoric bad French, I have lost everything. I have lost the car. I have lost the wife. I have lost everything but not yet life itself.' I laugh like anything and so do they, all but one baffled-looking man, and they get off and he says to me, '*Monsieur, parlez-vous anglais*?'

We have stopped at the third floor at that moment, and there, wonder of wonders, are the wife and the car, and I say, '*Oui, Monsieur, je parle anglais*,' and, typical heartless Frenchman, I leave *le pauvre anglais* to get on with it himself.

This time the slot accepts our ticket and the gate goes up and we are out, whether *except* or *only to* the *voie rapide* I could not care less, but we are on it and, blood up and full of fun together, we make a smartly perilous U-turn on the *voie rapide* and head up the Boulevard Carnot for Mougins and home. I know Carnot very well because of its large pollarded plane trees, so ruthlessly cut back.

There is little more to be said about the Côte d'Azur except that we do not think it to be quite our kind of place. The food is excellent, with all sorts of delicious sauces which I mop up with my roll. But to adore the stomach quite so much offends me; yet it is better far by far than the bloody inch-thick steaks of North America. It is a busy little world, nowhere peaceful and appealing to stroll about in and to watch a bird. It is true that behind the barbed wire, the meshed fence and the impenetrable hedge are immense lawns and handsome villas where the rich must come later to do whatever they may find to do to pass away rich time. At present most of their gates are barred and their guard dogs threaten. I am afraid of the guard dogs and I am bored with the endless columnar evergreen junipers or thujas, so graceful in isolation, so tedious in landscape gardeners' artificial plenitude. I am aware that it is not for us, though everyone is very kind to us, and there is one exceptionally appealing girl who spares me warm smiles from her varied computers at hotel reception.

It was early in the next year, 1949, that a unique thing happened. I was going for a potter with our second, Barclay, a merry child of one, not talking yet. The snow was sparse and we could walk on the golf course, with some jogging rides on shoulders, peals of laughter, a good cold winter day, and an idea hit me: *small boys want to be big.*

I think that every other book or story I ever wrote required of me hours and days, or weeks and months of sitting and of waiting for it. But *Geordie* came full-born. It was a very short book, about 35,000 words, and it wrote itself in six weeks.

Houghton Mifflin asked me in a gentlemanly way whether I would consider entitling the book *Wee Geordie*, and I said instantly, 'Sorry, Paul. Nothing doing,' and Paul Brooks as instantly yielded; you see what I mean about the club.

When it was made into a film a few years later (a very good film too, I loved almost all of it) it was *Geordie* in Britain but *Wee Geordie* in North America. *You wrote Wee Geordie? Yes I wrote Geordie.* The *Wee* was more cute than I could happily subscribe to.

It was set in Scotland again. No two books could be more different one from the other than *The Storm and the Silence* and *Geordie*, excepting only in devotion to my native land, land of my bones. Later I was to poke a bit of fun at sacred Scotland, which Scotland did not like at all. But *Geordie* was a fantasy, a down-to-earth fable, I called it, and it was just that.

Jonathan Cape, who had an option on my next book, had high hopes for me from the starkness of Tam Diamond's story and wrote about *Geordie*: 'We would like you to lay it on the table,' a publisher's euphemism for turning it down.

But Billy Collins in London heard of it and his brother Ian, who ran the printing end of things in Glasgow, came to meet me at

Prestwick near his house, wrested the manuscript from me, and that was that. They were Scottish too and they loved *Geordie* as most of the world seemed to love that simple story until Geordie became more real than me. As I wrote early on, I never knew a Geordie. He came full-born alive for me.

It was a short visit that summer, to stay at Rankeillour, to play golf with the Field Marshal on the Old Course, and to go to London on writing business – two books done, it was already business. I think that most of our meetings after India involved a game of golf, but he gave me lunch one day at the Athenaeum, club of clubs, and told me that he had been asked to visit The Canadian Black Watch that autumn and could I spare a day or two to help him when he first came over? So diffidently asked – if he had said Timbuktoo I would have been there to meet him.

It would be easier to write about a man whose character one could fault. But I saw no cracks in the Wavell rock. Or, if I saw one, it might be an excess of honour, too much: *take the blame and don't complain*. At Washington during the war he was asked by a reporter how he would account for his defeat in South–East Asia. After consideration, Wavell replied, 'Because I was out-generalled and out-fought.' But his cause had been hopeless from the start. Surely this was carrying self-depreciation beyond reasonable bounds. From a lesser man such a remark would ring false. And yet the strange, annoying and wonderful thing about Wavell is that he meant it, I have no doubt. It was simple though – too much the simple soldier.

The day Mountbatten came to Delhi he said to his private secretary George Abell (who served both the last Viceroys with high distinction): 'You know, Archie in a way likes to be thought a simple soldier, but if anyone thinks me a simple sailor, he can think again.'

History will judge Wavell as a commander of genius. History may well not agree in judging him as Viceroy. But history will also judge him as the good great man.

I spent a few more days at Rankeillour before flying back. One morning as I walked out of the front door I heard a barred owl hoot down in the woods toward John Keiller's cottage. A daylight owl was unusual, not particularly odd. But later, as I got into the driver's seat of the big green Ford to go with Thoms our chauffeur to catch the plane at Prestwick, an owl hooted again. An uneasy feeling, superstition to be dismissed, but I had lived with a man, John Arundell of Wardour, in whose family there had been an omen about owls. I spent that night with Ian Collins near the airport. Billy Collins, the chairman of Collins whom I had not met before, was also there, in bed with the flu, and he was reading *Geordie* with enthusiasm.

Billy was not particularly gifted intellectually, so far as I ever knew, but he had an extraordinary eye for the winning book. I remember, much later when he came to stay with us at St Andrews, he was absorbed in reading galley proofs of *From Here to Eternity*, hardly the book, one would imagine, for the staid house of Collins, the world's biggest publisher of bibles. But Billy bought the British rights.

Next day Ian took me to the Constellation of BOAC (successors to Imperial Airways of Hannibal days) to fly to Keflavik in Iceland and to Gander in Newfoundland, and on to Montreal. I forgot about owls until we had crossed the point of no return beyond Keflavik and lost an engine, reaching Gander without further trouble. We were held up for two days awaiting a replacement aircraft. I know nothing bad about Gander except its godforsaken bleakness, and nothing particularly good either except that an owl story incubated in me.

I called it *The Owl* and Diarmuid Russell sold it to the *Saturday Evening Post*, at which bullseye I had been aiming unsuccessfully for some time. It may be worth a brief aside to say that I wrote all the novels without a direct commercial intent. I tried to do as decent a job as I could, and then hoped for reward. They had to be readable or nobody would read them. Beyond that, I made no concessions, and never wrote with a thought to movie rights or to serialization or the like.

But most of the stories were written with direct commercial purpose, to pay the bills and provide for an increasing family. I evolved a technique: they had to be about places that I knew well. They had to have a strong plot, a carrot to encourage reader donkey on. They had to have action, which I was good at. They had to observe the house rules, which meant in the case of the

*Saturday Evening Post* that you could say *damn* but love must go no further than a kiss. I did not have to prostitute myself to write them but I did have qualms about writing deliberately for money.

The *Saturday Evening Post*, still at that time the most powerful magazine in the United States, paid extremely well, starting me off at $750 and raising me quite swiftly to their top rate of $2500 a story, and twice that for a novella, double-length. They were meticulous too as to content. They sometimes required me to cut a story but they never changed a word I wrote.

Titles were another matter. *The Owl* came out of a family superstition and nearly ended in disaster. The *Post*'s title was *Panic over the Atlantic*. There had been fear but no panic whatever. Titles were their prerogative, awful as their titles might be.

*Geordie* became a bestseller but no other novel of mine ever did. I later had two tremendous windfalls (in our terms anyway, not those of John le Carré) from the *Reader's Digest* Condensed Books. The idea of condensing what I had slaved at and pared to its bones horrified me, but I have to say that they did it brilliantly well, and built Strathcroix for us, thank you very much.

Lord Wavell wrote to me from the Athenaeum where he had read my *Atlantic Monthly* story. They called it *The Rescuers*. Not much of a title but a hell of a lot better than *My Strong Lambs*. He praised it highly, with encouragement. Somehow or other, and I don't know how, he believed that I could do it. His kindly contemplative eye watched always from behind my shoulder.

In October of 1949 Willa had our third son since the war. She was as good at having babies as at everything else, this one at the Charlotte County Hospital in St Stephen, twenty miles from us. We called him David Clibborn after the first David at Pitlair in 1657 or so and after the Clibborns of County West Meath of whom my wonderful spinster Cousin Sophie, who still rode to hounds at the age of ninety, had been a last survivor. David's godfathers were Patrick Campbell-Preston, my escaping partner, and Archie John Wavell.

There was still one boy to come, two years later again, those long cold winter nights. By then Willa had had enough Walker names or predominantly Walker names. We called him Julian Harry, possibly a link to Julian Gascoigne. Also a link to the Harry

Walkers of whom the most notable had been my cousin, Colonel Harry.

Julian edited our local newspaper for three years, not an easy job in a small town but he did it well, and his editorials, particularly about affairs of the larger world outside, were of outstanding quality. I do not write this as an admiring dad but with a cold critical eye. He has taken this year to work to a master's degree in politics at the London School of Economics, which he gained with triple distinction.

This is not a family chronicle and so I have written little about our four sons, their wives, their children. Giles, the film director, nominated for an Oscar; Barclay, the free artist with a rarely vivid visual imagination; David, the shrewd lawyer and countryman, unflappable; Julian, the political journalist. They are their own men, as I had always hoped, and they will go where they will go.

As for grandchildren, there are six and another on the way, the eldest of them not yet five. That would faze most grandparents of seventy-two and seventy. It fazes me, remote that I am, if amiable enough. Not Willa, though, who cares constantly for every one of them in her mind and doings.

The writing and the living, the plunderer, the plundered.

Lord Wavell arrived to a tumultuous Black Watch welcome in Montreal. They had served with gallantry and fame in two World Wars, so the enthusiasm was mutual. I attended the first days as an unofficial aide-de-camp, and then went home to get on with the job and he went on to speaking engagements in Canada and the United States. He sent me drafts of most of his speeches for comment. About only one, I think, I did help. In a speech to the Canadian Club in Montreal he stressed the quality of Britain and the unequalled contribution that the British had made to the world. This would be meat and drink to his English-speaking audience, who would be the majority, but might also offend by its neglect of a heritage from France. He adjusted that gratefully and gracefully, and also spoke a little French.

He was to sail from New York on December the second, and the evening before that to address the American Academy of Poets. But he had a further commission, to buy some things for his wife and daughters. He wrote to ask whether I could come to help him with both tasks. The poets' dinner was an illustrious affair with presentations, recitations, four eulogies and four main speakers. It was rendered even more protracted because the penultimate speaker, a Shakesperian scholar and former Prime Minister of Canada, who used no notes, came to a pained and painful dead stop after twenty minutes and went back to the beginning. The second time he romped right through for his full half hour. So it was midnight when the Field Marshal spoke of the soldier and poetry. It was difficult for him to reach an audience, but this subject kindled his fire.

He quoted from many poems, including 'Magpies in Picardy' by Cameron Wilson who was killed in the First War:

> '"A magpie in Picardy told me secret things –
> Of the music in white feathers and the sunlight that sings
> And dances in deep shadows – he told me with his wings.
>
> He said that still through chaos works on the ancient plan,
> And two things have altered not since first the world began –
> The beauty of the wild green earth and the bravery of man."
>
> *The beauty of the wild green earth and the bravery of man.* I hold that those should be the chief themes of the poet, who should open our eyes to beauty and lead us to face the dangers and difficulties of this world with bravery.'

So, late to bed and up betimes for the shopping expedition. I viewed this with more trepidation than the poets' dinner, never feeling much at ease among ladies' underclothes up for sale, whether on Fifth Avenue or elsewhere. But the warrior, monocle in remaining eye, went about his task with seasoned aplomb. He had strict written instructions from his womenfolk, but he also seemed to know his nylons and the other stuff. I never admired him more. He wrote later from England: 'The blouses were a great success with my daughters, so was the red belt. But there were one or two other things I was told I might have got. However, on the whole, I think we did very well. I am glad that your purchases for Willa were successful.' Emboldened by his sturdy presence I had also bought a blouse.

During that winter I sold one or two more stories to the *Saturday Evening Post* and began to labour with the idea for another novel. It was to be a 'straight' one again, like the first, but set in Germany. Thus, one straight, one fable, one straight, and next after that ahead would come an extravagance, *Digby*.

I do not think that I changed but the books did, and perhaps that ability helped me to recharge my batteries before the next non-mixture-as-before. A fairly eminent critic wrote later that I was perhaps the most versatile storyteller then writing. This was gratifying to me, although versatility and quality are by no means synonymous. In fact the former may be the ultimate enemy of the latter. But it kept me going, even if it cost our pockets dear. I could never be typed into any pattern that a reader could expect for next time. The stories had one thing in common only, a fondness for the natural world. Still, we were prospering already, as 1950 came.

On the last day of March, Wavell wrote:

> My dear David,
>
> Thank you very much indeed for the three copies of *Geordie* which I have now received. I gave one copy to Neil Ritchie just before he sailed to Washington, asking him to try and publicize it out there; and I have sent one copy to Archie John. Collins asked me to write a short 'blurb' which they could put on the cover on publication, and I have done so. I think that it will be a great success over here . . .

And then, after some comments about Wavell family doings, he wrote:

> I have been stricken by that foul plague jaundice, and have been in bed for the last week, I think the first time for about twenty years. I am not very bad, but very uncomfortable, as the irritation to one's skin is maddening.
>
> How is the new book going? I hope you resolved all the difficulties and that it is coming out well now.
>
> Love to you and Willa, I hope you are all well.
>
> Yours ever, W.

On April the 7th I wrote back:

My dear Field Marshal,

Thank you very much for your letter. I am glad the copies of Geordie arrived safely, and that you gave one each to Neil Ritchie and Archie John. There have been some really good reviews, some good, and some indifferent. The only thing which alarms me a little is that almost all the reviewers take Geordie as a serious contribution to the modern novel! which was far from my intention, as I meant it to be a lively and real fable, not a contribution to serious literature. Many thanks also for writing a blurb for Collins. That will make a great difference to sales. But please don't let them victimise you.

I hope you are getting better from the jaundice, which is a horrible complaint, and very depressing, I believe. I remember being thoroughly cantankerous when I had it as a small boy. The new book went wrong at the beginning of January; so I stopped writing it because I didn't feel the story was good enough; and I made some concessions to readability. But it may have worked out this week at last. My new idea is to take a mess of six people through prison from 1940; not very much escaping; but a try to get at the dreary irritating wonderful comradeship; and the whole thing by allusion in the eyes of each of them one after the other.

Willa and the boys are all well. We are moving to another house next month, this time at the edge of the town. We wanted to buy one but could not find anything under a fortune. I am planning to go down the Mackenzie river to Aklavik in the Arctic this summer, leaving in the middle of June. The Canadian government are being very helpful, and they are going to take me free most of the way.

I did not know when I wrote that letter that his last illness had already begun.

The book that he and I mentioned was to become *The Pillar*, the title coming from the six-sided pillar of their house. The task that I had set myself was an exceedingly difficult one – each of the six of them seeing the other five in turn. They were not real people taken direct from life (none of my major characters have ever been) but they each, of course, had traits of people that I had known in prison. Months later, after a long journey done, the plan did work itself out for me. Looking back at it now, I would not change any of the prison parts of *The Pillar* but I think that the five flashings-back to time before imprisonment were to some degree flawed, contrived from too brief a writing experience. The sixth man, the last and the oldest, had had so much dubious experience in life before that I did not try to write of it. He was my favourite man, named Busty, dissolute uncle to the rest of them. But as the spring went on I was still stuck for the plan that would bring it all together.

But the news of the Field Marshal's illness grew worse.

As I wrote at the beginning:

> The last time I saw Wavell was on December the second 1949. We were in a well-travelled New York taxi cab, sharing it with his well-travelled luggage which had accompanied him on many journeys. But the bags and the man still held together, a bit creased and battered, strong as ever. He had nothing to say and I had nothing worth saying, so we sat without speech.
>
> We were nearing the Battery and the liner *Mauretania* when a policeman stopped us and a long traffic jam piled up, with us as leaders of the queue. 'Some bigshot, I guess,' said the taxi-driver.
>
> We sat in silence, awaiting the arrival of the bigshot. Eventually there crossed our bows a large and explosive motorcycle escort, a police car or two and then a dignified Rolls-Royce. The hold-up of common mortals was explained; and here sat Wavell in a humble taxi, and there passed in exalted state another field marshal.
>
> Wavell smiled that wry grim smile of his and said, 'There goes Monty.' Neither rancour nor envy dwelt in him.

It transpired later that both of them were travelling in the *Mauretania*, and I am glad to say that when they met there was no doubt who considered himself the junior officer: Field Marshal Montgomery held Wavell in some awe.

This is the advertisement that appeared after he had written to Collins.

One of the last books read by Lord Wavell was Geordie, a novel by David Walker who had served in his old regiment, The Black Watch, and as his comptroller in India. He wrote us the following letter and gave us permission for its publication: 'Perhaps I am prejudiced about *Geordie*. The author is a personal friend and the scene of the story, the Perthshire Highlands, is familiar and nostalgic to me. But I believe that this simple, kindly and humorous tale will appeal to all who read it by reason of its light touch, the quality of the writing and the homely but keen observation. It has borne with me the best test of all for a tale: I have read it twice, and enjoyed it even more on the second occasion.'

*Geordie* will be published on July 31st.

That first advertisement appeared in the *Times Literary Supplement* on Friday June the 16th 1950, nine days after he was buried.

He was accorded the first state funeral by the river Thames since Nelson's in 1806. His body was taken upriver from the Tower of London, of which he had been the Keeper, to Westminster Pier and to the Abbey, where the world paid honour to him, and this was read:

> My Marks and Scars I carry with me to be a witness that I have fought his battle, who will now be my Rewarder.

At the end of the long journey, Archibald Percival Wavell came to Winchester to the Cloister Garth where he was buried.

He had included John Bunyan's poem 'The Pilgrim' in *Other Men's Flowers*. Let this flower speak for him:

> Who would true valour see,
> Let him come hither;
> One here will constant be,
> Come wind, come weather.

On that day, June the 7th, and because of time differences a good many hours after his body lay in the Cloister Garth, I flew from Edmonton to begin a first long Arctic journey. I kept a diary of that journey – one of the only two diaries I ever kept – and it began:

> You leave Edmonton and those fabulous oilfields, and you fly for the first time into the romance of the north country. You fly from the city – from the last of the cities of North America – over farmland where the young wheat is sprouting, over trees and smaller farms, over trees again and lakes and more trees; until now quite soon you have left the agreeable cultivated world behind, and you look down at a brown river winding in the forest. As you fly along the Athabasca river to the lake you should be thinking of Alexander Mackenzie who started from Fort Chipewyan on the third of June 1789 with his voyageurs and their Indian wives, with English Chief, his temperamental interpreter. He hoped to find a route to the Western Ocean. Instead of that, they paddled their canoes 1600 miles to the Arctic Sea and back in one short summer season. You should be thinking of this as you sit in a comfortable seat in a DC3.

I was thinking of the friend that I had lost, and I was thinking ahead, as he would have wanted me to do.

We landed at Fort Smith on the sixtieth parallel of latitude, the southernmost boundary of the North–West Territories. While we waited for Great Slave Lake to break up, I flew about a bit in a single-engined Beaver, over Wood National Park where buffalo had been re-introduced and flourished, and to Lake Athabasca, all the great north in that great name, and back down the Slave river above the fiendish rapids which some day might be tamed. As we neared Fort Smith again I asked the bush-pilot to fly low so that I might photograph them. He did, and I did, and suddenly we stood on our tail to avoid a startled flock of pelicans. My companions grumbled and we landed on smooth water at Fort Smith.

A few days later our river boat, festooned with barges, went down the last muddy miles of the Slave river, as brown and messy and tropical-looking as the Jumna is at Delhi, then across the lake where the candle ice tinkled pleasantly aganst my barge far up ahead, and to Wrigley harbour where the great green Mackenzie dips on its run.

That first journey or voyage was easy enough, five miles wide, or two or four, or narrowing at the Ramparts, and to Aklavik in the Delta, 1600 miles to the Arctic Ocean.

At Aklavik I met a bush-pilot named Dick Denison, a Canadian who had flown fighters all through North Africa with the RAF. He was to fly the bishop of the Arctic to Tuktoyaktuk, which means in Eskimo *the crossing place of the caribou*, and he thought that he could fit me into the Stinson Stationwagon, a four-seater aircraft. We had a preliminary spin off our floats, the windscreen suddenly opaque with oil. Dick leaned out of his window, put us down, and fashioned a wooden plug to replace the missing cap. Dick took on the other two passengers and we flew to Tuktoyaktuk, getting in with a whistle to spare before the north wind brought fog down from the ice. I used to be nervous of flying, except if flying myself in a rudimentary way or flying with a good bush-pilot. We were held up at Tuktoyaktuk in some comfort in the *Snowbird*, a ship that had wintered there. As can occur, Dick and I got to know one another quite well in those twenty hours or so until the weather showed some possibility of improvement.

'What do you think, David, should we go?'

'My God, Dick, don't ask me.'

We went, and the weather was all right with low overcast. Not unmindful of the Mackenzie mountains to the west, we dropped Bishop March off at Fort Mackenzie. As he stood on the bank of the Peel river in the rain he raised his hand in blessing, and we flew back to Aklavik. Dick was a great pilot, but risking his bets, as I had seen. The next winter his father wrote to me that he had tried to take off in an old twin-engined Anson with a thousand pounds overload. It was once too often.

Back up the murky Mammoth with a side excursion to climb the Bear river, a pure crystal blue with sizeable ice-floes from Great Bear Lake to respect, and so down and Out by air and across the continent by train to home, all in all a cushy journey.

Six years later I went back to the Arctic, which belonged to Canada, although Canadians did not belong to it. I was still wrestling with one book, but leave it for a while and seek experience for another. My second Arctic journey was not cushy. I left St Andrews in late February, one winter mostly gone, another much harder winter now to come.

# NINE

# 1956

We flew into Cambridge Bay, a main station on the distant early warning radar line, which was then being built, and back by light plane to Coppermine on the Arctic coast, starting point for a dogsled journey on the sea-ice. I had hired an Eskimo driver and team and was to accompany the annual RCMP patrol up by Victoria Island, past Cape Baring at the seventieth parallel, and on across Prince Albert Sound to a place called Holman.

There were a few days' delay at Coppermine while deft Eskimo ladies sewed my deerskins – so-called, but fashioned from caribou hides – one suit worn fur-to-skin, one identical suit worn fur outwards. There was airspace too, double parkas overlapping double trousers.

As soon became apparent, there were two essential keys to pleasure or purgatory in dogsled travel: they were wind and ice. Given still weather; given a clear smooth lead of ice, with a smattering of snow to cover the bare frozen sea, you could travel in a comfort as near to bliss as might be imagined, getting off every now and then to run a little to warm your feet, hop on the back of the sled again, to hear the hiss of the iceclad runners and the oddly melodious spittled voice of the driver calling direction to his lead dog in the team of twelve; perfect comfort, and so it was, except always a thought to my vulnerable feet. For a non-Eskimo the rest of me was good. You travelled – and in the true old north *travel* meant by dogsled – as warmly as summer butter at a temperature of forty degrees below zero Fahrenheit, which coincides also with minus forty degrees by that tiresome Celsius.

I am not much of a spitter, but writing of the Eskimo's spittled voice, an adequate description of that sound, I am reminded of a thing I used to do as diversion in the pleasant peaceful times. I would wait with gathered spittle for a patch of bare green ice and spit and watch the instantly frozen ball go rolling across the bare green ice. It was not a diversionary spittle-ball game to be played before or after that cold journey.

We travel peacefully on, some rough ice beside us, and in that ice I see shapes and tumbled figures such as were seen in my novel *Where the High Winds Blow*, finished at last some four years later. I saw the like of them, but they were seen by the man of the story, Simon Kepple Skafe.

> He lived a daydream on the trail. The hours dawdled by as he watched the forms and fancies of the ice that every traveller has seen – the bunny rabbit and the goose, green woman sprawling welcome on the ice, the wolf-cub keen as mustard at salute, the skyline of the crazy city, a Shinto gate, and on and on, they lulled him, slipping past him . . .

I do not suppose that the racketing speeding snowmobiles of nowadays permit mood or time for such imaginings.

There had been no chill at all to think about except for an occasional jog to bring warmth back to those weakling toes. But now it grew positively balmy at seventeen below or something, and even toes could be forgotten. I was soon to learn that a sudden rise in temperature was not a good sign but the worst. 'Blow comin',' said Peter Kamingoak, the Eskimo, guiding his team north of west on the smooth lead beside broken ice toward that paler rim of horizon that meant a blow.

Sometimes a blow might arrive out of nothing at the speed of an express train but the wind grew steathily that time, in fitful gusts that made snow-devils swirl just as hot gusts in the plains of India made dust-devils swirl. As passenger, I could turn my head for shelter from the wind but the driver had to face it. The wind grew, and grew faster now, and grew until Kamingoak could no longer see beyond his lead-dog thirty or forty feet ahead. 'Camp,' he said, shouted in the wind.

I was learning, but in all essential preliminaries to camping, arctic fashion, I was more nuisance than I was worth. My lowly task was to sit on the grapnel anchor lest the dogs scent Nanuk, the polar bear, and go berserk after it.

Alone, he pitched our tent far more quickly than with me

getting in the way, set out the dog-line, started the gas cooker to melt snow to freeze the toggles of the dog-line, and hustled the dogs to be chained to it at a safe distance one from the other so that war could not break out. They were not household pets but rough tough beasts, fed only to work.

At about that stage I began to be of some use, brewing up again, heating our frozen supper of stew and spuds and beans while he fed seal-meat to the dogs. But first lesson, hammered home and learned – get the snow off your deerskins before you go into the warmth of the tent. And while the gas stove burned, or the primus for the brew, it was warm in there within the buffeting pulsing thunder of the wind.

My man in the book that was to come from all that, S. K. Skafe – Husky Skafe, they called him – began as a young man in the north who went on to be immensely successful, to be honoured on his fiftieth birthday, and in his speech he said: 'A man who has sat out an Arctic blow the hard way in a tent, or has sat out enough of them to lose his first fear of them, will not forget that on his backside in an office chair.'

Skafe had dreams and pipedreams of the north. His dream about oil in the Arctic Islands would soon come true, all too true, some would say. His pipedream of Canadians as a truly northern people would remain just that.

The tumult of the wind was frightening against the walls of the warm tent, and more frightening when the time had come to put out the stove and be inside much-vaunted sleeping bag, proof against fifty below the makers claimed, but they had not sampled that. I did become inured to the thunder of that killer wind. Buried deep in my bag with the icicles of my breath I never slept soundly on the trail; but when a lull came in the wind I could hear Kamingoak snoring in the deepness of his sleep.

They said that Arctic blows never lasted longer than thirty-six hours, but my diary records that our worst blow began one afternoon and blew that night, a second day, a second night, a third day and a third night, sometimes easing but always waxing mightily again, until on the fourth morning it died away to stillness.

*

I wrote in my diary on the last afternoon that we were pinned:

> . . . It is perhaps the first timeless time of days passing that I have known since early prison.
>
> *19th March.* The wind fell in the night, and by five-thirty there was only a light blatter of canvas so I woke Peter and then went over to the police tent to stir them up. Visibility was sometimes a mile, sometimes much less, but as we were out of dogfood and very low on fuel, no question of waiting to see how the day developed.

The day developed all right in weather but poorly for the police team who broke their sled in rough ice. Kamingoak went to help with repairs while I sat on that anchor, hoping against polar bear. I could probably have coped personally with polar bear because I had my rifle (against regulations, but never mind). What I could not have coped with was a runaway dogteam hellbent after a scent of polar bear.

Kamingoak returned with a suggestion from the corporal, RCMP, that we should push on to Holman Island and leave them to follow after repairs. It was not the first time that their sled had broken, and if it should turn out to be the last time it would be somewhat less than sporting, not quite cricket, to travel on to the haven of a hard floor in a warm house at Holman Island, most northerly Hudson Bay Company post and Catholic settlement.

So there was one more night to camp, during which no part of me slept except my right foot, which was fast asleep. Most of it thawed out painfully at Holman and I lost only the first three toenails.

Before writing this I had to read the diary again. Except that it mentions Willa's cable about the film sale of my Indian novel *Harry Black*, there is no reference to writing, no word about plots for stories, no characters to put into books. It is a prosaic logbook. It was always like that for me. When I was doing, I gave no thought to writing. Indeed, I forgot altogether about my job, forgot even that I had ever written. But I did learn the hard way, than which there is no other way.

We had travelled north in loose tandem with the police patrol. But after a few days of waiting at Holman Island for the Company plane which was to come and never came, I wearied of that and decided to travel south alone. To be more accurate, I did the deciding but Peter Kamingoak and his dogteam did the travelling, with one rather more competent passenger than I had been at the beginning.

I have mentioned hardship on the trail but there could be danger too. On the way up we had run into some rough ice, bad enough to be troublesome, no worse than that. But going south was another story. We had been told at Holman that if we headed a little wide of Cape Baring we would have easy running through the pressure ridge – formed off the Capes as they always are when the wind and the sea clash at freeze-up time and break apart and pile again. Our informant may have found such a way but we did not.

In my diary for that day, which was March the 27th 1956, I wrote:

> We had plain sailing, lovely sailing, for about fifteen miles until we had to make for the coast to round Cape Baring. The pressure ridge, caused by the meeting of gale and tide, grew bigger and bigger, until the slabs were ten feet high, and Peter said it was the worst ice he had ever tried to cross. Certainly a bad affair, and I don't know how we, sled and dogs arrived on this side more or less complete. One time the sled (say 800 pounds worth) whipped over at me and the runner missed my head by less than I wd care to think of. Peter was terrific, and I not much good, but tried to help, puffing and panting in and out of ice slabs. Not the recommended treatment for frozen toes.'

It was dangerous, and we got through safely. That is why, nearing the end of Skafe's journey to the Nunangyak, the islands far from land where his people drilled for oil, I was able to write:

> They swung into the defile and round and up, the small man running by his sled, and once he leapt on top of his sled at a narrow place and off again, and his voice boomed in viridescent ice, between the walls, the slabs, the overhangs, the crazy columns . . .
>
> The sled had been guided up that cornice on the right, had slewed, and was now perched on the overhang while eleven dogs heaved at one garrotted dog.
>
> Skafe might have sensed it about to happen, or he might have

seen it happening. He did not know, and he would not know.

'Watch out!' he called to his smaller hero, Avakana, the Eskimo. But he called too late, or perhaps he should not have called, because the man heard him and checked below the sled as the overhanging cornice cracked, and the tail of the sled dropped free. Skafe saw it happen – he saw the runner, of wood, steel, frozen mud and ice smash Avakana's head against the hard green ice that framed that place. He heard the crunch. Then he saw the strangled dog and its mate, the two wheel dogs, the sled, go over the saddle of the pressure ridge.

Avakana, the square man, lightning quick, lay in that narrow cleft of ice. He wore his sealskin boots, his deerskin pants, his duffel parka. He lay on his face, and he was dead.

It was a pity that I had to kill Skafe's smaller hero, Avakana, but the story required me to bring Skafe to the come-uppance that awaits successful men. Unlike myself, he was a traveller in his own earned right and he did get through alone on foot to the small far islands called Nunangyak.

But after that one rough episode, our journey south was increasingly pleasant. As March grew into April the days were much longer and the weather less cold. It had been a fair long haul in and out and round about, seven hundred miles or less or probably more, growing easier along the homeward way.

We had camped always in a tent; but on the last evening I prevailed upon Kamingoak, much against his will, to build me a snowhouse. It took us more than an hour, as against five minutes for the tent, to cut the snowblocks, spiral them, chink them to make a windproof abode, much preferable to canvas, eerily quiet but for sounds of movement conveyed up through the ice.

It was a short final run in zero weather, no touch of wind. I sweltered in deerskins, took off my fur mitt, my leather and woollen mits, my gloves, and the touch of the deerskin was warm to a bare hand, and so back to Coppermine.

*May 1983*

It is a year since I began to write these slivers of memory. The facts have been as true as I could make them, and the few excerpts of fiction as true to the needs of those stories as I could make them.

Spring is here again, and I am home again in the same leather armchair that used to occupy a corner of the dining room at Rankeillour. Down there beyond my workroom window the same trees are coming into leaf and blossom.

In that novel of Canada and the north, which took ten years altogether in the learning and the making, Skafe's only son, who cared not a fig for worldly success, wrote a small poem:

Lean, wind, lean,
For summer has been.
Cry, plover, fly,
For the year must die.

But there is a saying among country people in these parts, that no seed should be sown until certain young leaves break to a certain size. So two lines may be added to John Skafe's verse:

The leaf on the birch is a mouse's ear,
And spring is here.

St Andrews
Mougins
London